Praise for Erica James

'A heart-warming, romantic story full of engaging characters, an emotional roller coaster' *Daily Express*

'A captivating read: beautifully written and heart-rendingly sad' *Daily Telegraph*

'A captivating novel of love, deception and misunderstanding' *Woman & Home*

'She writes with a wry sense of humour and this story quickly reels you in' *Evening Telegraph*

'A big hug of a novel that leaves you feeling warm and fuzzy' *Woman*

'An entertaining read with some wickedly well-painted cameo characters. It's a perfect read if you're in the mood for romance' *Prima*

'Delightful ... a blend of emotion and wry social observation' *Daily Mail*

'An extraordinary deftness of touch, coupled with some searing insights into both how relationships fail, and can work' *Daily Mirror*

'A wonderfully humorous novel' *Woman's Own*

'With the turn of every absorbing page, you'll find yourself caught in the rapture and despair of each character as they find their way through this beguiling drama' *Candis*

'A poignant read with plenty of laugh-out-loud moments' *Heat*

By Erica James

A Breath of Fresh Air
Time for a Change
Airs and Graces
A Sense of Belonging
Act of Faith
The Holiday
Precious Time
Hidden Talents
Paradise House
Love and Devotion
Gardens of Delight
Tell it to the Skies
It's the Little Things
The Queen of New Beginnings
Promises, Promises
The Real Katie Lavender
The Hidden Cottage
Summer at the Lake
The Dandelion Years

With an insatiable appetite for other people's business, Erica James will readily strike up conversation with strangers in the hope of unearthing a useful gem for her writing. The author of many bestselling novels, including *Gardens of Delight*, which won the Romantic Novel of the Year Award and the recent *Sunday Times* bestseller *Summer at the Lake*, Erica divides her time between Suffolk and Lake Como in Italy, where she now strikes up conversation with unsuspecting Italians.

Visit her website at www.ericajames.co.uk

The Dandelion Years

ERICA JAMES

An Orion paperback

First published in Great Britain in 2015
by Orion Books
This paperback edition published in 2015
by Orion Books,
an imprint of The Orion Publishing Group Ltd.
Carmelite House, 50 Victoria Embankment,
London EC4Y 0DZ

An Hachette UK company

13 15 17 19 20 18 16 14

Copyright © Erica James 2015

A CIP catalogue record for this book
is available from the British Library.

ISBN 978-1-4091-4613-1

Typeset by Deltatype Ltd, Birkenhead, Merseyside

Printed and bound in Great Britain by Clays Ltd, St Ives plc

The Orion Publishing Group's policy is to use papers that
are natural, renewable and recyclable products and made
from wood grown in sustainable forests. The logging and
manufacturing processes are expected to conform to the
environmental regulations of the country of origin.

www.orionbooks.co.uk

This book is dedicated to my long-suffering sons Edward and Samuel and their partners Ally and Rebecca. And, of course, my grandson who grows ever more gorgeous.

THANKS AND ACKNOWLEDGEMENTS

Being relentlessly curious about other people's lives, I'm indebted to my friend Elaine Betts for sharing an old family photograph album with me. It was while looking at those photographs that the character of Jacob Belinsky came fully formed to me. It was a true lightbulb moment!

I must also thank the staff at Bletchley Park who were so generous with their time and help and answered so many of my questions.

Many thanks to Chris and Liz Lawton for the chat over tea and biscuits, and for letting me snoop around their bookshop – I could have stayed all day!

Adèle Geras also needs to be thanked for guiding me round Cambridge so enjoyably on a chilly day in December. I should, however, point out that Cambridge is not home to Merchant College; it exists only in my imagination.

My imagination also played its part in adding a flourish of colour here and there to suit the purposes of the story. I hope my readers will allow me that small bit of artistic licence.

Lastly, I need to thank a few people I met last year on my travels – Ekaterina for giving me the name Katyushka, and Bob and Jean from Canada who became Uncle Bob and Auntie Jo – I hope they'll forgive me!

'*Seize the moments of happiness, love and be loved!*
That is the only reality in the world, all else is folly'

Leo Tolstoy

'*The world is indeed full of peril, and in it there*
are many dark places; but still there is much that
is fair, and though in all lands love is now mingled
with grief, it grows perhaps the greater'

J.R.R. Tolkien

Chapter One

Today was Saskia's birthday.

She was thirty-two years old and it would be true to say she was thoroughly out of step with most other thirty-two-year-olds. It would also be true to say that this was partly an inevitable consequence of still living at home with her father and two elderly grandfathers. But while the set-up would strike a lot of people as odd and far from ideal, Saskia never felt the need to defend or justify the situation. Besides, their domestic arrangements had been in place for so long now it was difficult to imagine living any other way: it was just the way it was.

From the cushioned window seat in her bedroom Saskia watched Grandpa O – wicker basket in hand and wearing an old gardening coat over his pyjamas – set off down the frosty garden at an unhurried pace on his recently replaced knee. It was a familiar sight: every morning, apart from a few weeks back in November when he had gone into hospital to have his arthritic knee sorted, he visited the chicken coop to relieve the hens of their eggs. Back in the kitchen he would place his plunder on the worktop next to the Aga and Grandpa Harvey would tut and mutter about him always leaving the basket in his way. His complaint made, Grandpa Harvey would then take what he needed to make breakfast. Scrambled or poached eggs on toast was their favourite way to start the day although Saskia and her father, more mindful of their cholesterol levels, rang the changes by opting for porridge or cereal. The kitchen was where Grandpa Harvey ruled supreme, just as Oliver was in charge of the garden.

They each had their point of command, and each had their well-honed routine. It was the way it was.

Maintaining her vigilant watch over the tall and slightly stooping figure of her eighty-six-year-old grandfather steadily making his way back up the garden towards the house, his breath forming in the wintry February air, Saskia could see it was going to be one of those magical days of bitter cold, when the whitened ground would be as hard as iron underfoot and the low sun would shine weakly from a pale sky but provide no warmth. Beyond the garden, the fields were also covered in frost and from the top of one of the nearby oak trees, a pair of rooks rose into the sky, cawing loudly.

When her grandfather had disappeared from view, she knew that meant he was safely back inside the house and so she stepped away from the window and continued dressing.

The day might have started just as any other, but today was different, and not just because it was Saskia's birthday. It was also the anniversary of the tragic accident that had thrown their lives into disarray and brought them here to Ashcombe. Twenty-two years ago her mother and both grandmothers went out shopping together and never came home, their lives brutally cut short in a horrific car crash.

Saskia was ten at the time, old enough to be grief-stricken but not old enough to deal with the trauma of so much loss. It was weeks before she could let her father leave the house without becoming hysterical with terror that he wouldn't return.

It had been Harvey – her mother's father – who had put forward the suggestion that it would help them all if they set up home together, that her father shouldn't be left to cope on his own, that actually *none* of them should be left to cope alone. Within eight months they had pooled their resources and moved here.

The moment Saskia had set eyes on Ashcombe she had fallen in love with it. It was the most beautiful house she had ever seen, a rambling Suffolk Pink cottage on the edge of the village of Melbury Green, flanked by open fields and the River Stour to the rear of the two-acre garden, and a minor road that twisted and turned through the softly undulating Suffolk countryside. To the west, the road took you towards Cambridge, and to the east, to the beaches of Southwold and Aldeburgh.

With its immaculate thatched roof and ornate ridge, its sloping pink walls covered with climbing roses and an orchard filled with apple, pear and damson trees, it was fairy-tale perfect. From the day they moved in, the house beguiled them and became their sanctuary, an enchanting and secluded oasis in which, very slowly, the healing process could begin.

'There you are!' her father greeted her when she pushed open the door to the kitchen and instantly felt the warmth from the Aga. 'We were thinking of sending a search party to find you. Happy birthday!'

'Yes, dear girl, happy birthday,' chimed in Grandpa O, taking her by the arm and steering her towards the table where a small pile of presents and cards had been laid out in front of her usual seat.

'Thirty-two,' Grandpa Harvey said with a chuckle, kissing her on the cheek, 'that sounds like a properly grown-up age to me.'

'It sounds worryingly ancient to me,' Saskia said with a grimace.

'What nonsense! Now sit down and your every birthday whim and desire shall be attended to. What can I make you for breakfast?'

'You know, I think I'll risk some scrambled eggs this morning.'

'Good choice, even if I say so myself. Would that be with toast? Maybe with a rasher or two of bacon on the side? Look lively, Oliver, don't just stand there, pour the girl some tea!'

'All right, all right,' Grandpa O said with a roll of his eyes, 'no need to nag.'

Saskia smiled fondly at the pair of them as they flapped and bustled and bickered around her in their pyjamas and dressing gowns in what she called their Laurel and Hardy routine. They were, she knew, giving an exaggerated performance for her birthday, in the hope it would distract her from the unavoidable shadow cast over the day. Despite their own loss – their wives and a daughter – they had always tried their best to make sure her birthday wasn't lost in the sadness of their collective grief. But in reality her birthday could not be anything but complicit in forcing them to look back and remember.

However, for Saskia the passing of another year was a reminder that the future was more of a concern to her than the past. Her grandfathers, though in reasonably good health, were not getting any younger, and the thought of one day losing them caused her immeasurable sadness. She looked at her father and could see from Ralph's expression that he knew what she was thinking. He usually did.

When she had been studying for her A levels she had announced one Saturday, while she'd been working in the family-run antiquarian bookshop, that she had no interest in going to university. 'Three years of pointless study would bore me rigid,' she'd said.

'And what exactly do you plan to do instead?' her father had asked, barely looking up from the catalogue he was preparing.

'I'll work here with you, of course,' she'd responded, 'and when I'm not doing that I'm going to learn how to restore books so you won't have to pay the exorbitant fees Franklin Reed charges you.'

Giving her his full attention, he'd said, 'How long have you been cooking up this little scheme?'

'Long enough to know it's what I want to do. Please, Dad, don't make me go to university just for the sake of it, I won't fit in and I'll be as miserable as hell. It would also be a shameful waste of money.'

With hindsight it hadn't been that difficult for her father to guess at what was really uppermost in her mind – after all, fitting in had never been a priority for her, not since the accident that had wiped out half her family.

The immediate shock of what had happened that winter's day, when a driver at the wheel of his lorry had fallen asleep and ploughed straight into her mother's car, had left her terrified of going to school. Overnight she became paralysed with fear and the irrational conviction that while she was away from home something awful could happen to what was left of her family, for she'd been at school when disaster had struck in the first place. To solve the problem of continuing her education, her grandfathers took on the job of home-schooling her, but when it came to A levels they said they were out of their depth and she reluctantly agreed to go to the local sixth-form college. She had enjoyed it more than she had anticipated, but at the same time she had accepted she didn't really fit in, not socially; she was too self-contained and too introverted to make any kind of an impact.

'So this has nothing to do with you worrying how your grandfathers and I will cope when you're not here?' Ralph had asked when she'd explained her plan to be a book restorer. He had gone straight to the heart of the matter, knowing precisely what was on her mind. She had denied it, of course.

In the days that followed he'd pestered her to reconsider, telling her that she mustn't make the mistake of living her life through him or Oliver and Harvey, or worse, sacrificing her future for their sakes. 'You're your own person with your own life to live,' he'd said. 'We'd never forgive ourselves if we believed we were responsible for denying you the opportunity to live your life to the full.' To hammer his point home, he'd finished by saying, 'You are not responsible for us, Saskia. That's not what your mother would have wanted or expected from you.'

She hadn't needed to reconsider, not for a single second. Keeping to herself that it was unthinkable for her to leave her family when they had done so much to provide her with a loving and stable childhood, she had waved goodbye to her small circle of friends as they set off for their universities of choice that autumn. She enjoyed hearing from them once term was under way, but didn't envy them or regret her choice to stay behind. She was exactly where she wanted to be and doing exactly what she wanted to do. Ashcombe was where she belonged, and restoring books was what she was meant to do.

Just as old and rare books had become a passion for her father, so they had for Saskia. She loved to hold one in her hands and breathe in the musty age of it, feeling through her fingers a sense of history, and of placing herself within the life of the book. How many people before her had turned its pages and lost themselves in the wonder of its words and pictures? What had their lives been like? What happiness had they experienced? What sadness had they suffered?

More often than not she preferred the company of a room full of books to a room full of people. Books were quiet and constant companions that brought nothing but solace. But best of all, she preferred the company of a book she was restoring and bringing tenderly back to life. And there was no need for anyone to point out that devoting herself to such a vocation – and she did see it as a vocation – was some sort of metaphor for being unable to bring her mother and grandmothers back to life.

It was something her ex-boyfriend had thrown at her at the beginning of last month when he'd called in unexpectedly one evening after work to share his good news with her: he'd been promoted. 'Fifteen other applicants, and I was the one they selected!' he'd said proudly. 'A brilliant way to start the New Year, don't you think?'

She had been genuinely pleased for him, but when Philip had gone on to say the new job meant transferring from the Ipswich office of the software company he worked for to Newcastle, and he wanted her to go with him – they could find a place of their own and set up home together – the conversation had taken a dramatic turn for the worst.

Amazed that he'd been secretly planning this without so much as a word to her, she'd said, 'But Philip, Newcastle is hundreds of miles away and you know I can't leave my family. I couldn't live that far away from them. I'm sorry, it's out of the question.'

'You could at least think about it,' he'd said, his face wreathed in disappointment. 'I thought you'd be pleased. I thought you'd see it as a way to escape.'

'*Escape*?' she'd repeated, stunned. 'Why on earth do I need to escape?'

'Perhaps escape is the wrong word,' he'd said, suddenly avoiding her gaze and looking around her workshop. 'I just meant this would give you ... give *us* ... the chance to be together properly.'

Conscious that she'd comprehensively ruined his surprise, not to say his moment of glory, she'd tried to placate him. 'I'm really happy for you, Philip, it's just that this has come out of nowhere for me.' But while she was saying the words, she was thinking that surely in the eight months they'd been seeing each other he'd come to realise what life at Ashcombe meant to her?

'You know how it is,' she went on, trying to appease him, and wondering if a long-distance relationship might actually be better – it would have all the convenience of having a boyfriend, but without the inconvenience of being forced to change her life. 'I can't drop everything at a moment's notice,' she explained, 'and leave Dad on his own when Oliver and Harvey are likely to need ... well, you understand, I'm sure.'

That had been too much for Philip. 'Your bloody family!' he'd snapped. 'It's all you ever think about! I thought we were—' He stopped himself abruptly and pursed his lips hard, causing them to whiten into an ugly hard line.

'You thought we were what?' she'd prompted, suddenly angry. *Bloody family.* Is that how he viewed Dad and her grandfathers? And after they'd always treated him so well. How dare he!

'I thought we were a *couple*,' he said sullenly. 'A couple that did things jointly, who planned things jointly.'

'Is that what you did when you applied for a job that would be in Newcastle?' she fired back, her patience gone. 'Or did you just think you'd present it as a *fait accompli* and expect me to tag along in your wake?'

'I expected you to accept that it's time you grew up and left home and joined the real world. You're thirty-one, Saskia, not twenty-one!'

Thirty-two as of today, Saskia thought glumly, recalling the childish way in which Philip had vented yet more of his angry disappointment before storming out of her workshop. He'd slammed the door behind him so hard it had bounced back open, giving her a perfect view of him stomping down the path to his car and then driving off with a gratuitous roar of engine. Transfixed, and reflecting how easily life could change, she had watched him go, the freezing cold air swirling in at her feet.

He hadn't spoken to her since. She imagined he was now fully absorbed in either planning his new life in Newcastle, or already enjoying it. Realistically, she doubted they'd had much more left in the tank of their relationship. Moreover, he'd begun to show worrying signs that he couldn't accept that there were certain conditions she came with. Conditions that might just as well have been carved in stone tablets and carried down from the mountaintop by Moses himself.

'Come on, Saskia, why don't you open your cards?'

Her father's voice put an end to her thoughts and returned her to the kitchen and those she loved most in the world.

Looking up at her father, she saw that he was staring at

her with one of his characteristically intuitive smiles. She smiled back at him, and at her grandfathers who so badly wanted her to enjoy her birthday.

Chapter Two

Later that day, standing in line at the post office, Ralph stared out of the window at the passing traffic. Car headlamps glowed in the fading afternoon light and people, bundled up in coats, gloves, hats and scarves, hurried past in the cold.

By stepping to his right and craning his neck, he had a clear view of the church and Granger's Rare and Antiquarian Book Shop across the road. Observing the three-storey building from this vantage point, he reminded himself that when spring arrived, hopefully bringing some warmer and drier weather with it, he really must arrange for Will Swinton to come and redecorate the shop front. Wouldn't do to let things slide, not when the town had such an illustrious reputation to maintain. Not only was Chelstead one of Suffolk's smallest and prettiest towns, it frequently made it on to the list of most desirable places to live in the county. An historic wool town on the south bank of the River Stour, it attracted a steady flow of tourists with its picturesque colour-washed and timber-framed buildings, along with an impressive medieval church, admittedly not on a par with the churches of Long Melford or Lavenham, but perfectly in keeping with the size and character of the town.

The woman at the front of the queue moved away, her business complete, and with three other customers ahead of him, Ralph inched forwards and switched the Jiffy bag he was holding from his right to his left hand – inside was a first edition of G.K. Chesterton's *Father Brown Selected Stories* which he was sending to one of his regular online customers. The Internet had transformed the nature of the business and accounted for a high percentage of what he sold. The time would come when he might well do away with the shop, but not yet. For now his market street position gave him an excellent footfall amongst locals and tourists alike, and owning the premises meant he had no worries about the rent being hiked into the stratosphere by a greedy landlord, as was too often the case these days.

The man immediately in front of him had resorted to passing the time by holding an intrusively loud conversation on his mobile. Ralph tried not to listen, but it was impossible not to be drawn into the one-sided exchange that revolved around a head office meeting in Colchester tomorrow morning, which apparently nobody was looking forward to. It was extraordinary how uninhibited people could be with that small device pressed against their head.

With the clock on the wall behind the counter helpfully informing Ralph that he'd so far been held captive here for fourteen minutes, he watched the second hand judder inexorably around the face of the timepiece; it seemed to say, 'I feel your pain, but here's another minute of your life gone forever.' Did the post office deliberately provide a clock to taunt its customers?

In common with anyone who had better things to do, Ralph hated to be kept waiting, but on the days when Pat, his long-standing part-time helper, didn't come in he had no choice but to put a 'Back-in-Ten-Minutes' note on the door of the shop and stand in line and patiently wait his turn. Oliver and Harvey used to help out on a regular basis, and occasionally still liked to lend a hand, as did Saskia when she had the time to spare.

He shuffled his feet for something to do and thought of Saskia opening her birthday presents that morning. He'd been pleased and relieved that she'd been so delighted with the bluey-grey cashmere cardigan he'd given her. He'd spotted it in the window of a new clothes shop in Long Melford some weeks ago and had been struck by how similar it was to the colour of her eyes. She had the same colour of eyes as her mother, but whereas Evie's had all too often sparkled with humour and mischief, Saskia's were more prone to a solemnity that quite belied her age. That difference aside, she was most assuredly her mother's daughter and had inherited the same wide cheekbones, the same chin that could rise with a defiance that told him in no uncertain terms to back off, and the same dark hair that curled when damp. Slightly taller than her mother had been, she had the same slim, long-legged build that never seemed to gain a pound in weight.

Whenever he thought of these similarities, he was filled with sad regret that Evie had never known her daughter as an adult.

At once the image of his wife wagging her finger at him popped into his head. 'Ralph,' he imagined her saying, 'stop it! No regrets and no living in the past because it's the safer option. You never used to be like that. You used to take matters into your own hands and make things happen!'

Whether or not it was Evie's stern voice chastising him, or merely the voice of his subconscious, he knew without a shred of doubt that the criticism was justified. But the simple fact was he wasn't the same man he'd once been. As clichéd as it was, when Evie died a part of him died as well.

They'd met in the time-honoured way at a party, a party that had taken place in London in the flat below his in Wandsworth. At the time Evie had been engaged to be married to someone called Magnus, but before that had been made known to Ralph, and after he'd introduced himself as their host's neighbour, he had believed himself to be more or less home and dry, having made her laugh with a self-effacing story about some disastrous faux pas he'd committed at work. But when he'd asked her if she'd like to risk an evening out with him sometime, she'd said that Magnus, her fiancé, probably wouldn't like that. She'd pointed across the room to where said fiancé was deep in conversation with a trio of men who were dressed as if they'd come straight from the office.

'So what's wrong with your fiancé?' Ralph had asked a few minutes later when she'd gone into more detail about the man who had just ruined his evening.

'What do you mean, what's wrong with him?' she'd replied with a frown and a distinct lifting of her chin.

'You've just told me you've been together for two years,' he replied, 'and despite being engaged, you've yet to set the date.'

The frown deepened. 'And from that you discern a problem? How about the old adage, marry in haste and repent at leisure?'

'If he truly loved you he'd have whisked you off to the altar by now, he'd have snapped you up fast before someone better came along.' He then indicated the ring on her finger. 'He would also have given you a decent ring, not fobbed you off with some shabby little thing he found in a cracker.'

Her eyes widened even more. 'Wow! You've got some nerve, haven't you?'

'I like to think so, yes. How about you? Or are you the type to settle for second best because you don't have the courage to expect better? And from where I'm standing, you absolutely deserve better.'

She stared back at him, her face ablaze with anger. 'I'll tell you the type of person I am. I'm the sort who doesn't waste her breath on a jerk like you. Have a nice life, why don't you? And good luck with finding someone mad enough to take on you and your colossal ego. Maybe they'll be able to teach you some manners!'

He'd had to admit that her description of him was fully deserved; he *had* behaved like an egotistical jerk. But for some bizarre reason something had got into him. Jealousy, perhaps. A need to impress her. A need to sweep her off her feet. Whatever it was, it was a new experience for him and left him baffled long after she had left the party with her fiancé.

A week later he heard through his neighbour, the host of

the party, that his old school friend, Magnus, had just been dumped by his long-term girlfriend. Which presented Ralph with a dilemma – without seeming insensitive, how could he get the necessary information from his neighbour so he could contact Evie?

In the end, he didn't need to; *she* contacted him. He came home from work one evening and found her huddled on the front doorstep. It was the middle of winter and she looked frozen half to death.

'You were right about Magnus,' she said simply. 'I've left him.'

'I'm sorry,' he said, getting down and sitting on the step with her.

She turned her head. 'Are you?'

'No, not really. You were too good for him. And without doubt you're too good for me, but I'd like the opportunity to see if I could raise my game.'

She smiled. 'I don't think anyone's ever had the same effect on me as you have.'

'You mean, annoyed you so much? I'm sorry for being such a cocky big-mouth who could learn some manners.'

'No, I meant someone who makes me feel the way I do. I haven't stopped thinking about you since that night.'

'That makes two of us; I've thought of nothing else but how I could get in touch with you.' Taking his gloves off, he held out his hand to her. 'How about we start over and pretend we're meeting for the first time?'

Her smile increased and she took off her woollen mitten. 'Evie Milner, pleased to meet you.'

He wrapped his warm hand around her slender, icy fingers. 'Ralph Granger,' he said, feeling as though he was jumping off a cliff straight into the unknown, 'I'm exceptionally pleased to meet you. But before you die of cold, let's get you inside and warmed up, and you can tell me all about yourself.'

'No,' she said, 'let's walk. I don't care where.'

That's how it always was with Evie. She could always find a better way of doing things. Hand in hand, they walked the dark streets hardly aware of their surroundings. He discovered she was exactly the same age as he was and that their birthdays were a week apart. 'I've never met a stylist before,' he said when she told him what job she did, 'what does one actually do?'

'Basically I help people to make the most of themselves.'

'Could you do that with me?' he'd asked.

She'd stepped away from him, tilted her head to one side and pressed her lips together while slowly raking him from top to toe with alarming scrutiny, taking in the new suit he'd treated himself to last week and which he vainly thought gave him an air of grown-up gravitas as a City accountant, along with the woollen overcoat his parents had bought him for Christmas last year. 'Hmmm ... I think I like you just the way you are,' she said finally.

'Really?'

'You seem surprised?'

'In my experience girls always want to change something about a man.'

'Then you've been mixing with the wrong kind of girls.'

It turned out her work as a stylist was a lot more involved and specialised than she'd implied and it made him doubly anxious about his appearance when they were together. Her clients weren't middle-aged housewives in need of a revamp, as he'd pictured, but included an up-and-coming pop star as well as a TV presenter. Her real love was designing clothes, but mostly she sourced outfits for photo shoots for magazines and television appearances.

Five months after meeting her, he blew his savings on the biggest diamond he could afford. Evie was furious that he'd gone to such expense. 'You're not trying to prove something, are you?' she'd asked.

'Only the extent of my love for you,' he'd replied, slipping the ring on to her finger.

They married three months later – a week before the wedding of Prince Charles and Lady Diana – and in contrast to the ceremony that took place at St Paul's Cathedral, they tied the knot without any fuss or bother in the church where Evie had been baptised as a baby, along with their immediate family and a couple of close friends. The following year they were back in the same church, this time standing at the font having Saskia baptised.

To this day he couldn't say exactly what it was that had made him fall in love with Evie. It could have been the way she looked at him so intently. Or the way her body was a natural fit with his, whether they were slouched on the sofa together or lying in bed. Or it could have been her laugh, the way it could magically flick a switch inside of him and make him feel like nothing would ever matter more to him than to hear that happy sound. Whatever the reason, the result had been that he'd been deeply and profoundly in love with Evie and knew that, by some incredible fluke of chance, he had found the one person in the world he was meant to be with.

So that was the man he'd once been. A man who saw what he wanted and went all out for it. Had Evie not been waiting for him on the doorstep that evening, he would have found her, even if it meant scouring the whole of London.

Now he was almost sixty, a man who spent his life taking the path of least resistance, a man who frequently capitulated and stood in line at the post office patiently waiting his turn.

At long last the wait was over and he'd made it to the front of the queue where he exchanged a few pleasantries with the woman behind the counter – a woman who had only started working there a few weeks ago and who seemed to have a permanently red and runny nose. The parcel safely delivered into the hands of the Royal Mail, he hurried out into the street and crossed the road.

His mobile started to ring in his pocket as he let himself in at the shop.

'Hi, Gil,' he said, shutting the door and removing the

note he'd stuck on it before he'd been trapped in Chelstead's equivalent of purgatory. 'What can I do for you?'

'Always a matter of what I can do for you, old son. I've another load of books you might like to have a rummage through.'

Ralph shrugged off his coat. Gilbert Ross's line of work was house clearance and he often gave Ralph the opportunity to have first dibs on the books that came his way. 'You mean you've got a ton of books you don't know what to do with?' he said.

'Don't be like that, Ralph – I've been good to you over the years and you've had a fair few nice little earners through me.'

It was true and in return Ralph had always given Gil a cut of anything that turned out to be of real value. 'The trouble is, I'm a bit stuck for space,' he said. Again this was true. He was way behind with sorting through Gil's previous deliveries. Much to Saskia's disapproval, after there'd been a small flood in the basement caused by a leaking pipe, he'd had to store some in her workshop. Actually 'some' was an understatement. There were about twenty boxes of books waiting to be sifted through.

'You know what you need,' Gil said, 'you need a lock-up.'

'I need that like a hole in the head,' Ralph said.

'So what's your answer, yes or no?'

As always Ralph couldn't say no, not when there was the chance that in amongst the mundane, there could be that elusive rarity that would give him the kind of thrill his job as an accountant all those years ago never had. He was a great believer in the theory that, more often than not, books, the special ones, found their way to the serious book lover.

Opening an antiquarian bookshop had been a secret ambition of his when he'd been a teenager, but unsurprisingly it didn't feature as an option on the school's career list. Evie was the first person to whom he'd confessed this harboured ambition – there were many things he shared with her that he'd never shared with anyone else – and her reaction was to tell him to get on and do it. 'What, ditch my job, just like that?' he'd responded, shocked.

'Why not?' she'd answered him.

'Money for starters. And stability. And a good pension. And—'

'All excuses stopping you from doing something daring and exciting.'

'Would it be exciting if we didn't have enough money to put food on the table?'

She'd tutted. 'Don't be so boringly bourgeois. And if it's slipped your mind, I'm capable of earning a decent wage. Come on, where's that cocky man I met who accused me of settling for second best?'

He was almost convinced he should do as she said when they discovered she was pregnant. Children had been a part of the equation, eventually, just not yet. Inevitably, the unplanned pregnancy had the accountant in him rising to the fore and he was forcibly reminded that money and stability and a good pension were of even greater importance now. Without a backward glance, all thoughts of the new life he'd begun to imagine were swept away in their combined excitement and trepidation at becoming parents.

His love of books – particularly old books – came from his mother's parents who'd lived in the Cotswolds and owned exactly the kind of establishment Ralph wanted for himself. The shop had been a home from home for him and he'd loved nothing more than to stay with his grandparents during the school holidays and be allowed to browse the walls of shelves that were chaotically packed tight with all manner of books. Through those dusty old books he travelled the world and filled his head with dreams and adventures. He went with explorers to Egypt to discover the tombs and pyramids; he lived with revolutionaries in Russia; fought the Greeks in the Trojan War in ancient Anatolia – and all without ever leaving the comfort of the chair in the corner of the shop.

But then his grandparents retired and sold up to go and live by the sea in Devon.

The shop might have gone, but its smell, redolent of aged books and everything they stood for, had worked its way into his system where it lay dormant, biding its time until it could be ignored no longer.

Evie's death taught him many things, primarily that he could never love anyone else in the way he'd loved her, but also to face up to the knowledge that working in the City for a large accountancy firm was never going to satisfy him. Yes, it would give him and his daughter financial security, but with the long hours expected of him it would mean he would never see Saskia; she would be in the constant care of a nanny. Then Harvey had suggested they combine forces and buy a house large enough to accommodate them all and thereby do away with a nanny. It opened their eyes to a radical change in lifestyle and, after careful consideration, they decided Suffolk would give them more for their money – it was actually the only county the three of them could agree upon as somewhere they thought they could live. So Oliver moved across from Bishop's Stortford, Harvey from Chelmsford and Ralph and Saskia up from London. It was a convergence of four heartbroken people desperately in need of support and a new start.

An hour later and Ralph had locked up and was on his way home. Arriving back at Ashcombe in the dark, he saw that the light was still on in Saskia's workshop. The studio had originally been a tumbledown collection of outhouses, which he'd had converted into one large, airy space for Saskia to work in.

Respecting that it was her private domain, he knocked on the door and waited to be granted permission to enter. He caught a vague response and turned the handle.

'Dad's just walked in,' Saskia said into the screen of her

laptop and waving him over. 'Do you want to have a word with him?'

'Sure, birthday girl, put him on.'

There was no need to ask who Saskia was talking to: Ralph's sister's voice was so recognisable and loud it could travel without the aid of Skype or FaceTime all the way from Calgary in Canada where she and her husband Bob had lived for the best part of thirty years.

'Hi, Jo,' he said, looking at the comically pixelated image of his sister. 'How's tricks?'

'We're freezing our butts off here. We've got three feet of snow and have resorted to drinking de-icer to keep warm. How do you think I am?'

Ralph laughed. Always the same Jo. No matter what, she never changed. It was one of the things he loved about her. That and the fact that she might live thousands of miles away, but she never forgot them, or Saskia's birthday.

Chapter Three

Harvey slung the tea towel over his shoulder, took an appreciative and, in his opinion, well-earned slurp of wine and looked about him with satisfaction: everything was coming together very nicely.

With the main lights dimmed, the table set with plates of smoked salmon blinis – some sprinkled with chopped chives, others with dill – was ready and waiting. Their main course of lamb shank casserole was in the bottom oven of the Aga where it had been for most of the afternoon, filling the house with the appetising aroma of garlic and rosemary. Pudding could only be one thing, Saskia's favourite chocolate cake, a cake he made for her every birthday, and always in a pantomime of secrecy – he never let on that he'd made it and in turn she never let on that she knew he'd make it for her.

Harvey liked to think that his wife was looking down and smiling to herself, and was maybe even proud of him. 'Who'd have thought it,' he imagined Ester saying, 'Harvey Milner knowing his way round a kitchen? Whatever next!'

Who'd have thought it indeed? Time was when Ester had only trusted him to help with the washing-up, and even then he'd put things away in the wrong place. It had been a different time back then, especially when they'd been newly-weds and their roles had been clearly defined into very much his and hers – he went to work, she stayed at home; that was how it was. It was better these days, he reckoned. Fairer, although not necessarily easier.

Their marriage had been a good one. It had been rock solid with a strong, loving bond between them. It was that bond that had seen them through some pretty tough times – a series of miscarriages before Evie was born, and another one two years later. They had then resigned themselves to the fact that there would be no more children and, as anyone might expect, their one and only precious child became the centre of their marriage and their love for each other.

Did they spoil her? Perhaps they did. But so what? She grew up to be a wonderful young woman, vibrant and funny, a loving daughter and an adoring wife and mother. And how he still missed her. Ester, too. He breathed in deeply and let his breath out slowly. Twenty-two years on and he could still feel the pain of losing his wife and daughter.

It was hardly surprising that today of all days he would be more vulnerable to that loss, a day that brought into sharp focus the terrible memories. It had been one of those arranged-at-the-last-minute days out that Ester and Nell and Evie often did – lunch together and, in this instance, a few last things to shop for in readiness for Saskia's party at the weekend. Taking the train into London, Ester had met with Evie who had then driven them to Hertford to pick up Nell. But they never made it to lunch. Ralph had been the first to be told the news and, poor devil, he'd been the one to break it to him and Oliver. They were two phone calls no one should ever have to make.

Selecting a vegetable knife from the wooden block, Harvey began chopping the carrots he'd just peeled. No maudlin thoughts, he told himself firmly. Not tonight. Not for Saskia's birthday dinner.

By rights she should be out celebrating with friends, but she always said she would spend this evening no other way. It pained him that her small circle of friends had become dispersed in recent years; they had either moved away, or had married and were now preoccupied with the demands of small children. In short, their lives had moved on and sadly Saskia's hadn't. Which meant, as anybody in the same situation would know, with increasingly less in common, friendship becomes harder to maintain.

Harvey knew from personal experience how easily that happened. In the aftermath of the accident, a few people who he had counted as friends suddenly didn't know how to be around him anymore, and before too long they stopped ringing or visiting. He had understood their reluctance to be around him, for what could you possibly say to a man who had lost so much?

Two more minutes and then he'd call everyone for supper. Harvey had heard Ralph's car earlier but not having heard him come in, he assumed his son-in-law was with Saskia in her workshop. The last he'd seen of Oliver was an hour ago when he'd gone for a bath after his usual fifteen-minute session in the garden, rounding up the hens and putting them to bed for the night.

Routine. It was all about routine and tradition at Ashcombe. That's how it had been from the day they moved in. Knowing what they were all doing at a certain time in the day had represented stability, not just for Saskia, but for the rest of them; it was a way to cope, a means to battle their way through the minefield of grief.

Friends had thought he'd been so brave to suggest they all live together – brave because what would they do if the plan went horribly wrong? But really it had been selfish cowardice on his part that had made him come up with the idea; he simply couldn't bear to be alone in the house where he and Ester had lived for the last twenty-eight years, the house that was crammed full of memories of their life together. He had badly wanted it to be a comfort to be surrounded by the familiarity of their home, but it had been the opposite. Everywhere he looked he was reminded of all that was gone and the awful silence and emptiness filled him with unrelenting sorrow.

Perhaps if the accident hadn't coincided with his recent retirement he might have coped better. But there was nothing to distract him, and with the deepening awareness that Ralph was in a worse state than he was, he saw a way to be of use and to feel needed.

With his days as a regional building society manager with a dozen branches under his control behind him, at Ashcombe he had a new role to adjust to, that of Domestic Technician, and he threw himself into it with gusto. Cooking was the Everest of his learning curve, but he eventually mastered it and came to find relief in the process. Chopping, grinding, kneading, mixing, stirring – it was all a way to keep busy, and to pour his love into taking care of what was left of his shattered family. United we stand, he would often murmur to himself as he stood at the sink looking out of the window and watching Oliver tending to the vegetable patch.

The carrots now chopped, it was time to rally the troops for supper. First he called up the stairs to Oliver and then went to the back door where there was a ship's brass bell hanging in the porch. He gave it a vigorous tug and watched in the darkness for a response over in the brightly lit workshop where he could see Ralph and Saskia talking. They turned simultaneously and gave him an acknowledging wave.

Back in the warmth of the kitchen, he uncovered the plates of smoked salmon blinis and took out a bottle of champagne from the fridge. Removing the cork, he carefully filled four flutes. This was another Ashcombe tradition to which they rigidly held. Saskia had been sixteen when she'd suggested they should drink a toast to Evie, Ester and Nell on her birthday, and that it should be champagne they drank. It was one of the many things Harvey loved about his grand-daughter, her absolute understanding of what mattered, of what was important to them as a family. Some people wanted to forget; they didn't. They wanted to remember.

Chapter Four

A week after his granddaughter's birthday and with March now upon them, Oliver was looking forward to getting cracking in the garden. But before then, he was helping Saskia sort through the boxes of books in the workshop. They had been at it for over two hours and apart from a couple of attractive clothbound Conan Doyle's they had found little of real interest. The reject boxes were mostly full of paperbacks and the ubiquitous assortment of Reader's Digest anthologies.

It was a job that was long overdue and one Oliver knew Saskia was keen to tackle now that she had some free time. Since December she had been absorbed in the painstaking task of restoring a collection of valuable leather-bound atlases dating from the mid-1700s to the nineteenth century. Some of the books had required no more than a cursory amount of restoration, such as mending split spines or the reattachment of boards, but others had been in need of a lot more specialised care. The client, a serious collector, had bought the atlases at an auction and yesterday, when he came to collect them, he'd been so delighted with the miracle Saskia had wrought that he'd returned an hour later with a large bouquet of flowers for her.

Oliver didn't know how Saskia had the patience to do what she did, but then, as Ralph was only too quick to point out, living with the three of them had taught her to have the patience of not just one saint, but a whole host of them.

Spooning coffee into two mugs while he waited for the kettle to boil, Oliver thought that increasingly there were days when he felt he could do with a bit of restoration himself. Having a new knee was just the start, he supposed. There again, at his age, and compared to a lot of folk, he was lucky to have got away with only an arthritic knee. It was amazing what the quacks could do nowadays. Although they still couldn't do anything for a common cold.

'There are biscuits in the tin, if you fancy one,' Saskia said to him as he bent down with a creak of bones in the cramped space to find the milk in the small fridge.

'Right you are,' he replied. He liked being in the workshop with Saskia; he liked the sense of containment it gave. He suspected Saskia did too; it was her private space, her little oasis away from the house. In their own way, they each had their special place – Ralph had the shop, Harvey had the kitchen, he had the garden, and Saskia had her workshop.

From the very start of living here they had agreed that the situation would only work if they knew when to keep out of each other's way and had somewhere to be alone. He would be the first to admit that he needed time alone occasionally as he could be a thoroughly miserable bugger when the mood took him, unlike Harvey who had an inherently upbeat personality. Harvey was their very own Pollyanna and could always be relied upon to find the positive in a situation; in contrast, Oliver's default setting was more inclined to the pessimistic leaning of the dial. His daughter said his problem wasn't so much thinking his glass was half empty as believing it would slip out of his hands and shatter into lethally sharp shards.

Jo was full of pithy remarks likes that. She was one of those people who always spoke her mind. All of it. You were never in any doubt where you stood with Jo. You also knew you could rely on her one hundred per cent in a crisis. He'd never been prouder of her than when she had flown over twenty-two years ago in response to the news of the accident and her mother's death. Somehow putting her own grief to one side, she had taken control of the situation and organised everything that needed to be done. Whereas the rest of them had been all but catatonic with shock she had been a tower of strength, an absolute godsend. Some weeks later, when she was back in Canada, Oliver had asked for her advice about Harvey's suggestion that they all live together. She was the only person he trusted to be completely honest and objective with him. 'What do you think?' he'd asked her on the phone. 'Good idea or not?'

'Misery loves company,' she'd said, 'so the danger is you'll all go under together.'

'So it's a bad idea?'

'On the other hand,' she had continued as if he hadn't spoken, 'it could be the best thing you could do. Best for Saskia as well. She needs people around her. She needs routine and stability. By helping her, you'll be helping yourselves. It's perfect. You have my full approval. Go ahead.'

She had been right; it had been the perfect solution. But much as Oliver loved Ashcombe – much as he knew it had saved them – he worried that it could be Saskia's undoing. She needed a life beyond Ashcombe, but stuck here with them she was never going to have that. He suspected she had secretly signed up for the job of official carer for them now, which she would see as a way to repay them for what they had done for her as a child. He wished there was a way to disabuse her of this sense of sacrificial duty, but he couldn't for the life of him think how to go about it, other than for them all rather conveniently to die. But even he could see that was a somewhat drastic solution.

'Kettle's boiling, Grandpa O.'

He turned round, startled, to see Saskia standing a few feet away from him with a concerned look on her face. Then he realised the kettle must have been boiling for some time because she was staring at him through a cloud of steam.

'I thought it switched off automatically,' he said, embarrassed, while wafting the steam away with his hand.

'It's started playing up,' she said, reaching over to flick the switch herself. 'You looked like you were miles away.'

'I was.'

'Anything you want to share?'

Mindful that she was still watching him, he paid extra care and attention to pouring the boiling water into the mugs. The last thing she needed was the worry that he was losing his marbles. 'I was thinking about you, if you must know, Miss Parker.' Miss Parker, as in nosy parker, was the nickname he'd given her when she'd been about four years old and had constantly bombarded him with questions – Where are you going, Grandpa O ... why do cats purr ... what's for tea ... why don't we have fingers all the same size ... where does the wind go when it's not windy?

'Me?' she said. 'Why should you be thinking about me?'

He stirred the coffee and passed a mug to her. 'I was wondering about that boyfriend of yours,' he improvised, making a quantum leap and grasping at the first plausible thing that came into his head.

Surprise flickered across her face. Then it was eclipsed by another expression, and one he didn't like the look of.

'I don't have a boyfriend,' she said, her voice measured.

'I know you don't,' he said quickly, feeling her eyes lasering the face off him. Damn, now she really would be worried that his mind was on the way out. 'What I meant was, I was wondering about ...' Oh hell, what was his name? Peter? No, that wasn't right. It was ... it was Philip, that was it! 'I was wondering if you'd heard from Philip recently. Perhaps a text message or maybe an email last week to wish you a happy birthday.' Dear Lord, dragging up an ex-boyfriend! Could he dig himself into a deeper hole? And why couldn't he just be honest and say what he'd really been thinking? Because he knew that as far as Saskia was concerned, there was no discussion to be had. He'd tried it before and had been given two very clear shades of short shrift. She could be scarily stern when she wanted to be.

He watched her help herself to a chocolate digestive and, as she held it poised to dunk into her coffee, she said, 'No,

Philip didn't get in touch and I really wouldn't have expected him to.'

Realising that he'd established himself on less than secure ground – Saskia had never gone into details why she'd stopped seeing Philip, other than to say they'd run their course – Oliver grunted. 'I never really took to that chap,' he said, 'he was rubbish at playing board games with us. Harvey and I could tell he did it under sufferance.'

The biscuit duly dunked and chewed on, Saskia gave him one of her unnervingly inscrutable stares and then she suddenly smiled. 'I don't think we can really hold that against Philip, can we? Not everyone enjoys that sort of thing.'

That was where Oliver wisely left it, respecting that Saskia was entitled to her privacy. But behind her back, it had not gone unnoticed amongst the rest of them that too many of her relationships apparently ran their course and ground to a halt. When pressed she would claim that she was choosy or bored easily, but Oliver reckoned that she was lying, that the truth was if a boyfriend got too serious and began to be a threat to the stability of life here at Ashcombe, she hit the ejector button.

Regarding his granddaughter now as he helped himself to a biscuit, Oliver made a sudden promise to himself. The next boyfriend who came along, and if he met with universal Ashcombe approval, Oliver would make damn sure Saskia didn't ditch him just as things began to get serious between them.

Which was easier said than done, he could see that, but he would make Saskia see sense if it was the last thing he did.

Chapter Five

The silvered mist of early morning lay like a shroud over the church and graveyard. It wouldn't be everyone's ideal outlook from their bedroom, but in common with the man who had slept in this room and woken to the view every morning for the last twenty-three years, Matthew had a fondness for it. Perhaps he did so because he associated it so greatly with Jacob Belinsky, the man who had played such a crucial and pivotal role in his life.

Matthew had been here the night Jacob had died in December. It was three weeks before Christmas and he'd come back for the weekend as he so often did, his visits increasingly more regular following Jacob's ninety-third birthday earlier that summer when the old man had sadly turned the corner from relative independence to discernible frailty. Mentally, though, there had been no disintegration; his mind had been as sharp and alert as ever and it remained that way right up until the end.

They had eaten supper together that evening, then played a game of chess, which Jacob had won. Having played so often together they each knew the other's moves, which, of course, provided its own entertainment and challenge. Matthew considered himself a competent player – he'd played for his college chess society at Cambridge – but he hadn't been in Jacob's league. Always gracious when he won, Jacob had taken a long, thoughtful sip of his whisky while watching Matthew replacing the pieces on the board. 'You very nearly had me,' he'd said, 'and to quote dear old Tartakower, the winner of the game is merely the player who makes the next-to-last mistake.' Savielly Tartakower, a Polish and French chess player from the 1920s and '30s, was Jacob's grandmaster of choice, if only because the man had been such a ready wit and left the world of chess with so many great aphorisms. 'An isolated pawn spreads gloom over the chessboard,' was a particular favourite of Matthew's.

Gloomy, was how Matthew felt this miserable Saturday March morning as he stood at the window and contemplated the task ahead of him, that of clearing out Jacob's bedroom. He'd left it till now, unable to face the depressing thought of sifting through Jacob's clothes. A man's underwear should surely be his own business?

A smile suddenly broke over his face as he imagined Jacob's scornful reaction to his squeamishness. 'Thirty-four years old, Matthew, and scared of some shabby old undergarments? You'll be frightened of your own shadow next!'

Turning away from the window, Matthew faced the bed where he'd found Jacob. One look at him that morning and he had known straight away that the old man was dead. He'd been much too still to be asleep; there was no laboured rise and fall to his breathing. His usual pallor was paler than normal also, and his mouth had dropped open, giving the impression that he was about to say something. With his head resting against the pillow, the bedclothes flat across his chest and just touching his chin, as though he'd lain perfectly still from the moment he'd got into bed, he had looked strangely childlike. It was an appearance hugely at odds with the man he'd been, a man of commanding authority and high intelligence. He had not been an especially big man, or physically strong; rather his strength had come from a fierce inner force. He had been as private and determined a man Matthew had ever known. But there had been a sensitivity to him as well and he'd possessed a deep understanding of the human mind and what it was capable of, good and bad.

Matthew was not ashamed to admit that he'd cried that morning when he'd found Jacob dead. The man had been the closest thing to a father he'd had. In fact, he'd been father, grandfather and mentor all rolled into one and Matthew would be forever grateful for everything he'd learnt from him. It wasn't an exaggeration to say that, apart from his mother, Jacob had been the single greatest influence in his life.

Matthew had been eleven years old when his mother had applied for the job in Cambridge as housekeeper to Professor Jacob Belinsky. The word housekeeper has a pretentious and ludicrously archaic sound to it in this day and age and even back then it did, but Mum didn't care; so long as it provided her with the means by which she could pay the bills in order to keep a roof over their heads, she would do it. That had been her attitude ever since Matthew was two years old and his father had decided he wasn't suited to married life, or fatherhood, and had vanished completely and utterly from their lives as if he'd never been there. His mother always claimed it was just as well; they were better off without him.

The job turned out to be perfect for Mum; her employer might have been a little eccentric, waving her away with a haughty wave of his hand when he didn't want to be bothered, or forgetting to eat the meal she'd cooked for him, but all in all, she felt she'd landed on her feet. But then her employer announced his intention to leave Cambridge and retire from college life – he was Professor of Slavonic Studies at Merchant College, his old alma mater – and move out of town to live in rural Suffolk. Disappointed that the job was to be so short-lived, Mum braced herself for another job search. But then Jacob Belinsky informed her he'd bought a house and wanted, for ease of continuity, to take her with him, saying the post of housekeeper could now be live-in. She refused on the grounds that it wouldn't be fair to uproot her son.

'You have a son?' Jacob had queried. 'Why is this the first I've heard of him?'

In the repeated telling of this story, and by Jacob himself,

Matthew's mother had politely explained that she had told him before, indeed she had mentioned Matthew many times before, but it must have slipped his busy mind.

For years afterwards Jacob liked to reminisce about that conversation, which proved to be a turning point for all three of them. 'I can remember her now,' he would say to Matthew, 'standing there, prickling with indignation beneath that veneer of politeness of hers and basically informing me that I was a blithering idiot! That taught me a lesson, I can tell you, it taught me to sit up straight and pay attention to your mother.'

Having insisted that she bring her son for him to meet, Jacob subsequently worked on Mum until he'd convinced her that they should make the move with him, stressing that there was a perfectly good school nearby for Matthew. 'Please,' he'd said, 'spare me the tiresome task of having to find a replacement for you, a replacement who won't run things half as efficiently as you.' Part of his persuasion included driving them out to see the house and surrounding area.

Mum had been horrified when she'd seen it. 'That's an awful lot to take care of,' she'd said, taking in the large and imposing building as they drove between two gateposts where a painted sign welcomed them to Glaskin House.

'Professor Belinsky needs somewhere big for all his books,' Matthew had said helpfully, staring in awe up at the mellow brick and thinking that it wasn't so much a house as a mansion.

Clapping his hands together with a loud emphatic laugh, the professor had looked pleased. 'Look at that, Mrs Gray; your son understands the situation perfectly. He's a smart boy.'

'Hmm ... well, it's not my smart boy who has to dust all those books.'

'Oh, I don't know, perhaps you could enlist his help?'

After sharing a conspiratorial wink with Matthew, the

professor had unlocked the front door of the house, which he'd explained was Georgian, solidly built and mercifully untouched by those of an ignorant disposition hell-bent on a ruthless mission to modernise when no such thing was necessary.

'I hope the kitchen's been updated in the last hundred years,' Mum had muttered.

'You might have to spruce up the roasting spit, but other than that I think you'll find it more than adequate.'

Matthew wasn't entirely sure what a roasting spit was, but he caught Mum's tut and roll of her eyes, which made him think that she knew she was being teased.

The hall was large, with what the professor described as original wooden panelling to the walls, and to their right was a wide, curving staircase. Looking about him as they moved towards a door on the far side of the hall, Matthew reckoned the flat he and Mum rented could easily fit into the hall alone. The professor pushed the door open and took them into what he said would be the nerve centre of the house: the library. The walls were covered in empty shelves, and having seen the professor's house in Cambridge, which was packed full with books, Matthew could easily imagine how this room would look once he had moved in. All that interrupted the flow of shelves was a stone fireplace and a large window with a view of blue sky and an endless lawn ringed with trees.

'I presume you're going to have a gardener,' Mum said.

'You presume correctly,' the professor replied. 'The previous owners have put me in touch with the man who worked for them.'

Their shoes clattering noisily on the wooden floors, Matthew's awe grew with each empty and high-ceilinged room they were shown round. When at last the tour was over, the professor took them outside. 'Now to see where you and your mother will live,' he said to Matthew.

He took them to a red-brick cottage tucked away at the

side of the house. 'Formerly there was a stable block here,' he said, opening the black-painted front door and letting them go in first, 'then some clever Victorian spark decided to convert it to this and renamed it The Coach House. Why don't you go off and explore and see which bedroom you'd like, Matthew?'

Matthew went up the stairs and, standing on the landing where a diamond-shaped stained-glass window overlooked a small walled garden, he turned and tried to listen to what was being said downstairs. He hoped his mother wasn't going to say no. He couldn't think of anything nicer than coming to live here with Professor Belinsky.

His mother didn't say no and they moved to Glaskin House four weeks later.

So began Matthew's relationship with a truly inspirational man, a man of infinite intellect, kindness and generosity. Twenty-three years later that generosity had led to Matthew being the sole benefactor of Jacob's last will and testament.

Realistically there was no way Matthew could live in the house himself; it just wasn't practical. Firstly it was too big, and secondly, while it was fine for a weekly commute to Cambridge where he worked, it wasn't ideal for a daily one. But whenever he considered selling the house he was overwhelmed with feelings of disloyalty and an unexpected desire to cling on to the last connection with his childhood.

Not once had Jacob ever spoken about his will, and naturally Matthew had never asked – he had simply assumed Jacob would leave the bulk of his estate to the various charities he supported, and maybe donate a large percentage of his books, particularly the specialised ones, to his old college library in Cambridge. If Jacob had planned to leave anything to him, Matthew would have guessed at a relatively small amount of money. Never had it crossed his mind that apart from making a sizeable donation to the church next door for any future restoration work required, Jacob would leave everything, lock, stock and barrel, to him.

He'd spoken at length to the solicitor handling the will and had been informed that there had actually been a previous will in which Jacob had left the house and contents to Matthew's mother, but after her death six years ago, he had instructed his solicitor to draw up a new document in favour of Matthew.

Mum's death had hit him and Jacob hard and had created an instant and massive void in their lives; it was an emptiness that seemed to create a vacuum that drew them towards each other, making them closer than ever. Mum was buried next door in the churchyard, where Jacob had now joined her.

Getting on for a year after his mother's death, and following a string of cleaning women who Jacob didn't take to, the old man had taken the decision to close off parts of the house and not bother with any help. He told Matthew he didn't want strangers poking about in his things. Matthew did his best during his visits to try and keep on top of the growing chaos, but it had been pretty much useless because the tide of disorder kept coming in. In Matthew's absence, the vicar and his wife – Mal and Jenny Allbright – called in regularly to keep an eye on Jacob and to shop for him, and occasionally take him out for the day somewhere. A gardener came sporadically, seemingly when it suited him, and as a result the garden was not what it once was. Nothing was.

Some mornings Matthew woke full of certainty that he'd reached an important milestone in his life and it was time to cut the tie with the past and, just as soon as probate had been completed, he would put the house on the market. But invariably, by lunchtime, he'd have convinced himself he should rent the house out, thereby delaying the final decision until he was sure of what he really wanted. However, by the time he was on his way home from work, he'd have talked himself out of that as well and would picture himself living at Glaskin House, reminding himself how much he liked this part of the East Anglian countryside, how the openness of the largely unhedged fields and the immense, far-reaching skies gave him a sense of space and freedom.

He supposed his inability to know what he should do spoke volumes and left him with the one very unambiguous option: he had to be patient and wait until his mind was clear.

Meanwhile, he was doing the one thing he could do and that was deal with all the clutter Jacob had gathered about him. With the solicitor's permission, he'd made a start early last month with the help of his flatmate, James. They had tackled the loft first where they had been confronted with junk on an industrial scale – rolled-up rugs (some with the remains of dead mice inside them), prehistoric television sets and record players, various pieces of furniture, moth-eaten coats, old shoes and boots, broken china ornaments, picture frames, battered suitcases, trunks of manky blankets, towels and curtains, tea chests of newspapers, correspondence and cheap paperbacks, and a ridiculous number of dented lampshades. Most of what they found was destined for the tip and the house clearance firm Matthew had engaged took the rest away.

James was firmly of the opinion that Matthew should sell the house immediately before it became a millstone around his neck. It always struck Matthew that, for a cardiologist, his friend had a singular lack of heart and saw everything in black and white terms.

Which should have been more his territory, seeing as he was a forensic accountant and trained to be hard-headed in the pursuit of looking beyond the numbers in order to deal solely with the bare bones of the business realities. He was currently coming to the end of a messy divorce case at work, his job to trace the assets the wealthy husband had endeavoured to hide from his wife in a complicated offshore web of deceit, and there were astronomical amounts of money involved.

*

Several hours later, and with the contents of Jacob's wardrobes and chest of drawers now in bin bags, Matthew heard the ring of the doorbell from downstairs. From his jeans' pocket, he pulled out the silver pocket watch Jacob had given him on his twenty-first birthday, and which Jacob had been given on his own twenty-first birthday. Worn smooth with age and use, it was like a shiny pebble in his hand. Often when he needed to think a problem through, he would reach for it in his pocket; it was his talisman.

The precious timepiece told him it was five minutes to twelve, which meant that the person at the door was probably the man from the antiquarian bookshop in Chelstead.

Chapter Six

Ralph's first impression of Glaskin House was that it was probably a while since it had looked its best, something he often saw in his line of work when he was called out to assist in a probate valuation.

This particular valuation had come his way via the usual solicitor's letter in these situations, along with the instruction to liaise directly with the young man with whom he'd just shaken hands. From the brief conversation they'd had on the telephone when arranging this appointment, Ralph had expected someone older ... quite a bit older. The voice he'd heard had been one of courteous maturity and seemed at odds with the person in front of him. Youthfully thin-faced with strong cheekbones and a sharp jawline, and casually dressed in grey jeans, canvas trainers and a black sweater with its sleeves pushed up to the elbows, he looked like the slightly sensible member of a boy band.

'Would you like a drink first,' Matthew Gray asked, 'or would you prefer to get straight down to business?'

'Maybe a drink later, after you've shown me what there is,' Ralph replied. 'You said on the phone there was a considerable collection for me to see.'

The young man nodded and led the way across the hall, the rubber soles of his shoes squeaking on the wooden floor. 'We'll start in the obvious place,' he said, 'the library.'

A 'considerable collection' proved to be a massive understatement. The floor-to-ceiling shelves of the library were crammed full of books, which spilled on to the floor in waist-high towers, as well as covering a large refectory table that dominated the centre of the large room. At the far end of the room was a pair of library ladders, which Ralph could see would prove invaluable for reaching the higher shelves. But where on earth to start?

An amused smile crossed the other man's face. 'Maybe you'd like that drink now,' he remarked.

'I think that's an excellent idea,' Ralph said, looking around him and trying to take stock. This valuation was going to take a lot longer than he'd anticipated.

'Coffee OK? It'll have to be instant, I'm afraid.'

'That's fine. Milk, no sugar. Thank you.'

Left on his own Ralph thought about the deceased man who must have devoted his life to amassing this incredible collection. The world of serious book collecting was a relatively small one in which people got to know, or know of, one another, and Professor Belinsky had actually crossed Ralph's path a number of times over the years, though not recently. Ralph had recognised the name when he'd read it in the solicitor's letter and after checking his records, he'd found the last purchase the professor had made from him had been four years ago when, for £1,850, he'd purchased an 1860 edition of John Bunyan's *Pilgrim's Progress* bound by Riviere and Sons. With that in mind he'd come here today intrigued to see exactly what kind of collection the professor had owned – but he hadn't expected anything on this scale.

Had the professor actually read all these books? he wondered. Or had it been more a matter of acquisition and the ownership of rarity and beauty? Just as some art collectors fed their addiction for works of art, had Professor Belinsky fed a voracious and insatiable hunger for the written word?

Ralph's visit today was merely to do a recce, to gauge just how much work would be involved in carrying out the valuation for probate, and based on this one room alone, he decided he'd better ask Saskia to help him.

*

Each with a mug of coffee in hand, Matthew Gray took him on a tour of the house, revealing the full extent of the collection; almost every room contained a hoard of books. When they were back downstairs in the library, Ralph said, 'Mr Gray, I have to be honest with you, I'm puzzled why I've been approached, why not one of the bigger set-ups in Cambridge? I'm very small fry in comparison.'

His question was met with a look of quizzical concentration. 'Are you saying you'd rather not do the valuation?'

Struck by the young man's assured manner, which was in no way arrogant, purely matter-of-fact and to the point, Ralph said, 'No, not all. I'm just curious, especially as you mentioned earlier that you live in Cambridge where there are some excellent specialist booksellers right on your doorstep.'

'Professor Belinsky specified in his will that you should be approached. I recall him speaking very highly of you, saying that you weren't one of the greedy dealers he'd frequently come across. I suspect he thought you could be trusted to handle things with discretion and fairness.'

'Thank you, that's good to hear.' And knowing that Matthew Gray was the sole beneficiary of the professor's will and thinking that a collection as large as this was a huge responsibility, if not a liability, for someone so young, he said, 'May I ask if you intend to sell the collection?'

'I think I'll have to. But not all of it, I'll want to keep some of the books.' He turned away from Ralph to glance about him at the crowded shelves. The sudden expression of sadness on his face was unmistakable. There was another emotion in his countenance that Ralph recognised all too well: loneliness. After a few moments had elapsed, Matthew Gray turned back to him. 'Do you have any guidance on what I should do?' he asked.

'I'd recommend selling them at auction. But you'd have to decide how you wanted the sale to be done, Mr Gray: do you want to try and keep the collection together, or divide it up into subject matter, for instance?'

'Please, call me Matthew, and to be honest, I'll take your advice on how to go about the whole process. Although I wouldn't have thought there'd be many collectors out there who'd be able to take on a library of this size in its entirety.'

'It would be highly unlikely, but what I would also recommend is that the rarest and most valuable books amongst the collection be sold individually. Again, that could be done at auction, or through private negotiation, which I could handle for you. May I ask you a personal question?'

'You can try,' the young man replied, now looking back at Ralph with a steady intelligent gaze.

'Is your motivation to raise as much cash as possible, or are you looking for a good home for the books?'

'Are the two mutually exclusive?'

'Not necessarily, but it is something I like to advise the client to consider.'

'In that case, I'll give it my full consideration. When can you make a start on the valuation?'

'I'm happy to fit in with your requirements, so as soon as you like.'

Chapter Seven

It had taken several days of ruthless sorting, but finally Saskia was down to the last of the boxes of books her father had stored in her workshop. She had come across only a few items of any interest and didn't hold out much hope this last box would yield anything but the usual tat.

Kneeling on the floor, she opened the cardboard box and found a jumble of paperbacks – Jeffrey Archer, Len Deighton, Frederick Forsyth and Jack Higgins. Beneath them was a large family Bible; it was the sort of hefty-sized Bible she and her father regularly came across. Mostly they were from the late nineteenth century, big solid items that, to the untrained eye, looked hugely impressive, if only for the sheer weight and size, but in terms of collectability they were in the category of two a penny. Anyone genuinely interested in collecting Bibles soon wised up to the fact that connoisseurship was the name of the game.

This one didn't look to be anything special; it was certainly no Gutenberg. It wasn't in especially good condition either: the corners of the front were badly scuffed and knocked about, what gilt had applied was rubbed away in places, and the spine was cracked and faded. A black ribbon had been tied around it, widthways as well as lengthways, suggesting that the spine was so badly damaged some of its pages had come loose. Or maybe there were long forgotten mementos of pressed flowers, letters or photographs tucked within the pages for safekeeping. Saskia was always finding things like that, and thinking of somebody wanting to capture a particular moment in their life, even if it was just a theatre ticket or a bus or train ticket, never failed to touch her.

Resting it on her knees, she untied the ribbon and opened the Bible. Disappointingly there was no family history page at the front and the title page was almost ripped in two. After carefully turning it over, she flicked through the first few pages that made up the book of Genesis, many of which were damaged and spotted with damp. She had restored countless family Bibles over the years, just like this one, and she liked the sense of history the book gave the family who, by virtue of wanting to have it restored, cared about the tradition of passing the Bible on to the next generation. But sadly this one must have reached the end of the family line, or perhaps had been inherited by somebody who didn't treasure the past.

She heaved the Bible over on to its front to check the back, and had it almost flat on her lap again when she had the oddest sensation; it was as if she'd felt something move inside the book. She gave the Bible an experimental shake and yes, there it was again, a barely perceptible little thud.

Her curiosity roused, she stood up and carried the Bible over to her workbench. She flicked through Genesis again, then through Exodus, Leviticus, Numbers and Deuteronomy. She then took hold of a sizeable block of pages and turned them over in one go. It was at 1 Samuel that a shiver worked its way up her spine.

For there, nestled within a deep rectangular recess cut into the rest of the pages of the Bible, was a black leather notebook. This was a first for her, never had she come across a find like this before. It was exactly the kind of thing she had tried to do as a child with an old phone book – she had spent days painstakingly cutting the pages with a pair of scissors only to give up in frustrated disillusionment at the hopelessness of the task.

But here somebody had gone to an inordinate amount of trouble to make a perfect job of creating a place in which to conceal a notebook. It was such a snug fit inside the recess,

44

she decided the best way to get the notebook out was to tip the Bible upside down. She did this and with a bit of a shake, the notebook was released from its hiding place and landed on the workbench with a soft thump, along with a faded buff manila envelope.

She opened the envelope first, feeling in some way it might explain what the notebook contained. But really it was an act of delayed gratification and was a typical example of her self-restraint, of keeping the best till last, for instinctively she was sure the notebook was going to be more interesting than the usual keepsakes she came across. Why else had someone gone to so much trouble and hidden it so cleverly?

What she retrieved from the envelope was a single sheet of paper: it was a letter. She placed it on the workbench and studied it in the way she would when assessing a book in need of repair. It had been folded in half inside the envelope. The paper itself was of good quality and had discoloured with age, as had the ink used. Very likely the ink had originally been blue, but now, faded with time, it was a faint bluey-black colour. There was no address at the top, only a date in the right-hand corner – September 1943.

My dearest darling,

What a fearful bore this has all been, stuck in bed for days on end and with no way of letting you know how I am. I feel so very queer I don't even know what day of the week it is!

I am now without that curious little thing called an appendix, which I believe serves no purpose other than to take one unawares and very nearly burst. I'm told that this was what happened to me and that I'm lucky to be alive. That's probably Mummy exaggerating matters, but I must say I hope never to go through a similar experience.

I have no idea when I shall return to work, but if you

should be able to visit me, I'm sure it would speed my recovery. I make a terrible patient, so please come at once to cheer me up! I miss you more than words can say, my darling.

With all my love,
Your very own Katyushka.

P.S. Give my love to Billy and the others.

P.P.S. Apologies for brevity, but Nanny Devine is waiting to post this for me.

Saskia read the letter through one more time and then reached for the notebook with eager hands.

Chapter Eight

The Dandelion Years

I had been at the Park for what felt like an eternity, but which in actual fact wasn't even a year, when I realised my life had been changed for ever.

At twenty-two years of age (and in comparison to my peers, an embarrassingly awkward and inexperienced man), I had reached this immense and momentous conclusion with a clarity of thought so sudden it took my breath away and made me shake my head as if to confirm that I was not imagining it. No, it really was as I thought: I was in love!

Ironically, I felt as though I had just deciphered the most complex of codes. I was filled with euphoria, to the extent I wanted to laugh out loud and dance around the lake, yet at the same time I was wholly bemused – why had I not realised the transparently obvious before now?

Being a cryptanalyst I was supposed to be good at unravelling the incomprehensible and making sense of it. It was this skill that had brought me here to Bletchley Park, otherwise known as Station X, along with thousands of others, many of whom had a thought process that was similarly wired – a love of crosswords and chess, of Scrabble and of anagrams, essentially anything of a cryptic nature. The prerequisite qualification being that one was in possession of what was viewed as an agile and freethinking mind, a mind capable of unorthodox thinking while also able to pay meticulous attention to detail.

In common with many of my colleagues, I was also a

linguist and had wound up at Station X after being covertly recruited and interviewed in what could only be described as an inscrutable manner.

It was hard for me not to think occasionally that I had come a long way for the grandson of Russian Jews who'd fled Nizhny Novgorod in the early 1900s to escape the latest series of pogroms. They came to England and settled in the East End of London. Dear old Grandpa Abraham, sadly no longer alive, had used what little savings he had and opened a barber's shop and together with his wife and two small children, they had lived in the flat above. Before long Grandma Lila was working alongside her husband, cutting and styling women's hair, and the business flourished at a rapid rate. With an influx of women wanting their hair done, Grandpa Abraham fled to the peace and quiet of the other side of the road and opened another barber's shop, leaving his wife in charge of the first, the clientele now exclusively women. The Great War saw Ezra, their eldest child, going off to fight, and in 1915 he was killed in action. When the war was over their daughter, Rebekah, married a local Jewish boy called David and in 1921 I was born, a scrawny baby with a thatch of almost black hair and a pair of unusually green eyes that my grandmother claimed would melt many a heart.

I was five years old when I carelessly fell down the stairs and broke my arm, specifically the top of my humerus; it was such a bad break I never regained full movement of my arm and shoulder. In spite of this small disability, or perhaps because of it, my parents brought me up with the strict belief that I was to make something of my life and that meant I was to work harder than any of my peers at school. I did, and to my family's pride and delight, I won a scholarship to Cambridge to read German and French, being already fluent in Russian and Hebrew. I became a member of the debating society and joined my college chess club, of which, in my second year, I became president. I received repeated invitations to join the University Jewish Society, but I eschewed this for although I was Jewish by birth, by inclination I was becoming progressively non-religious. My parents had also distanced themselves, much to Grandma Lila's chagrin – she was a staunch believer and vociferously chastised me, and my parents, for not attending synagogue regularly.

I was approached over a convivial glass of sherry in college one evening, immediately after I'd sat finals in the summer of 1942. With active service not possible due to the childhood injury to my arm, I was preparing to leave Cambridge for a teaching post in a small prep school in Derbyshire. I later learnt that this invitation for a glass of sherry was a typical recruiting move. Apparently I'd been singled out for some weeks, quietly observed by one of my tutors as a likely candidate for Bletchley Park – the headquarters of the Government Code and Cypher School, jokingly referred to as the Golf Club and Chess Club. Without being told what I would be doing, I understood enough from the level of secrecy involved to know that it would be intelligence work of some sort.

My first sighting of the Park was on a balmy and windless night. Owing to a delay with my train leaving Cambridge I arrived much later than planned and stepped into a world of blackout darkness that felt like the back of beyond, but which I knew to be a small railway town called Bletchley. I didn't know whether I was supposed to be met or not, but since there wasn't a soul on the platform, I carried my suitcase and followed my nose. In keeping with the wartime fear that there were German spies on every corner, there were no helpful signs to guide me, but hoping for the best, I kept going until eventually I came to a driveway and a manned sentry post. After my identity was checked, I was directed towards the house. It was then that the moon appeared fleetingly from behind the thick clouds and I glimpsed a lake and the looming outline of a monstrously large house. So this was to be my new home.

I was wrong. Just as soon as I'd signed the Official Secrets Act, I was driven to a nearby hotel where I was to be billeted for that first night and instructed to report for duty in the morning. Two days later I was given the address of a house that was to be my permanent lodging.

But that was then. This was now, eight months later in the spring of 1943, and I was a very different man to the unworldly fresh-faced specimen who had been thrown in at the deep end and assigned to join the code-breaking team whose Herculean task it was to read the intercepted U-boats' Enigma messages. Seemingly I had lived a whole lifetime in the intervening months. The work was exhausting and relentless and there had been frequent times when I had believed myself incapable of continuing.

But then Katyushka arrived and, just like that, things suddenly didn't seem so bad.

Chapter Nine

From across the garden Saskia heard Harvey ringing the bell for her to join him for lunch. It was just the two of them this Saturday; Oliver was helping at the shop while Dad was out on an appointment regarding a probate valuation. Closing the leather notebook she took it with her to show Harvey.

'I'll say this for whoever wrote it,' he said when he'd taken a quick look, 'he or she had the most awful handwriting.'

'That's putting it mildly,' Saskia said, 'it's almost illegible in places. I've spent ages reading just a couple of pages.'

Putting two bowls of soup on the table, Harvey said, 'Do you think it's a work of fiction, an attempt at a novel, or a genuine memoir written by somebody who was at Bletchley during the Second World War? It has an odd sort of title, doesn't it – *The Dandelion Years* – what does that mean, do you think?'

'I have no idea,' Saskia replied. 'Perhaps when I've read some more it'll become clearer. If it is a genuine memoir, I suppose that makes it an historical document, doesn't it?'

She told her grandfather about the letter she'd found as well, written by somebody called Katyushka. 'I'm convinced the two things are connected, otherwise why would they be hidden together?'

'Seems a fair enough supposition. Katyushka sounds Russian to me.'

'That's what I thought, but she doesn't sound at all Russian in the letter; she sounds a quintessential upper-class English girl. And since the man in the story is of Russian origin it's likely that Katyushka was a pet name he'd given her, a term of endearment.'

Harvey sat down opposite her. 'How about we give Google a whirl after lunch,' he said, 'and see if we can find the name? We might be able to find out what its British equivalent is.'

Saskia smiled, glad to have piqued her grandfather's curiosity, and knowing that he was a history buff and liked nothing better than to watch the History Channel, she said, 'What do you know about Bletchley Park?'

'It's claimed it was the nerve centre of the British war effort,' he said, pushing some bread towards her, reminding her to eat, 'and by all accounts the work carried out there in breaking the Enigma codes transmitted by the Germans helped bring about an early end to the war. But during the war, and for a long time after, the place was shrouded in secrecy; nobody was supposed to know about it and amazingly it wasn't until the mid-seventies that people who had worked at the Park began to tell their extraordinary stories.'

'There was a film, wasn't there,' Saskia said, suddenly remembering seeing it. 'Kate Winslet was in it. What was it called?'

'*Enigma*. But the book it was based on was much better.'

'You always say that about books and films.'

He smiled. 'And I'm always right.'

When they'd finished lunch, and instead of going back to her workshop – and resisting the urge to read some more of the notebook – Saskia stayed in the kitchen with Harvey and they spent the next few hours in front of her laptop reading all they could about Bletchley Park.

Saskia was fascinated by what she read. She'd had no idea that as a result of the code-breaking work that had gone on, it was effectively the birthplace of modern computing. But what struck her most were the individual stories of those who had worked at the Park and, just as Harvey had said, how they had never spoken of their contribution to the war;

indeed, outside of their circle, no one knew about this vital undercover work. The level of secrecy to which they had sworn was incredible, they weren't even allowed to tell their families what they were doing.

Saskia couldn't help but wonder whether a secret of that magnitude could be maintained in this day and age. People today were obsessed with the compulsion to share their every waking thought and action via social media sites, and equally they felt they had a right to know what everyone else was up to.

It made her question the moral rights and wrongs of her reading the notebook she had found and she put the question to her grandfather.

Harvey frowned and scratched his chin thoughtfully. 'In my humble opinion, if the author hadn't wanted to run the risk of someone reading what he'd written, he shouldn't have put pen to paper.'

'He could have done so solely for his own benefit,' Saskia countered, 'in the way most people write a diary. Unless, of course, you're a politician and intend to spill the beans when your political career is over.'

'True, but if it was so private he should have either left specific instructions as to what was to be done with the notebook, or he should have destroyed it.'

'What if he'd died before he was able to do that?'

Harvey smiled. 'As Oliver would say, there you go with your rapid-fire questions. But if you have any qualms about reading the notebook, I'd be happy to do it for you, in the interest of historical evaluation, of course.'

'Not a chance! I found the notebook, so if anyone's going to read it, it's me.'

Laughing, he pushed his chair back to stand up. 'With your moral compass appropriately reconfigured, I'll make us some tea, shall I? Slice of cake?'

'No, you stay there; I'll do it. It's not right you waiting on me hand and foot.'

'Hey, don't you come over all ageist with me. Anything but that.'

'Zip it, old man, and do as you're told!'

Harvey laughed again and returned his attention to the laptop while she filled the kettle. 'You know, Bletchley's not that far away,' he said, 'and since the Park is now open to the public as a museum, we could have a day out there. What do you think?'

'I can't think of a single reason why not,' Saskia said, taking the lid off the cake tin and inserting a knife into the beautifully light Victoria sponge her grandfather was such a dab hand at making.

While she waited for the kettle to boil, she thought of the notebook and where it might have come from. Odds-on the person who'd got rid of the Bible had been in ignorance of what it contained and he or she would surely be extremely upset if they knew what they'd thrown away. Which made Saskia think it was her duty to return it to that person. It would be wrong to assume the author was dead, but if that was the case, then potentially that still left a relative who might appreciate having the book.

That evening when her father and Oliver were back from the shop, Saskia once again went through the story of what she'd found. This time they were gathered in her workshop and were inspecting the Bible and its cleverly concealed hiding place.

'And you found it in amongst the house clearance boxes?' her father said.

'Yes,' Saskia said. 'So I was thinking, would it be possible to trace the owner through Gilbert?'

'It's worth a try, although there are no guarantees with Gilbert, especially now his sons are doing more of the work. It would be fair to say they're not the type to be overly keen on admin and keeping records.'

'But they must have something as basic as a diary for

keeping track of the houses they clear,' Oliver said. 'They must be able to run to that level of competency.'

'I wouldn't count on it, but I'll give Gilbert a call on Monday,' Ralph said. Then running his fingers over the cutaway section of the Bible, he said, 'You know, I've never seen anything like this before, it's the kind of thing you read about in books, or see in a film, but you never actually come across it for real. It's quite intriguing, isn't it?'

Everyone agreed, especially Saskia who couldn't wait to be alone with the notebook so she could read some more of it.

Chapter Ten

Matthew had lit a fire in the library and it was there he ate his supper, a ready-made, microwaved shepherd's pie. It wasn't bad, but the way he was feeling he would eat more or less anything.

Apart from the time spent with Ralph Granger, the entire day had been devoted to bagging up more of Jacob's life and it had left him wearily depressed. He'd been tempted to lock up and drive back to Cambridge, but that would have been stupid when he still had so much more to do here. Hiding in Cambridge wouldn't get the job done.

His plate empty, he put the tray on the floor next to the armchair, threw another log on the fire and heeled off his shoes. Stretching out his legs towards the hearth, he thought how appalled Mum would have been to know that after her death this was where he and Jacob would always eat together, their chairs placed either side of the fireplace, their trays balanced on their knees. Poor Mum, she had been a stickler for dining propriety – the dining or kitchen table had to be used, preferably the former. 'What's the point in having a dining room, and me going to the trouble of dusting and polishing it, if you never use it?' she would say to Jacob.

She had been the same over at The Coach House, insisting that the two of them ate in the kitchen, never in the sitting room in front of the television, although more often than not, Jacob had invited them to join him. 'No point in cooking two lots of meals,' he would say. Invariably he used the time to quiz Matthew over his schoolwork, testing him on what he did and did not know, while constantly encouraging him to help himself to any of the books in the library.

He taught Matthew many things over the dining table, but possibly the greatest skill he acquired from the old man was the ability to debate a point, and always with the benefit of fact and reason to support his viewpoint. 'Never go into battle unprepared,' was a frequent piece of advice from Jacob, and Matthew had taken it to heart.

It was after Mum's death that Jacob suggested Matthew should choose one of the bedrooms upstairs to use during his visits, rather than him sleep alone in The Coach House. Inevitably, without Mum around, The Coach House no longer felt like home and in time Matthew took the step to empty it and close it up. He couldn't remember when he last ventured inside but he supposed he ought to.

He was just contemplating fetching another beer from the kitchen when he heard the doorbell. He wasn't expecting a caller, not at half-past eight in the evening, but going out to the chill of the hall he could guess who it might be.

He was right: it was Jenny Allbright from the vicarage next door. A brisk, no-nonsense woman who gave the impression of always being in a tearing hurry, and of not wanting to put anyone to any trouble, she predictably shook her head when he invited her to step in out of the cold.

'No, no, I know you're busy,' she said, 'so I shan't keep you. Mal and I wondered whether you'd like to join us for lunch tomorrow after church. How does roast beef sound?'

'It sounds delicious, but I'll have to pass, I'm afraid.'

'Going back to Cambridge early, then?'

'No, I have somebody coming to make a start on valuing the books for probate.'

'On a Sunday?'

He smiled. 'Heresy, I know, but he said it was as good a day as any for him and since I planned to be here tomorrow anyway, I took him up on his offer. Which reminds me, would it be possible for you to let him in on Monday morning?'

57

'Of course, and if I'm not here, Mal can do the honours.'

'He strikes me as being completely trustworthy, so you could just give him your key and he can let himself in.'

'Whatever you say. What's his name?'

'Ralph Granger.'

'Right you are.' Eyeing the bulging bin bags lined up in the hall behind him, she said, 'You've been busy, I see.'

'It's Jacob's clothes,' he said. 'You wouldn't think somebody of his age would have so many.'

'I'm not at all surprised, he could never bring himself to throw anything away, could he?'

'True,' Matthew said with a wry smile.

'If it would be a help, Mal and I can take the bags to the charity shop for you.'

'Really?' said Matthew. He'd been wondering about the logistics of getting rid of the bags. 'That would be an enormous help,' he said 'but are you sure?'

'Don't be silly; it's no bother. Just let me know if there's anything else we can do. Goodnight!'

Matthew watched her march briskly down the drive, her shoes grinding the gravel beneath her feet in the darkness, a beam of light from the torch in her hand lighting her way. Not for the first time he was reminded that he should get the security lights fixed which illuminated the driveway. But then there was so much of the house that needed fixing.

Back in the library, after taking a bottle of beer from the fridge, he made himself comfortable again and thought of Mal and Jenny's thoughtfulness towards him. It was of the sentiment-free, practical kind, the sort he could bear knowing that it was genuine; they had both been extremely fond of Jacob and Matthew's mother.

Mum had never been a churchgoer until they'd moved here and it was out of a vague sense of curiosity that made her venture across the threshold of St Margaret's. Before she knew it, she was roped in by the then vicar's wife – a fearsomely efficient woman to whom no one dared say no – to help deliver the parish newsletter around the village as well as polish the brass and help with the flowers.

Mum never forced Matthew to go with her to church, but he went occasionally as an act of solidarity. When the Reverend Maxwell Hartley retired, taking with him his fearsome wife, Mal and Jenny arrived, along with their daughter Laura who was sixteen and two years older than Matthew.

Born fifteen years after her older twin brothers, Mal and Jenny referred to Laura as a late and very special delivery. She was also the object of Matthew's first crush. Falling for her caused him to undergo an experience that would have knocked St Paul's road to Damascus conversion into a cocked hat; suddenly he was very much interested in attending church and became an overnight convert. He volunteered to help Laura in the Sunday School Club when she was home from boarding school, along with anything else that meant he could be near her. She knew, of course, in the way girls always know, how he felt about her and, very likely at her parents' request, she let him down as gently as she could, explaining – after she had kissed him very thoroughly one evening in the graveyard – that really it would be better if they could just be friends. They had remained so to this day and, much to her parents' pride, Laura was now a deaconess in Winchester. His own so-called religious fervour didn't last, which surprised no one at all.

It would be true to say that when it came to girlfriends, his track record did not stand close scrutiny. Fliss, his last girlfriend, would doubtless have plenty to say on the matter. His friend, James, who thought she was perfect in every way for Matthew, had introduced her to him. Matthew had queried that if she was so perfect, why wasn't James interested?

'Not my type,' his friend had responded offhandedly, 'too perfect.'

'And you think that's *my* type?'

'I just know how bloody fussy you are and that you can always find some reason to say you're not interested.'

'Discerning is what I like to call it.'

He agreed to meet Fliss, a radiologist at Addenbrooke's where James worked, and to his surprise they hit it off. The next thing he knew, they were coming up for their twelve-month anniversary. It was then that he began to feel they were nearing a tipping point: if they continued it would lead to something more, something ultimately permanent. He also sensed an emerging carefulness on Fliss's part, as though she was consciously avoiding hinting at what all couples become aware of in the course of a relationship – The Next Step. It wasn't long before he felt her carefulness had somehow become a physical presence between them.

Then Fliss began to drop hints about how little she saw him some weeks. On one occasion she joked that she now knew how it felt to be in a relationship with a married man. When he asked her what she meant, she laughed and said he was married to his work, which left her as his mistress, his convenient bit on the side.

He'd been shocked. Yes, he knew he worked long hours, but he'd believed he'd got the balance between his work and private life right. Something else he'd believed was that his aptitude to throw himself one hundred per cent into a task was a strength, but now he was effectively being told his ability to lose himself in the absorption of a challenge – the more in depth and all-consuming the better – was actually a weakness. As accusations went, it didn't sit comfortably on him.

It was seeing Fliss wandering round Glaskin House after the funeral that crystallised his feelings and brought matters to a head. She had visited the house before, but in this instance she seemed pre-emptively to be sizing the house up, as if picturing herself living in it with him one day. In the kitchen she had given a despairing little shrug and made the observation that it was in desperate need of modernisation, that no one in their right mind would tolerate such antiquated fittings. His hackles up, he'd taken it as a personal slight against Jacob. And his mother. For years they had managed perfectly well here without any outside interference.

He had planned for the two of them to stay the night, but rigid with grief and a growing sense of outrage he suddenly wanted Fliss – with her disapproval and her assumptions – out of the house, away from everything that was important to him. He hadn't wanted her tainting the place. 'Change of plan,' he'd said abruptly, 'let's go back to Cambridge now.'

Her face was a picture of surprise. 'Really? But why?'

Seized with an anger so intense he couldn't speak, he'd begun switching lights off and shutting doors.

Once they were in the car and on their way, he'd thought he might regain his composure, but he didn't. She told him to slow down, that he was driving too fast.

'Is this how it's going to be?' he muttered, gripping the wheel and pressing his foot to the accelerator while pulling out to overtake the car in front. When there was sufficient clearance between him and the car, he swerved back in but didn't slow his speed.

'What do you mean?' she asked, her right foot twitching as though in search of a brake pedal in the footwell.

'You know exactly what I mean,' he snapped, relishing the anger coursing through him. More than anything he wanted a row. He wasn't the argumentative sort, but right now a blazing row would make him feel so much better.

But Fliss wasn't the argumentative sort either and instead of rising to his bait, she allowed a long, awkward moment of silence to pass between them.

'Please, Matthew,' she said finally, 'you're scaring me; slow down and tell me what's wrong.'

He did as she asked, realising that it was forgivable to scare one's passenger, but not oneself. And for a second or two back there, he had scared himself, had for the briefest time wondered what purpose there was in living when ultimately it all ended with a wooden casket shoved into a deep hole.

But he couldn't bring himself to apologise. If he did that, he would lose the precarious balance of self-control he'd managed to hang on to for the day. Lose that and he might give in to that black hole of grief he'd done his damndest to avoid being sucked into. Raw, choking anger was better. It kept the emotion he was most scared of in check. So he made the decision there and then to put his anger to good use and at a time when he didn't have to look at Fliss, when he could say the words and stare resolutely ahead at the road and not have to watch her reaction.

He told her that being with her wasn't working for him anymore, that it hadn't felt right for some time. It was plain to him that they wanted different things, he explained; she was obviously ready for the settling down stage, probably thinking about a baby, while he was nowhere near that stage.

When he'd finished, she said, 'You've been thinking all that but never once thought to discuss any of it with me?'

'We're discussing it now,' he said flatly.

'No we're not. You're telling me you've reached an assessment based on nothing more than what you suspect I'm thinking. Is that fair?'

Undeterred, he said, 'On a scale of one to ten, how right am I?'

She didn't answer him, but said, 'I had no idea you felt this way. I thought ... I thought we were good together, that we had a future.'

The sad disbelief in her voice gave him cause to hesitate and from nowhere he was overwhelmed with shameful disgust at his behaviour, of his urgent and desperate desire to be free of Fliss. Guilt, combined with knowing that he had been needlessly cruel, now made him apologise. 'I'm sorry,' he said, 'perhaps for a while I thought the same.'

'What's changed?'

'I don't know. But something has.'

'You're sure it's not just a reaction to Jacob dying? Death

can make a person think in ways they might never normally do.'

'I don't think so.'

'So you want to end it between us?'

'I think it's best, don't you?'

'Yes,' she murmured. 'It probably is.'

Sitting here in the soft light cast from the lamp beside him and the flickering flames of the fire, Matthew knew that, self-ishly, he would forever be grateful that Fliss had made it so painless for him to walk away.

In the weeks that followed he had often found himself missing her and been tempted to send a text or an email to see how she was. And to apologise again. But he never did, deciding it wouldn't be fair. It was better to cut the tie completely. He wished her well, he truly did. He knew from James that she hadn't started seeing anyone else, but it was early days. James reckoned Matthew had probably put her off men for good.

If he had to justify himself, and James had insisted he did, Matthew reasoned that if he'd been ready for the next stage in his relationship with Fliss, he would have embraced it all too readily, and he most assuredly would not have reacted the way he had the day of Jacob's funeral.

When Fliss had asked him what had changed between them, he honestly hadn't known the answer. Now he did. For the first time in his life, he'd become unsettled; he was restless and bored and he needed a new challenge, something different to excite him. He had reached a crossroads and needed to decide what he did next. And not just whether he sold Glaskin House or not.

Chapter Eleven

April 1943

I promised myself many things when I embarked upon this enterprise, one of which was not to go into too much detail about the work I did as a cryptanalyst at Bletchley Park. Call it habit if you will, but everything each and every one of us did was cloaked in secrecy because it was absolutely vital there was no danger of the Germans discovering we had found a way to break their codes and were thus able to keep apace or outmanoeuvre them. I must also stress that I was essentially a very small cog in an astonishingly large and effective piece of machinery, surrounded by intellects far superior to mine, the like of which I doubt I will ever encounter again. Not on that scale at least.

Another promise I made when I decided to write this down was that I was to resist the temptation to succumb to any needless sentimentality or mawkishness. The purpose of the exercise, as I have had regularly to remind myself, is to record and preserve a special time and special place in my life, but above all to honour my dearest Katyushka, and in a way that she would approve. I can picture her now, rolling her eyes and threatening me with dire consequences if I were to step out of line and resort to soppiness of any sort. 'Darling,' I can hear her say, 'I expressly forbid you from making me out to be some kind of plastered saint. Paint a true picture by sticking to the facts and you'll be all right.'

So these are the facts.

Fact One: I loved her.

Fact Two: I had never met anyone like her.

Fact Three: I have never met anyone like her since.

But now to breathe life into those facts and to explain how it happened, how I came to know the ecstasy and the torment of being in love.

I had been on my way back to Bletchley after a day off to visit my family in London. They had no idea, of course, what work I did and knew better than to press me. Amusingly, my mother and grandmother had initially assumed they would be exempt from any rules that required me to keep quiet about the nature of my job and took it as a personal slight when I remained firmly tight-lipped. But I knew all too well, much as I loved them, that to confide in either of them would have been tantamount to air-dropping detailed leaflets over the neighbourhood. As it was, they had to make do with the ubiquitous two-word explanation, that the work was *Hush, hush*. That in itself was code for – *please don't ask me again*.

My family weren't the only people to be curious; I was frequently treated to hostile stares outside of the Park, as were many of my colleagues. A man of my age, not dressed in uniform, was to be viewed with instant suspicion of cowardice. I looked healthy enough – my wonky arm was not immediately obvious – so surely I should be doing my bit fighting for King and Country? But as the war went on and the small railway town of Bletchley filled up with a veritable army of billeted recruits for the Park, the townspeople learnt not to ask any questions and accepted that the ever-growing influx of odd-looking boffin types were not all conscientious objectors. It was only natural that eventually they would make the assumption that the Park was an important secret establishment and, as a result, a sense of respect and patriotism set in.

That April evening on the packed train from Euston Station to Bletchley, I stepped around, and in some instances over, sleeping soldiers, kitbags and gas masks, and eventually found a space in which to stand. I didn't mind; it was not a long journey, only an hour, and cramped travel conditions were hardly a privation in the circumstances.

It was then, as I stood in the busy corridor of the train with that day's *Daily Telegraph* precisely folded so that the crossword was before me, that the carriage door behind me slid open and I saw a strikingly pretty girl with dark, alert eyes and a wide, smiling mouth beckoning to the soldier beside me to have her seat. His head was partially bandaged and he looked exhausted, ready to drop. At first he declined her offer, but she was having none of it. 'Please,' she said in a low voice that was unmistakably upper class, 'I insist. I couldn't possibly sit there while you're standing here. It wouldn't be right. Not right at all.' And with a touch of her small but noticeably elegant hand on his arm, he gave in, muttering his thanks.

Everything about her was small and elegant, I observed, from her well-shod feet to the top of her chestnut-brown hair that was doing its best to escape being pulled into a bun at the nape of her neck. There was a string of pearls at her throat and her clothes – a lightweight two-piece suit with a cameo broach pinned to one lapel – were stylish, yet not showy. Her jacket was open and I could see she had the smallest waist. She looked young – younger than me – but supremely sure of herself.

'I know what you're thinking,' she suddenly said, directing her comment at me.

I felt my face colour, knowing that I must have been caught blatantly staring at her.

'You do?' I said.

'You're thinking I made the poor wretched man feel even worse by offering my seat.'

'Not at all,' I said quite truthfully, 'it was a kind gesture on your part.'

'Kindness be blowed!' she said vehemently. 'It was no more than I should have done. In my opinion one has a duty to do all that one can to help, and offering my seat to a poor bedraggled soldier who's brave enough to put his life on the line to fight is a small price I'm more than willing to pay.'

'Quite,' I murmured. I then returned my attention to the crossword in my hand. Anyone else would have made the effort to be friendlier, but I was rarely at ease around pretty girls. I was socially myopic when it came to the fairer sex, blind to the thought that I might be of the slightest interest. I always assumed they were either making fun of me for my shyness and tendency to be too serious, or merely being polite by engaging me in small talk. The upshot was I tended to be too taciturn and often said the wrong thing. However, try as I might, I was unable to concentrate on the newspaper in my hand, sensing that the girl had something else to say.

'You haven't got very far, have you?' she said. 'Or are crosswords not your thing? I'd be happy to help. I'm rather good at them.'

I smiled politely. 'I'm sure you are.'

She tutted. 'Now you're teasing me, aren't you? Which I call jolly unfair. I expect you're one of those ghastly old-fashioned types who doesn't approve of girls with half a brain.'

'Quite the contrary,' I said, desperate to make amends for my clumsiness. 'I strongly approve.'

She smiled. It was a smile that seemed to contain an expression of endearing innocence, but in contrast her eyes were twinkling with something that appeared to me in that warm and stuffy train carriage dangerously mischievous. Was she mocking me? Of course she was.

'Go on then,' she said, leaning in closer, so close I caught a waft of something sweetly fragrant, 'let me help with your crossword, it'll help pass the time.'

Disconcerted, I allowed her to do as she asked, keeping to myself that I had already completed most of the crossword in my head – actually applying pen to paper and filling out the boxes lessened the enjoyment of the exercise for me. Even so, as I pulled a pen out from my jacket pocket, I was impressed

67

with the swiftness of her thought process as she rattled off the answers to the cryptic clues and it wasn't long before I had a strong feeling that she was bound for the same destination as myself.

She was probably a fresh new recruit, brimming with enthusiasm and excitement with not a clue as to what lay ahead. Her healthily clear complexion certainly didn't have the greyish colour most of us old-timers had, a sure sign of the sleep-deprived. I had come across plenty of young women like her at the Park – they were well-bred daughters of well-to-do families, some of them debutantes, and with a strong sense of duty they were eager to do their bit for the war effort. Hadn't this girl already revealed how keenly she felt that sense of duty in giving up her seat to the injured soldier?

Just as I had, she had most likely been informally interviewed and then sent a telegram with no more information than: *You are to report to Station X at Bletchley Park, Buckinghamshire, in five days' time. Your postal address is Box 111, c/o The Foreign Office. That is all you need to know.*

Not that I voiced any of this, and bearing in mind how many men and women worked at the Park, combined with the weekly rotation of shifts, the chances of our paths crossing again were slim. I knew that once we alighted at Bletchley we would go our separate ways – she directly to the Park to register, and I to my digs.

I was to learn that for a supposedly above-average intelligent man I was exceedingly proficient in underestimating fate. Not to say the determination of a highly spirited young woman.

It was my great misfortune to be billeted with Mrs Aida Pridmore, a widow in her mid-fifties whose husband had died shortly before the outbreak of the war in an accident on the railway line. She spoke about the deceased Mr Pridmore a lot, as though he was still with us. In many ways he was:

his ashes were in an urn and stood pride of place on the mantelpiece in the front room, a room I seldom ventured into. If we were to believe his widow, Mr Pridmore would have more than thrown his weight into the war effort and rushed off to fight the Boche at the first opportunity.

It was an oft-repeated remark, uttered, I was sure, to make clear our landlady's displeasure at having three billeted men occupying the top two floors of her house when, to her mind, we should have been engaged in active service. At the same time, she was more than happy to commandeer our ration books, though what she produced for us to eat bore no reflection on what we were entitled to.

Supper tonight consisted of something thin and watery masquerading as Scotch broth and as I sat alone at the table in Mrs Pridmore's dismal dining room with only the patched linoleum and the loud ticking of the clock on the mantelpiece for company – Griffiths and Farrington were on the four o'clock till midnight shift, whereas mine began at midnight and ended at eight o'clock tomorrow morning – I felt un-accountably morose. And not just because what I was trying to eat was so unappetising. Wartime rationing was a fact of life and I was more than used to it.

No, it had nothing to do with the Scotch broth; it was annoyance with myself. Why was I so socially inept? Why couldn't I have chatted more easily with the girl on the train? Griffiths and Farrington would have had no such problem; they probably would have asked her out for a drink by the time they arrived at Bletchley. All I had managed to do was offer to carry her suitcase off the train. That done, and spotting an army captain stepping forward on the platform to meet her, I had hurried away, not even bothering to say goodbye. Almost certainly she had thought me the rudest man she had ever had the bad luck to meet.

Normally I wouldn't care how others viewed me, but in this instance I cared deeply for the poor impression with which I had left her.

To put a stop to my increasingly gloomy mood, I marshalled my thoughts in the direction of what awaited me later that night in Hut 8. The ongoing German U-boat threat to the Allied convoys in the North Atlantic was still our priority and last month more than 600,000 tons of shipping had been lost. In those awful weeks the intensity of the workload had resulted in an endless cycle of sleepless nights and when I did manage to sleep, I was woken by terrifying nightmares of U-boat wolf packs hunting down their prey and of bodies floating in the freezing waters of the North Atlantic. Sometimes I dreamt those bodies of the dead men, women and children were in the lake at Bletchley Park and it was my job, and my job alone, to fish them out.

Yet it wasn't the threat of U-boats and the long hours ahead of me spent decrypting enemy messages that occupied my thoughts as I cycled from my digs to the Park in the blackout darkness, with only the weak glow of light from my cycle lamp to guide me as it began to rain, it was that girl on the train and the gently mocking look in her eyes.

Chapter Twelve

Sunday morning and Saskia was awakened by the sound of the wind gusting at her bedroom window. Through the gap in the curtains she could see it was raining, and raining hard.

Relishing the warmth of her bed and in no hurry to leave it, her thoughts turned to an earnest young man cycling to work in the rainy darkness a little over seventy years ago. Whatever happened to him? she wondered. Was he still alive? He'd be in his nineties if he were. And what about the girl on the train? Was that his 'dearest Katyushka'?

On her bedside table lay *The Dandelion Years* notebook, put there last night when, too tired to read any more, Saskia had been forced to turn out the light. Not surprisingly, the pages she'd read had seeped into her subconscious and she had dreamt about the author and the secret world he'd inhabited. In one dream, she had been trying desperately to decipher the author's atrocious handwriting, repeatedly rereading sentences, but the more she read, the more incomprehensible the words became.

She was tempted to try again now before going down for breakfast, while her eyes and brain were still fresh, but glancing at her alarm clock, she saw that far from having the luxury of time to lie there, lazily cocooned in the comfort of her bed, she'd actually overslept. Having agreed to spend the day helping her father with the probate valuation at Glaskin House, she roused herself and pushed back the duvet. Other than attending book fairs, they seldom worked on a Sunday, but her father had decided to make the most of a free day and get the ball rolling on what he was convinced would be a protracted task.

By the time they'd eaten breakfast and were on the road, it had stopped raining and, as though a switch had been flicked, the sky had magically cleared. Driving by hedgeless, wide-open fields of rolling pastureland, the sun shone down with a luminous radiance. But for all the brightness of the sun, a bracing cold wind was blowing in straight off the North Sea.

They passed through Long Melford, then on to Lavenham and then picked up the Stowmarket road. Entering the village of Old Brawton and turning right at the triangular village green that was bordered with pretty period cottages, some of them beautifully thatched and traditionally painted, they passed a road lined with parked cars and a church on their left. Immediately afterwards, and precisely at ten o'clock, just as the church bells sounded, they drove through the gateway of Glaskin House.

Scattered along the length of driveway valiant clumps of pale yellow daffodils and snowdrops pushed staunchly through a wilderness of overgrown laurel and rhododendron bushes. The house itself looked equally unkempt and a lot more foreboding than Saskia had expected, and as they stepped out of the car and were met with a blast of bitterly cold East Anglian wind that whipped at her hair and sliced through her coat, she had a feeling she wasn't going to enjoy the day that lay ahead.

Her father rang the doorbell and it was a while before the door was opened, which again didn't fill Saskia with gladness that she'd come. Frankly, she'd much prefer to be back at home reading *The Dandelion Years*.

'I hope you don't mind, Matthew, but I've brought my very able assistant with me, my daughter,' her father said when they were at last invited over the threshold by a distinctly cross-looking individual who had a face on him like the wettest of wet weekends. He also had a smudge of something across his right temple. Was this really the Matthew Gray of whom her father had spoken so highly? The Matthew Gray who her father thought was about the same age as she was and with whom she would get on so well? What was her father thinking? 'Saskia's as knowledgeable as I am,' he continued, 'if not more so.'

'He's exaggerating, of course,' Saskia said lightly, thinking that, like the house, Matthew Gray in no way matched her expectations. She extended her hand, but frowning and wiping his on the back of his jeans, he said, 'Better that you don't; mine are filthy. Come on through.' His voice and demeanour were about as welcoming as the cold wind had been outside on the doorstep. Hey, Misery Guts, Saskia wanted to say, I've given up my Sunday to be here!

Her father must have read her mind for he shot her a look and she reminded herself of what he had told her, that Matthew Gray had obviously been very attached to the man who had recently died here. Grudgingly cutting him some slack, she followed behind the pair of them as they crossed the large hallway where, pushed against the wall opposite the wide, curving staircase, was a row of black bin bags. While her father was perfectly relaxed and was chatting away happily with their host, Saskia gave an involuntary shiver. The house was Arctic cold, and about as hospitable as old Misery Guts ahead of her. Her premonition that this was not going to be a fun day was turning out to be a little too close to the truth.

'I'm sorry the house is so cold,' Misery Guts said, turning abruptly to face her. 'The boiler's not working. I've spent the last hour arm-wrestling it. But the library's at a bearable temperature – I lit a fire there earlier.'

'I'm sure it'll be fine,' she said stiffly.

Thankfully he was right; the library was blessedly warmer than the hallway and she automatically went over to the fireplace where a log fire was burning. The wood popped and crackled invitingly in the grate, the flames giving off a pleasing smell of woodsmoke.

With her back to the fire, and standing on a faded hearth-rug, Saskia let her eyes wander over the immense room with its packed bookcases and the overspill of teetering towers of books on the floor and yet more covering the large table in the middle of the room. Generating an air of academic disorder, which to many might feel oppressive – almost certainly to a non-book person it would – the room had a comfortable lived-in feel for Saskia. Observing the laptop and the plate of what looked like toast crumbs on the table by the armchair to the right of the fire, she guessed that this was where Misery Guts liked to hang out. Or maybe it was because the boiler wasn't working and this was the only warm room in the entire house.

But this, she thought, taking in the library of books again, was not the whole story. Her father had told her that apart from the kitchen and bathrooms, there wasn't a room in the house that didn't contain a stash of books. Clearly the owner, Professor Belinsky, had been a true bibliomaniac.

'I'll make you a drink, shall I?' Matthew Gray offered. 'Coffee all right?'

'Coffee would be great,' Ralph said with an excess of enthusiasm and rubbing his hands together. 'Saskia?'

Unwinding the scarf from around her neck, and recognising that her father was trying to jolly things along, Saskia nodded her agreement. 'Thank you, I'll have the same.'

When they were alone, she went over to the window and, leaning across the desk, looked out at the garden. It was entirely laid to lawn with a slightly off-centre cedar tree of majestic proportions. There were no flower borders to speak of, just the one directly beneath the window and that appeared to have been left to its own devices, as she imagined a lot of the house had. 'I suppose he'll sell the place, won't he?' she said quietly.

Her father came and joined her in front of the desk. 'I

74

should think so; it's not exactly ideal for a young single chap, is it?'

'Is he single?'

'I have the feeling he is, he's not mentioned a partner.'

'Any reason why he should?'

'I suppose not.'

Still looking at the garden where a squirrel darted out from behind the cedar tree and then shot up the trunk and disappeared from view, Saskia said, 'He doesn't strike me as being overjoyed to have us here, does he?'

'I think he's annoyed that the boiler isn't working. It can't be much fun being stuck here without any heating, other than this one log fire.'

'I guess so.' She turned decisively away from the window. 'Right, where shall we start?'

'I suggest the table. Let's clear it so we have a decent workstation and then we'll crack on.'

They had just cleared the table when the door opened and Matthew Gray reappeared with a tray of drinks. Wordlessly, he put the tray on the table, then went over to the fire and threw a few more logs into the grate. Saskia watched him take hold of the poker and after some careful prodding, when he appeared to be satisfied that the logs were where they should be, he put the poker down and straightened up. Resting a hand on the mantelpiece and staring into the flames, he drummed his fingers in an abstracted way as if deep in thought and completely oblivious to anyone else in the room with him. Rarely had Saskia seen anybody so uptight. 'I'll leave you to it, then,' he said finally, turning round.

He was across the room with his hand on the door when Saskia's father said, 'If this is the only warm room in the house, we can't very well kick you out of it.'

'That's OK.' He shrugged. 'I'm going to have another look at the boiler, see if I can't bully it back into life again. Jacob used to revert to cursing it in Russian when it played up. *Ti menia dostal* was a favourite of his, followed up by *unbju!* Which roughly translates as, I've had enough of you, I'm gonna kill you!' He smiled unexpectedly and the transformation in him caught Saskia off guard. He suddenly went from unfriendly and nondescript to a lot more interesting and gave her cause to look at him properly.

Tall and slim, with shoulders slightly hunched, his chin unshaven, and his light brown hair, thick and loose-curled, all combined to give him an air of youthfulness. But beneath eyebrows that were slightly drawn, his hazel eyes, a little narrowed as if squinting, struck her as intelligent and all-seeing. There was, she sensed, a depth to him that previously had been masked by a fit of bad temper over the faulty boiler, she supposed.

But perhaps it wasn't only the faulty boiler that had rattled him and made him appear so uptight. Saskia and her father were always mindful that when they were asked to do a job of this nature, they were being charged with putting a figure of worth on a deceased person's possessions, often that person's prized possessions. For some of those left behind to deal with the aftermath of a death, it was a horrible intrusion, a rubbing of salt into the open wound of their grief.

Feeling an unexpected surge of empathy for the man before her, Saskia suddenly realised that those intelligent eyes of his were observing her. Embarrassed, she looked away quickly before he could see that she was blushing.

'If you can't get the boiler to work, Matthew, please don't feel you can't join us in here,' her father said.

'Thanks, but hopefully it won't come to that.' He grimaced. 'I'm sorry,' he said, 'that came out badly. I meant that hopefully I can get the boiler started. I didn't mean that I didn't want to be in the same room as you.'

'No offence taken,' her father said with a laugh, adding milk from a small jug on the tray to the mugs of coffee. He passed one to Saskia, then picked up the other for himself.

When they were alone, Saskia remarked in a low voice,

'He's not the most easy-going of people, is he?'

Looking at her over the rim of his mug, her father said, 'He has a lot on his mind, I expect. I feel sorry for him.'

'Well, so do I,' she said, aware that she was being gently admonished. 'Of course I do. Given the circumstances.'

Her father smiled. 'Come on; let's get on with the job we're here to do. You take this end of the room, and I'll go down the other end.'

Taking a sip of her coffee and letting his comment go, Saskia knew perfectly well what her father was getting at. Her quickness to judge was a trait inherited from Grandpa O. In her defence, she was invariably right when it came to first impressions; it was just that now and again she was proved wrong, much to her family's satisfaction.

With her sleeves now mentally rolled up, and iPad in hand ready to log the necessary details, she went over to the bookcase to the left of the fireplace – her father was already absorbed in a large leather-bound book at the far end of the room.

Generally speaking, a large percentage of the average book collection had no value at all, and it didn't take Saskia long to categorise the lower bookcase shelves as the kind of thing they would sell in the shop around the five or ten pound mark. There were a lot of historical biographies ranging from Richard II to Elizabeth I, and from Napoleon to Lord Mountbatten and Montgomery. Samuel Pepys and Dr Johnson were there amongst the diarists, along with political diaries and memoirs by Kissinger, Benn, Thatcher, Blair, Bush and Clinton. The usual suspects, in other words. But the higher the shelf, the greater the value she soon found. Here there was a batch of first editions – Evelyn Waugh, H.E. Bates, Joseph Conrad, Ernest Hemingway, John Buchan and P.G. Wodehouse – and all with their dust jackets in premium condition. She smiled. Most people didn't realise the significance of the dust jacket and yet for many collectors it was the most important element. In the shelf above was a row dedicated to the great poets – Keats, Shelley, Byron, Tennyson, Wordsworth and Blake. These were beautiful editions – leather-bound, gilt-edged and again in excellent condition with minimal scuffing to the corners of the boards.

From the other end of the room, she heard her father let out a long whistle.

'What have you found?' she asked.

'*The Adventures of Sherlock Holmes with the Memoirs of Sherlock Holmes* in two volumes and published by George Newnes – 1892 and 1894. First edition.'

She went over to take a look. Her father handed her one of the two volumes. The spine and boards were of light blue cloth complete with pictorial decoration. A careful turning of the pages revealed there was only a light amount of foxing to the paper.

'There's even a solander box with chemises,' her father said. 'The last set I saw like this fetched over twelve thousand pounds. I'd say that our Professor Jacob Belinsky was the most discriminate of collectors. What's more, I think we can safely say this is just the tip of the iceberg.' He pointed to the glass-cased bookshelves. 'Heaven only knows what gems are there under wraps.'

'Bad news I'm afraid.'

They both turned to see Matthew Gray standing in the doorway. 'No dice as far as the boiler's concerned,' he said. 'I've tried ringing round for a heating engineer but there doesn't seem to be anyone available, they're all busy. So if you don't mind, I'll get on with the work I need to do in here.' He indicated his laptop on the small table next to the armchair. Noticing the books they were holding, he added, 'Found something interesting?'

Leaving her father to explain, Saskia went back to her end of the library. 'Are you sure?' she heard Matthew Gray say when he heard what the two books might fetch if sold. 'But Jacob let me read them when I was a teenager,' he said, disbelief ringing out from him.

'He clearly trusted you to take care of them,' Dad said.

'He always said books were to be read and enjoyed, not to be shut away, and he never spoke of their value. I know some collectors buy because of the investment potential, but Jacob wasn't like that; for him it was the joy of reading a good book, especially a beautifully produced book. Mind you, he drilled it into me from a young age to respect them, no turning over of the corners, and absolutely no breaking of a spine, not even with a cheap paperback.'

'Quite right too,' Saskia piped up, approving of all that she was hearing.

Dad smiled. 'Saskia's forte is restoring books, so she sees a lot of neglect and abuse in the course of her work.'

Matthew Gray was about to respond when he put a hand to his back pocket and pulled out a mobile phone that was ringing. 'Sorry,' he said, 'with a bit of luck it's somebody who can come out to fix the boiler after all.'

His hope was in vain. 'Nothing doing,' he said a few minutes later. 'Not until tomorrow when I'll be back in Cambridge.' He sighed, his frustration plain to see. 'There's always something, isn't there?'

The hours slipped by while Matthew got on with whatever it was he had to do on his laptop, at the same time keeping the fire fed with logs. He also provided them with more coffee and biscuits, and some ham sandwiches for lunch. For a lot of the time the three of them worked in a comfortable silence, the only sound in the library that of the logs burning in the grate.

At five o'clock Saskia's father called it a day. They were packing away their things when Ralph said, 'Matthew, if you're not rushing back to Cambridge straight away, why don't you join us for supper this evening? I can guarantee a fully functioning boiler and a warm house. Not to mention roast chicken followed by apple crumble care of my father-in-law, who's an excellent cook.'

Saskia didn't know who was the more surprised by the suggestion, her or Matthew. Dad really did feel sorry for him, didn't he? Or was there, she suddenly wondered, something more to it? Something that didn't bear thinking about?

Chapter Thirteen

After waving them off in the fading light, Matthew immediately regretted turning down the unexpected invitation. A warm house and a roast dinner seemed like a hell of a good idea.

But the look on Saskia Granger's face had warned him off. Obviously she hadn't wanted to prolong the time spent around him any longer than was necessary. He couldn't blame her; he hadn't exactly been the best of company today. Waking up to a freezing cold house had not got his day off to a good start. Nor had his mood been improved when the bloody useless boiler wouldn't respond to his repeated and furious attempts to make it work. He'd eaten a hurried breakfast while sorting out the fire in the library and had just fetched in a basket of logs when Ralph and his daughter were at the door, catching him thoroughly on the hop. So no, he hadn't been an overly receptive host.

He had hoped as the day wore on that he'd made good the worst of his irritability, but that look on Saskia's face when supper was mentioned told him otherwise. Which was a shame because he'd quite liked her. She'd struck him as being a little on the reserved side, but interestingly individual. He'd like to know more about the work she did as a book restorer; he imagined it to be incredibly rewarding.

While he'd been working in the library preparing for a day in court tomorrow, he'd had plenty of opportunity to observe her and, for the most part, her expression, had been one of intense concentration. He'd noticed an almost unnatural stillness about her at times, the only movement her eyes. Occasionally, from behind the curtain of long hair that partially covered her face when she leant forward, he'd caught a glimpse of a wide and appreciative smile as she inspected a particular book. He'd watched how carefully she would handle the books, never rushing, always taking her time and treating them as gently as a mother would a newborn baby. He liked that about her, that she respected – *revered* – what had been important to Jacob.

Putting out the fire in the library and packing up his things, Matthew decided Jacob had chosen well when he'd requested Ralph Granger be the one to carry out the valuation on his collection of books.

He drove back to Cambridge thinking about how much he had inherited from Jacob, not in financial terms, but in personality. Jacob had frequently allowed the small things in life to get the better of him – he would have ranted for hours about the boiler had he been here – and Matthew knew that at times he was prone to reacting the same way.

Of course he hadn't inherited anything from Jacob genetically, but he was convinced certain things had rubbed off on him, such as the way Jacob had always spoken his mind, claiming he had neither the time nor inclination for shilly-shallying around what needed to be said.

Matthew was the same and his frankness had more than once got him into trouble at work, usually when he'd had his fill of being polite to someone who was senior to him and who also happened to be a complete jackass. He was all too aware that being so direct would ultimately blight his chances of ever being made a partner at the accountancy firm he worked for, should that be something he ever wanted – but he doubted it was. Also, like Jacob, he wasn't a natural team player; he preferred to be left alone to get on with the job in hand.

On the upside, being so focused and to the point worked to his advantage whenever he was called to be an expert witness in court: it enabled him to deliver the facts clearly and succinctly. To date, no smart-arse lawyer had ever successfully derailed or run rings around him.

Undoubtedly the experience of having such an extraordinary mentor had formed the core of Matthew's learning and had propelled him to achieve in a way he might not have done without Jacob's contribution to his education.

When Jacob had proclaimed Matthew as having an above average level of intelligence, he had offered to pay for him to go to a private school where he would receive more individual attention and be stretched more. But while Mum was eager for him to do well at school, she put her foot down, insisting that the local school was more than good enough for her son. She openly admitted that she didn't want him to be educated out of her life. Matthew's response had been to say he'd happily stop going to school altogether and have Jacob teach him at home. Mum had met that with equal short shrift and told him not to be so daft. 'And what about making friends?' she'd wanted to know. 'I'm not having you turn into an eccentric recluse like the Professor!'

Poor Mum, she hadn't realised then that he was already considered an eccentric at school. He was the nerd, the freak. Then a teacher pondered the theory to Mum during a memorable parents' evening, that he might be borderline autistic and had she thought of having him tested? It was a suggestion that went down like a brick being hurled through a window. Mum was outraged and demanded the accusation was retracted. No son of hers was going to be given a label that, in her opinion, would disadvantage him for life!

Matthew hadn't been able to see what all the fuss was about. He knew there was no getting away from the fact that he was different – he was the tall, lanky one who wore glasses and was always sitting in the corner with his head in a book, the one obsessed with the tiniest and seemingly insignificant of details and who wasn't afraid to correct those who got something wrong. What a tosser he must have been!

He was also the one who was pathetically useless at anything that involved hand–eye coordination, which pretty much ruled out him having any competency when it came to sports. Yet winning approval from those around him had never been a priority. Nor was he overly fussed about forming friendships amongst his peers; as far as he could see, it was a minefield of complications that he could happily avoid. Although Laura was the exception, and he fully believed that was down to her knowing him outside of the school environment and with an absence of peer group pressure dictating how she should treat him. They had merely taken each other at face value.

He hadn't gone out of his way to be unsociable at school, but the truth was, he simply didn't fit in and people didn't want to associate with him for fear of being tainted by association. The surprising thing was, he wasn't bullied – not to any great extent at least – perhaps he wasn't worth the effort.

Things changed, just as Jacob predicted they would, when he went to Cambridge. There, and with the benefit of relative anonymity, he found any number of social misfits like himself and discovered that being different was perfectly acceptable, that, in fact, to be normal was considered a far greater crime. It was there he met James, a medic student, and in their second year they ended up sharing a house together.

All in all, he'd had a great childhood and he would forever be grateful to his mother and Jacob for that.

It was typical of the self-sufficient to be content with their lot, Jacob always used to say, and time was when Matthew would have agreed all too readily with the statement. But now he felt his self-sufficiency wasn't enough. Whether or not it was Jacob's death that was the cause of his equilibrium being disturbed, he didn't know, but he was no longer content with his lot and with each mile he drove away from Glaskin House, and which took him nearer to Cambridge, he had a growing sense that he was heading entirely in the wrong direction. The feeling made him recall what he'd thought last night, that he had reached a crossroads in his life.

*

'One question, Dad,' Saskia had said, the minute they'd driven through the gateposts of Glaskin House. 'What's got into you? You have never, *ever*, in the history of carrying out a probate valuation, invited the benefactor, client, customer, call him what you will, to dinner. Why this one?'

'Why not this one?' Ralph had replied. He'd known as soon as he'd invited Matthew to join them that Saskia would question his motives.

'Because I have the awful suspicion that you're up to something.'

'What? I can't feel sorry for somebody without being up to something? Really, Saskia!'

'That you feel sorry for Matthew Gray is not in doubt,' she'd said, 'but inviting him for dinner, that's ... that's altogether different.'

'I just thought, stuck there on his own in that miserably cold house, a damned good meal inside him and some cheerful company wouldn't go amiss.'

'Well, let me know when we go into the meals-on-wheels business, won't you?'

Now, and only a couple of miles from home, Ralph risked a look at his daughter and ventured to say, 'Was there something about Matthew in particular you didn't like, Saskia?'

She frowned. 'What are you really asking me, Dad?'

He swallowed uneasily, knowing he was heading into dangerously choppy waters. Even so he unwisely pressed on. 'I honestly thought the two of you might ... you know ... that you might ...' His words fell away. It was all very well thinking it, but saying it out aloud was another matter.

'I knew it!' she exclaimed. 'You were trying to set me up! Dad, that's outrageous!'

'Saskia, he's a decent young man, on his own, about your age, good-looking and intelligent, why not consider him date-worthy?'

She visibly cringed. 'Date-worthy?' she repeated with a

85

shudder. '*Date*-worthy? What sort of language is that?

'It's a perfectly reasonable expression in my opinion,' he said defensively, wondering himself where on earth it had come from. 'Just as Matthew Gray is a perfectly reasonable young man.'

'So you admit it! You were trying to fix me up?'

'Not really.'

She snorted at that. 'Hmm … when I need anyone to set me up, I'll let you know. Or better still, I'll reciprocate and fix you up with somebody wholly inappropriate. See how you like it, eh?'

'Got anyone in mind for me?' he said after a long silence.

'Yes,' she said. 'That awful woman who's fancied you since forever, the one with the dyed red hair who's always coming into the shop smelling of eau de gin and asking if you have any erotic fiction.'

He laughed, relieved that Saskia had resorted to threatening him with the woman they referred to as Nympho-Lil. Just as he couldn't, Saskia could never stay cross for long. 'I'm sorry,' he said, 'but hand on heart, I didn't ask you to help me with the valuation with an ulterior motive. It was only when we were there at the house that I thought the two of you might get on. What didn't you like about him?'

'It's not a case of not liking him.' She shrugged. 'He just seemed so uptight. And don't forget, he's still grieving, which means his head will be all over the place and therefore not exactly ideally suited to getting involved with anyone new right now. So seriously, Dad, no more getting any ideas, OK? I'm fine as I am. As I expect he is.'

But Ralph did have ideas. He had lots of them if he were honest. His greatest fear for Saskia was that she would make the same mistake he once had, that to preserve the status quo at Ashcombe, she would deny herself the chance to lead the life she deserved.

Chapter Fourteen

I was finishing lunch in the canteen when I found myself embroiled in a lengthy and heated argument over Rachmaninov who had died a few weeks ago in the US. Chatterton-Jones had put forward the hypothesis that if Rachmaninov had remained in Russia he would have continued to write music of the highest calibre, that moving to America he had lost his artistic integrity.

It was one of those senseless arguments that had us all determined to have our say, but which predictably reached no satisfactory conclusion. What it did do was provide a temporary distraction from the horror of knowing that we were still failing to make any real impact in saving lives in the North Atlantic. What kept us sane was the knowledge that little by little we were making progress of sorts and gaining ground on the threat posed by the U-boats to the Allies. However, it was cold comfort in the face of so much death.

What felt more personal to me were the terrible reports coming through of the systematic murder of Jews by Hitler's SS in Warsaw. It was being referred to as a massacre and I knew that my grandmother, who followed the news avidly on the wireless, would be greatly distressed. She and my grandfather had fled Russia in fear of their lives, now there was a much more ruthless enemy to fear.

It was when I was on my way back to Hut 8 and lagging behind the others who had found some other topic to argue about, that I spotted a face I didn't expect to see again. To my surprise, and bearing in mind it was now nearly a fortnight since we had met on the train, she recognised me straight away. Breaking away from a couple of Wrens with whom she had been chatting, she waved and came towards me. In an instant I experienced an inner panic. What could I say to her? It was absolutely forbidden to discuss the nature of what we did here at the Park. What if, as a recent and naïve recruit, she broke that rule?

'How was lunch?' she asked, 'I'm on my way there now.' She spoke as if we were old friends.

'Even more disgusting than usual,' I replied. 'I think it was whale meat. But I wouldn't swear to it. It might even have been something worse.'

She wrinkled her pretty nose. 'I wish now I hadn't asked. Are you going to the concert tonight?'

It was the concert this evening that had instigated the heated debate around the table during lunch. I hadn't planned to go, my only thought for when I finished my shift was to go back to my digs and do nothing but sleep. I'd had a vicious headache for the last three days and every square inch of my body felt pummelled with exhaustion.

'I hear the orchestra here is rather good,' she said, 'and a girl I work with plays the violin and is a member. Are you a fan of Rachmaninov?'

'Yes,' I responded.

She smiled. 'In that case I'll see you there. Cheerio!'

She raised her hand in a jaunty gesture of farewell and rushed to join the Wrens who had gone on ahead towards the canteen.

When I entered the hut, Chatterton-Jones was setting about the business of filling his pipe in preparation to starting work again. He claimed he couldn't concentrate unless he smoked it. 'Who was that you were talking to?' he asked.

I shrugged and replied quite truthfully that I had no idea. 'I met her on the train a couple of weeks ago,' I said.

'Pretty girl,' he said in his languorous drawl, while wedging the pipe into the side of his mouth. He struck a match, applied it to the tamped-down tobacco in the bowl and sucked hard. It took him a couple of attempts to get the thing going and when he'd managed it, he peered at me through a dense cloud of foul-smelling blue smoke. 'I wouldn't say no to you introducing me. She's new, isn't she? I must say, she looks familiar, can't place her though.'

I'm not surprised, I thought, the wretched man probably knew far too many girls to recall them in any detail.

Known for his fondness for the opposite sex, Charles Chatterton-Jones had acquired himself quite a reputation at the Park. A tall, athletic man two years my senior and oozing a debonair and careless charm, he had been vaguely familiar to me at Cambridge where he'd been captain of the college rowing club. Here at Bletchley he was known for his ferocious competitiveness on – and off – the tennis court. He also regularly frequented the Scottish Reels Club, along with various other clubs and societies, all of which gave him access to any number of women.

If you were so inclined, and had the energy and appetite, you could lead an extremely active social life at the Park, which Chatterton-Jones most certainly did. A man for whom the expression burning the candle at both ends had been coined, he was possessed of the hearty self-assurance of one who knew, with a cast-iron conviction, that he was devastatingly attractive to the female sex. For some reason, in this precise moment, his overly confident manner and his perfect poise and ability to wear a pair of corduroy trousers, a Fair Isle pullover and a scarf tied loosely around his neck and look like a film star, incensed me to the point I could have happily punched him.

Removing my shabby and shapeless tweed jacket I sat down purposefully at my desk, mentally cursing the infuriating man's lofty sense of entitlement which came with his class and background, and which always brought out the worst in me. Knowing that he was watching me and waiting for a reply, I muttered, 'I'm sure you don't need me to make an introduction.'

I arrived back at the Park that evening hot and perspiring just a few minutes before the concert was due to start.

Despite how exhausted I was, I had rashly decided to attend and, having made that decision, I had cycled home to my digs in Peck Street for a wash and to change into fresh clothes. I had been brought up to believe that a clean shirt and a wash were two of the most important things in life. More important than this was a decent haircut and a well-trimmed beard and it goes without saying that I had the latter two by dint of the family business.

As soon as I had emerged from the bathroom where I'd had to make do with cold water – the hot water was strictly rationed by my landlady – the woman herself had pounced on me in her crossover apron. For an age Mrs Pridmore kept me talking about something so inconsequential I have no memory of what it was, other than to digest that it was a complaint about something, or somebody. Probably it was me. Then with a twitch of her nose, she had wafted the air with one of her fat white hands. 'What's that smell?' she'd demanded. Reluctant to admit I had splashed on some precious cologne from the bottle my grandmother had given me last Christmas, I denied I could smell anything. The nose had twitched again. 'It smells foreign to me,' she said with disgust. Mrs Pridmore considered anything that was foreign as the wickedest of crimes, and I knew all too well that she suspected me of exactly this offence.

Unused to me breezing in and out of an evening, she'd then demanded to know when I expected to return. 'I won't be late,' I'd replied with the supreme certainty of one who knew he was on a fool's errand.

The evening's entertainment had attracted a large crowd and there was standing room only when I entered the ballroom. I squeezed through the noisy throng and took up a position on the sidelines – my usual position in life – and, feeling like an insignificant speck orbiting the universe, I surveyed the audience for The Girl on the Train, as I had come to think of her.

There was no sign of her and disappointment and the utter absurdity of my actions caused my head to pound to the point of nausea. What was I doing here? What had compelled me to do something so irrationally out of character? A few words from a pretty girl and I had dispensed with every ounce of my common sense.

Yet I knew I had made the effort to come because I wanted to see her again. I wanted to know more about her, her name at the very least. I had liked it earlier today that she had made the effort to acknowledge my presence and speak to me. I had especially liked knowing that the exchange had not gone unnoticed by Chatterton-Jones who, doubtless, had assumed she was out of my league.

Being the grandson of a Russian Jewish barber I knew I would never be like the Chatterton-Joneses of this world, but I was not without a modicum of fight within me. Maybe it was that which had brought me here this evening, to prove to Chatterton-Jones, and myself, that I was not entirely unattractive to the opposite sex.

But all I was currently proving, fifteen minutes into the concert, was that this was the last place I should be. I should be back at Mrs Pridmore's lying on my bed resting. No matter how fond I was of Rachmaninov, the music wasn't helping. In fact, I could barely recognise what the orchestra was playing, I felt so ill. Worried I might make a ghastly exhibition of myself by fainting, I knew I needed to get out. I managed to wait until an appropriate moment, when the audience burst into thunderous applause, and then pushed through the crowd to reach the door and the way out. I was almost there when I felt a hand on my arm. But in my rush to escape I ignored it and pressed on, not caring who I was rudely barging past.

I had been ill like this before. It was the pressure we were under that was the cause. Some were better at coping, but I knew of men who'd gone clean off their rocker. Only last week poor old Sykes had collapsed in the hut and had to be carried out. We'd been informed that he was now 'resting'.

Once I was outside, I took deep breaths of the cool evening air.

'Are you all right?'

I turned at the sound of the voice, and there she was – The Girl on the Train.

I couldn't speak. I was too overcome with the fear that I was about to be physically ill, right there in front of her. Clamping a hand over my mouth and hoping she would leave me alone, I disappeared into the fading light of dusk, whereupon I promptly threw up behind the nearest bush. It was such a violent spasm of retching that there was no chance of disguising the revolting noise I was making and, as my stomach roiled and I gasped for air, I felt my whole body break out into a clammy sweat. Frightened I was going to lose consciousness, I fought the light-headedness that was compelling me to fall to my knees. Breathe, I told myself. *Breathe!*

Finally the nausea passed and closing my eyes with relief that it was over, I steeled myself for the revulsion that was surely due to come. That's if she hadn't slipped away to avoid witnessing such an appalling scene.

'Here,' I heard a soft voice say in the shadowy half-light of dusk, 'take this.'

I opened my eyes and there she was, The Girl on the Train. In her outstretched hand was a handkerchief. It was small and dainty and edged with lace. 'Thank you,' I murmured, my gratitude outweighing my embarrassment. But instead of taking the handkerchief, I pulled my own out from my jacket pocket. 'I'd hate to ruin yours,' I said, wiping my mouth. Then: 'I'm sorry you had to see that.'

'Don't be silly. I did a first-aid course, so I've seen far worse. Do you think you can manage to walk a little?'

Conscious of the vile smell coming from behind me, I forced myself to move. 'Thank you,' I said when we'd put some distance between ourselves and the scene of my humiliation, 'you're very kind.'

'Nonsense.'

Then with equal straightforwardness, she took hold of my arm with surprising strength and slowly led me towards a bench overlooking the lake. 'There,' she said, 'how do you feel now?'

'Better,' I admitted. Which was true. My head had stopped thumping and the nausea had definitely passed. 'But please, if you want to go back to the concert, don't feel you have to stay.'

'I only came this evening because I wanted to see you.'

Her candour startled me. 'Why?'

'Why not? And you were right, by the way; it *was* whale meat at lunch and quite possibly the most disgusting thing I've ever eaten.'

I shuddered. 'I'd rather you didn't mention food just now.'

She laughed. 'I'm sorry. How very silly of me. Do you think you're suffering from food poisoning?'

'I doubt it; otherwise almost everyone here would be ill. I'm afraid it's nothing more than a bad headache brought on by tiredness.'

'Daddy suffers from headaches; usually it's anxiety that brings it on for him. He works at the Foreign Office. That's where I was before it was suggested I be transferred here. You knew when we met on the train that I was coming to Bletchley, didn't you?'

I nodded. 'It was fairly obvious.'

'Oh dear. Rather defeats the whole purpose of me being here, doesn't it? What with all the secrecy we're sworn to.'

'No harm done, I'm sure.'

'And don't worry, I'm not going to ask you what you do.

Although I do know you work in Hut 8, so that is a bit of a clue.'

I looked at her closely. 'How do you know that's where I work?'

'One of the Wrens you saw me with at lunchtime told me. You're the subject of much speculation, you know.'

'In what way?'

'Don't look so alarmed! I think it's rather sweet, they've got it into their heads that you're fearfully shy and a terrible grump. But I don't think you're at all grouchy. You chatted happily enough with me on the train. Do you think that when you're feeling better you might agree to meet for a drink some time?'

There was patently nothing shy about her and once I'd recovered from the shock of her question, I muttered something that I think implied that I would. Though I wouldn't swear to it because, and to my shame, I was too busy picturing the expression on Chatterton-Jones's face when he heard about this.

But my crowing was short-lived as I then wondered if this girl's newly made friends had put her up to a prank. Had I become the target of a cruel joke?

'By the way,' she went on blithely, 'my name is Katherine, but everybody calls me Kitty.'

Trying not to dwell on the thought that this was all some sort of elaborate ruse, and she was merely playing her part, I said, 'Presumably you already know my name?'

She grinned. 'Oh, yes.'

Chapter Fifteen

Saskia had decided that the author of *The Dandelion Years* was a natural storyteller and knew just how to craft his narrative. He hadn't pieced it together in actual chapters, but in segments, and rather conveniently those built-in pauses lent themselves to Saskia taking a break from deciphering the appalling handwriting. If it wasn't so bad, she would happily race through the notebook in one sitting, but putting it on the bedside table, she turned out the light, glad to be able to close and rest her eyes. At this rate, by the time she finished reading it she'd need to start wearing glasses.

In the late-night quiet of the house – it was almost one o'clock – she heard her father trying unsuccessfully to creep up to bed without making a noise. Being as old as the cottage was, it was impossible for anyone to move about without the tell-tale creak of a floorboard. Ever since Mum's death, Dad had become a committed night owl. Immediately after the accident he hadn't been able to sleep at all. None of them had, but unlike Dad, the rest of them had eventually readjusted and adopted their normal sleeping patterns again. Dad used this late night-time to study the online auction catalogues. She did it herself in fits and starts, but wasn't addicted the way he was. Something she could become addicted to with no trouble at all, and which they both really enjoyed doing together, was bidding for books online. Firing off bids to a saleroom at the click of a button, and without having to leave the comfort of home, made buying at auction dangerously easy, and a lot of fun.

The trouble with Dad was that he frequently became too

attached to the books he bought and hated to part with them. Though she wasn't much better herself. Luckily Harvey and Oliver would remind them both that there was a business to run and there was no point in buying books if they weren't prepared to sell them.

'A little hard-headed business sense wouldn't go amiss,' Harvey would say.

Oliver, on the other hand, would go straight for the emotional jugular. 'Heaven only knows what you two will be like when Harvey and I have gone!'

'At least we'll get some peace and quiet,' Saskia would say, brushing his comment off with humour rather than confront the idea of her beloved grandfathers not being around any more.

Out on the landing, she heard footsteps and the creak of floorboards. The footsteps stopped outside her door, which was ajar.

'I'm awake, Dad,' she said, 'you can come in if you want.'

'I didn't wake you, did I?' he said, stepping into the room.

She sat up. 'No, I'd only just switched off the light. What's on your mind, then?'

'Who says anything is?'

'I do. All evening you've had that look on you; the one you think hides what you're really thinking. So come on, out with it.'

He smiled and sat on the edge of her bed, the soft light from the lamp on the landing spilling into the room and falling across his face. Not for the first time she thought that her father didn't really look his age. In recent years he'd filled out and gained a little weight, which he attributed to Harvey's cooking, but in no way was he overweight. There were more lines creasing the corner of his eyes, but that was to be expected, as was the amount of grey that was liberally sprinkled through his fair hair. For as long as she could remember he'd worn his hair in the same style – collar length and pushed back from his forehead – making him look, a friend of Saskia's once said, a dead ringer for Bill Nighy. While Saskia could see there was a passing similarity to the actor, to her mind it was only really evident when her father was worried, as he seemed to be now.

'You're not in any way still cross with me, are you?' he asked.

'What about?'

'That whole Matthew Gray thing today.'

She smiled, loving him for his concern. 'Dad, it's fine, don't worry. And really, I owe you an apology, I overreacted.'

'But I do worry about you, Saskia. I worry about you being stuck here with us oldies when you should be—'

'Dad,' she said firmly, cutting him off. 'I'm happy here with you "oldies", as you put it; if I wasn't, I'd be somewhere else, wouldn't I?'

He frowned. 'I keep thinking what your mother would say—'

Once more, Saskia stopped him from going on. 'She'd tell you to stop worrying, that's what she'd say. What's more, if Mum were in my shoes, I know she wouldn't want to be anywhere else but here. Now trust me, this is not a conversation we need to have. Or ever have again. But if it puts your mind at rest, I promise you that if I decide it's time to ship out, I will. I'm not here under duress, or because of any misplaced sense of duty. OK?'

She could see he wasn't finished on the subject, but wanting to put an end to it, she pointed to the notebook on the bedside table. 'I managed to read some more,' she said.

'Any clues as to who wrote it?'

She shook her head. 'None. I almost feel as though the author deliberately concealed his identity. Which would be perfectly in keeping with the secrecy of the world he inhabited at Bletchley.'

'You still believe it's real, that it's not a work of fiction?'

'It feels too real and personal to have been made up.'

His gaze still on the notebook, he said, 'You know, you

97

could just flick through the pages scanning them for names or likely references that might help to identify the author?'

She feigned a look of horror. 'What? And spoil the fun of reading the story as it was written? That would be cheating, like suggesting I begin a murder mystery by reading the last page first.'

He smiled. 'I should have known better than to suggest something so outrageous. You never could break one of your own carved-in-stone rules, could you? Remember how you used to tackle a tube of Smarties? You'd eat them systematically, one by one, but in strict order of colour as determined by you.'

She returned his smile. 'There's a right and a wrong way of doing things, that's all. Nothing wrong in that.'

He stood up. 'Do you still want me to speak to Gil tomorrow and see if he can tell us the house clearance jobs he's carried out recently?'

'Sure, why not?'

'It won't spoil the fun of your own particular sleuthing methods?'

'Who knows, maybe by the time Gil gives you an answer, I'll have cracked the mystery myself.'

'If there is any mystery, of course. I wouldn't rule out an aspiring author with a vivid imagination. It could be a woman, have you thought of that?'

'Yes, but even if that's the case, the notebook belongs to somebody. Or somebody's family if the author's dead. I can't believe anyone deliberately chucked it away.'

'But you know as well as I do, sometimes there just isn't anyone left, not if the family line has run out.' He bent to kiss her on the forehead. 'Sleep well, sweetheart.'

'You too, Dad.'

When he'd gone, lying back down in her bed Saskia thought about her father's comment regarding family lines running out. As things stood, the Granger family line would come to an end with her death. It was hardly the most cheering thought to go to sleep with, but she did. She dreamt of a large tube of Smarties she had tipped out and was carefully sorting into neat rows according to colour. But then she was back at Glaskin House in the library and was explaining to Matthew Gray that he could have the green Smarties as they were the ones she least liked. Ignoring her, he took all her favourites – the red ones. She was furious with him.

Chapter Sixteen

Monday morning and the day wasn't going well for Ralph.

Pat, his long-term helper, had just made their first coffee of the day and had broken the news that she wouldn't be able to continue working for him. After much thought she and her husband had volunteered to mind their ten-month-old twin grandchildren now that their daughter was returning to work.

'I'm sorry,' she said, 'I've been dreading telling you. As much for myself as anything, as I know I'm going to miss all this.' She cast her gaze about the shop. 'It's like a second home for me. And you've always been so good to me.'

'I'll miss you too,' he said, his own gaze sweeping over the bookcases that Pat ensured were immaculately ordered with everything clearly labelled and displayed to its best. She knew the stock as well as he did, if not better. She was also particularly creative when it came to the window display, which she took great pride in arranging, regularly selecting a theme of her own choosing. This month's theme was gardening. It had seemed a good idea last week when the weather had begun to warm up with the promise of spring, but since yesterday, when a bitterly cold wind had swept in from the North Sea bringing with it another lashing of rain in the night, gardening pursuits felt a long way off. It was raining now and only the hardiest of shoppers were out and about in the town.

'I hate to leave you in the lurch,' Pat said, 'but Denise is desperate. She was all set to put the twins in nursery, but when push came to shove, it was going to cost too much.'

'Don't worry,' Ralph said, 'I'll find somebody else.'

Like who? he wondered gloomily. Who would replace Pat? She was the best part-time member of staff he'd ever had and without her the place would soon fall into rack and ruin – shop housekeeping, such as keeping the place in apple-pie order, wasn't his forte. He knew exactly what would happen this evening at home when he told the others that Pat was leaving; they'd all rush to say there was no reason why they couldn't lend a hand and do more hours at the shop. None of which would be right. Not in the long-term. No, he would have to be very firm about this. Saskia needed to concentrate on her own work and his father and Harvey needed to take things easier. Fair enough it wasn't necessary for them to grind to a halt completely, but a little winding down wouldn't hurt them. Though neither would ever admit that.

Pat's news had been the second disappointment of the day. First thing that morning before leaving Ashcombe, Ralph had received a call from Matthew Gray to say the heating engineer was due late that afternoon and not that morning as arranged, so perhaps it would be better for Ralph and Saskia to return to Glaskin House tomorrow when, hopefully, the central heating would be working. Ralph had mentally geared himself up to get stuck in again today with the probate valuation and had said he'd be happy to wear extra clothes to keep warm, but Matthew had said he wouldn't dream of putting him and his daughter through the ordeal of spending the day in a house which would be colder still now. 'I'll let you know how the engineer gets on,' he'd said before ringing off.

The day passed slowly, which did at least lend itself to Ralph doing some online research regarding a number of art books from Jacob Belinsky's collection, in particular a study in the original language of the nineteenth-century Russian landscape artist Isaak Levitan. He had next to no knowledge on the subject, but by the time he'd finished reading up on-line he was a good deal wiser.

Next he tackled some paperwork and then took a look at a bag of books brought in by an elderly gentleman. Ralph hated turning people away, especially the elderly who always believed they had something of special interest and value to sell. This chap didn't have anything out of the ordinary, but given that he'd battled his way here in such awful weather, Ralph took pity on the old boy and offered him a fiver just to make him feel his journey hadn't been wasted.

It was at the end of the day, when Pat had already left, and Ralph was getting ready to close the shop, that he remembered he was supposed to have phoned Gil. He'd got as far as reaching for the telephone, when the door opened and a blast of cold air swirled in. He almost dropped the receiver when he saw who it was beneath the canopy of a purple umbrella.

'Hello,' she said, pushing the door closed behind her. 'I bet you didn't expect to see me today, did you?'

He hurriedly locked up and took her over the road to The Crown and, after he'd settled her at a table in a cosy corner where they could talk in private, he went to the bar.

While he waited to be served he corralled his wits. The last time he'd seen Libby he had upset her terribly. But then he'd upset himself too. Finishing their affair had not been easy, but guilt and the constant skulking about had finally got the better of him.

They'd met at a book fair. She'd had a stall next to his and not recognising her face amongst the regular exhibitors and members of the PBFA – the Provincial Booksellers Fairs Association – he'd gone over to chat with her during a lull. She was new to the area, she'd explained, having recently moved from Worcester to a village on the outskirts of Cambridge. He saw her again at the Woodbridge fair, then again in Long Melford the following month. After that event, they went for a drink and she told him that things weren't going well between her and her husband – they were arguing non-stop, mostly because he drank too much, which was a symptom of bouts of depression.

'He hasn't always been this way,' she told Ralph, 'he used to be fun. I just wish it could be how it used to be between us.'

It was the oldest story in the book – providing a shoulder on which to lean, until eventually it was more than a shoulder that was being offered. Ralph didn't bother justifying the affair to himself – he just went with the flow, telling no one what he was getting up to. Who could he tell? Who wouldn't hesitate to point out the glaringly obvious: that he was skating on the thinnest of ice?

The trouble was he had known he and Libby were falling in love and that their clandestine meetings would soon no longer be enough for either of them. When she started talking about leaving her husband to be with him, to be a part of his life and his family who she'd heard so much about, he knew he had to confront the situation head on and make it clear that things weren't that simple. The truth was that he couldn't give Libby what she wanted without disrupting life at Ashcombe – and he wasn't prepared to do that.

He just couldn't do it. It wouldn't be fair to Harvey and Oliver who could have easily remarried a long time ago, but had chosen not to consider it as an option. Instead they had put aside their own needs and put those of his and their granddaughter before anything else. Quite frankly, Ralph hadn't had the guts to break the pattern set in place by their stoicism. He especially couldn't bring a woman home to parade under the nose of his father-in-law.

There had been a number of women before and after Libby, all of whom he'd seen on what could only be described as a casual basis. None of them had lived on the doorstep. In the early years they had been nothing more than an attempt to prove to himself that he could love again, but they proved no such thing. They had been no more than acts of sexual release which only left him wallowing in the bleak betrayal of his actions, both to Evie and the women with whom he had slept.

But then that changed when he met Libby Henshaw. Libby had got to him, had made him realise that he could be in love with someone other than Evie. And it very nearly broke his heart knowing that. Now, ten years later, here Libby was again.

Still waiting to be served, he threw a quick glance over his shoulder to where Libby was reading something on her mobile phone. The same age as he was, the years had treated her well. Her hair was shorter than it used to be, softly layered, the colour of caramel shot through with golden highlights. The style and colour suited her. Unlike him, she hadn't put on any weight; in fact he'd say she had lost some. Which all went to make him feel conscious that perhaps he hadn't fared so well in the intervening years.

Finally he was served and their drinks paid for – a glass of red wine for Libby and a single malt whisky for him – he rejoined her.

'Is that whisky for shock?' she asked with a smile when he sat down.

'Of course not,' he lied.

'Oh, Ralph, you never could lie convincingly.'

He shrugged and held his glass aloft. 'To you,' he said. 'It's good to see you.'

She tapped her glass against his. '*Is* it good to see me?' she asked, after she'd taken a sip of her wine.

'Why shouldn't it be?'

She sat back in her seat and stared at him. 'I might be here to remind you how devastated I was when you ended our relationship. I might be here to make trouble.'

'Ten years is an awfully long time to plan your revenge. I don't think I could be worth that amount of thought and effort, surely?'

She laughed abruptly. 'I'd forgotten how self-effacing you could be. But you needn't worry; I'm not here to rock the boat. We were both acting out of self-preservation back then: I needed somebody to fill the void my husband was creating and you needed whatever it was you needed.'

He drank some of his whisky. 'It was more than that,' he said quietly. 'Much more.'

She looked at him intently with her soft brown eyes and her full lips pressed together. 'It was for me,' she said, after a pause, 'but was it for you?'

'It was. It really was.'

She took another long sip of her wine as if contemplating his sincerity. At length, she said, 'Why don't you bring me up to date. How's your family and have you taken the plunge and remarried?'

He did as she asked, giving her a broad brushstroke picture of the last ten years and categorically denying he'd ever been remotely tempted to marry again. When he'd finished, he said, 'What about you? Did you and your husband sort things out?'

'No. I divorced him just as I said I would and moved back to Worcester where I still had friends and family.'

'Ah, so that's why I never saw you around on the circuit again.' Without meaning to, his gaze slid towards her left hand. There was no ring.

'I'm single,' she said. 'And not on the look out for Husband Number Two, so you can relax.'

He smiled, remembering with fondness how candid she could be. 'So what brings you back to Suffolk?' he asked.

'My parents are no longer alive and I decided I needed to shake things up. I'd always liked it round here, so I decided to move back. I'm renting a sweet little cottage in Long Melford until I can find something to buy.'

'Where are you thinking?'

She laughed again. 'Drink your whisky, Ralph, you look like you're about to go into cardiac arrest.'

He laughed too. 'I'm not in shock, I'm pleasantly surprised, that's all.'

And the thing was, he genuinely *was* pleasantly surprised. He felt as though the day had suddenly got a whole lot better.

Chapter Seventeen

Saskia was out of sorts.

She blamed it on a frustrating day spent unsuccessfully trying to chase down a particular type of goatskin leather she needed in order to restore an exquisite first edition of *A Christmas Carol*, but she knew that wasn't the sole reason for her grumpiness. She had woken up in a bad mood, and for the most irrational of reasons – a dream. A dream about, of all things, a tube of Smarties. Except it felt so much more than that.

She was now driving back from the supermarket in the pouring rain with Harvey and Oliver. Once a fortnight they went to Sudbury to do a big shop, stocking up on all the things which Oliver claimed were cheaper there than buying locally. Calculator in hand, and coupons cut from the newspaper at the ready, he would spend an age inching his way along the aisles running to earth the best deals. He could happily spend an entire afternoon absorbed in wringing the most out of the system. It was a personal crusade for him, an us-versus-them situation. Saskia's preferred method was to be in and out of the supermarket in the fastest possible time. If she could set the fastest record for getting the job done, she would. A penny extra on a loo roll, who gave a—

'Hobnobs!'

'Sorry, Grandpa O?' she said in response to the bellowed proclamation from the back of the car.

'We forgot to buy chocolate Hobnobs.'

'For the love of God, don't let him make us go back for them,' muttered Harvey beside Saskia.

'What's that, Harvey?' Oliver demanded.

'I've told you before,' Harvey answered raising his voice, 'you need to get your hearing tested. You're as deaf as a post these days.'

'I'm no such thing!'

'That's why you keep shouting at us when we're no more than a few inches from you. You're like a foghorn. I keep telling you, but you won't listen, and that's because you can't hear! Tell him, Saskia, tell him he needs to get his ears checked. He probably needs them syringing. God only knows what he's got bunged up in them!'

'I'll have you know I heard every word of that,' Oliver snarled.

'A check-up wouldn't do any harm, Grandpa O,' Saskia said diplomatically. She had been thinking much the same as Harvey, that in the last few weeks Oliver's hearing wasn't as sharp as it could be.

'My arm? What's that about my arm?' he asked.

Harvey tutted and shook his head. 'See what I mean,' he said under his breath. 'Deaf as a post and driving me round the bend into the bargain.'

Usually the more upbeat of her grandfathers, Harvey, like Saskia, was far from his normal self today. In the post this morning he'd received a letter with the news that an old and dear friend had died. Given their age, it was to be expected he and Oliver would hear news of this nature with escalating regularity, but it didn't make it any less upsetting for them.

The appalling weather and fading light was adding to the overall gloom of Saskia's mood and, as the wipers worked double-time to cope with the monsoon-like rain lashing down, she gripped the steering wheel and concentrated hard on the road.

When they were back at Ashcombe, Oliver rushed off in the rain to put the hens away for the night, while Saskia and Harvey dealt with the shopping.

In the kitchen, and shrugging off her wet coat and surveying the numerous carrier bags they'd lugged in, Saskia said, 'Why don't you go and sit down and let me deal with this?'

Harvey frowned. 'No need to mollycoddle me,' he said gruffly. 'I may have lost a friend, but I haven't lost the ability to pull my weight around here.'

'I wasn't suggesting anything of the kind,' she replied. 'But a little cosseting never did anyone any harm. Give me your coat and I'll hang it up. Then I'll make us all a cup of tea.'

'You're becoming bossier by the day; you know that, don't you?'

'Coat?' she said, holding out her hand.

Rolling his eyes, he did as she asked and when she returned from hanging their coats in the boiler room, the telephone was ringing. 'Probably Dad saying he's on his way,' she said, picking up the receiver.

She was wrong.

'I'm afraid he's not here,' she said in answer to the request to speak to her father, at the same time gesticulating to Harvey to leave the shopping alone and sit down.

'Is that Saskia Granger?' the caller asked.

'Yes, that's me,' she said, just as the back door was thrown open and Oliver burst in.

'What a bloody awful day it is!' he roared at an unnecessarily loud volume. 'The wind's getting up again and it's like the end of the world out there!' He snatched off his sopping hat and stomped over to the Aga to hang it on the hook where he liked to dry it, despite Harvey's protestations that it stank like wet dog and was a health hazard. Turning round he saw that Saskia was on the phone. He pulled a face of apology and began removing his dripping coat with exaggeratedly silent care.

'I'm sorry,' Saskia said to the caller, aware that he'd been speaking but that she hadn't heard a word. 'Who did you say you were?'

'It's me, Matthew. Matthew Gray, we met yesterday at Glaskin House.'

She did a double take, for here was the cause of her bad mood. Here was the cause of that stupid, stupid, *stupid* dream she'd had last night, and which had left her feeling so irritable. She knew it was about as irrational as it got, but she just hadn't been able to shift the groundless feeling throughout the day that something precious had been taken from her.

'Oh, hello,' she said, determined to overcome the absurdity of her emotions. 'Sorry about all the noise. That was one of my grandfathers announcing the latest weather forecast to the greater part of East Anglia.'

'The weather's bad over there, is it?'

'You could say that.' She forced an extra cheerful bounce to her voice. 'Don't tell me Cambridge is enjoying a heatwave?' *It was only a dream. Nothing but a dream. It wasn't real. It wasn't his fault. He didn't really steal anything from you.*

'To be honest it could have been as hot as the Sahara and I wouldn't have noticed,' he said. 'I've been in court since early this morning and have only just emerged. I just wanted to let you know that the boiler's been fixed. I tried ringing your father's mobile to tell him, but didn't get a reply, so I tried this number he gave me as backup. I'm sorry if I've disturbed you at home.'

'No worries. I'll tell Dad you called and that we can resume work again tomorrow. Do we still collect the key from your neighbour?'

'Yes, Jenny said she'd come in with you to make sure the heating really is working.'

'OK, thanks for letting us know.'

She was about to say goodbye and take Harvey to task for ignoring her instructions – he was bending down to yet another bulging carrier bag – when Matthew said, 'There's something else I wanted to say. I ... I want to apologise to you.'

'Oh?' she said. 'What for?'

'I think I may have given you the wrong impression about myself yesterday; I'm not normally that miserable, I just wasn't in the best of moods. I'm sorry if I came across as less than hospitable. I'd hate to think I'd offended you.'

His apology couldn't have surprised her more. But as his words sank in – *I think I may have given you the wrong impression about myself ... I'd hate to think I'd offended you* – she felt uncomfortably aware that her quickness to judge had been horribly exposed. For yes, her first impression had been to dismiss him as an uptight misery guts and she'd therefore treated him accordingly. But on what had she based that conclusion? On nothing more than a terse manner perhaps, because in this precise instant she couldn't think of any other crime he'd committed. No wonder, in the car driving home, Dad had asked her why she hadn't liked Matthew.

Had Matthew picked up on that? Had he just apologised because he'd been genuinely concerned that he'd inadvertently upset her? If so, what in her behaviour had led him to think that? A look on her part, a gesture, a turn of phrase? If that was the case, she had acted less than professionally and it was she who should be apologising.

She opened her mouth to say something when the silence in her ear was broken by Matthew saying, 'I'll let you go, then. Goodbye.'

To her disbelief, the line went dead. He'd ended the call. And before she'd had a chance to respond. That wasn't fair. Not fair at all. He should have given her the opportunity to explain herself.

But to explain what, exactly? That she'd taken against him because he hadn't been entertaining enough? Given what a moody doomster she'd been today, that was rich coming from her! She sighed and banged the receiver back into place.

'Something wrong?' Harvey asked.

'Yes,' she snapped. 'Which bit of sit down and let me put the shopping away did you not understand?'

Taken aback by the sharpness of her voice, both her grandfathers stared at her across the kitchen. And with good reason; she was taking her frustration out on them and that was wrong.

Oh, what was the matter with her? Why was she behaving so badly with everyone?

It was Oliver who was brave enough to speak first. 'I think it's you who needs to sit down and take it easy. What's troubling you?'

Sapped of energy, she sighed and her shoulders sagged. 'I don't know. I'm just not very nice to be around at the moment.'

'Baloney,' Harvey said, coming over to her. 'It's us, we're enough to try the patience of the most saintly of saints.'

'You're very sweet to say that, but it's not you two. It's me. I'm turning into a miserable old grouch.'

'Then we need to do something to stop the rot,' Oliver said. 'You need to get away from us decrepit old fogies and have some fun. When *was* the last time you went out of an evening and enjoyed yourself?'

Harvey shot him a warning look. A warning look that was too late.

'Sorry,' Oliver said. 'Big mouth syndrome. Forget I said that.'

Saskia smiled tiredly. 'Nothing to apologise for,' she said. 'And please, the pair of you, no tiptoeing around Philip – he's long gone and as good as forgotten. OK?'

They nodded unconvincingly.

'I wonder where Ralph is,' Harvey said, looking up at the clock on the wall, as if clutching at the nearest diversion. 'It's not like him to be so late and not let us know.'

His desk submerged beneath a swathe of documents and files, and with another day in court to get through tomorrow, Matthew's mind should have been on the case, but it wasn't. Swivelling his chair from side to side, he was thinking about the conversation he'd just had with Saskia Granger.

He hadn't expected to speak to her, but hearing her voice, and recalling that awful look on her face when her father had invited him for supper, he had felt compelled to blurt out an apology. Unfortunately he was now left thinking that ending the call so abruptly had not furthered his cause. He was tempted to ring her back and issue yet another apology for his offhanded manner, but he suspected that would merely make him look an even bigger fool.

He'd ended the call the way he had because of that long and very telling silence from her, during which he had pictured her rolling her eyes and thinking: *Offended me? Well, hell yes, you offended me from the get-go! Come to think of it, you're offending me now, so why don't you just get off the line and leave me alone?*

He found a pencil from amongst the papers on his desk and twirled it round between his fingers. The real question in all of this was why did he care so much when normally that kind of thing slid off him without a second thought? Why did he give a damn what Saskia Granger's opinion of him was?

He tossed the pencil back on to the desk. What the hell did any of that matter anyway? He had more important things to deal with. Like going over the evidence he needed to present tomorrow morning. Removing his glasses, he rubbed his eyes. Normally he wore contacts, but often for a day in court he preferred the effect a pair of spectacles gave: they cranked up his maturity and gravitas ratings in front of a jury while being cross-examined.

Hearing the sound of his colleagues in the surrounding offices preparing to go, he checked what time it was on his pocket watch. It was later than he'd thought. Even so, he'd prefer to work here for another couple of hours than at the flat where James would be there to distract him.

Just as soon as the coast was clear – when Saskia had gone upstairs for a bath – Harvey enlisted Oliver's help and together they tackled Ralph in his study.

'What's this,' he asked, turning away from the computer on his desk, 'a deputation?'

'Something's wrong with Saskia,' Harvey said, closing the door after them. 'She's not herself. You must have noticed it.'

Oliver joined in. 'Not to put too fine a point on it, she's miserable, and we think it's our fault.'

'We're not good company for her.'

'We need to do something about it.'

'Before it's too late.'

'Before things get any worse.'

'We need to shake things up.'

Later that night, sitting up in bed, Saskia was annoyed and upset that she had effectively ruined a perfectly good day by succumbing to a bad mood, over absolutely nothing. She was furious with herself for snapping at poor Harvey, especially as she knew both he and Oliver would worry about what was making her act so out of character. She hated the thought of them watching their every word for fear of upsetting her.

Tomorrow, she told herself firmly, she would wake in a far better frame of mind. There would be no snapping. No grumpiness. No childish moodiness or outbursts. In short, she would be a model of smiling positivity and would make amends for today. She would do it, if for no other reason than to stop her grandfathers worrying about her.

To ensure she didn't dwell a moment longer on her dismal shortcomings, she reached for the notebook from her bedside table and opened it to the page where she'd stopped reading last night.

Making herself comfortable, she began to read and within minutes she was happily lost in the world of *The Dandelion Years*.

Chapter Eighteen

May 1943

A week after that excruciating evening when I'd been ill in front of her, and knowing we were on the same shift, Kitty proposed we go for a picnic and a bicycle ride together.

It was a glorious May afternoon and in the bright sunshine even the railway town of Bletchley had managed to shrug off its normally drab appearance. The sun could do nothing about the smell of the brickworks, however.

She asked me to meet her at her lodgings where she was billeted with a woman and her four rambunctious children, plus an invalided elderly father who, every time he set eyes on Kitty, asked her who she was. The only lavatory was outside and she giggled about there being no lock on the door and that the slightest gust of wind could blow it open. Far from complaining about her digs, Kitty merely laughed and called it all rather a lark. I was fast coming to know that her resilience and unshockable nature was all part and parcel of her upbringing. An upbringing that was vastly different to mine.

Her family home – Fanley Manor – was in Sussex and was, I guessed, something akin to a small estate. She had casually mentioned that it was referred to in the Domesday Book. There was also a house in London. Her father worked at the Foreign Office and had fought in the Great War and, according to Kitty, was simply furious that it was happening all over again. Her older sister drove a mobile canteen round the East End, having been taught to drive by the family chauffeur, just as Kitty had. 'That's what I wanted to do,' Kitty told me, 'but Daddy put a stop to my plans and said that he had something far more important for me to do. That's when I was dragged off to the Foreign Office and ended up here.' By here, she meant Bletchley, where I now knew she worked in Hut 4 translating decrypted German messages. She was fluent in the language, having spent time in Berlin before the outbreak of war to learn the language.

Though she was careful never to speak of what she did in any detail, she was what my mother called a 'real talker' and I could only wonder what Mum would make of my fraternising with a young woman who, as a debutante, had been presented at court to the King and Queen.

We cycled out of the town and, as seemed to be the pattern of our friendship, I was happy to let Kitty take the lead and decide upon our destination. With few cars on the road, due to strict fuel rationing, we had the quiet, winding country lanes to ourselves and the only other traffic we saw was a horse and cart and a motorcyclist roaring by. With the warm spring sun on my back as we freewheeled down the other side of the hill we'd just pedalled hard to climb, I experienced a lightness of spirit I scarcely recognised. All thoughts of the gruelling shift of decoding that awaited me that night were forgotten; I could not remember when I had last felt so free or unburdened. If, in fact, I ever had.

With no road signs – a precaution against German spies knowing their whereabouts – I was equally clueless to where I was. In front of me Kitty stuck her hand out and waved, indicating a field to the left. For much of the time I had endeavoured to keep my eyes on the burgeoning hedgerows and verdant farmland on either side of us, but I have to confess the sight of her light floral dress fluttering in the breeze and revealing her long bare legs was too strong for me to ignore entirely.

We rested our bicycles against a large oak tree next to a wooden stile and, from the front of my bicycle, I unhooked the basket that contained our picnic. I carried it over the stile and fell in step alongside Kitty. To my surprise, though really I should have learnt by now not to be surprised by anything she did, she slipped her arm through my free one, the arm I had broken as a child, and with careless ease she tipped her head back with a happy laugh. 'Isn't this utterly glorious?'

I nodded and murmured a shy yes.

'I'm so glad you agreed to come,' she said, giving my arm a squeeze. 'I didn't think you would.'

'Really?'

'I thought perhaps you weren't the country sort.'

'You think I'm strictly a town-dweller?'

'Aren't you?'

'You hardly know me, so I find it difficult to believe you could judge me one way or another.'

'But one can make an educated guess,' she said with a smile. 'After all, I'm absolutely certain you will have made all kinds of judgements about me based on what I've told you.'

'A few,' I conceded.

'I knew it! Now let me guess.' She whipped her arm free of mine and sprang in front, blocking the way along the footpath we were following. 'You think I'm a toff's daughter who doesn't take anything too seriously, don't you? You also think that by the time this ghastly war is over, I'll have fulfilled my destiny by marrying some toff of my parents' choosing. I'm right, aren't I?'

I stared at her, her exquisite face just inches from mine, her eyes bright and shining, her lovely lips smiling playfully at me.

'Which would upset you more,' I said, 'to know that you're right, or that you're wrong?'

She laughed, exposing her neat white teeth. 'You see, that's exactly it,' she said, tucking her arm through mine again and resuming our pace along the path, 'you've made sufficient judgement about me already to know that I hate to be proved wrong. How clever you are!'

Not clever at all, I thought; just too cowardly to answer a leading and compromising question.

We continued to climb the gentle rise of the field, and after a few minutes I turned to look back at the way we'd come – the oak tree and our bicycles along with the stile were nowhere to be seen.

'Where are we going?' I asked.

'Not far now.' She pointed to a large and ancient chestnut tree at the summit of the hill. 'We can have our picnic up there.'

'Have you been here before?'

'No. I'm just following my nose. It's what I do. When we were children my sister and I were allowed to go off on our own all the time on our bicycles. I never got us lost.'

When we reached the chestnut tree, I once again turned to look at the view. It stretched out for miles and miles, an endless swathe of green dotted with hamlets and villages, each with a church spire rising into the cloudless sky. Far in the distance was the town of Bletchley; it seemed a very long way off, as did the war.

After the recent spell of fine weather, the ground was dry enough to sit on at the base of the tree and with the contents of the basket now laid out on a square of red and white gingham cloth, I had to pinch myself. I hadn't seen a spread like this in a very long time. There was a pie the size of a tea plate, a wedge of creamy yellow cheese, some water biscuits, two Scotch eggs and a small jar of pickled onions. 'Where did you get all this?' I asked in stunned astonishment.

'Nanny Devine visited me yesterday and, at Mummy's insistence, she brought me some emergency rations in case I wasn't eating properly.'

I eyed the bottle of champagne she was thrusting at me to open. 'That's an emergency ration?'

'Now don't be like that,' she chided, reaching into the basket and pulling out a pair of china teacups wrapped in a tea towel. 'I expect Daddy thought I'd earned a treat.'

I laughed. How could I not? 'I like the sound of your father.'

'He's a sweetie, he really is. So long as you don't cross him, that is. Then he turns into a monster. He once got so cross with Uncle Richard over some argument or other, he pushed him out of a window.'

'A ground floor window, I hope.'

'Actually no, it was upstairs.'

'And your uncle?' I asked, instantly reviewing my opinion of her father.

'The bushes below softened his landing. It was terribly funny, really. He came limping back into the house covered in leaves and whatnot as though nothing untoward had happened.'

The stoic upper-class bearing for which the aristocracy was famous, I thought, trying inexpertly to remove the cork from the bottle of champagne. I'd never opened one before, but was damned if I was going to let on. 'What had your uncle done to deserve being pushed from a first floor window?' I asked, mentally cursing the wretched cork for resisting my efforts and making me look a callow fool.

She shrugged and sank a knife into the pie. 'I've no idea, it was just one of those things.'

To my enormous relief I felt the cork give and, gripping it in the palm of my hand, I pulled on it hard, determined to show it who was boss. The next thing I knew, a stream of froth spurted from the bottle straight into my face and with such unexpected force I let out a yelp of alarm.

The bloody cork had won, I thought miserably, dashing a hand across my reddening wet face. Opposite me Kitty was trying not to snigger. But then she snorted and let out a thunderous hoot of unfettered laughter.

I had never enjoyed the experience of being laughed at – I had been on the receiving end of too many taunting jibes at school and Cambridge about my Jewish background to relish so-called harmless quips made at my expense – but there in the dappled shade of the chestnut tree, with a radiantly beautiful girl at my side who had chosen me to spend the afternoon with, I could do nothing but give in to the ridiculousness of what I'd done and see the funny side. Once I started to laugh, I laughed so hard, my sides ached and tears ran down my cheeks to mingle with the champagne. It felt like a release and made me laugh uncontrollably until I feared I resembled a madman.

'I'm sorry,' I managed to say, when at last I pulled myself together and caught my breath. 'I'm afraid that was a terrible waste of champagne.'

She took the bottle from me and shook her head. 'Not at all,' she said, carefully filling the two teacups, 'it was worth it to see you so happy.' She waited for the bubbles to settle in the cups, then added some more. Clearly she was perfectly at home with the task of pouring expensive wine. Settling the bottle back in the safety of the basket, she passed me a mug.

'Sorry I couldn't run to glasses,' she said. 'Now then, a toast to our very own dandelion years.'

I cocked my head. 'What do you mean by that?'

'It's how I think of the war and the effect it's having on everybody. The hopes and certainties we used to live by have been swept away. We live in a time when all it might take is one little puff and everything could be gone. You. Me. Everything we hold dear.' Her expression was suddenly grave. 'These could be our last moments here on earth.'

'That sounds a very pessimistic view to take.'

She wrinkled her brow and drank some of her champagne. 'It's the reality, though, isn't it? I'm not afraid to die, you know. Not when I believe in an afterlife. And before you say anything, if there isn't an afterlife, I shan't be around to complain that I'd got it wrong, shall I?'

'Let's hope that's something you don't need to worry about for a very long time yet,' I said.

She smiled. 'Why, darling, I do believe you're more of a sentimentalist than I am.'

Brushing aside her comment, I said, 'Are we going to eat any of this food your divinely devoted nanny provided you with?'

'No joking about Nanny Devine, I won't have it!'

'Tell me about her,' I said, dodging the knife Kitty was now brandishing in front of my face in the manner of a swashbuckling pirate. 'Did she look after you when you were a baby?'

'Yes. And my sister, Ruthie, too. She's practically a member of the family. I love her to bits and can't imagine a world without her. She's desperate for Ruthie and I to have children so she can look after them. Tell you what: I'll take you to meet her. She'd love to meet you.'

I tried to picture the unlikely scenario of me arriving at some vast mansion set in the rolling Sussex countryside, but all I succeeded in achieving was conjuring an unwelcome image of Kitty's disapproving father hurling me from the nearest window.

'Oh, I don't think Nanny Devine would be remotely interested in meeting me,' I said lightly.

She passed me a slice of the pie, which I could see was made of pork and encased in a mouth-watering layer of jelly and pastry. 'Why do you say that?' she asked with a frown

Where to start, I thought. Could she really be so obtuse? 'Well,' I said carefully, 'we come from very different backgrounds.'

'Are you talking about me being a Roman Catholic and you being a Jew?'

This was the first I'd heard about her Catholicism. For some reason I'd assumed religion played no part in her life. Now here she was talking about an afterlife and declaring herself a Catholic. Choosing my words with yet more care, I said, 'I wasn't referring to that difference between us, although I would say that I'm culturally Jewish, and very much aware of my roots, but am not in the least bit religious.' I indicated the slice of pork pie I was eating. 'If I were, I wouldn't be eating this. But I'd hazard a guess that your parents would not approve of you associating with somebody like me.'

'Oh, what tosh! You absolutely don't know what you're talking about! What's more, I'll prove it to you one day.'

You can try, I thought. But I knew with unreserved conviction that an aristocratic Roman Catholic family would look upon me with no more than polite tolerance. That would be to my face. Behind my back, I would be nothing more than that upstart Jew from the East End of London with whom their daughter had taken up.

But for now that didn't matter. I was never going to meet them, so why not continue to enjoy the afternoon?

We ate until we were full and when we had drunk every last drop of the champagne – how did that happen? – I suddenly felt incredibly tired. We both lay on our backs staring up at the limpid blue sky, the sun on our faces. Then crossing my hands behind my head, I closed my eyes. The air was still and warm and thrummed with insect noise, and the sound of birdsong. Far off in the distance I discerned a train whistle and then nothing at all as I slept. It was the most peaceful sleep I'd enjoyed in a long while, a deep sleep of sublime oblivion. There were no tormenting dreams of never-ending encrypted messages, no heart-stopping dreams of bodies floating in the lake, just the pleasurable relief of a mind abandoning itself to a blissful unconsciousness.

I had no idea how long I slept, but I stirred eventually to the sensation of something tickling my lower lip. An insect, I assumed, and brushed it away with my hand. Seconds later, it was back again, this time to annoy my top lip. With reluctance I roused myself and opened my eyes.

'I thought you were never going to wake,' Kitty said with a small laugh. She was leaning over me and in her hand, she held a dandelion, its fluffy seed head perfectly intact; it was that with which she had been tickling me. I was about to apologise for rudely sleeping so long, when she lowered her head and very tenderly kissed me on the mouth.

Chapter Nineteen

May 1943

That night I turned up for my shift with something akin to the original enthusiasm and determination with which I had first arrived at Bletchley Park. That was when I had believed no code was unbreakable, not even the Enigma. That was when no matter the enormity of the task, I believed we would overcome it. I'd as good as had these two mantras woven into the fabric of my being. Sadly, it hadn't taken long to feel defeated and for the naivety of those words to haunt my every waking thought, as well as those when I slept.

But now, magically, I had something of my old self about me, I was no longer wound so tightly I felt I was on the point of shattering into a thousand pieces. Instead, I felt reinvigorated, buoyed up with happy optimism. In fact, I believed the intensity of my happiness was so palpable it had to show like an aura around me, that it was as visible as the cloud of smoke that Chatterton-Jones was producing from his pipe as he walked into the hut just seconds after I'd sat at my desk. Par for the course, he wore his habitual expression of self-satisfied superiority while greeting us all with a jovial hello as though we were old friends gathered for a social occasion and he was the guest of honour. I acknowledged him with a nod and took out my pad of paper and sharpened my pencil. I was ready to get down to work.

But I was halted by his approach. Resting his backside against the end of my desk, he removed the pipe from his mouth and waved it in my general direction, as if determined to gain my full attention. 'I've just bumped into that delightful girl you said you met on the train,' he drawled. 'Turns out our fathers know each other and our paths crossed several times as children. Didn't I tell you there was something familiar about her? I think it only jolly well right I invite her to go for a drink for old times' sake, don't you?'

'I'm sure you'd have lots to talk about,' I said through gritted teeth.

'Oh, I don't doubt it, old boy.'

And with that, he sauntered off to his own desk leaving me to smoulder in a heap of miserable desolation while mentally cursing him. How I wished he were anywhere but here – somewhere far away where he could not apply his considerable charm and handsome good looks to snatching Kitty from under my nose. God help me, I even wished he were in the North Atlantic with a pack of German U-boats hunting him down!

I heard a sharp crack and saw that I'd snapped the pencil I was holding clean in two. Oh, how easily my wretched insecurities had been laid bare, cruelly exposing the bald truth that I was a fool – a jealous fool at that.

The shift dragged on with encrypted messages pouring in relentlessly. No matter how hard we all tried, we could not get that elusive lucky break we depended upon. It would take only one such break to buck everybody up, to inspire and give us the necessary stamina to see the shift to the end without falling asleep through the sheer repetitive tedium of getting nowhere.

By general agreement, a group of us broke off for something to eat and by the dim ineffectual light of my torch I stumbled around in the blackout darkness to the canteen. Having earlier looked forward to the chance of seeing Kitty again in the canteen, I now dreaded spotting her, sure in the knowledge that Chatterton-Jones would have beaten me to it. I had been so absorbed in what I was doing, convinced at last that I was on to something, that I hadn't noticed he had already left the hut ahead of me.

I was right to be concerned. I saw him straight away taking the last remaining seat at the table where Kitty was sitting. My stomach lurched, both at the inevitability of his attention and its outcome, and the smell of the food being served.

I took a tray and lined up with two of my colleagues, Craggs and Bennett. I barely noticed what was put on my tray and following them to a table, I gave thanks they'd chosen one that was mercifully a safe distance from Kitty's.

'I see Chatterton-Jones is putting his magnetism to good use,' Bennett said with a grin as he began shovelling food into his mouth no more than a few seconds after we'd sat down. I had never seen anyone eat as much or as fast as he did. He claimed that being the youngest of five children, he had learnt from a young age not to let anything hang about on his plate for too long.

Glancing over to the other side of the noisy room, Craggs squinted through the thick lenses of his tortoiseshell-framed spectacles. 'I can't say I blame him,' he observed, 'she's a beauty.'

I lowered my head and thought of the moment this afternoon when Kitty had kissed me. It had been no more than the lightest touch – a butterfly's wing brushing against my lips could not have been lighter – but the recollection of it was so scorched on my memory I could feel it now.

My experience of kissing was severely limited. My first kiss had been with the daughter of one of my mother's customers at the salon. She had been eleven years old to my ten and had cornered me at the party for her brother's bar mitzvah. I hadn't enjoyed the encounter in the slightest, but two years later when I decided I'd like a repeat performance and tried to kiss her, she slapped me hard. The next girl I kissed was at Cambridge and while this time I was spared a slap, I was not to be rewarded with a second kiss.

The thought that I might never experience a second

kiss with Kitty, if Chatterton-Jones and his sickening self-possession had his way, caused the last vestiges of my appetite to dwindle and I pushed my tray away from me.

'Aren't you eating that?' Bennett asked, his hand already stretched out towards my discarded food.

'Be my guest,' I said mechanically.

Craggs, forever the more aware to subtle nuances going on, as well as being predisposed to mothering the rest of us if given a chance, looked at me. 'Everything all right with you?'

I shrugged. 'I'm just not hungry.'

'You should eat something. Give the jam tart a go, it's usually the least offensive thing on the menu.'

In spite of my foul mood brought on by the odious Chatterton-Jones, I smiled at Craggs. 'You've missed your calling,' I said, 'you should have been signed up to be matron here.'

'Ho, ho, very funny. Now do as you're told and eat something or you'll be of no use to anyone.'

Of all of us in Hut 8, Craggs was, in his quiet undemonstrative way, the one who believed wholeheartedly that we could defeat the Germans. Such was his positive outlook, not for a minute did he doubt that our intelligence work was superior to theirs. He could also be relied upon to stop us from falling foul of ill temper brought about by despair and exhaustion. And seeing the sense in what he was saying now, I removed the tart from my tray before Bennett could demolish it.

I took a mouthful of what I knew would taste like sweetened cardboard and, not proved wrong, I chewed on it with grim resolve. Washing the mouthful down with a gulp of water, I risked a look over towards Kitty's table. She was up on her feet saying something to Chatterton-Jones. Then turning away, she carried her tray to the area where uneaten food was scraped into the pigswill container. After she'd done that, she looked about the room as if searching for somebody. I snatched my head round to face Craggs and

Bennett: I couldn't let her see that I was watching her. I had to pretend I didn't care that I'd missed the opportunity to sit with her.

So what if we had had a wonderful afternoon together?

So what if we had recklessly had too much champagne and got a little drunk?

So what if she had kissed me?

So what if she had then lain back against the grass beside me and held my hand?

So what if she had said, 'Tell me about your family, and your time at Cambridge. I want to know everything about you'?

It meant nothing. Any of it. More than likely she was amused by my awkward and obvious inexperience and had taken pity on me. Perhaps she saw me as nothing more than a pet project, someone to educate in the ways of the world.

This was her doing her bit for King and Country.

Chapter Twenty

At Glaskin House again, Saskia and her father were making good progress in the library.

As instructed, they had called in at the vicarage and had been told by Jenny Allbright that she had already popped over first thing to make absolutely sure the heating was working, which it was. She had also relayed a message from Matthew that they were to make themselves at home. At his request, she had very kindly put some milk in the fridge for them to use if they wanted to make themselves a hot drink.

It was late afternoon now and in the kitchen waiting for the kettle to rumble to a boil, Saskia looked out of the window on to the front garden and the drive where Dad had parked the car. It had been another miserably wet and windy day, just like yesterday, but here, inside this cavernous house, with the gusting wind and rain lashing at the window panes making them rattle in the casements, the weather seemed worse. The house was as draughtproof as a sieve and blasts of cold air whistled through every gap it could find. And unlike Sunday, when they'd been here before, there was no fire lit in the library, and without the comforting crackle and pop of logs burning in the grate, only the occasional lament of the wind howling down the chimney, the room felt empty and less lived in.

Matthew's absence from the house also had an effect; it made Saskia feel like an intruder as she helped herself to yet more coffee from the jar on the counter.

Despite her intention to be full of smiling positivity today, Matthew's apology on the phone last night still rankled with her. Her annoyance wasn't directed at him, but at herself, for he had left her with the unpleasant knowledge that she really wasn't a nice person to be around at the moment. She'd go so far as to say she suddenly no longer felt she was the person she used to be. It was as though all the softness in her was slowly dissolving, revealing, she feared, the sharp, hard and brittle stuff she would rather keep hidden.

The kettle came to the boil and clicked off, and after she'd filled the mugs and added milk and given them a stir, she thought of the author of *The Dandelion Years*. How well she could empathise with the agony of the man's insecurity – the debilitating pain of liking Kitty, but not daring to allow himself to believe that she might return his feelings. Saskia had not only experienced the same apprehension, but had suffered from the additional anxiety that truly to love someone put her at risk of having to deal with a greater torment, of losing that person, just as she had lost her mother and grandmothers.

She knew that everybody experienced this anxiety to some extent, but she had yet to find a way to believe that the risk was worth taking, that it was better to have loved than not. A deep dark place in her soul held her back from taking the necessary blind leap of faith. How did anyone entrust their heart and their life to another?

Love was all too frequently held up as being the cure-all to many of life's difficulties, but was it? Her head wanted to say it wasn't, but her heart said otherwise; it reminded her of the fiercely protective love that bound her and her father and grandfathers together. What would have become of them without that bond of love?

Back in the library, her father was talking on his mobile phone. She placed his mug of coffee on the table near him and took her own down to the window overlooking the sodden garden. Giving it no more than a cursory glance, she turned her attention to the stack of photograph albums on the desk in front of her. She had noticed them on Sunday, but with

Matthew around she hadn't wanted to be caught being so blatantly nosy by having a look through them. Now, with no danger of being accused of snooping, she opened the album on the top of the pile.

The first page was blank, but turning it over there was a double-page spread of faded black-and-white three-inch-square photographs. They were all of the same man and appeared to have been taken at the one sitting. With his discernibly wavy dark hair, cut short and parted on the right of his head, he sported a natty, well-trimmed beard and moustache that wouldn't have looked out of place today.

From what Saskia could see of his clothes, he was wearing a shirt and tie and a tweed jacket. But the most striking element of the set of eight photographs was the pose he had assumed in each one. Whether he was turned to his right, or his left, or facing straight into the lens of the camera, his expression was of wry amusement as he alternated between smiling and raising an arched eyebrow that caused a couple of deep lines to crease his broad forehead.

Studying his face, Saskia was left with two thoughts: he'd either enjoyed having his picture taken and had played up to the camera, or he hadn't wanted his picture taken and had adopted a mask to hide behind. Inclined to believe the first possibility, she wondered if this was the deceased Professor Jacob Belinsky as a young man in his twenties, or even thirties; it was difficult to pin an exact age on him. People invariably seemed older than they really were in photographs from years ago, especially in black-and-white, or very formal portrait pictures.

Taking a sip of her coffee, Saskia turned the page of the album. Here there seemed to be a collection of group shots, one of which showed a collection of smiling women gathered around a shop front. They were all dressed in the same outfit, a sort of smart overall. A uniform, perhaps? On closer inspection, the women each had the same logo fixed to the breast pocket of their outfits. In another photograph there was a man in what looked like a smart double-breasted white overcoat standing in the middle of the same group of women.

Peering closer still, Saskia noticed the writing beneath these two photographs. If it was meant to be helpful in identifying who these people were, it failed hopelessly. But more crucially, and with recognition tugging at her consciousness, the faded spidery scrawl reminded Saskia of the appalling handwriting she had been struggling to read these last few days. It was the same. No question. She had spent too many hours deciphering the damn near illegible scribble to doubt that she was again face to face with it.

She twisted round to her father to share her discovery with him, but he was still talking quietly on his mobile at the far end of the room and with his back to her.

Waiting for him to finish his conversation with whoever it was, she flicked through a few more pages, looking for yet more handwritten inscriptions. She found plenty and with each one she felt the thrill of her certainty grow.

But did it mean that the author of *The Dandelion Years* and Professor Jacob Belinsky were one and the same? If so, why had the notebook become separated from the deceased man's belongings?

She forced herself to be objective, telling herself that while it was an obvious conclusion to reach – that the professor had written the notebook – there was always the chance that the photograph album had belonged to somebody else, a relative or a friend, and had merely ended up here at Glaskin House. As theories went, Saskia didn't like it one little bit and flicked through the pages looking for something that would give her irrefutable proof of what she believed to be true – a photograph of a young man with a girl at Bletchley Park with their names clearly shown would do very nicely!

She had just turned the last page of the album when her father ended his call and came over. She told him what she'd found, explaining that the man in *The Dandelion Years* was the grandson of Russian Jews who immigrated to England. 'The professor's name was Jacob Belinsky,' she said, 'which you have to agree sounds Russian, doesn't it?'

'Yes, but the name could also be from almost any East European country.'

'What about all those books of Russian art, history and poetry we've come across?' she said. 'And didn't Matthew say the professor used to curse the boiler in Russian? It adds up, Dad, I'm sure of it; it's too much of a coincidence for it not to. Do you suppose Matthew knows anything about the notebook?'

Her father looked doubtful. 'He doesn't strike me as the sort who would knowingly throw away something like that. Don't forget, it was hidden inside that Bible, so very likely he knew nothing about it.'

'But why did he get rid of the Bible when he knew a valuation had to be made of the books for probate?'

'You know as well as I do most benefactors start the job of clearing out the junk before probate is complete; it's the stuff that has potential value they're not supposed to touch. I'd say that in view of all those bin bags in the hall, Matthew's made a start already. Maybe the Bible simply slipped through the net.' He paused to drink some of his coffee. 'You know what this means, don't you? We have to tell Matthew about the notebook.'

Saskia knew her father was right, but the thought of parting with the notebook before she'd finished reading it – before she knew the outcome of the story – made her hesitate to agree. 'Perhaps I could tell him at the end of the week when we've finished the valuation here?' she said, realising that she would have to admit that she'd been snooping through the photograph album. How else could she explain the connection she'd made? Unless the notebook itself revealed Jacob Belinsky as its author …

*

An hour later they decided it was time to finish for the day and they stopped off at the vicarage to return the key.

This time it was the vicar himself who came to the door. Dressed in jeans and a grey clerical shirt with a dog collar, he asked how they'd got on. 'That house is a devil to heat properly,' he said. 'I used to tease Jacob that it was in his genes to withstand the cold so well.'

Saskia couldn't resist the opening the comment gave her. 'Did his grandparents emigrate to England from Russia at the turn of the last century?' she asked.

He regarded her for a beat, plainly surprised by the question. 'Well yes, as a matter of fact they did. Why do you ask?'

Saskia smiled. 'Just joining up the dots on a man who put together such an interesting and diverse collection of books,' she said.

'Shame on you for lying to a vicar,' Ralph said with a laugh when they were in the car and driving away.

'It was only a small white lie,' Saskia replied, 'and perfectly defensible under the circumstances.'

'Oh yes, and what circumstances would they be?'

'I'll think of something, I'm sure.'

Ralph laughed again. 'That notebook's really got a hold of you, hasn't it?'

'Let's just say it's piqued my interest. By the way, who was that you were talking to on the phone? I forgot to ask you earlier.'

'A friend,' Ralph said. 'Someone I hadn't seen for the best part of ten years until yesterday when she surprised me at the shop.'

Ralph had been wondering when Saskia was going to ask him about the call. Yesterday when he'd been having a drink and catching up with Libby, they had swapped mobile phone numbers and he'd promised to stay in touch. Libby had told him not to make rash promises he couldn't keep, so to prove her wrong, he'd rung her when Saskia was in the kitchen making coffee. Her surprised delight at hearing from him had been oddly pleasing and he'd found himself slipping in to the easy, light-hearted banter they'd always enjoyed.

'Anyone I know?' Saskia asked.

'No,' he said, fixing his eyes on the red taillights of the car in front of them. 'Her name is Libby and she's recently moved back to the area. I had a drink with her after I'd locked up the shop. That's why I was late home.'

'Oh.'

He wasn't fooled by the nonchalant cadence of his daughter's response. 'I'm going to have dinner with her tomorrow evening,' he said.

'Taking her anywhere nice?'

'No, I thought I'd take her somewhere horrible.'

Saskia snorted. 'So, is this Libby someone you would describe as *"date-worthy"*, then?'

He slid his gaze towards his daughter. 'Ten years ago, very much so.'

'Oh.'

His eyes back on the road, Ralph said, 'How can anyone pack so much meaning into that one small word?'

'I'm just wondering why I'm only hearing about her now. I don't recall her name cropping up back then.'

'It didn't. I didn't tell anyone I was seeing her. Her situation was what you'd call ... complicated at the time.' He waited for Saskia to work it out.

'You mean she was married?' she said at length.

'I'm not proud of it,' he said quickly.

'Hey, I wasn't judging you.'

'Perhaps I'm judging myself.'

'Is she still married?'

'No, she's been divorced for a long time now.'

There was another pause from Saskia. Then: 'Do we get to meet her?'

And that was the million-dollar question, thought Ralph.

134

After Harvey and Oliver had shared their concern with him last night about Saskia, he had thought long and hard about how he had to try and shoehorn Saskia out of the rut she had got herself into. Not that she would ever see it that way.

The answer had come to him while he'd been chatting with Libby on the phone this afternoon. What if he led by example and showed Saskia that things didn't have to stay the same? What if he did what he should have done ten years ago and introduced Libby to the family? After all this time, what could be the harm?

The only problem he could see with the idea was that, having denied Libby access to Ashcombe ten years ago, she might not feel inclined to cross the threshold now. Especially if she thought Ralph was using her. Which he wasn't. He absolutely wasn't. He wouldn't do that to her.

It was extraordinary, but within twenty-four hours of seeing her again, he was thinking how good it would be to have Libby in his life once more. And properly this time – without the secrecy, without the skulking around to snatch illicit moments together.

'Dad? I asked you when do we get to meet this Libby?'

'Sorry,' he said, 'I was miles away. Let me see how dinner goes tomorrow evening. Who knows, she might not want to see me again by the end of it.' Then changing the subject, he said, 'Never mind tomorrow, do you have any plans for this evening?'

'Since it looks as if I'm going to have to tell Matthew about the notebook when we've finished the valuation, I think I'd better get on and read it.'

Chapter Twenty-One

May 1943

Over the following days I engineered things so that there would be no danger of accidentally bumping into Kitty.

The effort I poured into doing this brought home the disturbing realisation that before the day of our picnic I had somehow got into the habit of casually hanging about in the proximity of the hut in which Kitty worked. When I hadn't been doing that I had been loitering in the canteen for longer than was necessary as well as going for extended strolls around the lake in the spring sunshine, all on the off chance I might catch sight of her and strategically place myself in her line of sight so she would speak to me.

But after the day of our picnic, after witnessing Chatterton-Jones making a play for Kitty, the extent of the naïve foolishness of my behaviour was fully exposed. I then swore not to humiliate myself further and so, despite the warmth of the weather, I joined in with none of the usual outdoor leisure pursuits at the Park, thereby lessening the chances of our paths crossing. I studiously avoided the rounders' matches that took place on the front lawn, a game I rather enjoyed playing and could do so quite decently. I also eschewed watching any of the tennis matches, a game I couldn't actually play because of my left arm. Kitty, I knew, had grown up with her own court at Fanley Manor and loved to play, as did Chatterton-Jones. The last thing I needed was to stumble across them playing a cosy game of mixed doubles together.

Instead, as soon as my shift was over, I would head

back to my digs on my bicycle, thus avoiding all chance of social interaction. Besides, work was my real priority. Amazingly we were winning the battle with the U-boats in the North Atlantic; for the first time the Allies had the upper hand and the sinking of seventeen U-boats already this month was a much-needed boost to our flagging morale. It was this change in our fortunes that I tried to focus on. In comparison, nothing else mattered. Saving lives was what counted. That was why I was here. It was why we were all stuck in this dreary backwater steadily going mad. Some madder than others judging by the behaviour of a few of my colleagues who thought there was nothing odd in turning up for work in their pyjamas. I'd as good as done it myself on one occasion when, after days of gruelling tension and lack of sleep, I'd finally slept one night and so deeply that I overslept. Upon waking to the sound of children playing in the next-door garden – they were always playing in and around the Anderson shelter at the end of the garden – I'd stumbled from my bed in such a blind panic that I shoved my coat on over my pyjamas and started for the Park on my bicycle. Had it not been for Mrs Pridmore shouting after me, outraged that I was still wearing my slippers and for all the neighbours to see, I wouldn't have noticed.

Lying fully clothed on my bed tonight listening to Griffiths singing to himself in the bathroom – he was giving a lusty performance of 'Don't Sit Under the Apple Tree', having moved on from 'Danny Boy' – I wondered if any of us would survive this experience with our sanity fully intact.

This less than cheery thought brought me full circle to Kitty and to what she had called the dandelion years and her stark explanation that with one single puff it could all be over, our lives simply blown away on the wind as though we'd never existed. 'But the nature of the dandelion is for its seeds to scatter and take root, so all is not lost,' Kitty had further explained when we were walking back down the hill to where we'd left our bicycles.

My hands clasped behind my head as I stared up at the ceiling, tracing the cracks creeping across from one side of the room to the other, I asked myself what seeds would I have scattered in my life if it were to be cut short today, tomorrow or next week?

None, was the depressing conclusion I reached. Other than what I could achieve here at Bletchley. If I could make a worthwhile contribution in my work, then that would at least be some kind of legacy.

I was still pondering this when I heard heavy footsteps lumbering up the stairs, followed by a sharp rapping on the bathroom door and Mrs Pridmore demanding that the singing stop at once. 'This is a respectable house,' she yelled through the door at Griffiths, 'I'll not have it turned into a cheap music hall!' In the sudden silence there was a loud *thump* on my door; it was so loud I half expected the door to crash to the floor.

Swinging my legs off the bed, I stood up and opened the door.

'You've a visitor,' Mrs Pridmore announced without ceremony and in a voice as disapproving as the expression on her face. 'She says it's important. That it's personal. And I told her I didn't care if she was a messenger from Churchill himself, she wasn't coming up here at this time of night. There might be a war going on but there are decencies to be upheld. I put her in the front room, I said it wasn't right for—'

'Did she say who she was?' I cut in abruptly, bringing an end to the woman's nerve-grating diatribe.

'No, and I didn't ask. This might come as a surprise to you,' she stabbed a beefy finger at me, 'but I'm not here at your beck and call to relay messages backwards and forwards. I've better things to do with my time, thank you very much!'

'I'm sorry you've been so inconvenienced,' I said smoothly, stepping on to the landing, and at the same time flattening my hair and straightening my clothes.

'And don't take that clever tone with me, young man. I've just about had my fill of you lot messing up my house. If you're not using all the hot water, or grumbling about the meals I go to the trouble to cook for you, it's one of you giving me smart-alec lip. And let's not forget the constant comings and goings, and at all hours. I'm surprised I can get a wink of sleep with what I have to put up with. If I'd known it was going to be as bad as this, I'd never have agreed to take in lodgers. Some days I think it would be easier if those blasted Jerries just came over here and put us all out of our misery. At least then I'd get some peace and quiet!'

In that precise moment I couldn't have agreed with her more. Frankly I would personally welcome the Germans at Dover if it meant Mrs Pridmore would just cease her endless babble!

Sliding past her repulsive bulk, I slipped down the stairs to see who needed to see me at this late hour. All I could think was that there must be an emergency at home in London, that one of my family had been taken ill. Or had the East End been bombed again?

Such was my fear and dread that in the time it took me to cover the short distance to Mrs Pridmore's front room, I had my parents and grandmother if not practically dead and buried, then certainly gasping their last. With my heart crashing in my ribcage, I all but flung myself into the room, ready to hear the awful news.

'Oh, there you are, darling! I thought perhaps your land-lady wasn't going to let me see you. Lord, she's a stickler for propriety, isn't she?'

Shocked and alarmed, I swivelled my head round to check Mrs Pridmore wasn't there to hear. Mercifully she was still plodding her way down the stairs. It gave me a second or two to catch my breath before forming the words, 'What on earth are you doing here, Kitty?'

'To see you, of course. How else was I going to talk to you and find out why you've been avoiding me?'

'I ... I haven't.'

She smiled. 'Please don't think of ever becoming a spy, you're a terrible liar. Ah,' she said, glancing over my shoulder, 'here's your wonderful landlady. Now, why don't we make amends for the trouble we've put the dear lady to and go for a walk? How does that sound?'

It sounded unreal, as though I were still lying on my bed caught up in a weird dream.

On her way towards the kitchen, Mrs Pridmore muttered something indistinct, but wholly meaningful, and closed the door behind her with equal emphasis.

Kitty giggled and taking hold of my arm, led me out of the house. Dumbly, I said, 'How did you know where I was billeted?'

'I asked one of your chums in Hut 8. I think he said his name was Bob Craggs. Please say you're not cross with him? Or with me for that matter.'

'I'm not cross,' I assured her. Then: 'Where are we going?'

'Anywhere, so long as it's somewhere we can talk.'

With the weak glow from Kitty's torch guiding us, we walked through the quiet streets of Bletchley in the darkness, the thick, low cloud denying us even a hint of helpful moonlight. A car drove slowly by with blackout masks attached to its headlamps, followed by a man on a bicycle with no light at all. I had always found the streets eerily quiet in the blackout, almost to the point of disorientating me, but with Kitty at my side, I strode purposefully in the direction of the nearest café that would be open at this time. Once there, I ordered two cups of coffee, only then realising that in my haste, I had no means with which to pay for them. To my enormous discomfort, Kitty came to the rescue and pulled out her purse from her handbag. Red of face, I sat down at a corner table with her and apologised.

She laughed. 'My fault entirely for turning up unannounced and kidnapping you.'

'I'm glad you did,' I said cautiously.

'Are you? Are you really?'

'Yes.'

My reply hung between us while we each concentrated on drinking our coffee, which, compared to the stuff up at the Park, was reasonably palatable.

Unsurprisingly it was Kitty who spoke first. 'Why were you avoiding me?' she asked. 'Was it something I did? Or said?'

I put down my cup and cleared my throat. How could I possibly tell this extraordinarily confident girl that I was not made from the same bold stock as she, that I was riven with inexperience and insecurity when it came to this sort of thing.

'No, it wasn't something you did,' I said guardedly. 'It's just that ... well ... I find it difficult to comprehend why you would choose to spend time with someone like me when you could ...' Under her fixed and unnervingly penetrating gaze, I hesitated while I sought to choose the right words. 'When there are any number of far more interesting people at the Park with whom you could socialise,' I managed.

'Do you have anyone particularly in mind whose company I might prefer?'

I swallowed nervously, suddenly sensing that it would be futile to lie to her. She was, I realised, perceptive enough to see right through me, beyond the defences I'd so carefully erected since I was a child to combat my shyness. 'I would hazard a guess that you would have more in common with a fellow like Charles Chatterton-Jones ... for instance,' I added feebly. There, I'd uttered the name, and in one swift step had therefore revealed not just how green I was, but the degree of my crippling jealousy, something to which I had hitherto not known I could succumb.

She placed her cup carefully into its saucer and dabbed an elegant finger at the corner of her mouth. 'The Charleses of this world are two a penny,' she said, 'I meet his kind all the time and, not to put too fine a point on it, he's far too full of himself for my taste. Whereas you—'

'Whereas I'm a novelty for you,' I supplied, and before I'd even consciously articulated the words in my head.

Her eyes widened and she sat back from me, plainly stung. 'Goodness, I had no idea you regarded me so poorly.'

At her obvious upset, I rushed to apologise. 'I'm sorry. That was clumsy of me.'

'Yes, it was. And very hurtful. I'm shocked that you could think such a thing.'

'I'm sorry,' I repeated. 'Chalk it up to being out of my depth. I'm not used to beautiful girls taking an interest in me. And you *are* beautiful. You're charming, too, and perfectly delightful and enormous fun to be with. Whereas I'm just a verbally ham-fisted idiot masquerading as someone with half a functioning brain.'

She shifted her position again, but this time she leant in across the oilcloth-covered table. 'No you're not. You're just shy, there's nothing wrong in that. What's more – and I can't tell you what a refreshing change this is – you're not full of self-congratulatory hot air, you actually listen to what people say rather than rush in to brag about yourself.'

'That's because I have nothing, or have done nothing, to brag about.'

She smiled. 'There you go again, you're so splendidly modest.'

'I assure you it's genuinely meant, it's not an act I've mastered.'

'I know that, my darling, you have no side to you whatso-ever, you're as honest as the day is long and as transparent as glass. That's what I like about you. And I love it that you always look so grave.' She lightly tapped my forehead. 'I'm fascinated by what goes on in there.'

At her touch, and beneath the strength of her intense gaze exploring my face, I felt so intoxicated by her attention I gave in to the sensation that the rest of the world no longer existed, that it was just we two who existed. It was the same sensation I'd experienced during our picnic and it reminded me of the moment she'd kissed me. The memory emboldened me to put a hand to her soft cheek and kiss her on the mouth.

I kissed her for what felt like a very long time and when finally, and reluctantly, I leant away from her, she gave me one of her wonderfully wide and joyful smiles.

'And now that we've cleared all that up,' she said, 'will you walk me home, please?'

It was that memorable night that she became known to me, and forever afterwards, as Katyushka. My darling Katyushka.

Chapter Twenty-Two

June 1943

Three weeks later Kitty took me to meet Nanny Devine.

I had tried to resist the proposed outing, fearing it would amplify the cultural chasm that existed between us, a chasm that Kitty either pretended to be in ignorance of, or was determined to flout. For my own part, I was utterly convinced that our relationship could only ever exist within the parameters of life at Bletchley where we lived in a world that played by different rules. But the combination of my curiosity to see where she had grown up, and my desire to spend as much time in her company as was possible won out, so off we went.

An elderly chauffeur called Andrews met us at the small station in the Sussex village of Fanley and greeted Kitty formally yet with obvious fondness. 'It's a pleasure to see you again, Miss Kitty,' he said, doffing his cap while she climbed into the back of a gleaming Austin Eighteen, 'the place just isn't the same without you.' In contrast he regarded me with the upmost suspicion, especially when I made the mistake of holding out my hand to him. His disapproval was such that I might as well have been offering him a dead rat.

The station was three miles from Fanley Manor, half a mile of which covered a long sweep of drive that sliced through lush green parkland ridged with woodland. Nestled within a wide sloping valley, it was a perfectly bucolic scene and quintessentially English, complete with grazing sheep and gambolling lambs bathed in golden sunlight.

I had promised myself that I would not be so gauche as to be overawed by my first sighting of Fanley Manor; after all, I was used to the grandeur, despite the questionable taste, of Bletchley Park, and of course there had been the splendour of my surroundings while up at Cambridge. However, I had severely underestimated just how exquisitely beautiful the Elizabethan mansion would be. With magnificent Tudor barley-twisted chimney stacks, mullioned windows and pleasingly ornate brickwork, it made Bletchley Park look very much a tactless architectural interloper.

Having deposited us at the entrance, Andrews drove round to the side of the house. Grabbing my hand, and smiling happily, Kitty sprang up the steps to the front door and pushed it open. Her simple delight at being home was as apparent to me as my own queasy nervousness. It was an enormous relief knowing I wouldn't have to endure meeting her parents – they were both in London – but even so, and having made a fool of myself with Andrews, I was now doubly on edge about meeting Nanny Devine, a woman who clearly meant the world to Kitty and who I knew would judge me and doubtless find me wanting.

Led by the hand, I followed Kitty across the oak-panelled hallway and up the stairs, which creaked noisily like cracking bones beneath our feet. I would have liked to linger a while to take in the house fully, but Kitty, who had dismissed it as 'boring old home' during our train journey, was intent on only one purpose, reaching the nursery at the top of the house as fast as she could. We were on the first landing when I managed to slow her down long enough to look out of the open window. Peering out I saw a knot garden.

'It's not half as good as it used to be,' Kitty said beside me, her breath warm against my neck. 'The gardeners all had to sign up to fight. Andrews does his best, but it's hardly a priority these days.'

'Who's that?' I asked, pointing towards an impressively large glasshouse where a girl dressed in boots, brown breeches and a shirt with the sleeves rolled up to the elbows was emerging with a heavily laden wheelbarrow.

'That's one of the land girls. Daddy says we have about half a dozen of them now. The kitchen garden has been tripled in size and it's practically a market garden. I'll take you to see it if you like.'

'Where do they stay?'

'Here, of course, where else? There's plenty of room for them. We had a couple of evacuated children for a bit, but they kept running away back to London. Poor Mummy, she was at her wits end trying to make them feel at home, but they said they were frightened by the quietness, especially at night. Extraordinary, don't you think? One would imagine with all the chaos going on in the East End they'd be glad of the peace and quiet.'

'I expect they missed their mothers and the familiarity of home more than anything.'

Once again she took hold of my hand. 'How sweet you are! Come on, Nanny awaits!'

Seated to one side of a fireplace, a friendly-faced woman looked up from her knitting when we entered her large and cluttered room. Behind her was a window with a view over a tennis court and the Sussex Downs in the far distance.

'I thought you were never coming,' she greeted her grown-up charge. 'And just look at the state of you! You look properly worn out. You're working too hard and not eating enough, I shouldn't wonder. There's scarcely a scrap on you!'

Kitty kissed the woman on her cheek. 'Nobody's eating as they should, Nanny, there's a war on, didn't anyone tell you?'

'Don't you take that cheeky tone with me, little missy. You're not too old to have your ears boxed. Now, who's this anxious-looking young man hiding behind you?'

'You know jolly well who he is; he's the very dear friend I told you about. So be nice to him.'

I stepped forward and after a split-second hesitation – during which my mother's clear instruction that manners cost nothing boomed in my ears – I stuck out my hand. Andrews may have felt disinclined to shake my hand, but surely this woman, whom I had heard so much about, wouldn't humiliate me in the same way? I was rewarded with a warm handshake and a direct stare through a pair of wire-framed spectacles.

'I'm very pleased to make your acquaintance,' she said. 'It's always a pleasure to meet Kitty's friends. Now, why don't you both sit down and I'll make us some tea. I have a Madeira cake which Mrs Enstone made when I told her you were coming.'

Kicking off her shoes and sinking into a small sofa and indicating I join her, Kitty said, 'And how is dear old Mrs E?'

'Complaining as always about the lack of butter and eggs and anything else she feels she's being cruelly deprived of. Bless her heart, she takes rationing very personally, as though she's been specifically singled out for extra punishment and denial.'

I listened to the exchange between the two of them while watching Nanny Devine set about the business of making tea in the furthest corner of the room where there seemed to be a small area dedicated to the task. Taking a box of Swan Vestas, she struck a match and put it to a gas ring, then put a shiny aluminium kettle to boil. In an instant, the room was filled with a comforting and familiar smell that reminded me of home.

Still keeping up her happy chatter with Kitty, she opened the doors of a display cabinet that was crammed full with ornaments and a bone china tea service. Seeing the woman selecting cups, saucers and plates, I was touched that our visit warranted the best china.

The whole of the room felt just as crammed full as the cabinet, for every bit of space had been filled with some piece of furniture or other. There was a single bed with a bedside table, two armchairs, a number of occasional tables, a bookcase, a wardrobe and a dressing table, along with the sofa Kitty and I were sitting on. There was also a raft of framed photographs everywhere I looked, most of which contained children, very likely Kitty and her sister. My eyes drifted back to the bed where I noticed a crucifix with a set of rosary beads hanging from it.

'Nanny's more or less self-sufficient,' Kitty said, breaking into my thoughts. 'I used to love sneaking up here to be with her. Isn't that right, Nanny?'

'You did indeed. I think you did it to hide from your sister mostly, which was very naughty of you.'

'Lord, yes! Ruthie is the bossiest sister conceivable,' Kitty said to me. 'She's quite the monster when she wants to be.'

'Now, now,' Nanny Devine said sternly. 'We'll have none of that talk. Do you have any brothers or sisters?' The question was directed at me.

I shook my head. 'No,' I replied, omitting to say that I had had a younger brother but he'd died as a baby of meningitis when I was four years old. It would be fair to say my parents had never recovered from the pain of losing him. They'd never forgiven God, either.

'You don't know how lucky you are to have escaped the torture of an older sibling,' Kitty said. 'How I envy you. Were you spoilt rotten as an only child?'

'Not at all.'

'But I bet you were given lots of extra attention, that's why you've turned out to be such a clever boffin.'

'I'm no such thing,' I retaliated.

Ignoring me, Kitty leapt to her feet and went over to Nanny Devine. 'Nanny, he's so clever he can do *The Times* crossword puzzle in his head. In his head! Can you imagine such a thing?'

'Perhaps if you stayed quiet for more than two seconds, you might be able to do the same,' the older woman said, giving me a friendly wink and making me warm to her.

'Now take this tray and behave yourself. If I didn't know better, I'd say you were showing off, young lady. And you know what little misses who show off deserve, don't you? A smacked bottom!'

'What a perfect beast you are to me!'

'Somebody has to be to keep you in order, as heaven only knows what you'd be getting up to otherwise.'

The repartee continued between them and I drank my tea and ate the generous slice of cake Nanny Devine had lavished on me, savouring every delicious crumb while thinking on what Kitty had said. *He's a very dear friend.* Was that what I was to her, a friend? Did friends kiss in the way we did? Did they hold hands and lie on the grass together wrapped in each other's arms? Perhaps in her world they did.

But I was being absurd. To introduce me as anything other than a friend would have invoked all manner of questions and consequences. And was that what I wanted? No it wasn't. I didn't want anything to spoil my happiness. And if that meant I had to accept the role Kitty had cast me in for appearances sake, so be it.

Nonetheless, I could admit to myself that deep down I wanted more. I wanted so much more. I wanted her to shout from the rooftops that we were courting, that we were a couple. I wanted the world to know that I had never been happier. I wanted every day to be filled with those intimate moments we shared on our rare time off together. I wanted to tell anyone who would listen that she was my darling Katyushka.

When I had first called her by this name she had giggled and asked me what it meant. 'It's the Russian equivalent of your name,' I explained, 'the diminutive form of Katharine. It can also be spelled without the last k, but I prefer it with.'

'Katyushka,' she'd said, experimenting with the sound of it on her tongue, 'my very own Russian pet name, how perfectly wonderful!'

Since that night when she had come to my digs we had

managed a trip to the cinema and another cycle ride and picnic together. On each occasion we had kissed and held each other close, causing my body to respond with alarming desire to the softness and warmth of hers; it was a strong and animal-like desire that craved greater intimacy between us. As yet, and despite the temptation, I hadn't dared cross that line with her.

It pained me to admit that Kitty brought out a range of emotions in me I hadn't known I was capable of feeling. On the one hand I experienced a lightness of spirit when with her, but the flipside was that I experienced a debilitating undercurrent of jealousy and the inability to be content with things as they were. Resembling a greedy child, I was in a perpetual state of wanting more from her.

And perhaps that was because I knew ultimately my happiness could not last, that it was fleeting and any day now it would be snatched from me.

We had finished our tea and cake when Kitty sat up straight and cocked her head towards the door that was ajar. I followed her gaze and discerned voices.

'I don't believe it!' she exclaimed.

'What is it, dear?' Nanny Devine asked.

'I can hear Ruthie's voice downstairs. Honestly, trust her to show up and muscle in on our time together.'

So I'm not the only one who's susceptible to jealousy, I thought as the voices from beyond the door grew louder and more distinct, at the same time accompanied by the clatter of hurried footsteps. One of the voices belonged to a female – presumably Ruthie – and the other to a man. 'Nanny, are you there?' the girl's voice called up the stairs.

'Of course I am, where else would I be?'

The door was thrown wide open and in burst a thickset young woman who looked nothing like Kitty. I rose quickly to my feet but Kitty stayed where she was, her arms folded across her chest and a small yet perceptible frown drawing her brows together.

'So here you all are! Andrews said you'd popped down for the day, Kitty. Mmm ... that cake looks heavenly!' She bent down to help herself to a slice.

Quick as a flash, Nanny Devine slapped her hand. 'Manners, young lady! Say your hellos properly and then I'll make a pot of fresh tea.'

'Quite right, Nanny,' Kitty said. 'And there's no need to shout, Ruthie. Hello, Cordy, what brings you here?'

This was directed to the square-jawed, fair-haired man standing next to Ruthie. Dressed in an RAF uniform, he smiled at Kitty and came round to the back of the sofa where he leant over and planted a kiss on her cheek. 'When Ruthie summons, what's a man to do other than carry out her bidding?'

'Try ignoring her, it's what I've learnt to do.'

Nanny Devine tutted and gave her a scolding roll of her eyes. 'Really, Kitty! You are the limit. Please, just introduce everybody and try to act like the lady you're supposed to be.'

Rolling her own eyes, Kitty did as she was told and introduced me first to Cordy, aka Simon Cordale, and then her sister.

With a look of cool courtesy, Ruthie shook my hand with such a limp touch I suspected she would rather have not bothered. Whereas Kitty was all softness and laughter and spontaneity, her sister was measured and aloof. 'And where exactly have you sprung from?' she asked me. Her voice had all the refinement of her sister's, but it lacked the cheerful warmth; instead, there was a bristling air of authority to it.

'How astonishingly rude of you to ask, Ruthie. Now kindly leave him alone.'

'I'm sure he can answer for himself.' Ruthie turned back to me. 'You can, can't you?'

'When given the chance, certainly.'

Kitty laughed and slipping her arm through mine, she said, 'Come on, why don't I give you a guided tour of the garden? It's much too stuffy to stay inside a moment longer.

Toodle-pip, Nanny, we'll come and say goodbye before we leave.'

A hint of disappointment on her face, Nanny Devine said, 'You be sure you do. And don't think about leaving without saying hello to Mrs Enstone.'

'Will do,' Kitty said. 'Cheerio, Cordy, take care, won't you?'

He smiled and gave her a small wave. But there was no mistaking the regret in his face. Another man slain by Kitty, I thought.

'You're not at all like your sister, are you?' I said when we'd made it downstairs and had emerged into the bright sunshine.

Her hand now resting in mine, she said, 'That, my darling, is the sweetest thing you could ever say to me. Had I known Ruthie would be visiting I wouldn't have put you through that excruciating encounter. She grows more imperious every time I see her. The war has simply gone to her head. I blame her being in the ATS; ever since she joined up and put on a uniform she's become unbearable. Mind you, it started when we were at school; the nuns at the convent foolishly gave her too much power and authority.'

'You went to a convent?' I said, struggling to digest the image of this vivacious and outspoken girl being taught by nuns.

'You sound horrified. But yes, it was where Mummy went as a girl. It's the done thing in our family to send the girls off to be taught by the nuns.'

'Would you do that with your own daughter?' I asked.

'Heavens, yes! That way I'd know she would learn to question and disobey at a very young age, just as I did.'

I laughed. 'So that's where you learnt it.'

She squeezed my hand. 'But seriously, you're not to take any notice of Ruthie. She can say some pretty unpleasant things sometimes without really understanding what she's talking about.'

'And by that you mean what exactly?'

She shrugged and let out a long sigh. 'Oh, forget I said anything, my sister's far too boring for words. Let's go round to the kitchen garden and see what we can pinch to take back to Bletchley with us. There might be some rhubarb and lettuces ready to pick.'

Sensing she was deliberately changing the subject, I said, 'So where does Cordy fit in? Is he your sister's boyfriend?'

Kitty laughed. 'Lord, no! He's a long-standing family friend. He used to be terribly sweet on me. In fact, he asked me to marry him eighteen months ago.'

I tempered my reaction and did my best to sound nonchalant. 'Really? What did you say to him?'

'That I would make the most appalling wife for him and that he would be better off with just about any other girl in the world rather than me.'

'Have you received many proposals of marriage?'

'Just the two.'

'Two?'

'Well, perhaps the first one doesn't truly count as I was only fourteen and the boy in question had drunk a few too many glasses of beer and didn't know what he was saying. He was a boy from the village I'd known since I was six years old. He taught me how to kiss, as it happens.'

'Would it be very indiscreet of me to say he taught you exceptionally well?'

'Darling, you couldn't be indiscreet if you tried!'

But as we passed through an archway of yew topiary and disappeared from view of the house, I took her in my arms and proved to her that I – Jacob Belinsky – could be exceedingly indiscreet.

Chapter Twenty-Three

Libby Henshaw was coming for dinner and Dad was massively on edge. Whether or not it was self-generated or because the rest of them were generating so much tension between them, Saskia couldn't be sure. What was abundantly clear was that her grandfathers were the main cause of the mayhem.

Harvey had decided to impress their guest with an ambitious dish he'd never cooked before and as a result he'd holed himself up in the kitchen for most of the day with only the clatter of pots and pans for company. Oliver's contribution was to grizzle endlessly that he couldn't find his favourite shirt – the pale blue check one Saskia had given him. For some reason no other shirt would do.

After locating it in the utility room under a pile of towels, Saskia was now ironing it for him and hoping that nothing would go wrong for Dad, that they would all settle down and treat their guest as though she were a perfectly ordinary visitor and in no way somebody they were on tenterhooks to meet.

Which was a lie. Behind Dad's back they had spoken of little else since he'd revealed his secret affair with Libby ten years ago. When he'd returned home last night from having dinner with her, and had immediately tried to slope off to his study, probably knowing he'd be met with the equivalent of the Spanish Inquisition, Grandpa O had quickly intervened and all but physically dragged him into the sitting room to be debriefed.

'How was your evening?' he'd asked Dad.

'Very good, thank you.'

'And the food?' This was from Harvey.

'Equally as good.'

'Anyone there we know?'

'No one I noticed, Dad.'

'No, I suppose not. Your attention was otherwise occupied.'

There was a short pause from her father while he picked up a book from the console table behind the sofa where Harvey was sitting. Without even looking at it, he put it back down while casually glancing at *The Dandelion Years* notebook Saskia had in her hands. 'Don't you have a question about my evening, Saskia?' he'd asked.

Suppressing a smile, she'd said, 'I think Harvey and Oliver have it pretty much covered, thank you. But I'll let you know if anything else springs to mind.'

His mouth twitched and, pushing a hand through his hair, he'd cleared his throat as if preparing to deliver an important announcement. 'Would anyone object to Libby joining us for dinner tomorrow evening?' he'd asked.

In their rush to support and encourage the suggestion – Object? Good Lord no! … Whatever made you ask such a thing? … Since when have you needed our permission to invite somebody for dinner? – Dad's face had flushed and he'd fled from the sitting room as fast as he could.

Now, with only a few minutes to go before Libby was due to arrive, he was upstairs getting ready and wisely keeping his distance from the rest of them, and the pressure-cooker tension that was building. While it was true they rarely had guests for dinner, it was not exactly uncharted territory inviting someone to Ashcombe, yet this particular guest's arrival was causing an altogether unwarranted amount of kerfuffle.

Of course, what was uncharted territory for them was the idea of Dad with another woman. Which was crazy; it was actually crazier for him not to be involved with another woman. Auntie Jo had regularly rebuked him for living his life like a monk, though privately Saskia had taken it for granted there had been the occasional encounter with the opposite sex. It wasn't the kind of discussion her grandfathers would have with her, but she had assumed they had thought the same as she did.

Perhaps it wasn't fair to Dad, but Saskia had emailed Auntie Jo, a woman known for her forceful interrogation methods, and asked if she had known about this Libby Henshaw. Apparently she hadn't and was just as keen as the rest of them to know more.

Saskia knew that the very fact her grandfathers were turning the evening into such a big deal reflected how much they cared about Dad; his happiness mattered to them. But there was a danger they cared too much and would do or say something very silly in their desire to do and say the right thing.

To take her mind off the evening ahead and how best to rein in her grandfathers, Saskia switched her thoughts to her delight and satisfaction last night when she'd got to the part in *The Dandelion Years* when the author stated his name unequivocally to be Jacob Belinsky. She was in bed at the time and knowing her father was still downstairs, she had rushed down to him in his study. 'Look!' she'd said triumphantly, showing him the page in the notebook. 'I knew I was right! I knew it, I knew it, I *knew* it! What's more, my guess is that Gil cleared away a load of stuff for Matthew and the Bible was hidden in amongst the dross, and that's why it ended up with me.'

'Nice work, Miss Marple,' Dad had said with an amused smile on his face.

'And I know exactly what you're going to say next, now I definitely have to mention it to Matthew.'

'I think it would only be fair, don't you? The longer you keep hold of it without saying anything, the more awkward it will be to admit it to him that you've been secretly reading it.'

'I could always say I'd only just come across it in my workshop.'

'You could.' As mild as his tone was, the look her father had given her said otherwise.

So today, when they'd been at Glaskin House continuing with the probate valuation, Saskia had rung the number Dad had for Matthew. But as luck would have it, he hadn't answered, so she'd left a message on his voicemail. He hadn't got back to her, so she felt fully justified in holding on to the notebook a while longer so she could finish reading it, hopefully tonight when she was in bed.

Taking the ironed shirt through to the kitchen where Oliver was standing in front of the telly watching the news in his vest and trousers and at the same time vigorously polishing his shoes with a blackened brush, Saskia decided to have a quiet word with her grandfathers. As quiet as was possible given Grandpa O's inability to hear properly.

'Don't take this the wrong way,' she said, 'but we've all got to calm down, or we'll ruin the evening for Dad.'

'What's that?'

'She says we've got to be on our best behaviour tonight,' said Harvey, raising his voice from where he stood at the Aga in a cloud of steam as he stirred the contents of a large saucepan.

'Best behaviour,' Oliver repeated gruffly, attacking the shoe in his hand with an energetic swipe, 'I don't know what you mean!'

'Yes, you do, Grandpa O. Remember what you were like the first time I brought a boyfriend home?'

'That was different,' Oliver said.

'How so?'

'We knew he wasn't right for you,' Harvey answered, turning round from the Aga and wiping his forehead with a corner of his butcher's apron.

'That,' she said, pointing her finger at them both, 'is

precisely my concern. We mustn't make that kind of knee-jerk judgement tonight, OK?'

'But what if we don't like her?' asked Oliver.

'We're going to have to do everything in our power to ensure we do. Yes? I don't expect you to salute me, a nod will suffice.'

Before they had a chance to respond, all three of them started at the sound of the doorbell ringing.

'For heaven's sake, Oliver, get your shirt and shoes on!' ordered Harvey. 'We don't want this woman thinking she's walked into some kind of home for the lost and bewildered who can't even dress themselves!'

'What's that you say?'

Harvey rolled his eyes. 'Saskia, please, take him to get his hearing tested.'

Ralph pushed a nervous hand through his hair, took a deep breath and opened the door.

'You found us all right, then?' he said at the sight of Libby smiling back at him.

'No problem at all, thanks to the combination of your excellent instructions and my very assertive satnav.'

When she was inside and he'd closed the door behind her, he kissed her lightly on the cheek. 'I think I should warn you; they're in a very strange mood. I hope you've brought your sense of humour with you.'

'I never travel without it. I've also brought these.' She held out a bottle of wine and a box of chocolates.

'You needn't have done that.'

'As though I'd blot my copybook by turning up empty-handed.'

'Well, it's very kind of you, but I'll let you present Harvey with them – he's the one in charge tonight.'

'He's your father-in-law and the chef, right?'

'Well remembered. And the slightly grumpy one is Oliver, my father. You might need to make a few allowances for his hearing, he refuses to accept he has a problem and it's driving Harvey round the bend.'

She gave him a wry smile. 'And what allowances do I need to make for you?'

'That I was mad enough to think it would be a good idea to put you through this.'

She rested a hand on his arm. 'Relax. It'll be fine. Why wouldn't it be?'

'You're right,' he said, 'I'm acting worse than a teenager. By the way, dinner last night was great. Really great.'

'I know.'

'You do?'

Removing her coat, she handed it to him. 'You told me so in your text this morning. It was great for me too, in case you were wondering. And I'm sure this evening will be just as enjoyable.'

He hung up her coat, and with his nerves settled by her calm assurance, he put his hand to the small of her back and guided her through to the kitchen where he knew everyone was gathered and waiting expectantly. 'Brace yourself,' he murmured in her ear. Though in truth he was saying it more to himself; he hadn't been this nervous in a very long time.

Harvey could remember the day Evie had brought Ralph home to meet him and Ester for the first time like it was yesterday. The poor devil had been so nervous he'd tripped over the step going into the conservatory, and as he'd crashed to the floor, he'd banged the side of his head on the corner of the coffee table and had ended up at casualty, having four stitches put in his bonce. Ester had been mortified, but he and Evie, once Ralph had been stitched up, had seen the funny side and teased him for providing such an entertaining icebreaker.

'Glad to be of service,' Ralph had said, 'I'll see what I can do next time. If there *is* a next time; maybe you won't trust me to set foot over the threshold again.'

Evie had hugged him with a laugh. 'Of course you'll be invited for a return visit. Mind you, if you'd smashed the table, I'd have my doubts. What do you think, Dad, dare we risk it? Can Ralph come again?'

'Oh, I think we can risk it, especially if we keep a better eye on him.'

In many ways, as odd as it sounded, given how old Ralph was, that's what Harvey had been doing ever since, keeping an eye on his son-in-law, looking out for him. He had made a promise to himself when he'd lost Ester and Evie that he would do all he could to help Ralph and Saskia, and Oliver. He'd vowed he would sacrifice whatever it took to make life better for them, because that's what he believed Evie and Ester would have wanted.

And while he had never actively discouraged Ralph from finding a replacement for Evie, he had never actively encouraged him to do so. Selfishly, once they had established their new life together here at Ashcombe, he hadn't wanted anything to alter it. He still didn't, if he were honest. But he knew that was wrong. Just as he knew Saskia had to fly the nest and create a new life for herself. Both she and Ralph deserved their share of happiness, which meant life at Ashcombe had to change.

Surreptitiously observing their guest as he ate the starter he'd cooked – risotto with three types of mushroom and a truffle sauce – he had to acknowledge that Libby Henshaw was a very pleasant addition around the table. She had patently been put in the picture about Oliver's poor hearing and sitting on his right for his good ear, she was making sure she spoke clearly and loud enough for him to hear. She was also a good sport with a lively and spontaneous sense of humour and seemed perfectly at ease chatting with them, almost as though they were old friends.

But then she and Ralph *were* old friends – quite a bit more than friends in actual fact. Taking a mouthful of wine, Harvey thought that what surprised him, and hurt him to a degree, about Ralph's confession was that he hadn't been straight with them ten years ago. But then, as Saskia had said, how could he when Libby had been married at the time? He had probably feared they would judge him and tell him to get the hell out of such a potentially messy situation. That would almost certainly have been Harvey's advice. He couldn't help but wonder how different life might have been if Libby hadn't already had a husband. Would Ralph have considered marrying her? Would she have lived here with them? Or would she have wanted Ralph to herself? And what would happen now if the two of them picked up where they'd left off?

Harvey suddenly felt unutterably miserable at the thought of Ralph being taken from them. He could accept that it was time for Saskia to move on, but if Ralph went as well, then it would be just him and Oliver left. Would Ralph do that, after all they'd done?

No, no, *no*! he thought angrily. He mustn't think like that. Ralph owed them nothing. Harvey and Oliver had chosen to throw in their lot to help; it had been their choice, they had not been forced.

Cutting into his thoughts, he heard Libby say, 'Harvey, this risotto is out of this world; it's the best I've ever eaten.'

'Thank you,' he murmured. 'I'm glad you like it.'

'I don't suppose you'd give me the recipe, would you? Or is it a chef's secret? A case of what goes on at Ashcombe stays at Ashcombe?'

Harvey smiled. 'Not at all, I'll happily give it to you. Ralph, perhaps you could photocopy it for Libby before she leaves?'

'Consider it done.'

So far so good, thought Saskia as she stacked the dishwasher in the kitchen while Harvey put the finishing touches to the black cod dish he'd been fretting over. 'It really should have had longer to marinate,' he muttered, more to himself than her.

'It'll be perfect,' she said soothingly, 'just as everything you cook is. And your risotto really was fantastic. There wasn't a single grain of rice left on any of the plates. So what do you think of Libby?'

Saskia knew that of all of them, it would be Harvey who would find the situation hardest to deal with. Mum might have been dead for all these years, and inevitably the memories were no longer as strong as they once were, even for Saskia, but she imagined for Harvey, as Mum's father, they were as clear and sharp as they'd ever been.

'She seems nice,' he replied absently.

Saskia was about to agree when she heard the sound of a mobile phone ringing. She went over to the dresser where they tended to put their mobiles when they were in the house: it was hers that was ringing.

She was tempted to ignore it, but thought better of it.

'Hello,' she said, not recognising the number.

'Hi, is that Saskia?'

'It is.'

'It's me, Matthew. Matthew Gray. You left a message for me to ring you. Sorry I'm only now getting back to you, but I was in court all day again. Is there a problem at the house? The boiler didn't go wrong again, did it?'

Taken by surprise, as she so often seemed to be when Matthew Gray was concerned, she said, 'No, nothing like that. It's … it's something a bit personal … erm … the thing is I came across something that—' From behind her an almighty crash followed by 'Damn, blast and buggery to hell!' had her spinning round to her grandfather. On the floor at his feet was a smashed serving dish.

'Is there a problem your end?' Matthew asked.

'Yes, I'm sorry, we're in the middle of dinner here. Can I call you back later?'

'If it's nothing important, perhaps it could wait until the morning? I've decided to work from Glaskin House tomorrow and stay on for the weekend. I'm on my way there now.'

Relieved not to have to make her confession right now, Saskia said, 'OK, that sounds fine. We'll see you in the morning, then. Would you rather we didn't come too early?'

He laughed. 'Depends on what you mean by early. Any time after eight is OK with me. See you.'

Saskia rang off and went over to Harvey who was quietly swearing to himself while bending down to pick up the pieces of the smashed dish. 'Let me do that,' she said, 'you get back to the important stuff.'

'Careful' he warned, 'it's hot from the oven. I stupidly picked it up without the oven gloves.'

'In that case, get your hand under the cold water.'

He blew on his fingers. 'No need, I'll survive.'

'Come on, do as you're told.'

She led him to the sink and turning his hand over so it was palm up, she saw a vivid pink stripe across his fingers. 'Ouch,' she said, turning the tap on, 'that looks painful.'

'My own dim-witted fault, my mind was elsewhere.'

Concerned, she said, 'What were you thinking about?'

'About us. You, me, Oliver, and your father.' He paused a beat while Saskia continued to hold his hand under the tap. Then: 'Saskia?'

'Yes.'

'It hasn't been so bad us all living together, has it?'

Knowing instinctively why he'd asked the question, she said, 'It's been wonderful us all living together. Truly it has. It's hard for me to imagine it any other way.'

'But you realise it can't stay like this forever, don't you?' His voice was suddenly subdued.

Feeling a rush of intense love for Harvey, and wanting to reassure him, she said, 'Nothing's going to change any time soon.'

'You're wrong, Saskia, it has to change. It would be wrong for it not to. That's enough cold water; my hand's completely numb now. Will you help me carry the plates through to the dining room, please?'

'You don't think I should wrap your hand in something to protect it?'

He shook his head. 'If it's still hurting later, I'll do it myself.'

Soon they had everything together for the next course. Following behind her grandfather, Saskia wondered what sort of changes he was referring to. Had the reappearance of Libby Henshaw in Dad's life triggered Harvey's comments, or was there something more going on inside his head?

When the coast was clear – when her grandfathers had both gone up to bed and when she could no longer hear her father's lowered voice speaking on the phone in his study – Saskia knocked on the door and went in. 'I've brought you a mug of tea,' she said.

Looking at the pair of mugs she was carrying, he raised an eyebrow. 'And a detailed post-mortem report to prepare as well, I presume?'

She gave him one of the mugs and, going over to the fireplace, she sank into the lumpy squashiness of the battered old armchair that, by rights, should have been resprung and reupholstered many years ago. But Saskia wouldn't hear of it ever being changed; she had too many fond memories of sitting in it as a young child, cuddled up with her father while he read to her, to contemplate it ever being altered. The same went for the room. She loved the shabby familiarity of it – the packed bookshelves, the worn carpet, the soft glow of the picture lights behind Dad's desk, and the framed photographs charting their lives here at Ashcombe.

'I think post-mortem might be going too far,' she said, taking a sip of her tea. 'An opportunity to share and reflect on the evening would be a better way of putting it. And to set your mind at rest, and based on my ability to make instant and snap judgements when I meet people, I liked Libby. I thought she was lovely.'

'Really? You're not just saying that?'

'Dad, watch my lips – I liked her. As do Oliver and Harvey, if I'm not mistaken. All things considered, they behaved pretty well in the end. The question is, what did Libby think of us?'

'She thought you were all as mad as a box of frogs.'

'That's a little harsh on frogs,' Saskia said with a smile, 'but I'm glad we made a lasting impression on her.'

Her father drank some of his tea and smiled back at her. 'Actually, she didn't say anything of the kind; she said she hadn't had a more enjoyable evening in a long time. Which, as I told her just now on the phone, doesn't say much for my company last night.'

Saskia laughed. 'You're out of practice, that's all.'

Her father suddenly looked serious. 'I am, Saskia. We all are, aren't we? We're all out of practice when it comes to sharing our lives with other people.'

Taking a moment to consider his remark, Saskia said, 'Is this going somewhere?'

'I'd like to see more of Libby,' he said simply, 'a lot more of her. Would that bother you in any way?'

'Dad, please don't be ridiculous. Of course it wouldn't bother me. Why on earth would you ask such a thing?'

'Because my seeing Libby on a regular basis might have the potential to change things here.'

Thinking of Harvey's comments in the kitchen earlier, Saskia said, 'I'm sure we'll all get used to whatever changes lie ahead. You really mustn't worry about us.' She hauled herself out of the sunken depths of the armchair. 'And now I'll leave you in peace, I have Jacob Belinsky's notebook to finish reading.'

She kissed her father goodnight. 'I'm not afraid of change, Dad, if that's what you're worrying about.'

Chapter Twenty-Four

August 1943

Over the course of the summer Kitty asked repeatedly to meet my parents, to see for herself where I'd grown up. Personally I saw no point in doing this but, as I was rapidly coming to realise, Kitty was as determined a person as anyone I knew: once she set her mind on a course of action she wouldn't rest until it had been achieved. All I was doing was putting the day off.

'Are you ashamed of me, darling?' she said one evening when we had drifted away from the main throng of concert-goers up at the house. 'Is that why you keep putting me off?'

I was quick to reassure her that she couldn't be more wrong, but secretly I was nettled by her perseverance and beginning to feel that I was some sort of social experiment for her, that she was merely curious to see how we mere mortals lived. Or did she think that my family's Russian Jewish roots made us even more of a curiosity?

The other assumption she might well have made, though she never voiced it, was that maybe I was ashamed of where I was from and was hell bent on denying my roots. Which wasn't true. I was immensely proud of my family, for them-selves and for the opportunities they had given me. The fact was, I didn't want the spell broken – life at Bletchley had become so much more enjoyable since Kitty had arrived and I didn't want anything, certainly not the reality of the world beyond, to burst the bubble of my happiness.

In contrast to this fixation of Kitty's to meet my family,

my thoughts, when they weren't fully occupied with work, drifted all too often to my growing desire for her. It was extraordinary, but the more relaxed and easy-going she was around me, the more arousing I found her. We had progressed no further than kissing and, not to put too fine a point on it, it was no longer enough for me. I wanted us to be lovers.

Gossip abounded within the hut about our friendship, mostly generated by Chatterton-Jones I suspected, and I'd be a liar if I didn't admit to a degree of *schadenfreude* knowing how Kitty regarded him. But as ever, two steps behind my smugness, was the constant fear that this beautiful girl would suddenly view me as I viewed myself – as an impostor who would never be entirely accepted into her world.

Oh yes, people – including Kitty – were full of talk about the war changing everything, that it was the great leveller of our time, but I knew some things would never change. On a daily basis this was confirmed to me in numerous and various little ways, whether it was a patronising remark from Chatterton-Jones about my personal knowledge of the East End of London, or a more blatant display of undisguised hatred from Mrs Pridmore.

One day I had heard her discussing me over the garden fence with her neighbour. She claimed to have her eye on me and wouldn't be at all surprised if I turned out to be a filthy German sympathiser, or a spy. I was foreign, after all, she told her neighbour, a sly foreigner who would probably murder her in her bed if she lowered her guard.

Never did I hear her talking about her other lodgers in the same way. I also knew that she regularly snooped through my few possessions while I was at work. On several occasions I had put this to the test and proved myself right when on my return I found the book I'd been reading not in the same place I'd left it and my few neatly folded clothes rifled through. I was tempted to hide something vaguely suspicious just to see what the ghastly woman would do.

As luck would have it fate provided a welcome distraction from Kitty's ongoing wish to meet my parents when, out of the blue, she was told that she had to move digs as her landlady had been forced to take in an extra relative suffering from ill health and needed the room Kitty used. She was immediately assigned new digs at Broad Acre Farm, some four miles from Bletchley Park.

The following day, and with an afternoon free before doing the evening shift, I helped her move. With no car at our disposal, we had to balance her two cases – she had somehow gained an extra case since her arrival at the Park – on the handlebars of our bicycles and slowly push them to her new billet. With each mile we covered in the strong August sunshine, I silently mourned the distance that would now separate us. It seemed to stretch on indefinitely.

We eventually arrived at the farm, hot and perspiring. There was no one to greet us, other than a panting collie dog that wagged its tail in a desultory fashion. With the brief instructions Kitty had been given, we followed a rutted track away from the farmhouse until we came to a squat, tumble-down building with a sagging tiled roof, most of which was covered in honeysuckle. There was a horseshoe nailed to the wooden door and tied to this was a note informing Kitty that this was her new home.

Leaving our bikes and suitcases resting against a low wall to the side – where I spotted a cast-iron hand pump and water trough – Kitty turned the handle on the door and, stooping considerably, we went in.

Her billet had been described as a cottage, but this was a colossal exaggeration. We were standing in what was effectively an outhouse that had been given a coat of paint and aspirations of grandeur. Pushed against the wall to our right was a narrow metal-framed bed covered with a sickly pink candlewick bedspread, its fringe nearest to us coming away. Opposite the bed, no more than two feet away, was a small mahogany wardrobe leaning at a precarious angle. Next to it was an armchair with the stuffing oozing out of the ripped seat cushion and a washstand with a small cracked mirror above. A rag rug partially covered the uneven floor and a flimsy bit of yellow cotton masqueraded as a curtain at the small, grimy window, beneath which was a paint-splattered table bearing an enamel jug containing a few sprigs of welcoming honeysuckle, the smell of which lost out to the stronger smell of Jeyes Fluid.

With her usual propensity to see the positive in anything, Kitty was delighted with her new accommodation. 'Just look at the view,' she enthused, taking me by the arm to look out through the open door to admire the meadow the other side of the rutted track. 'One could truly believe there isn't a war on looking at that.'

Right on cue, as if to make it even more enchanting, the sound of a woodpecker thrummed in the distant copse of trees. 'It's breathtaking,' she said softly. 'Simply breathtaking. Imagine waking up to that every morning!'

It was on the tip of my tongue to say that waking up to see her every morning would be far more breathtaking, but refrained. 'There's no bathroom,' I said, boringly matter-of-fact.

'I expect there's an outside lavatory somewhere,' she responded with a happy shrug, her gaze still focused on the view.

'There's always the water trough or the stream to wash in.'

We turned to see who had made this suggestion and saw a tall, broad-shouldered girl coming towards us. She had a bright and cheery face and was dressed in boots, dungarees and an off-white shirt. Curls of springy red hair peeped out from beneath a scarf tied around her head and dangling from her left hand, their lifeless bodies stretched long and lean, were two rabbits.

'You must be the new girl we were told to expect,' she said. Wiping her free hand against the leg of her dungarees, she thrust it towards Kitty. 'I'm Peggy and I'm sorry to tell you but you're stuck with me as your nearest neighbour.' She indicated another outbuilding further along the rutted track, and where a dusty red tractor was parked. 'That's my home sweet home up there,' she said, 'Beryl and Dorothy, the other two land girls, live in luxury and share a room at the farmhouse. You'll meet them later I expect.'

Kitty introduced herself.

'How do you like your accommodation?' Peggy asked.

'It's perfect,' Kitty said, 'better than I could have wished for.'

The girl let out a hearty laugh. 'Then all I can say is that you must have very low standards. This your boyfriend?'

On the receiving end of an enquiring stare and a firm and callused handshake to rival that of any man I had encountered, I paused long enough for Kitty to reply and to see how she would introduce me so I could follow her lead. After much discussion we had agreed to keep our relationship a secret in case it caused problems at work. 'Lord, I'd simply hate to get into any trouble and be sent home,' she'd said. 'Or worse, put you at risk.'

While I could see the sense in concealment and maintaining the pretence that we were just good friends, I was aware of a number of relationships going on at the Park that hadn't caused any eyebrows to be raised, quite the contrary. But Kitty knew of a Wren who'd got herself pregnant and had disappeared in a blink of an eye. Another girl who was a bomber operator was quickly spirited away after a relationship with a cryptographer had ended badly. The theory was she'd gone off her head after a half-hearted attempt to drown herself in the lake. It was widely known that if a person, for whatever reason, was considered emotionally unbalanced they were deemed a risk to security and would be quietly removed. It was just one of the many rules by which we lived.

'This is Jacob,' Kitty said brightly, 'he's been an absolute saint in helping me transport my things here, I couldn't have managed without him.'

'We could do with more saints round here,' the girl said with a generous smile. She looked at our bicycles and cases. 'You don't travel lightly, then?'

'Oh, it's just silly stuff, mostly things my mother sends me thinking I can't possibly manage without. Stupid really. But what can you do?'

'Now that's the kind of mother I could do with!'

Sensing I was rapidly becoming a spare part, I said, 'Well, I'll leave you to it, I should be getting along.'

'Don't feel you have to rush off because of me,' Peggy said, 'stay and have a drink. Billy's managed to barter a side of ham for some cider which we're all keen to try.' To Kitty, she added, 'A proper welcome drink would be just the ticket, don't you agree?'

With several hours to go until my shift, I said I'd stay for a short while and after Kitty unpacked we retraced our steps to the farmhouse where we met Billy.

Billy wasn't the man I'd pictured, but a formidable woman in her fifties called Winifred, who, according to Peggy, preferred to be known as Billy. With wild iron-grey hair and muscular forearms, and dressed in a baggy shirt and a pair of voluminous dungarees with a red neckerchief at her throat, she looked a force to be reckoned with.

'Don't be scared, come in, come in!' she boomed with a Woodbine poking out from the side of her mouth as we stood hesitantly on the threshold of the kitchen, letting Peggy make the introductions while she deposited the dead rabbits on the wooden draining board.

Punishing a lump of pastry with a hefty-sized rolling pin on the floured table in the middle of the room, Billy apologised to Kitty for not being around earlier to greet her, but she'd been busy making raspberry jam. The sweet smell that filled the kitchen, together with the sight of half a dozen jars of ruby-red jam at one end of the table, gave testament to this.

Looking about me, I surmised that this large and untidy room was the hub of the house, in the same way the kitchen was in the terraced house where I'd grown up. On the range next to a copper pan, presumably the one in which the jam had been made, there was a blackened kettle that was identical to the one we had at home. Above the range was a long green-painted shelf that held a plethora of dented pans, jugs and mixing bowls. On the adjacent wall, a hulk of a dresser contained a jumbled assortment of crockery, including some oily bits of machinery on sheets of newspaper that looked as though they had been taken apart and were yet to be put back together. With years of use the worn stone flags of the floor were smooth and shiny in places, but also scarred and pitted in others.

'As you've no doubt discovered, your accommodation isn't up to much,' Kitty's new landlady said, while taking the Woodbine from her mouth and flicking ash into the sink behind her, 'but it's the best I can do in the circumstances. On the upside, you'll find the food more than adequate.'

Peggy smiled and nudged Kitty with her elbow. 'That's the advantage of being billeted on a farm; you won't go hungry. I've actually gained weight since coming here.'

Billy waved the rolling pin at Peggy. 'You should have seen her when she first stepped on to the platform at Bletchley – she was nothing but skin and bone, barely had the strength or energy to pick up her own shadow. I took one look at her and nearly put her straight back on the train. She'll be no use to me on the farm, I said to myself.'

'And she's been fattening me up like a goose for Christmas from that day on,' laughed Peggy.

Swivelling her gaze round to Kitty and then to me, Billy said, 'You both look like you could do with a decent feed inside you as well. You look properly starved the pair of you. Bit pasty in all, especially you, young man.'

This latter comment was emphasised by the pointing of the rolling pin at me.

'I suppose you're also at the Park, aren't you,' she continued, 'and rarely see the light of day. I hear you're kept in hutches like rabbits. It beggars belief. I've heard rumours that they carry out experiments on you, keep you starved and deprived of sleep, just to see if you'll go raving mad.'

Kitty laughed. 'Nothing like that, I can assure you. It's all terribly boring work, just typing mostly.'

'I don't see him as the typing sort,' Billy said, her attention, and the rolling pin, now back on the circle of pastry.

'Paperwork,' I said quickly. 'The war generates reams of it.'

She glanced up at me through the smoke of her cigarette and I knew she didn't believe me for a second. But thankfully she left it at that. 'Pegs,' she boomed, apparently deciding the pleasantries had been dispensed with, 'fetch the cider; it's in the pantry. On the shelf above, there's a tin of sausage rolls, bring those as well. You,' she pointed at Kitty, 'you'll find four glasses in the cupboard over there. I'll have no standing on ceremony here, everybody mucks in. After all, there's a war on and it's pulling together that'll enable us to put that mad Hitler in his place.'

Armed with nothing more than her acerbic tongue and a rolling pin, I couldn't help but think Billy would be a match for Hitler and the Third Reich any day. In that respect, she reminded me of my Grandma Lila.

I later cycled back to Bletchley, wishing I could also be billeted at the farm instead of being stuck with Mrs Pridmore.

Far from mourning the four miles between us, I soon delighted in the happy idyll of Kitty's new digs. Amusingly, she'd named the ugly little outhouse Honeysuckle Cottage and with Peggy's help she dug over the small patch of earth to the front and planted her very own vegetable patch, growing late-season lettuces, radishes and spring onions. She was already planning for next year when she would grow potatoes and onions, and peas and beans.

But what I liked most about her new surroundings was

the privacy it offered us. It sounds calculating on my part, but one way or another, I had decided this newfound privacy was going to be put to good use.

That moment came on Wednesday 8 September, 1943. It was the day Italy surrendered to the Allies. We heard the news on Billy's wireless in the kitchen and in response I was dispatched to the pantry to fetch a bottle of gooseberry liqueur so we could drink to the Italians. The four of us – Kitty, me, Billy, Peggy, and the other two Land Girls, Beryl and Dorothy, kept on drinking to the Italians until the bottle was empty and we were all quite merry. I was then invited to stay for supper, and with Kitty and I both working the midnight shift, I all too readily agreed.

It was a beautiful evening and at Billy's instruction we heaved the kitchen table and chairs outside to the garden where we feasted on corned beef hash with another bottle of gooseberry liqueur and a good deal of high spirits.

Afterwards Kitty and I went for a walk down to the stream, which, following Peggy's example, she had indeed used to bathe in on several occasions. Lying on the bank together in the dusky twilight, and quite uninhibitedly, owing to the gooseberry liqueur, I began singing, a song that from nowhere had come into my head.

Kitty raised herself on to her elbow and looked at me. When I finished, she said, 'That was lovely. I've never heard you speak Russian before. You sounded so different. What was the song?'

'It's from Rachmaninov's opera, *Aleko*, and is based on Pushkin's poem *The Gypsies*. My grandfather taught me to sing it when I was a child.'

'What's it about?'

'A doomed love affair.'

'Oh,' she said, pulling a face, 'I don't think I much care for the sound of that.'

I laughed. 'A true Russian's soul is but a smile or a tear away from maudlin melodrama.'

She looked thoughtful, so deep in thought, I could not resist taking her face in my hands and kissing her. The next thing I knew, I was rolling her gently on to her back and my hands began exploring her body, which was invitingly soft and yielding. Finding no resistance, I went on exploring, undoing the buttons on her blouse and slipping my hand inside to touch her smooth warm skin. At my touch, a small moan escaped from her mouth and I kissed her some more and explored some more, my head spinning and my breath quickening. But then beneath me, she suddenly slid her head to one side so she could look at me.

'Jacob,' she said softly, 'are we finally going to do it?'

I swallowed anxiously. 'Do what exactly?' I whispered.

'Are we at last going to make love? I do hope so, because I really don't think I can take the suspense any longer.'

I didn't need asking twice.

Chapter Twenty-Five

It was just the two of them in the library at Glaskin House when Saskia gave the letter and notebook to Matthew. A moment passed while he read the letter, then going over to the window where morning sunlight streamed in across the desk, he sat down and read the first page of the notebook.

With his back to her, Saskia watched him anxiously, not knowing how he would react. Would he be angry that she, a virtual stranger, had read something that was so personal? Or would he, she hoped, be happy she had discovered it and saved it?

Throughout her explanation of how she'd come across the notebook, and that she had only realised the other day who the author was, he had said nothing, other than to confirm that he had indeed used Gilbert Ross to take away most of the junk from the attic and garage. His worryingly taciturn manner made her glad that Jacob had revealed his name in the telling of his story and had therefore spared her the embarrassing admission that she'd been snooping through personal photograph albums.

She watched Matthew silently turn another page, but still nothing in his manner gave her a clue to his thoughts.

It had taken her until almost two in the morning to finish reading it – or rather, that was when she had reached the final page in the notebook, just as Jacob and Kitty had at last got it together. As much as it had made her smile when she'd read that part, Saskia had been disappointed to turn the page and see it blank. What? She'd wanted to cry. It can't end there. No! What happened next?

And now, as she stood patiently waiting for Matthew to say something, she was hoping he might know the answer to that question.

'It's definitely Jacob's writing,' he said quietly, and without turning to look at her. 'I'd know his awful scrawl anywhere. It used to drive my mother crazy if he ever left a note for her because it would take her ages to make sense of it. Fortunately I became quite adept at deciphering anything he wrote.'

Thinking he didn't appear to be too annoyed with her, Saskia ventured to join him at the desk. 'Did you know he worked at Bletchley?' she asked. 'Was it something he talked about?'

Now he did turn to look at her, and in that distinctively measured way she was coming to know – head slightly tilted, eyes perceptibly narrowed. 'He never mentioned Bletchley, not a single word. Not ever. This is a complete surprise to me. I had no idea. I'm stunned.'

'Perhaps that's not so very surprising,' she said, 'given the level of secrecy to which everyone at Bletchley was sworn. I've read that for some people, even back in the seventies when stories first began to emerge about the work carried out there, and how vital it was to the war, they still wouldn't talk about their contribution, or if they did they felt guilty and disloyal.'

Matthew seemed to reflect on her words, then shook his head and let out a small sigh. 'It's so typical of the old devil; he loved secrets. And playing games. He particularly enjoyed leading people up the garden path.'

'Do you think that's all it is?' Saskia asked. 'A cleverly concocted story?'

'I'd have to read the book properly before I could really answer that, but my gut reaction is that it's real.'

Glad that he felt the same as she did, she said, 'For what it's worth, I believe it's genuine; it feels too raw and honest for it to be a work of fiction. What's more, I don't think he finished telling his story; it ends too abruptly. I'm rather hoping there's a second notebook somewhere here in the house.'

He looked at her with a shrewd gaze. 'Meaning you'd like to read it if such a book exists?'

'Guilty as charged,' Saskia said with a placatory smile. 'Which I know makes me sound horribly nosy, but I just feel … oh, I don't know, and maybe this sounds a bit crazy to you, but I really like the man I've been spending time with. I've become attached to him and want to know what happened next between him and his first great love.'

'I don't think that sounds crazy; I'm sure Jacob would have been amused and flattered by your interest. But as to another notebook, I certainly haven't come across one. I haven't even found a diary. Jacob always claimed that diaries, other than appointment diaries, were strictly for the self-indulgent – or the maliciously inclined with an axe to grind. And I can assure you, he was neither.'

Her disappointment that he knew of no other notebook must have been so clearly stamped on her face that he quickly added, 'But I promise you: if I do find something, you'll be the first to know. Chances are, though, if it was caught up with the junk that Gilbert Ross took away, and wasn't passed on to your father like the Bible, then it's probably long gone and lost forever.'

Glancing at the notebook on the desk, Saskia said, 'That would be such a shame when Jacob went to so much trouble to write the story, and then hide it the way he did. I can't help but think he must have hidden a second notebook equally well. And for all we know, there might even be a third.'

A hint of a smile appeared on Matthew's face. 'You're quite the sleuth, aren't you?'

'An incurable nosy parker more like it.'

His smile widened, went all the way to his eyes. 'As far as I'm concerned you can be as curious as you like, because if it weren't for you, this,' he tapped the notebook, 'might never have seen the light of day again. So thank you. Thank you very much.'

There seemed nothing else to be said on the matter, and thinking that he'd probably like to be alone to carry on reading, she said, 'Right, well, I'd better get on with some work and join my father upstairs.'

'He seems to think you'll be finished here today, is that right?'

'That's the plan.'

Which was now a huge disappointment to Saskia, because in her belief that there was more of *The Dandelion Years* to come, she would love nothing better than to return tomorrow and ransack the house to find the completion to the story she wanted. But as she trudged upstairs to look for her father, she had to accept that she might never know what happened to Jacob and Kitty.

At the top of the landing she stopped to look at a framed antique map of Cambridge. She followed the direction of the River Cam from south to north, marking its progress along the Backs, the stretch of land between the riverside colleges, one of which was Merchant College where she knew Jacob Belinsky had been a professor. She wondered exactly where in Cambridge Matthew lived.

Beneath the map was a handsome mahogany glass-fronted bookcase and in common with all the bookcases throughout the house, it was crammed full. Saskia, having already catalogued and valued the books, knew the shelves contained a fascinating first-edition collection devoted to the great Russian writers – Tolstoy, Pushkin, Dostoevsky, Gorky, Gogol, Lermontov, Turgenev, and many more that Saskia and her father had never come across before. A number of the books were leather-bound and in the original language.

Moving further along the landing, she called out to her father.

'In here,' he called back.

She found him in what had been Jacob's bedroom – it

was at the front of the house and overlooked the church and graveyard. On either side of the sash window were two floor-to-ceiling bookcases, one of which her father was kneeling in front of. 'How did it go with Matthew?' he asked, his voice lowered.

'He was fine, not a word of recrimination thrown at me.'

'See? Just as I said he would be.'

'Tell me, Dad, how does it feel to be such a clever know-it-all?'

'It feels great. Always has. Did Matthew know Jacob was at Bletchley Park?'

'No, he didn't have a clue. I've left him downstairs in a state of stunned amazement.'

'Interestingly I've found a couple of recently published books here about the people who worked there. I've just been checking through them to see if Jacob features.'

'Does he?'

'I'm afraid not.'

All thought of work now gone from his mind, Matthew remained seated at Jacob's desk and stared out of the window at the garden where two squirrels were chasing each other across the sunlit lawn. A fat wood pigeon looked on from the branch of a tree.

But Matthew saw none of this; all he could see was Jacob – Jacob as an old man sitting quietly by the fire engrossed in a book, or thrashing Matthew at a game of chess. Or Jacob teasing Mum about something or other, or complaining bitterly about the poor standard of English now spoken on the radio and television. Had that same man really worked as a code-breaker at Bletchley Park? The only work he had ever discussed with Matthew had been his academic life in Cambridge and for some reason Matthew had never given any thought to the old man having a life before then. Let alone a romantic life.

Again, as far as Matthew had been aware, or as he had

simply assumed, Jacob had been a natural and confirmed bachelor. Not once could he ever recall Jacob speaking about there having been any women in his life.

But Bletchley Park, how extraordinary. And what a pity Matthew hadn't known this before; he would have loved to have heard what Jacob had to say about his time there.

He had the next best thing, he supposed, lowering his gaze to the notebook in front of him. Thank God it had fallen into the hands it had and that Saskia had been interested enough to read it. Another person might have given up trying to decipher the shocking handwriting and thrown the book away, not realising its significance.

As to how the notebook had left the safety of Glaskin House, all Matthew could conclude was that maybe he and James had been overly zealous when clearing the attic. It was possible that the Bible Saskia had described had been inside one of the many old trunks and boxes they had got rid of. Maybe they hadn't been as thorough in checking the contents as they should have been.

He'd been reading solidly for over an hour when he sat back in his chair to contemplate what he'd read. It was the weirdest thing, but the voice speaking to him through the pages of the notebook was that of a man he didn't know, yet at the same time he had never felt the old man's presence more acutely or more poignantly.

It brought home to Matthew just how close he had been to Jacob and how much he missed him. Just like Mum, Jacob had always been there for him, ever ready with a pertinent word of advice and encouragement. He'd been particularly supportive during Mum's illness and then when she died. It had taken Matthew a long time to get over her death and he suspected the same was going to be true of Jacob's passing. He slid his hand into his pocket and reached for Jacob's fob watch, thinking that not since the day of the old man's funeral had he felt this depth of isolation and sadness.

He stood up abruptly, knowing that to dwell on Jacob and his mother wouldn't help.

Out in the hall, he called up the stairs to see if anyone wanted a drink. Suddenly he didn't want to be alone. He wanted company.

Chapter Twenty-Six

With considerable reluctance Saskia was slowly coming to terms with never knowing how *The Dandelion Years* ended.

Common sense told her she should agree with Matthew that the wartime romance must have been nothing more than one of those typically intense but brief affairs. He claimed that if it had lasted for any length of time, or culminated in marriage, then there would be some evidence of it: a marriage certificate within the professor's papers, for instance. Saskia's counterargument to that theory was that Jacob had worked at Bletchley Park and yet, to all intents and purposes, there was not a shred of evidence at Glaskin House that he had. In Saskia's opinion, if he'd kept that secret, he was more than capable of keeping a relationship, maybe even a marriage, secret.

But when, one Friday afternoon in the first week of April, Saskia answered her mobile in her workshop and recognised Matthew's voice asking how she was, she straight away hoped he had good news for her. It was the first time she had heard from him since the day she'd given him the notebook and immediately she couldn't think why else he would be ringing her, other than with the news he had found the concluding notebook. With the probate valuation carried out and their fee paid, there was no other reason to contact her, unless, of course, he now wanted Dad to sell some of Jacob's book collection for him.

'I'm sorry to bother you but I wanted to ask you a favour,' he said. 'Do you still have the Bible in which Jacob's notebook was hidden?'

She looked guiltily across her workshop to the shelf where she'd kept the Bible all these weeks. Many a time she had thought she really should hand it over to Matthew, seeing as he was the rightful owner, but she'd hung on to it in the vague hope that, like a lucky charm, it might bring about the chance for her to read the rest of Jacob and Kitty's story. 'You're in luck, I do still have it,' she said.

'Excellent,' Matthew said in response. 'Would you mind if I came and took a look at it, please?'

'Of course I don't mind. It's yours by rights anyway. When would you like to come?'

'It's short notice, but how would this evening suit you? I'm just about to leave Cambridge to spend the weekend at Glaskin House, so I could come to you first. I promise I won't keep you for long, I just need to satisfy my curiosity.'

'That's OK, I have nothing planned. By the way, and assuming you read the whole of the notebook, what did you think of it?'

'I've read it through twice now and am inclined to take your view on it: there has to be more. Jacob would not have left such a meticulously written story hanging in the air like that. He was an infuriatingly pedantic man who liked all his Ts crossed and his Is dotted.' Matthew gave a short laugh. 'I know this to my cost because somewhere along the line it rubbed off on me.'

Delighted that he agreed with her, Saskia said, 'I'm the same; I can't bear for anything to be done in a slapdash fashion. But you know, I can't stop thinking that somewhere in that large house there's another notebook hidden away. Have you looked for it?'

'No, annoyingly I haven't had time; I've been up and down to Carlisle on a new case. But that's why I want to see the Bible you found the notebook in. I know it's a long shot, but I'm hoping it might give me a clue where Jacob hid the second part.'

'Or the third and fourth,' she said, delighted he was taking up the challenge to pursue the matter further.

He groaned. 'Don't say that, there are only so many needles in haystacks I can deal with! I'll see you then. About seven o'clock, depending on the traffic. If it looks like I'm running seriously late, I'll call you.'

'No problem, I'm not going anywhere.' Then, and because she was warming to Matthew, glad that he wasn't the sort to sit on his laurels and just let things lie – and with a bit of luck would share anything he found with her – she said, 'You could always join us for supper if you want. It's our night for fish and chips.'

There was a pause. 'Are you sure?'

'Am I sure we're having fish and chips?'

He laughed. 'No, that I'd be welcome to join you.'

'I wouldn't have suggested it if I wasn't. We'll see you at seven, then. Goodbye.' She rang off hastily, fearing her invitation might have sounded a bit odd to him.

Within seconds her mobile rang again.

'It's me again, sorry.'

So yes, she'd been right, it had sounded weird. Cue the apology that he had a prior engagement for the evening, which he'd just remembered.

'I don't have your address,' he said.

'Oh. Right. Sorry. I'll text it to you, shall I?'

'OK, thanks a lot. See you later then.'

She rang off, texted him the necessary information, then going over to the shelf where the Bible was, she took it down and automatically wiped it for any potential dust, even though she kept her workshop in pristine order and as dust free as possible. She couldn't abide working in a mess, she liked everything to be in its proper place and scrupulously clean.

Making a space for the Bible on the workbench, and opening it to the cut-away oblong where the notebook had been hidden for so many years, she felt a little sad knowing that she would have to part with it this evening. She had become quite attached to it; irrationally, it made her feel connected to Jacob and Kitty, as though she had become a part of their story.

Her sadness was tinged with a flicker of irritation – did she really have so little going on in her own life that she was obsessing about two people she had never even known? It was a question she was reluctant to answer for fear of giving in to the treacherous worry that had begun to take root recently, a worry that whispered an unpalatable truth, that beyond her family – beyond Ashcombe – she didn't have a life. For as long as she could remember, her world had revolved around Ashcombe and it had given her all the fulfilment she had needed, but now a part of her had begun to ask if that was still the case.

Very likely the reason for these thoughts could be attributed to the comments Harvey had made the night Libby came for dinner, and her numerous visits since that evening. In no way did Saskia object to her presence; quite the contrary, she liked Libby, she liked her a lot. The woman had a lively and engaging personality and was unfailingly friendly and considerate towards Saskia. She was also sincere in her interest in anything Harvey and Oliver had to say. An enthusiastic cook herself, she had swapped recipes with Harvey and, as a self-confessed novice gardener, explored the garden with Oliver while listening to his tips and advice on the easiest vegetables to grow. But as enjoyable as it was having her around, Saskia was aware that, just as Harvey had predicted, there were changes now taking place – changes that anyone observing the family would say had been a long time in coming.

Libby had also come to the rescue and offered to help Dad at the shop, Pat having left last week, and from all accounts the arrangement was working well. Dad had twice referred to Libby as a godsend. And with Harvey now keeping a box of her favourite green tea in the cupboard, and a place at the kitchen table assigned as hers, Libby had very much become a fixture, and all in a relatively short space of time.

In the last couple of weeks Saskia and her grandfathers had got used to Dad staying out late some nights and, logically, the next step would be for him either to stay over at Libby's, or for her to stay the night here at Ashcombe. Only yesterday Saskia had overheard her grandfathers discussing the probability of this happening. When they'd realised she had heard what they'd said, they'd both looked embarrassed and had quickly busied themselves with opening that morning's post. Never had she seen them so interested in what was ostensibly junk mail and which they normally threw in the recycling bin without a second glance.

No child at any age wants to be confronted with the thought of a parent having a sex life and Saskia was no different, but she wasn't stupid and knew that her father would not be playing Jenga or tiddlywinks when he stayed late at Libby's. She sensed, though, that Dad would probably find it awkward to have Libby stay the night here. Maybe Libby would too.

Saskia could sympathise – it couldn't exactly make for the perfect romantic moment knowing that his father and father-in-law, not to mention his daughter, were sleeping just a few yards away. She herself had only once had a boyfriend to stay over; she had been nineteen at the time and had sneaked him in late one night in the hope she'd be able to get rid of him before anyone was up, but they had both overslept. The whole awkward business of facing her father and grandfathers over the breakfast table with the boyfriend in question, as they had all tried too hard to hide their surprise and make their guest feel welcome, had been far too embarrassing to repeat.

Not that there had been a string of boyfriends queuing up to stay the night with Saskia, but that was probably down to her; she was choosy with whom she got involved. Plus working from home lessened the chances of meeting anyone. She had met her last boyfriend at, of all places, the garage where her car was having a new exhaust fitted. She had been sitting in the bleak, rubber-floored waiting room with only some grubby copies of the *Sun* and the *Mirror* to read, when he'd walked in to wait for a new set of tyres to be put on his Ford Focus. He was the one to strike up a conversation with her, and by the time their cars were ready to drive away, he had asked if she'd like to meet for a drink some time that week.

She couldn't drive by that garage now without thinking of Philip. But not in a regretful way: their relationship had never been destined to go the full distance. It sounded awful, but really he had been an example of the misplaced idea that it was better to have somebody in her life rather than nobody.

Looking back on it there had been nothing of the romance, or the intensity of emotion between them that she had felt when reading *The Dandelion Years*. There had been no sense of longing, just an easy-going, predictable, and comfortable safeness to their relationship. She had thought this was what she had wanted, that stability over uncertainty was preferable. But once things had ended with Philip she had realised that actually he'd just been plain dull. In fairness, and given her adamant refusal to consider moving away with him, perhaps he now thought the same of her.

Was she dull? And was there a worse condemnation of a person?

Auntie Jo in Canada had been on at her the other day in one of their regular Skype chats. Most of the conversation had centred on Saskia briefing her aunt on the latest news regarding Dad and Libby. But once that had run its course, her aunt had suddenly switched direction and demanded to know when Saskia was going to visit her and Uncle Bob. 'And don't give me any of your usual excuses about being busy with work because I'm sick, sick, *sick* to death of hearing that. Nor do I want to hear that you can't leave your father and grandfathers on their own, blah, blah; they're more than capable of managing without you for a few weeks!'

'Is there anything I *can* say?' Saskia had asked her aunt.

'You can tell me what's bugging you. I hear from Oliver

that you've been distinctly off colour lately – as snappy as an alligator with toothache, is how he put it. You're not getting all angsty because your father's finally found himself a woman, are you?'

'Of course not!'

'No, I didn't think you'd be that stupid. So what's going on?'

Knowing her aunt wouldn't let it rest, Saskia had gone on to explain that recently she had indeed been feeling snappy.

'A clear case of being stuck in a rut, I'd say,' her aunt had interjected. 'Mind you, I'd feel like ripping a few heads off if I were stuck with my stubborn old father for too long. Well done for finally getting him to have his ears tested, by the way.'

This, if nothing else, was Saskia's proudest achievement of the year so far, persuading Oliver to make an appointment with a hearing specialist. He now wore a discreet hearing aid and, despite still getting used to it, he had grudgingly admitted he could now hear a lot better and was often telling the rest of them not to shout.

'But forget about Oliver,' her aunt had said, 'what do you propose to do about your situation, apart from stagnate there at Ashcombe?'

There was no one like Auntie Jo for calling a spade a spade and Saskia could only smile at her aunt's chutzpah. 'I'll let you know when I've decided.'

What she had decided following on from that conversation was that she needed to inject some spontaneity into her life, which meant she had to throw away her naturally cautious predisposition and be more impulsive. This decision had come to her after thinking how like Kitty she wished she could be, a girl who seemed not to worry about anything and who Jacob described as the most determined person he knew once she set her mind on a thing. She seemed so refreshingly positive and uncomplicated, a girl from whom Saskia could learn a lot, she felt.

She wondered if inviting Matthew for supper this evening counted as a first step in learning to be more spontaneous, like Kitty.

Chapter Twenty-Seven

While Saskia apologised for the interruption and dealt with a phone call, Matthew examined the cutaway section of the Bible and found himself agreeing with her; it had to have been a professional job. The task of creating a hiding place for the notebook had not been done with a pair of scissors and time on one's hands; a machine must have been used because nothing else explained the precision of the work carried out.

He closed the Bible and studied the front of it, then the spine followed by the back. Considering its age – printed in the late nineteenth century – it wasn't in bad condition. Saskia had explained that most of the Bibles that came her way were in a far worse state and in need of extensive restoration.

During the drive here from Cambridge he had hoped he might recognise the Bible, that it might jog his memory in some way and magically help him find the remaining notebook. If indeed it still existed all these years later. It was always possible that it had got lost or thrown away a long time ago, just as this one so very nearly had. But trust Jacob to hide something so well it could be so easily lost! Had that been his intention, an amusing and elaborate ruse on his part? Or with the passing of years had the notebooks simply lost their importance to him and been abandoned to obscurity?

Matthew had asked James if he could remember seeing the Bible, or anything similar, when he'd helped with clearing out the loft and all his friend could come up with was that there were a couple of trunks which he hadn't exactly gone through with a fine-tooth comb, having decided they were full of manky old blankets and curtains.

Try as he might, Matthew couldn't recall seeing this Bible before, but for that matter he couldn't recall ever seeing Jacob reading a religious book of this sort, whether it was the Torah, the Koran or the Bible. He had to wonder why Jacob had picked this particular tome for a hiding place. Was it merely that the size of it lent itself so readily? In which case, had he used another Bible in the same manner? Or was its use a clue in some way that would lead him to the second instalment of the story?

Jacob had always maintained that he was Jewish by birth but agnostic by inclination. He spoke often about the fundamental need in the human psyche to believe in something bigger than oneself, if for no other reason than to hold somebody else accountable when things took a nasty turn. True to his contrary nature, he would sweepingly condemn organised religion of any kind, but then say he believed in people who had a faith, no matter the source or direction. He also happily admitted to a fondness for the ritual of religion, which he referred to as his vice for spiritual theatricality. No finer example was the siren call of evensong at King's College in Cambridge in his opinion. He would also visit the synagogue in the city now and then. A spiritual awareness had nothing to do with institutional doctrine, he would say when Matthew questioned him on the myriad contradictions he espoused. His bottom line was that a person should be allowed to benefit from mysticism if he so chose, yet not be forced to deny himself the ability to think for himself.

The freedom of disciplined thought had been one of Jacob's great obsessions and as a tutor at Cambridge his sole mission had been to instil in his students a hunger to think for themselves. It was something he drummed into Matthew as well. He abhorred students who were happy to follow the path of least resistance, to do only what was necessary to pass exams. 'The country needs original thinkers, not sheep,' was a frequent grumble of his whenever he came across what he perceived to be a decline in educational standards. But Jacob was always gracious in anything he tried to teach Matthew; he never ridiculed, he never humiliated, instead he gently encouraged with persuasive argument and razor-sharp thinking. Matthew counted himself privileged and extremely lucky to have been on the receiving end of Jacob's attention from so young an age.

But it was an eye-opening discovery for Matthew to realise that when Jacob had been young he had suffered acutely with a lack of self-confidence, and that he saw himself as a misfit. Mostly Matthew could see it stemmed from the combination of his ethnic background and growing up in the East End of London. And, of course, the times in which he lived would have shaped his thinking or, more precisely, the thinking of those around him.

When had it changed for Jacob? Matthew wondered. When had Jacob decided he was anybody's equal? Did that come when he returned to Cambridge, not as a student, but as a tutor?

Matthew would never have believed it, but there were unmistakable similarities between Jacob's younger self and his own – the feeling of not fitting in, and the social awkwardness that that perceived inadequacy generated. Had Jacob recognised those feelings in Matthew when he'd been a boy? Was that why he'd taken him under his wing and appointed himself his mentor?

The question Matthew found most difficult to answer was the obvious one – for whom had Jacob written *The Dandelion Years*? For his own benefit, or had he had a recipient in mind? Had he imagined Kitty reading it? Or subsequent generations of a family he assumed he might have one day?

Matthew had taken the notebook with him while he'd been working in Carlisle, and it was one evening as he lay on the bed of his hotel room rereading part of it that he received a phone call from the last person on earth he expected to hear from.

'I just thought I'd give you a ring,' Fliss said, 'to see how you were.' She sounded upbeat, not at all like a girlfriend who had been heartlessly dumped. 'How are you?'

'Stuck in a depressing hotel room in Carlisle,' he'd said, doing his best to hide his shock that she'd phoned him. 'How are you? You sound well.'

'I'm fine. I'm in London for a few days for a radiologist conference.'

'How's it going?'

'I'm one of the speakers tomorrow, so I'm feeling a bit on edge.'

'You'll be fine.'

'That's what you always used to say.'

'And was I ever wrong?'

They'd spoken at length, mostly about work-related things, until finally, Fliss said, 'I miss you, Matthew ...'

Hearing the simple honesty in her voice and knowing that he'd hurt her badly and wanting to make amends, he said, 'I'm sorry for the way things ended between us. I was pretty shitty to you. You didn't deserve that.'

'No, I don't believe I did, but you were upset at the time. It was understandable; you'd lost somebody you loved. Do you think you might like to meet up again, just for a drink, maybe?'

They did, a few days later when they were both back in Cambridge. They went out for dinner and sitting across the table from her, remembering how it had once been between them, Matthew told himself he'd been a fool to end it with her. The evening had ended with a tentative kiss, almost as though they were on first-date terms. There had been two subsequent nights out together since then, both of which Matthew had enjoyed.

Across the workbench, Saskia was mouthing another

apology at Matthew and rolling her eyes in a would-the-caller-ever-stop-talking expression? He gestured that it was fine for her to carry on and, leaving the Bible on the work-bench, he moved away to go and take a look at something he guessed was some sort of press. Either that or it was an instrument of torture.

Saskia's work intrigued him. As indeed the girl herself did. Initially he had found her to be a bit cool and aloof, quite different to the friendly openness of her father, but gradually he had seen a thaw in her. Certainly she couldn't have been more pleasant on the phone earlier when he'd phoned to ask if he could call in. Inviting him to join her family for supper was a definite improvement on that first meeting at Glaskin House and having turned down her father's invitation, he'd felt it would be rude to say no this time round. Besides, it would be good to have the opportunity to discuss the future of Jacob's book collection with Ralph.

But that aside, he was amused and touched by her obvious interest in Jacob, a man she had never known. Moreover, it might be fun to enlist her help to find the concluding part to the story.

'I'm sorry about that,' she said, her call now finished.

'No worries, business is business.' He'd caught enough of the conversation to understand that it was someone wanting to discuss the binding of a dissertation. 'What's this for?' he asked, indicating the machine that looked like a press.

'It's what we call a nipping press.'

'It looks old.'

'It's Victorian. My grandfathers bought it for me on my twenty-first birthday.'

'Is that when you decided to become a book restorer?'

'No, I'd already been doing it for some time. I suppose you could say it was inevitable I'd end up doing something book related.'

'I have to say it all looks and sounds a lot more inter-esting than anything I do.' He pointed to another piece of equipment that had caught his notice. 'And what's that?'

'It's a hot foil blocker – I use it for decorative finishes.' But as if bringing an end to his nosiness and getting down to the purpose of his visit, she stepped around the workbench towards the Bible. Joining her, he opened it to reveal the cutaway compartment. 'Have you found anything like this before?' he asked.

She shook her head. 'Only the usual kind of thing such as letters and photographs tucked inside the pages. More often it's very dull stuff, such as bus and train or theatre tickets. Shopping lists turn up all the time, and dried flowers. But never anything so deliberately or so well hidden.'

'Do you think there's a chance something else could be hidden in any of the books you valued at the house? And please don't think I'm suggesting you overlooked anything when carrying out the valuation.'

She nodded her head thoughtfully. 'It's possible something could have slipped through the net. For instance, with a particularly sizeable set of books we often only look at one or two of them because that provides us with sufficient information to make an overall valuation.'

'So that's my first starting point, then,' he said, closing the Bible, 'to hunt through the shelves for any likely candidates large enough in which to hide a notebook.'

'I'd be happy to help.'

He smiled. 'Funnily enough I was hoping you might say that. You're not free tomorrow by any chance, are you?'

'I have nothing pressing, so yes.'

He hesitated. 'Was that a joke?'

She looked at him blankly.

He pointed to the Victorian cast-iron press.

'Ah,' she said with a small smile, 'I see what you mean. But no, no joke or pun intended. I'll give you fair warning when that happens. Shall we go across to the house now?'

In the low evening sunlight he walked with her across the lawn towards the attractive Suffolk Pink thatched cottage.

Climbing roses that were yet to flower covered the sloping walls and Matthew could imagine how they would add to the idyllic charm of the place. Rounding the far side of the house and heading for the back door, he presumed, a couple of hens appeared, their heads down as if competing in a race as they rushed towards them. A few yards behind, and pausing from their pecking at the grass around a hencoop, another four raised their heads to take a look. Unimpressed, they went back to their pecking. Beyond the hencoop there was a greenhouse and then a row of tall Lombardy poplar trees that formed the boundary between the garden and a large field of rapeseed that was on the verge of flowering. With a soft breeze rustling the leaves on the poplar trees and making them sound as if they were whispering amongst themselves, Matthew slowed his step to try and take in as much of the view as he could; it really was quite beautiful.

'How long have you lived here?' he asked.

'We came here when I was ten years old,' Saskia said quietly, also slowing her step to match his. 'And by we, I mean my father and two grandfathers.'

Noting the absence of any mention of a mother, Matthew wasn't sure what to say next. So he said nothing, just continued to enjoy the stunning view and the sound of birdsong from all around.

'We came here to recover from the shock of a car accident that killed my mother and grandmothers,' she said.

He turned to look at her, but before he could think of anything remotely appropriate to say, she said, 'Please don't feel the need to comment, I just thought it would be better that you know some of our history, rather than spend the evening contemplating our less-than-conventional set-up here.'

Wondering if it was ever possible for a family to recover from such a profoundly devastating shock, it struck Matthew that every time he came in contact with Saskia Granger, he was presented with a new impression of her.

Chapter Twenty-Eight

The next morning, Saskia arrived at Glaskin House precisely at ten thirty.

'Exactly on time,' Matthew said when he opened the door to her.

'I'm a bit OCD when it comes to punctuality,' she said. 'I hate to be late.'

'Me too. What would you say to a bacon sandwich before we get started?'

Having bypassed Harvey's Saturday breakfast special in favour of getting here on time, her answer was: 'I'd say thank you very much.'

He smiled. 'Correct response as otherwise, and out of politeness, I would have been forced to forego one myself.'

He led her to the kitchen where she took off her jacket and slipped it over the back of a chair. 'Anything I can do to help?' she asked, surveying the antiquated cupboards and appliances while watching him place rashers of bacon on an ancient and seriously blackened grill pan.

'You can make the coffee if you like. The kettle's not far off boiling.'

Remembering where everything was kept, she did as he said.

'I have two confessions to make,' he said, sliding the grill pan into place.

'Oh yes?'

'I made a start on our search last night when I got back.'

'You're perfectly entitled to search through your own book collection, you don't need my permission to do it.'

'True, but I sort of feel this is your search as much as mine. You're the one who set this thing in motion and if it wasn't for you, I wouldn't have this new and extraordinary insight into Jacob. So I guess sharing the hunt is my small way to thank you for that.'

'You're not just humouring me because of what Oliver said last night, are you?' To her embarrassment her grandfather had gone on just a little too much for her liking about her fascination with the notebook. 'She was like a dog with a bone when she found it,' he'd told Matthew more than once, 'she wouldn't let anyone else get a look at it.'

'Not at all,' Matthew said. 'He's quite a character, isn't he? Harvey too. It was a fun evening, so thanks again for inviting me.'

She poured milk into their coffee and slid a mug towards him. With the appetising smell of coffee and bacon cooking now filling the kitchen, she watched him at work, buttering four slices of bread. When he'd done that he went back to the grill and, using a fork, he began turning the bacon over, each rasher exactly the same distance from the other.

Observing how methodical he was, and approving of it, Saskia thought of her father's comment last night immediately after Matthew had left, about how nice it was having him join them for supper. 'Nothing loaded in that statement, then,' Saskia had muttered, deliberately not pausing in wiping down the kitchen table and stacking the mats.

'Nothing loaded at all,' he'd said with a shrug that was just a bit too careless to be anything but forced. 'Just merely stating the case as we all saw it.' He looked to Oliver and Harvey for backup, who, as though primed and ready to agree with anything her father said about Matthew, nodded enthusiastically.

'I've warned you before about matchmaking, Dad,' she'd said, 'so why don't you leave me be and tootle off to have a chat with Libby on the phone – it must be all of five hours since you last spoke to each other.'

This had caused Harvey and Oliver to laugh, and with his face reddening fast Dad had had the grace to leave her alone. He was almost out of the kitchen when he flung one last remark at her. 'All I'm saying is you might like to consider why he's invited you back to Glaskin House. It's not as though he couldn't look for the missing notebook on his own.'

'It's a fair question,' Harvey said, when her father had closed the door after him. 'The lad obviously enjoys your company.'

'Don't you start as well. Honestly, what is it with you lot? Suddenly you all seem intent on fixing me up.'

Pouring himself a nightcap of whisky, Oliver had said, 'We'd just like to see you with the right young man, somebody who deserves you. We're not going to hand you over to any old idiot, you know.'

'And who says Matthew Gray isn't an idiot?'

'He struck me as a very decent sort,' Oliver had said. 'A decent sort' was the highest accolade Grandpa O could bestow on a person.

'A conclusion based on a couple of hours spent in his company?' Saskia had challenged him.

'I pride myself on being a pretty good judge of character,' he'd asserted, his bushy eyebrows practically standing to attention with dogged conviction.

Exasperated, she'd given up on the conversation. But a small part of her had mulled it over in bed last night and again when she drove here. Was she merely, for the sake of it, being stubborn in dismissing the idea that Matthew might actually enjoy her company? And didn't she, if she were honest, like him a lot better now she was beginning to get to know him?

'What's your other confession?' she asked, remembering that Matthew had said he had two to make.

'It's not really a confession, more of an oversight of something I forgot to tell you last night. I've been doing some poking around online and firstly I've found that Jacob's name appears on a roll call of people who worked at Bletchley.'

'Does that mean you found Kitty's as well and we now have a surname for her?'

'I'm afraid not. There are no specific Kittys that I could find, but quite a few Katherines, or the equivalent name with slightly different spellings. I also searched for Fanley Manor in Sussex, and drew a blank. Which is odd, given that Jacob referred to Kitty telling him the family home was mentioned in the Domesday Book. Which leaves me with the only conclusion: Jacob made up the name of the house.'

'To preserve some kind of anonymity, do you think?' Saskia said, fearing that Matthew was going to say that perhaps that wasn't the only thing Jacob had made up. For some reason she wanted to believe in *The Dandelion Years*; she didn't want Jacob and Kitty's romance to be reduced to the level of a fairy tale.

'I'd say so, yes. It could be that Kitty wasn't her real name, either.'

'Then why would he give her the equivalent pet name in Russian?'

'Makes for a good story, I suppose, and it made it more personal for Jacob perhaps, an echo of his roots.' He took a sip of his coffee. 'The truth is, I don't know. And maybe we never will.'

Not if I have anything to do with it, thought Saskia.

Their bacon sandwiches and coffee finished, they started work in the library, carefully and systematically checking any books of a size that could conceal a notebook in the same way the Bible had. They worked well together, slipping into a quick and efficient rhythm and chatting easily. He told her about the first time he came to Glaskin House with his mother and Jacob, how it had been a visit to convince her to take on the full-time job as Jacob's housekeeper. He spoke of her death and how it had affected not just him, but Jacob as well. 'Life was never the same again here,' Matthew was now explaining. 'That was when I began staying in the house with Jacob rather than The Coach House on my visits back.'

'Was Jacob lonely?'

'Yes, although he'd never admit as much. And before you ask, there was never anything but friendship and respect between him and Mum.'

'Did she not ever want to marry again? From what you say, she'd been on her own ever since your father left you both.'

'I guess she fitted into that category where for some people remarriage just isn't a priority. Or rather, her priorities changed. I think she got used to her new life and didn't want it to change. She was very happy here. She had friends in the village and an active social life. I think there was also an element of loyalty and gratitude towards Jacob that she felt. He did so much for us.'

'What about Jacob? For some reason I can't quite imagine him as the sociable sort, but was he actively involved in the village?'

'He showed his face when he wanted to, but in essence he was a natural loner and liked to perpetuate the myth that he was a grumpy old sod. Which he wasn't; he had a great sense of humour, he was just very particular with whom he spent time.'

'He seems to have lived a very ...' she hesitated, wanting to find the right way of putting it, '... a very comfortable lifestyle. Is that normal for a retired Cambridge professor?'

'He never liked to discuss money, but I gather he inherited a fair amount from his parents and invested wisely.'

'But his parents were hairdressers. Surely they didn't have that much money?'

Matthew laughed. 'Initially that was the case but from owning a couple of salons in the East End they went on to open one in Mayfair, and from there they branched out with a chain of salons around the country. Have you heard of a hairdresser called Mr Teasy-Weasy?'

She smiled. 'Is that a Beatrix Potter character?'

'Sounds as if it should be, but his real name was Raymond Bessone and he was the first real celebrity hairdresser, even had his own television programme back in the sixties. Jacob's parents saw the effect he had on the hairdressing world and shrewdly decided to get in on the act and raise their game. It was a decision that changed their lives and fortunes dramatically.'

Enjoying this new insight into Jacob and his family, she said, 'Do you know if they were disappointed that Jacob didn't follow them into the business, especially once it was so successful?'

'Jacob never said as much, but then, as he often observed, they'd educated him out of it so could hardly grumble when he showed no interest in being a hairdresser. And whenever he spoke of his family, I had the feeling he was immensely proud of them and what they achieved. They were a close-knit family from what he told me, and his Grandma Lila was probably the most influential character in his young life. She was the one who stressed the importance of having a proper education. He regularly quoted her, especially towards the end of his life.'

Storing away all this new information about Jacob, Saskia was spurred on with a renewed sense of purpose to find the concluding part to *The Dandelion Years*.

She had moved on to another area of shelves when Matthew said, 'I know it's not quite the same thing, and I don't want to sound insensitive, but how about your father and grandfathers: didn't they, once they'd recovered from their grief, want to remarry?'

It was a question she'd been asked many times over the years. 'Like your mother, their priorities changed and I think before they knew it, it was too late. Although perhaps not for my father.' She explained about her father and Libby, though skimmed over the details of their relationship ten years ago.

'And how do you feel about that?'

'I'm pleased for him. I am, really. I have no plans to turn into a monstrously possessive daughter with a psychotic hatred of stepmothers.'

'Hmm ... interesting choice of words.'

She was about to retaliate, when she saw the smile on Matthew's face and realised he was teasing her. 'And there was me thinking you weren't so bad after all.'

'Oh? How bad did you view me? And why was that?'

Annoyed that she'd walked into a trap of her own making, she concentrated on sliding a large and heavy cloth-bound book back into place. 'No reason,' she said, 'just a turn of phrase.'

'I don't believe you. I think we got off to a bad start the first day you came here with your father. I think my mood over the boiler affected your judgement of me, which I readily accept was understandable. But are you always so quick to judge?'

Surprised at his candour, she stopped what she was doing and looked at him. 'And are you always so direct?'

'Touché. But I'm right, aren't I?'

'Is that important to you, to be right?'

'I just like to know where I stand.'

'Even if it's on the precipice of rudeness?'

'Oh, especially so!'

She suddenly laughed. 'Then you're lucky my judgemental temperament is counterbalanced by such an abundantly forgiving nature.'

'Phew,' he said with a smile, 'that's a relief.'

When they'd finished checking all the likely candidates in the library, they moved on to the drawing room. Finding nothing there, they started on the dining room, a dark and dismally oppressive room that Saskia suspected probably hadn't been used in a very long time.

Drawing a blank in it, they ventured upstairs.

'I'd hate to think we're on a fool's errand,' Matthew said

when they were on the landing, 'but the more places we search, the more I can't help but think that if there'd ever been a continuation to the first notebook, it must have been taken away by the house clearance people and is now buried deep in some landfill site.'

'Trust me, if a book had been involved, Gil would have sent it Dad's way.'

'But only if he came across an *actual* book. If it was wrapped in something that looked so worthless he just threw it away, we're scuppered, aren't we?'

'Direct as well as defeatist,' Saskia said with a smile. 'Didn't have you down as that. I thought you were the tenacious type who had to keep on digging until you found the answer.'

He gave her a rueful smile. 'I hadn't realised until now what a painful business it is to be hoisted by one's own petard.'

'You'll get over it, I'm sure. But let's think about the matter in hand logically. You thought the Bible could have been inside a trunk of old blankets in the attic, yes?'

'Based on what James said, it's a possibility.'

'So let's forget about searching books for a moment. Who would have put trunks of junk up there? Jacob? Or maybe your mother?'

'Jacob hated to throw anything away, so odds-on he'd have put stuff in the loft rather than the bin, if only to defy Mum and her quest to keep things in a manageable state. As far as I know, she never went near the loft. She certainly wouldn't have been able to put a trunk up there on her own. As a child I went up there a couple of times, just out of curiosity, because it was somewhere to explore on a rainy day.'

'So odds-on the notebook had been hiding there in the trunk for years and years.'

'But that doesn't explain why the second notebook, or however many more there might be, weren't hidden together.

Knowing how Jacob revered order and method, it all seems a bit half-cocked to me.'

'But maybe Jacob *did* hide them together and somebody else either deliberately split things up, or in the process of a tidy-up didn't realise what they were doing. Maybe the books were carefully stored out of sight by Jacob in his bedroom, away from prying eyes and then—'

'Hang on,' interrupted Matthew, 'what about the removal men who moved Jacob here from Cambridge? What if they just threw what they thought was a load of old blankets into a trunk and ... '

'And that trunk was then stored in the attic,' Saskia finished for him. 'Yes, that could work. Or it could have been done in a previous move.'

'It's a likely scenario, just as so many could be, but it doesn't help us find the next instalment, does it?'

Having got carried away with the conclusion they'd reached, Saskia felt slightly deflated at Matthew's comment. 'What else is up there in the attic?' she asked. If there were straws to be clutched, she was going to grab every last one of them.

'Nothing. I cleared it all out with James.'

'Is there anywhere else where old blankets and the like are stored?'

Looking directly at her, Matthew did that head-tilting thing of his and narrowed his eyes. Except this time he'd added a small frown that creased his forehead. 'If you don't mind me saying, you're beginning to sound obsessed with blankets.'

'Humour me. Where's the most obvious place anyone stores that sort of thing?'

He frowned. 'I haven't a clue.'

'An airing cupboard, of course. Where is it? You do have one here, don't you?'

'Yes, it's next door to the bathroom at the far—'

But before he'd even finished, she'd set off to the furthest end of the landing. 'This door?' she asked.

He caught up with her and pulled the door open with a hefty tug. Within minutes they had everything out and spread over the landing floor. Just as Saskia had imagined, there were towels, sheets, blankets and any number of old bed coverings. But no sign of any books. Disappointed, and feeling foolish for her outburst of certainty, she muttered an apology and began putting things back where they'd been.

'It was a perfectly plausible idea,' Matthew said, dealing with the highest shelves which were out of reach for her, 'you had me convinced.'

'Close but no banana,' she said, taking off her cardigan, the warmth of the hot water tank having got to her.

'Maybe we should check all the cupboards and wardrobes for blankets.'

'I've gone off the idea of blankets now,' she said. 'Besides, how many can a bachelor have?'

'Worth a look all the same. Come on, where's your Sherlock spirit?'

'I suppose the most obvious ones to search would be in Jacob's room.'

'I've emptied those, and it was just clothes. Let's try this room.'

She followed him into the nearest bedroom where opposite the bed was a colossal mahogany wardrobe. She remembered thinking before, when she and Dad were here to do the probate valuation, that it was so large it wouldn't fit through the average doorway – it certainly wouldn't fit anywhere at Ashcombe.

'You take the right side, I'll do the left,' Matthew said.

'You know I asked you to humour me earlier?'

'Yes?'

'Well, you can stop now.'

'And there were you calling me defeatist. Get on with your side of the wardrobe, and after we've searched through all the other cupboards, we'll revert to Plan A and go back to checking books.'

They searched through the age-old undisturbed contents of the wardrobes, the air rapidly becoming tainted by the musty smell of old pillows, eiderdowns and household junk that hadn't seen the light of day for goodness knows how long. 'Oh, what's this?' asked Saskia, finally coming across something of interest. It was a box containing some sort of candleholder. On closer inspection she realised it was a seven-branch brass menorah. She handed it to Matthew, then bent down to the remaining item in the box. 'Is this a samovar?' she asked, holding up a badly tarnished urn about two feet tall with a tap at the bottom.

'I think you might be right.'

Going over to the dressing table, Saskia set it down so they could get a better look at it. 'It needs a good clean and a polish,' she said, 'but I'd say it's worth keeping. It's rather lovely.'

Unlike the rest of the stuff now littering the carpet, she thought, while Matthew inspected the samovar more closely.

And still there was no sign of a second notebook.

Chapter Twenty-Nine

Any misgivings Ralph had initially experienced about Libby working in the shop with him had long since been dispelled; he couldn't believe now that he'd questioned the wisdom of agreeing to her offer of help.

'I know what you're thinking, Ralph,' she'd said when she'd first come up with the idea, 'you're worried what will happen if we have a falling out. Well, why don't we worry about that if it actually occurs? Meanwhile, Pat's retiring and you need somebody reliable and enthusiastic. Guess what, that person's me!'

It was one of the many things about Libby that he liked, her pragmatic and wholly refreshing what-the-hell attitude. It brought home to him how cautious and risk averse he was. Not to put too fine a point on it, he suspected that having become ruled by habit, he'd turned into a very boring man who'd forgotten how to have fun. Thank God Libby seemed to be on a mission to put that right. And how ironic that the very thing he'd been worried about happening to Saskia – being stuck in a rut – had already happened to him.

He watched Libby listening to a customer explain that she was looking for a birthday present for her husband – the man was a keen collector of angling books and she wondered if they had anything suitable.

Since coming to work for Ralph, and in no time at all, Libby had thoroughly memorised the stock so she knew exactly the best book to show this customer. It was one that was kept in the pair of locked glass-fronted cabinets at the back of the shop where the more valuable books were kept.

The Compleat Angler by Izaak Walton, with its green cloth and gilt lettering, was a first edition in near-mint condition, but its real joy lay in the exquisite colour illustrations by James Thorpe. The plates were so beautiful that it was enough to make Ralph take up fishing himself!

He liked to think his books, especially the high-quality editions, were meant to stay in his safekeeping until just the right customer came along who could offer the book a good home. Observing this particular customer and noting the way she was handling the book as she carefully turned the pages under Libby's watchful gaze, Ralph decided she was a safe bet. At five hundred pounds, the book wasn't cheap, but he hoped the woman was feeling generous towards her husband.

She was, and offering the new personal service of gift-wrapping, Libby completed the transaction with the kind of friendly warmth that had attracted Ralph to her in the first place.

When the woman had gone, after thanking Libby for solving the problem of what to get her husband, Ralph went over to Libby and kissed her.

'That's called sexual harassment in the workplace, you know,' she said, kissing him back.

'Even if it was to say thank you for clinching such a great sale?'

She tutted. 'Rewarding an employee with a sexual advance? I fear you're adding to your crime.'

He held her in his arms. 'Then I have bad news for you, because with what I've got in mind for us this evening, you might just as well lock me up now and throw away the key.'

'Mmm ... tell me more.'

'I thought we'd go out for dinner and then maybe I'd come back to your place and—' He leant in to whisper in her ear, but out of the corner of his eye he saw a familiar face pressed against the window of the shop. It was Gil and he had a grin on him a mile wide.

'Oh hell,' Ralph muttered, 'I think the whole of Chelstead is about to be told about us.'

Libby turned in his arms. 'What else do you expect if you insist on smooching in full view of the window? And you're kidding yourself if you think the town hasn't already sussed us.'

The door opened and carrying a cardboard box, Gil came in. 'Hello, hello,' he chorused cheerfully. 'Business must be picking up nicely for you, Ralphy-Boy, if you have time for canoodling in the middle of the day. Or is it a slack time?' Without waiting for a response, or expecting one, he nodded at Libby. 'Gilbert Ross, house clearance specialist to the rich and famous, and at your service, should you be requiring anything cleared out.'

Completely unfazed, Libby said, 'I've heard about you.'

'All good reportage I hope.'

'Exemplary reportage.'

'Now, Ralphy-Boy, if you could take your mind off the charming lady for a minute, I have something here for you. I was having a bit of a tidy-up and came across this little lot shoved under a pile of things my sons must have dumped in the lock-up. I reckoned in view of your pestering about that clearance job I did at Glaskin House some time back – oh, and sorry I never returned your calls. How many messages did you leave me?'

'A couple,' Ralph said, his eyes firmly on what Gil was holding. 'I was beginning to think you were avoiding me.'

'As if. Anyway, in view of your pestering, I thought this might be of interest to you.' He held out the box to Ralph. 'A less-than-reputable dealer would have kept it to himself, but I'm a believer in playing fairly, so let's just say you owe me.'

Chapter Thirty

'What's this?' asked Fliss, when Matthew returned from the bathroom to his bedroom and found her half-dressed and holding the black leather-bound notebook he'd left on the chest of drawers. Seeing how carelessly she was flicking through the pages, he had to curb the strong impulse to take it from her.

'It belonged to Jacob,' he said matter-of-factly.

Still flicking through the pages, she said, 'And they say doctors have bad handwriting! It's as good as unreadable. What is it, a diary?'

Now he did take the book from her, and pulling open his sock drawer, he slipped it inside. 'Not as such,' he said, evasively, 'and sorry to hurry you, but I have an eight-forty-five meeting.'

She smiled. 'You told me that earlier when your alarm went off and you started hustling me out of bed.'

'Hustling's a bit unfair,' he said with a frown.

'I'm joking.' Still smiling, she watched him remove the towel that was tied around his middle. For some reason she had always enjoyed watching him dress or undress. Apparently he did things in an illogical order which she found endearing, like putting his socks and shoes on before his shirt. Before she'd brought this to his attention he'd never been aware of putting his clothes on in any particular order. As far as he was concerned, he simply got dressed. Subconsciously OCD, she'd once remarked. The recollection made him think of Saskia and her admission that she was punctually OCD.

It was now Wednesday and three days since he'd last seen Saskia and her family – three days since he'd been in possession of the second notebook, which had shown up inside a large antique and very ornate Russian Orthodox Bible, together with a ring. Matthew had personally phoned the house clearance man – Gil Ross – to thank him for handing over the Bible to Ralph. Had it not been for the good relationship that existed between the two men, who knew where these precious items would have ended up?

Much to Matthew's frustration, circumstances had annoyingly conspired against him in the last three days, preventing him from having the time to read what happened next in Jacob's story. Knowing how keen Saskia was to continue, he regretted now not insisting that she take the book to read first, but she'd been adamant that he was the rightful owner and therefore he must read it before her. He'd accused her of succumbing to an attack of extreme and misplaced politeness, but she had refused to budge, probably taking it for granted that he'd have the book read in no time and would hand it over to her. But since Saturday evening when he'd returned to Ashcombe to collect this latest find, and had then been invited to stay for supper again, just about every minute of each day had been snatched from him. Sunday morning at Glaskin House he'd overslept, then after getting through the work he'd brought with him to do, Mal and Jenny had invited him over for a late lunch. Before he knew it, it was time to drive back to Cambridge. It was during the drive home that Fliss had called him and said there was a week of Hitchcock films on at the Picturehouse and did he fancy seeing *Vertigo* the following evening. He wasn't a big Hitchcock fan, but to say no would have given her the wrong message and besides seeing Fliss again would be no hardship.

So that was Monday evening and then last night they'd had dinner and afterwards, knowing that James would be staying the night with a new girlfriend, Matthew had invited

Fliss back for a coffee. 'Is that a euphemism for what I think it is?' she'd asked.

'Just coffee,' he'd replied lightly. 'I wouldn't presume to think you'd be fooled by such an obvious ploy.'

'Maybe I wouldn't view it that way,' she'd said.

Whether he took the initiative or Fliss did, he couldn't really remember, but the evening had been rounded off with them in bed together and her staying the night. Probably just as they had both thought it would.

Having selected a white shirt – all his work shirts were identical in style and colour – he pulled it on and looked at Fliss as she slipped the dress she'd worn last night over her head. How many times had they previously enacted this very same scene, the hurried shower and dressing before a quick breakfast and then rushing off in their different directions to work? The comfortable familiarity of the moment made him think it was as if the last few months of not seeing each other had never happened. He was still ashamed of his petulant outburst on the day of Jacob's funeral and whenever he referred to his behaviour, Fliss told him to stop beating himself up over it.

'Grief made you angry and upset, I quite understand,' she'd said. Perversely, her understanding served to make him feel even more ashamed.

He went over to her and, doing the zip up on the back of her dress, he quietly said, 'I don't deserve your forgiveness.'

She turned around and faced him, clearly surprised by his words. 'I thought we'd covered that.'

'We did, but I can't—'

She placed a finger to his lips. 'Whatever it is you keep thinking, don't. We're fine now. Aren't we?'

He gently pushed her finger away from his mouth. 'Yes,' he said. 'We're fine.'

She smiled. 'Good. Shall I see you tonight?'

He thought of Jacob's notebook in the chest of drawers

behind him. It would keep another night, surely? But then he thought of Saskia patiently waiting to read it.

'I'll probably have to work late tonight,' he said. 'How about tomorrow evening?'

Why, he wondered, much later that day, had he lied to Fliss?

He was sitting at his desk, absently scratching his chin while staring out of the window on to the street below, his eyes tracking the progress of a girl in a pair of ridiculously high wedged shoes as she wheeled a pink-and-purple suitcase in the direction of the station that was a short five-minute walk away. Five minutes in normal shoes, he thought.

Why hadn't he told Fliss about Jacob's notebook and his desire to have a quiet evening in to read it? Perhaps because in so many ways Jacob had been at the heart of their bust-up and he didn't want to appear as though he was choosing an evening in with Jacob in preference to one with Fliss.

Even so, the question he really needed to ask himself was why hadn't he shared *The Dandelion Years* with her? Why had he felt such a strong, protective need to stop her from casually flicking through it? Did he think she wouldn't be sensitive to what Jacob had written?

Or was it merely he felt so protective of Jacob and the memory of the man he'd loved that he couldn't bear to let just anybody glimpse the vulnerable man Jacob had once been?

But Fliss wasn't just 'anybody', she was his girlfriend.

That they had managed to repair their relationship was something he hadn't thought would ever happen. Or, indeed, if it was what he had ever wanted. Their getting back to-gether was something that had just fallen into place, simply and naturally, as though he'd played no conscious part in the manner of its happening. Which was nonsense. Of course he'd played his part. It was just that it didn't feel as if he had.

He was jolted out of his thoughts by the unwelcome manifestation of a cumbersome figure in his doorway. Jim

Rycroft, a blunt-speaking bear of a Yorkshireman with an ego the size of his county of birth, was the most senior of the partners and for the most part, being low enough down the food chain in the firm, Matthew had managed to avoid too much direct contact with him. On the few occasions their paths did cross, it was rarely a pleasant experience.

Matthew had been working at the firm for less than a week when he'd been accosted by a mighty roar that had stopped him in his tracks. Having cycled into work that morning, he'd been on his way to the gents to swap his jeans and T-shirt for his suit.

'Where'd do you think you're going?' Jim Rycroft had bellowed the length of the carpeted corridor. 'Come here at once!' It turned out he'd mistaken Matthew for a courier he was expecting with important documents. There had been no apology, just a curt instruction that Matthew should smarten himself up and get his hair cut so there'd be no further incidents of mistaken identity. Matthew ignored the instruction. He didn't care who paid his wages, his hair was his own business and whatever the style or length, it in no way affected how he worked, or the results he produced.

'A man who has time to stare out of the window hasn't enough to do,' the thickset Yorkshireman growled from the doorway.

'I was thinking,' Matthew said quite truthfully.

The man came further into the cramped office, instantly crowding it with his considerable bulk. 'Word is you do a lot of that.'

'I find it generally helps.'

The man's eyes bored into him as though assessing the strength of insubordination contained within the reply. The corners of his mouth dropped and he emitted a snort, but apparently satisfied that Matthew hadn't stepped too far out of line, he said, 'I hear also that despite all outwards appearances your approach generates good results. The client up in Carlisle was very happy with the outcome of the case last week. I also hear that you're an inscrutable bugger in court, so that's why I want you assigned to work on a case with my team.'

Masking his surprise, Matthew said, 'What about the Rawlins' case I've just started work on?'

'You can leave that. I've cleared it with Doug.'

'Who's the client?'

'Sir Desmond Leamington, the chairman of the Leamington Manufacturing Group. He's accusing his old Cambridge college of fraud.'

His attention now fully engaged, Matthew sat forward in his seat, rested his elbows on his desk. 'It's a brave man who takes on the university. Which college is it?'

'Merchant College.' A meaty paw raised, Jim Rycroft slapped the large, three-inch-thick file he'd been holding on to Matthew's desk. It landed with a heavy thud, displacing the other papers Matthew had been going through. 'Read that and be at my office nine-thirty tomorrow morning for a full briefing. Don't be late.'

What were the chances, thought Matthew when he was alone and had pulled the file with its Rorschach-test tea or coffee stain on the front cover towards him, Jacob's old college?

His next thought was one of annoyance as he realised the time he'd set aside this evening to make a start on Jacob's second instalment of *The Dandelion Years* had been snatched from him. Served him right for lying to Fliss, he supposed.

But thinking again of Saskia, patiently waiting her turn to read the book, he decided there was nothing else for it, he'd just have stay up extra late.

Chapter Thirty-One

September 1943

Such was my newfound happiness with Kitty it was almost possible to forget there was a war on. Even the harridan that was Mrs Pridmore, with her undisguised disapprobation, failed to bother me in my blissful state.

Without intentionally meaning to, I had taken to whistling or singing to myself, a hitherto unknown activity on my part. On this particular morning, as I fairly bounced down the stairs with a tune on my lips, and entered the dining room to endure yet another diabolical breakfast before setting off for my daytime shift, Farrington looked up at me from the book he was reading at the table. 'I don't think I can take much more of your jollity, Belinsky! Do please kindly refrain in future.'

From the mildly amused expression on his face I knew his comment was not meant unkindly, so I pulled out my chair, sat down and asked if there was a song he'd prefer I hummed.

Griffiths appeared at that moment in the dining room and heard my question. 'Oh, for pity's sake, he's not at it again, is he?'

'The man's in love, what else can we expect of him?'

Despite our strongest efforts to keep our relationship a secret, rumours had begun to circulate at the Park about Kitty and me, rumours that we neither confirmed nor denied. We took the view that an enigmatic response was best; let people believe what they wanted to believe.

'I'll tell you what *I* expect,' said Mrs Pridmore, crashing against the half-open door with a tray loaded with rattling crockery and cutlery, 'I expect a bit of decorum in my house. What I don't expect is to have my eardrums bombarded at all hours, morning, noon, and night. What was that dreadful noise I heard as you came down the stairs?'

'It's a song called "Katyushka",' I answered good-humouredly, determined to prove nothing could dampen my spirits.

She shuddered with distaste. 'Sounds foreign to me.'

'Upon my word, Mrs Pridmore, how very perceptive you are this morning! Top marks to you! It is indeed a little medley from Russia about a young girl pining for her soldier husband.'

Banging the crockery down on the table in a declaration of open warfare, she said, 'I'll mind you not to take that tone with me, Mr Belsinky.'

'Bel*insky*,' I enunciated with such pointed clarity it drew forth a snigger from Farrington across the table. 'My name is Bel*insky*.'

Shooting a look at Farrington who was now clearing his throat exaggeratedly and returning his attention to his book, the woman's nostrils flared. 'Porridge,' she said, spitting the word out as though it were a curse. 'That's what's for breakfast. Take it or leave it. And there's no sugar or jam, so don't waste your breath asking for any.'

'By God, you're living dangerously these days, Belinsky.' This was from Griffiths, and muttered *sotto voce* when we could hear the elephantine tread of the woman thumping her way down the hallway to her lair in the kitchen.

I laughed. 'We've all kowtowed to that woman for far too long. It's time for an uprising of the troops!'

Farrington and Griffiths exchanged looks of bewilderment, the latter saying, 'Frankly I'd sooner have the old Belinsky back, we knew where we stood with him. At least then we weren't punished by being deprived of our meagre rations of sugar and jam.'

'Yes,' joined in Farrington, 'there's nothing more annoying

than blatant cheerfulness at the breakfast table when one feels so utterly wretched.'

I bowed my head. 'I apologise profusely and will endeavour to rein in any future outbursts of cheerfulness.'

The horror that masqueraded as our porridge duly arrived and forcing the bland, half-cooked lumpy gruel down, I further insulted my palate with a cup of tea that was so weak it very likely had never made the acquaintance of a single tea leaf – or if it had, it had been a fleeting and forlorn association.

And forlorn was the best way to describe the room in which we were expected to partake of Mrs Pridmore's culinary delights. It was a room that contrived to feel both dismally featureless yet depressingly claustrophobic. Heavy net curtains at the windows kept out the light and the dark, badly patched linoleum floor added to the gloom. There was a cheap-looking sideboard on which an array of photographs of the deceased Mr Pridmore observed our every move – a man who, having died prematurely had got off lightly, I often thought. Faded prints on the walls of sunny seaside cottages did nothing to lift the mood, rather they chimed like an out-of-tune bell in the depressing reality of the dismal room.

None of which I cared a jot about. Why would I, when I knew that when Kitty and I finished our shift today we would cycle over to the farm with the prospect of a delicious meal cooked by Billy to look forward to? Afterwards Kitty and I would then go for a walk, dodging the noisy foursome of geese – the latest recruits to arrive at the farm – and meander our way to the cluster of trees on the furthest westerly point of the meadow to wait for the nightingales to start singing. Then we would make our way back to Honeysuckle Cottage and lie on Kitty's narrow bed and make love.

Since moving to the farm, her skin had turned a golden colour from spending what free time we had outside in the fresh air; the bridge of her nose, much to her dismay and my enchantment, was sprinkled with freckles. 'I look like I did as a child!' she would complain.

But there was nothing of the child about her when we were in bed together. I still couldn't quite believe that this wondrous creature would allow me to touch her, much less make love to her. It was enough to make me believe that there really was a God, a God who had bestowed this miracle of unimaginable good fortune upon me. Of course, our initial attempts to make love were not without a few embarrassed fumblings, mostly on my part, but if nothing else I was a fast learner and to my pride I soon got the hang of things and knew exactly how to give Kitty the most pleasure.

It was a blissful existence, and for the first time in my life I understood what it felt to be genuinely happy. I truly believed that so long as I had my darling Katyushka to love, the war could do its worst, and I would still be content.

It was now the end of September and throughout the month there had been regular reports that the Red Army were continuing to make gains and free more of the territories that had been under German occupation. The latest news was that Smolensk had been liberated. When we heard the news in Hut 8 a cheer had gone up and Chatterton-Jones had called out to me, 'Hey, Belinsky, old chap, that's your lot showing the Germans what a bloody nose feels like! Let's hope they can keep up the good work.'

Though the remark emphasised that Chatterton-Jones and those of his ilk would never regard me as one of them, it rated as the least patronising or condescending utterance the man had ever said to me.

Kitty said I was far too sensitive when it came to Chatterton-Jones, that I should shrug him off as I did the ghastly Mrs P, as she referred to Mrs Pridmore. I supposed, with her innate sense of always wanting to think well of people, Kitty was blind to the fact that I was jealous of a man like Chatterton-Jones who would sail effortlessly through life on a wave of confidence born of privilege and good breeding, oblivious too that I was jealous also of his every fibre that came into close proximity with Kitty herself.

But then I wanted no man near her; I wanted her entirely to myself. I had never known an emotion so powerful. Yet I still had sufficient wit to recognise and accept that I had to fight it, because a possessive nature was a wholly destructive nature, not just to the person possessed, but to the possessor. I had to master and curb the emotion before it got the better of me and put me at risking of losing Kitty.

I was delayed in getting to lunch by a meeting with the head of our Hut and glancing round the noisy canteen while standing in line, I could see no sign of Kitty. We didn't always have our meals together, however today we had arranged to do so. Disappointed, I took my tray over to a table and was joined by Bennett and Craggs. They had to have known what I was thinking as I surreptitiously watched the entrance of the canteen to spot her arrival, but they made no mention of it; instead we talked about the advances made by the Allies in Italy.

With lunch over, and on my way back to start work for the afternoon, I made a detour in the direction of Hut 4 where Kitty worked. I spotted Rachel Burgess, one of her colleagues, walking purposefully along the cinder path, and asked as casually as I could if she knew where I could find Kitty. 'She's not in today,' Rachel said, 'apparently she was ill in the night.'

'Nothing serious, I hope,' I said calmly. As calmly as a man suddenly fearing the worst could sound.

'That's all I know, I'm afraid. Our section head got a call just before lunch, so we're having to cover for her.' Her gaze slid to the watch on her wrist. 'I really need to get back,' she added. 'I'm sure she's all right, though. It's probably just a case of exhaustion. It happens to everyone sooner or later.'

When I'd left Kitty last night she hadn't seemed any more tired than usual, but thinking about it, she had been a bit quiet and hadn't eaten as much supper as she usually did. Both Billy and Peggy had teased her, saying that being in love did that; it took your appetite away. Their teasing had not been confined to Kitty, I'd come in for my share with Billy saying, 'There again, Jacob here doesn't seem to have lost his appetite, so I wonder what that says about him?'

'Men are different,' Peggy had asserted. 'They have stomachs made of cast iron, and emotions to match.'

'I beg to differ,' I'd said, 'I just wouldn't dare to incur Billy's wrath by refusing to eat anything she's gone to the trouble of cooking for me.'

Billy had laughed at that and offered me a second helping of mashed potato. 'Diplomatic bugger, aren't you?'

After my shift was finished, I climbed on to my bicycle and hurtled off through the Park gates, across the town and out into the countryside.

I arrived at the farm breathless and sweating profusely. In the distance, I spotted the red tractor with Peggy at the wheel ploughing a field. She saw me and waved. I waved back at her, then resting my bike against the water trough I knocked on Kitty's door.

Getting no reply, I moved to the window and peered in through the gap in the curtains. I could see that her bed was unmade and poking out from under the pillow was Hamish, the teddy bear she'd had since she'd been three years old and which she'd been so embarrassed about when I'd found him hidden under the eiderdown. Hamish wasn't the only childhood keepsake she'd brought with her; above the bed were her rosary beads and crucifix, both of which Nanny Devine had given her on her first communion. It had taken me a while to get used to making love to her with a crucifix above our heads.

Strewn across the shabby armchair were her underclothes and stockings, and the dress I recalled her wearing yesterday. Her handbag was there as well, on the floor by the chair. But though I could plainly see the room was empty, I tried the door and stepped in. She definitely wasn't there.

Back on my bike again, with swifts swooping overhead in the fading light, I cycled along the lane the way I'd just come and turned into the farmyard where the platoon of geese made a raucous honking rush for me. Fending them off, I leant my bike against the wall and was about to knock on the back door of the house when Billy appeared from the nearest barn.

With a vigorous thrust of her powerful arms, she threw the greyish-coloured contents of a bucket on to the ground. Taking hold of a broom, she began brushing the yard, the smell of Jeyes Fluid filling the air. 'I thought you might show up,' she said.

'Where's Kitty?' I demanded, not caring how rude I was being. 'What's wrong with her?'

'Hold on to your horses now, don't go getting yourself into a state. She's in hospital and—'

'Hospital? Oh my God, it's worse than I thought!'

She leant the broom against the wall and gave me a pitying look. 'You'd better come inside,' she said.

I followed her into the kitchen, but when she told me to sit down, I refused, preferring to stay on my feet so I could shake the truth out of her should I need to. 'Tell me!' I demanded again. 'Tell me what's happened to Kitty.'

She went over to the sink to wash her hands, looking at me over her shoulder as the tap ran. She reached for the scrubbing brush. 'I had to call the doctor out in the night,' she said, 'and he reckoned it was a case of appendicitis. I drove her to the hospital myself.'

'Appendicitis,' I repeated. 'But does that happen out of nowhere? Without any warning? Wouldn't she have shown symptoms before last night?'

'How would I flipping well know, I'm not a doctor.'

'Have you heard anything from the hospital since?'

'No, but then I wouldn't expect to. Her parents will have

been informed and they'll probably be there now.' She dried her hands on the towel hanging from the rail on the range. 'Now sit yourself down and let me pour you a drink, you look like you could do with one. If not several.'

The next twenty-four hours passed in a blur of worry and frustration because I had no way of knowing how Kitty was. The hospital where she'd been admitted was too far for me to reach by bicycle and with no car at my disposal, and with Billy down to her last few gallons of rationed fuel, I had no choice but to wait for news to arrive from Kitty herself.

We were also on full alert again at work, with all leave cancelled – German U-boats had returned to the Atlantic and had successfully sunk several ships. The fear that more ships could be lost, along with the lives of men, women and children, brought back a flood of terrifying nightmares. I tried to channel all my energy into the decoding work that would save lives and valuable supplies, but never far away was the distraction of my anxiety for Kitty. I took to hanging about Hut 4 in the hope of bumping into Rachel Burgess and finally, five whole tortuous days later, I did.

'She's gone to Sussex,' Rachel told me before I'd even asked my question. 'Her parents took her home just as soon as the doctors said she was well enough to be discharged and could travel.'

'How do you know that?' I asked.

'We were told this morning, to shut us up, I think. You know what this place is like: gossip was circulating that she was either pregnant or had some sort of breakdown, and as we all know, somebody going off their rocker is bad for moral.'

'Any idea how she is?'

Rachel shook her head. 'Sorry, no.' Then: 'You're very fond of her, aren't you?'

I nodded.

'Don't look so worried. Kitty's a tough nut; she'll be fine. Just you see.'

In search of familiar comfort, I cycled out to the farm the next morning – I was on the midnight shift, so planned to stay in Kitty's little cottage if Billy would let me. It would serve the purpose of feeling close to the girl I loved and maybe distract my subconscious from giving in to the nightmares that were once more disturbing my sleep. I would go to the farm on the pretext of telling Billy the news I'd just heard from Rachel.

I found Billy in the farmyard, a Woodbine jammed into the corner of her mouth while threatening one of the geese with a pitchfork and telling the bird it deserved a damned good roasting and a dollop of apple sauce if it didn't mend its ways.

'Sounds good,' I said, hopping off my bike and propping it against the wall.

'And by the looks of you, you could do with a nice bit of roast goose. You look bloody awful.'

'I'm not sleeping,' I admitted.

'Nor eating, I'll be bound. Go on in and put the kettle on, I've got something for you.'

She came in some minutes later, toeing off her muddy gumboots and kicking them out of the way with a stockinged foot that had a gaping hole in the heel of the sock.

Washing her hands at the sink, she said, 'Over there on the dresser – there's a letter for you. It came this morning. Postmark says Sussex. Know anyone in Sussex?'

I smiled and threw caution to the wind by hugging her.

'Get off, you daft beggar,' she said, pushing me away. 'It's only a letter. Beats me why she sent it here, though.'

I was about to explain that Kitty had probably sent it to the farm to avoid using the official postal address which would mean it would be read by somebody as a safety precaution, when I thought better of it. After all, Billy wasn't supposed to know that the work we did was top secret.

Although odds-on she had long since guessed and was astute enough not to ask any questions. I kept to myself also that Kitty had broken a rule by sending me the letter the way she had and would be in big trouble if anyone ever found out.

I took the letter over to the table where I sat down to read it.

My dearest darling,

What a fearful bore this has all been, stuck in bed for days on end and with no way of letting you know how I am. I feel so very queer I don't even know what day of the week it is!

I am now without that curious little thing called an appendix, which I believe serves no purpose other than to take one unawares and very nearly burst. I'm told that this was what happened to me and that I'm lucky to be alive. That's probably Mummy exaggerating matters, but I must say I hope never to go through a similar experience.

I have no idea when I shall return to work, but if you should be able to visit me, I'm sure it would speed my recovery. I make a terrible patient, so please come at once and cheer me up! I miss you more than words can say, my darling.

With all my love,
Your very own Katyushka.

P.S. Give my love to Billy and the others.

P.P.S. Apologies for brevity, but Nanny Devine is wait-ing to post this for me.

'Good news from Sussex?' Billy asked, when I had finished reading.

I nodded. 'She sends her love to you and the others.'

'I should think so too. Any mention of when she'll be back with us?'

I shook my head, unable to speak, suddenly overcome with the relief of knowing the girl for whom I'd willingly give my life was alive and well enough to write to me.

Chapter Thirty-Two

October 1943

I couldn't get away until five days later when it was my day off. I arrived at the railway station and, as arranged by Kitty, Andrews met me off the train. I detected a slight thaw in his cool manner towards me and sitting self-consciously in the back of the car, I enquired after Kitty.

'I believe she's feeling a little better today, sir,' he replied deferentially.

'That's good,' I said.

His gaze slid briefly to look at me in the rear-view mirror. 'Indeed it is, sir.'

We neither of us spoke again until we reached our destination and Andrews brought the car to a halt alongside a number of other cars and let me out. 'Thank you,' I said.

He made no response, other than to touch his cap and get back behind the wheel and drive round to the side of the house. I couldn't help but feel he was playing his part just a little too much to the hilt.

Conspicuously alone, I gave a discreet tug on the bell pull. Hearing no bell sound, I realised I had presented myself with my first dilemma – had I pulled sufficiently to alert the occupants within of my arrival? To risk trying again when actually the bell had been heard by someone would certainly be a faux pas guaranteed to wrong-foot me for the duration of my visit. But then to be honest, I was already wrong-footed merely by being here.

Oh what the hell, I thought, and gave the bell pull a firm

wrench just as simultaneously the door was opened.

'Darling, you're here at last!'

Looking as beautiful as ever and not at all like the wan invalid I had pictured, Kitty took me by the arm and led me over the threshold and into the grand hallway where she kissed me. And not a peck on the cheek, but a surprisingly long and lingering kiss on the mouth. It would have been more enjoyable had I not been aware of voices coming from somewhere in the house.

'It's so good to see you,' she said when anxiety forced me to stop kissing her. 'I've missed you terribly.'

'I've missed you, too,' I said. 'You're looking so much better than I expected. But how are you really?'

'Bored out of my mind. I'm *desperate* to get back to Bletchley. I need you to convince Mummy and Daddy that I'm needed there.'

At the mention of Mummy and Daddy I swallowed apprehensively. 'Are they here?'

'Yes, and they're dying to meet you.'

I bet they are, I thought grimly, and trying not to show my disappointment gave Kitty my coat, which she threw on to a large oak coffer behind us. I had naïvely imagined having Kitty all to myself. Absurdly the image I had contrived in my head during the train journey here involved her lying decorously on a sofa with a blanket covering her and me sharing amusing tales with her about Mrs Pridmore and Billy at the farm. I could see now I had been mad to think she would be here alone while convalescing.

She suddenly grabbed my hands. 'Come and say hello to my parents, we were just finishing lunch.'

My heart took a further plunge as I realised my arrival meant disturbing my hosts at lunch. 'I'm happy to wait until they've finished eating,' I said. Happy too to make a cowardly escape back to Bletchley, content in the knowledge that I had seen for myself that Kitty had made a good recovery.

'Don't be so stuffy, the more the merrier, have some coffee

with us. Oh, but how silly of me, you're probably hungry, aren't you? Let me go and see what Mrs E has left in the way of—'

'I'm not hungry,' I lied, hastily interrupting her. Such was the escalating state of my nerves I would be lucky to force down a few sips of coffee, never mind food.

'Well, if you're sure. But just say the word and I'll find something for you.'

Her arm now linked through mine, she took me across the hallway and along a panelled corridor lined with sombre oil paintings, which did nothing to lift my spirits. What had possessed me to involve myself with a girl of this background? Why had I not done the sensible thing at the outset and walked away? Why, when I had first heard the flawless cut of her vowels, had I not had the wit to heed my common sense?

Because my heart had ruled my head and defied my every instinct. And because I had allowed my ego to be thoroughly flattered by the slightest attention bestowed upon me by this extraordinary girl. Oh, the sheer folly of my vanity! Was there ever a more ridiculous spectacle than a wretch of a man hopelessly in love?

We came to a stop outside a door that was ajar and through which I could hear a man's brusque voice. I couldn't make out exactly what he was saying, but he didn't sound like a man whispering sweet endearments to a loved one. The tone was that of a man used to barking out orders. With Kitty's hand pushing the door open for us to enter, a bolt of alarm ripped through me as I recalled the story about her father ejecting an uncle from an upstairs window.

Stepping into the room I was met with yet a further blow of disappointment – Kitty had failed to inform me that her parents were not alone, they had company. Although in fairness, hadn't she said the more the merrier? And hadn't I seen for myself the cars on the drive when I arrived?

True to my naturally reserved nature my preference

would have been to slip in amongst the diners with the least amount of fuss, but true to Kitty's more extrovert nature, she announced my arrival with all but a trumpeted fanfare. 'Everyone, say hello to Jacob!'

The room instantly fell quiet and all eyes homed in on me. I spotted one familiar face – Nanny Devine – but the rest, as to be expected, were all strangers. They didn't exactly look hostile, but neither did they look friendly in their studied observation of me. A woman sitting at the nearest end of the long rectangular table and who I took to be Kitty's mother spoke first. She was wearing a cream silk blouse with a string of pearls, her hair stylishly coiffured and with not a sign of grey – and thanks to the family business I knew enough about hair to know it wasn't natural. 'I'm afraid you've caught us at a most inopportune moment,' she said, 'we've just finished eating.'

'That's all right, Mummy,' Kitty said, 'I've already asked him and he says he's not hungry.'

'Don't be ridiculous, darling, the poor man's travelled all this way, he must be starving. I shall go and speak to Mrs Enstone.'

'No really, I'm fine,' I managed to say as the woman rose elegantly from her chair.

She raised a hand. 'Not another word, I insist.' She swept out of the room giving one more instruction. 'Kitty, find Jacob a place at the table and introduce everyone.'

I was seated between Nanny Devine and Kitty, and was introduced first to her father who, from his position at the head of the table, gave me close-quarters scrutiny, all the time stroking a drooping moustache – a moustache that seemed to sag on his stern face as if cowering in fear. Trying to act as though I was completely unaware of his beady-eyed gaze, I took in the other guests who were now being introduced to me. The first was a thin-faced, spectacled priest, Father Frank Fiennes, followed by a grizzled Cedric Manning visiting from London who worked in the City, then an overweight Major

George Allenby and his wife Helen who lived nearby, and lastly, and by no means least, Hector and Ursula Chatterton-Jones who were, I was told, old acquaintances and currently houseguests of the Allenbys.

'I believe you know our son Charles,' Ursula said, 'and that you work together.'

Her husband rattled his throat, which I took to be a warning for his wife to be careful in what she said.

'That's right,' I said and threw in a deflection. 'I knew him at Cambridge. By sight, really. He was a couple of years ahead of me.'

Hector laughed. 'That's our Charles for you, always ahead of the pack. *I've* not heard him mention you, though. What did you say your surname was?'

'Belinsky,' I said. 'Jacob Belinsky.'

'Russian, eh? Word is the Red Army's making some pretty good advances on the Germans along the Dnieper. Would never have thought the Bolsheviks had it in them, quite frankly.'

I had noticed all too frequently that so long as Stalin and the Soviet Army were making gains on the enemy, my stock was high, when not, I was treated as though I was personally responsible for any of Stalin's perceived mistakes or miscalculations.

'Jacob's as British as we are,' Kitty said staunchly beside me. 'He's never even been to Russia.'

'And your people?' asked her father. 'Where are they?'

I had never understood the affected use of the word 'people' in this context and I could feel my hackles rising. 'My parents live in the East End of London,' I replied, 'where I grew up and went to school.'

'Did you now?' Major Allenby said, peering at me as if I were a specimen in a jar. 'And what did you read up at Cambridge?' I knew without a doubt the real question this bloated man with his red-veined bulbous nose wanted to ask was: how did a nobody from the East End get to Cambridge?

My reply was lost in the reappearance of Kitty's mother who presented me with a plate of sliced pork, carrots, a couple of boiled potatoes and some apple sauce. 'All home-grown,' she said cheerfully, 'from the garden. Even the pork.'

Her husband laughed. 'Never thought I'd see the day when I had pigs on my land. But there you go, we're all doing our bit, aren't we?'

'Thank you,' I said politely to my hostess as she resumed her seat. As appetising as the food looked, I knew it would be a challenge to overcome my nerves and eat it in front of everybody without succumbing to some embarrassing mishap or other. I then had the misfortune to recall a mortifying occasion at a formal dinner in college when I had sent a particularly hard potato skidding across the table. I willed the knife and fork in my hands to do as I bade them.

Thankfully a diversion was provided in the form of a diminutive young girl in a maid's uniform bringing in the coffee for the other guests. She looked about fourteen and the large tray seemed far too heavily laden for someone of her stature and young years to carry. I noticed that when she set it down on the oak sideboard she let out a small, but discernible sigh. Nobody else seemed to be aware of her presence, the conversation having now turned to the matter of a poaching. Major Allenby, a local magistrate, was of the opinion that in these difficult times anyone caught poaching, particularly on his land, should be severely punished, no matter what age. Only last week he'd caught a nine-year-old boy red-handed with a couple of rabbits about his person.

'So no matter how hungry these people are, Major,' Kitty queried, making me want to cheer her, 'you'd still want to punish them?'

'Lawlessness is lawlessness,' her father said, grimly banging the palm of his hand on the table. 'No matter the difficulties we're facing. We'd be in a sorry mess if everyone broke the law for their own selfish greed. It's selfish greed that ensures the black market thrives the way it does.'

'Here, here!' agreed Chatterton-Jones senior, taking the offered coffee cup from the maid without so much as a glance at her. 'We're all having to make sacrifices; why should some lazy young ne'er-do-well think he's entitled to help himself to what's not his?'

Wondering what sacrifices he and his wife were making to further the war effort, I carefully speared a piece of pork and had it almost to my mouth when there was a sudden cry from the other end of the table.

'Oh, Mr Belinsky, I'm so sorry, I don't know what I was thinking!'

The piece of meat dropped from my fork as I turned to look at my hostess.

'Please don't force yourself to eat that out of politeness,' she said, 'I shan't be offended. I know it's against your religion, isn't it?'

Ah, so Kitty must have mentioned I was Jewish. Or perhaps she had been interrogated about this unknown friend of hers. 'It's quite all right,' I said as a silence fell on the room and the young serving girl closed the door softly behind her. 'I may be Jewish by birth, but I'm atheist by choice.' As though to prove my point comprehensively, I scooped up the piece of pork and popped it into my mouth.

As I knew it would, my comment had the attention of the priest sitting opposite me. The bespectacled man roused himself from the apparent stupor he'd hitherto been consumed by, presumably brought on by a hearty lunch and several glasses of good wine, the remains of which I could see in the decanter in front of Kitty's father. 'Come, come,' the man of the cloth said, peering at me through the thick lenses of his glasses, 'what sort of talk is that?'

'I'm sorry,' I said, 'but I simply can't believe in any kind of God that would go to the trouble of creating a world in which he would then allow men to go to war and treat each other with such wanton cruelty. Why? Why would any deity do that?'

To my right Nanny Devine sucked in her breath.

'My dear fellow,' the priest said, 'if we are to take away belief what does one have left?'

'And I put the question, what do we have *with* belief? A world completely at war with itself, that's what.'

My words had the effect of making Major Allenby inhale deeply, then puffing out his chest, he said, 'I say, you're not some sort of Bolshevik Communist, are you?'

Next to me, Kitty tutted. 'Of course he isn't! Why, Jacob's the most patriotic man you'll ever meet.'

'Patriotic to what or whom, I should like to know,' her father muttered, while narrowing his eyes and giving me a cool look.

'To England, of course!' Kitty asserted vehemently. 'Why else would he be entrusted with the vitally important work he does at—' Realising her mistake, and receiving a sharp warning look from her father, she stopped abruptly. 'Oh dear,' she said with a laugh that was entirely false, 'we seem to be getting so awfully serious all of a sudden, and for no reason. Jacob, come on, let's go for a walk in the garden. I feel badly in need of some fresh air.'

'Are you sure you're quite well enough?' asked Nanny Devine.

'Quite well, thank you, Nanny.'

'Darling, where are your manners,' her mother chided her. 'You could at least show your guest the courtesy to let him finish his lunch first.'

'I told you, Mummy; he's not hungry. He said he wasn't, but you wouldn't listen!'

To my horror I heard a tremor in Kitty's voice and recognised it as the sound of somebody on the verge of crying. I had never witnessed her cry before and had no intention of letting it happen now. As she pushed back her chair and stood up, I did the same and addressing her mother, said, 'Thank you for lunch, it was kind of you to go to so much trouble for me. I'm sorry for any disturbance I've caused.'

My apology was devoid of any real sincerity and uttered in the full knowledge that I would never see these people again.

We deliberately avoided the rose garden, which would give the occupants of the dining room a clear view of us, and instead wandered round to the kitchen garden, but seeing the Land Girls hard at work there, Kitty took me into the greenhouse.

'I'm sorry,' she said, closing the door behind us. 'I don't know who's behaved more beastly, that stuffy lot in there, or me.' It was the first time she'd spoken since we'd grabbed our coats and left the house. I hadn't said anything either.

'It's my fault,' I said now, 'I should never have come.'

'Why ever not?' Her eyes were soft and imploring.

I took her hands in mine. 'Because you know as well as I do, I'm the last sort of man your parents will want in your life. I have too much going against me – my family and upbringing, not to mention the suspicion that I must be a Communist at best, a spy at worst. It's called good old-fashioned prejudice.'

'But if they'd only take the trouble to get to know you they'd soon realise how ridiculous they're being.' Tears now came into her eyes. 'It's so unfair!'

I took her in my arms. 'Life is, I'm afraid, my darling.'

'No,' she said fiercely, tilting her head away from me. 'I'm going to prove you all wrong. Life *can* be fair. I'm going to make it fair. Just you see!'

I smiled and wiped the tears away from her cheeks. 'And how do you plan to go about that, my Katyushka?'

'You're going to ask me to marry you, of course. And I shall accept.'

Chapter Thirty-Three

November 1943

It was nearly six weeks later that I finally decided it was time to take Kitty to meet my family.

During the train journey from Bletchley I read in the newspaper that Oswald Mosley's internment had been lifted due to ill health, but that he would be kept under house arrest. The claims that he was no longer a security risk rankled with me. As far as I was concerned, he was a perniciously dangerous man.

I had been fifteen years old when, in 1936, Mosley and his strutting Blackshirts had attempted to lead a march through the heart of London's Jewish community in the East End. It was a march designed expressly to antagonise and promote their cause, a cause that was perilously aligned with that of Hitler. I could still remember my poor grandmother's terror at what might happen if the British Union of Fascists gained in popularity. 'It is always us Jews who people attack when times are hard,' she had wept, when one night our windows had been pelted with stones. She could remember all too clearly the threats and violence she and my grandfather had fled from in Russia and which had brought them to England.

Despite my mother's wishes for us not to get involved, I had gone to Cable Street with my father and neighbours. My pockets full of marbles to throw under the horse's hooves if they charged at us, I had stood side by side with those others prepared to stand up, not just to Mosley and his Blackshirts, but to the police who were known to support the fascists.

The Jewish community wasn't alone that day; the trade union movement was there as well, along with the Labour Party, the Communist Party and the Irish dockers, some of whom lived in our street. It was an extraordinary display of solidarity, a day I had never forgotten, when a force for evil on our own doorstep had been denied a further foothold.

Yet now the man who had orchestrated that day had been released from internment following a decision made by the Government.

'I can't believe so many people supported that awful man,' Kitty said quietly as she leant against me to read the newspaper.

'That's the danger of charismatic speakers, they're wholly convincing,' I said, 'they pinpoint a scapegoat and let the mob do the rest.'

'Yes,' she said softly, 'look what an orator that monster Hitler is and what he's done. He's mad though, isn't he? He has to be.' She gave a little shiver, either from cold or the thought of what Hitler might yet inflict on the world.

I stuffed the newspaper into my coat pocket, put my arm around her and changed the subject. 'Just think,' I said, 'this was the way we met; standing together in a crowded carriage just like this.'

She smiled. 'And you were so severe with me.'

'I was tongue-tied with nerves.'

'How silly you are. But you know, I've never forgiven you for making me look so foolish.'

'Really, what did I do?'

'You pretended you hadn't already worked out all the clues for the crossword.'

I held her closer. 'I was just being polite.'

She tilted her head back, which I took as my fortunate cue to kiss her.

Then with my arm still around her, and with the sound of a nearby soldier whistling Glen Miller's 'In the Mood', we stared out of the grimy window and the passing scenery.

It was the last week of November and winter was upon us. Which meant that along with the usual challenges working at Bletchley Park brought us, we now had the added challenge of staying warm. It was bad enough that the huts we worked in were freezing cold, but I also had Mrs Pridmore's parsimony to cope with. A woman who firmly believed in sacrifice and self-denial, especially when inflicting it on others, she had taken to rationing the use of the two-bar electric fire in my room to just the one hour in the evening. Not that I complained about this, not when Kitty's living conditions at Honeysuckle Cottage were far worse. Billy had found a small electric fire for her, but it barely took the chill off the floor and walls that now felt damp to the touch; there was a layer of mould growing on the wall behind the wardrobe. To Billy's credit, she had invited Kitty to move into the house during the winter, but reluctant to squeeze in with the two girls already sharing a room and lose our moments of being entirely alone together, Kitty had declined the offer. It went without saying that Billy had to have known what we were getting up to in the privacy of Honeysuckle Cottage, now renamed Chilblain Cottage by me, but thankfully she turned a blind eye to it.

Kitty had returned to Bletchley a fortnight after my disastrous visit to Fanley Manor, a visit we never referred to again. I had not formally proposed to her, but was planning to do so when I felt the time was right. And more importantly, when I had a ring. My taking her to meet my family today was a two-fold plan: I wanted them to meet the woman I loved, but also I wanted to ask my grandmother for the ruby ring she had promised would be mine when I was ready to marry. It had belonged to my great-grandmother – on my mother's side of the family – a woman I had never known. She had given it to her daughter Lila on the proviso it would always stay in the family and would one day be given to a betrothed. I had told Kitty nothing of this and intended to keep the ring a secret until I asked her to marry me, which

I planned to do on New Year's Eve. Staring out of the train window, my chin resting gently on the top of Kitty's head, I smiled to myself as I considered how romantically devious I was being.

But there was a practicality to our decision to marry. Kitty had confided in me that for some days before she had been taken to hospital with appendicitis she had been experiencing pain in her stomach accompanied by waves of nausea. Her first thought was that she was pregnant and, scared how I might react, she had kept her suspicion to herself. 'It was a relief to know it was only my stupid old appendix playing merry hell with me,' she'd said. Since then we had been extra careful and I had equipped myself with the necessary French letters. They were fiddly to use, but I saw now how irresponsible I had been previously. The thought of her parents' reaction to my getting her pregnant outside of marriage was enough to eradicate every last trace of my desire!

Equally, the thought of their reaction to our marrying was just as terrifying, but having stood up to the likes of Oswald Mosley and his Blackshirts when I was fifteen years old, I was certainly prepared to stand up for the woman with whom I wanted to spend the rest of my life. We would marry and to hell with the consequences!

We spoke often of the life we hoped to live when the war was over. Kitty wanted us to live in the country. She pictured herself in a cottage with a small garden where she could grow some vegetables and a few flowers. It was a far cry from Fanley Manor and the expectations she must have grown up with.

'We'll till and weed the soil together like a couple of happy peasants,' Kitty once said with her typical enthusiasm for an idea when speaking about our future home.

'But I know nothing about growing things,' I told her.

To which she chastised me with the words, 'Didn't you tell me that if you scratched the surface of a Russian you'd find a peasant not far below? And peasants work the land, don't they, so that means it's in your genes, Jacob!'

'But not yours,' I countered.

My parents had arranged things so that they could take the afternoon off work, something they rarely did. Mama was furious with me, though, when we arrived earlier than the agreed time; plainly she had wanted everything to be perfect and we had caught her still wearing an apron and giving the front door knocker a polish. She gave me a scolding look, then kissed me warmly, saying, 'You look better than you did the last time we saw you.' She prodded my chest, the polishing cloth still in her hand. 'You've put on some weight, thank God! But your hair! Just look at your hair! Papa must tidy you up before you leave. And if he doesn't, I will.'

Embarrassed, and catching sight of old Mrs O'Sullivan watching from next door, I gave her a friendly wave and said, 'Mama, please, we could be here all day on the door-step putting my many imperfections right, but perhaps you might like to take us into the warm and say hello to Kitty.'

She tutted. '*Feh!* Such rudeness from my own son; who'd have believed it possible?' But she was smiling all the same. 'Kitty, you are most welcome, I would shake hands, but—'

'That's all right,' Kitty said, proffering her own with a happy smile, 'a bit of Brasso never hurt anyone.'

Mama's approval was gained in an instant and with Mrs O'Sullivan still openly watching us, she was introduced to Kitty, my mother proudly describing her as 'Jacob's young lady friend'.

Once ushered inside, we gathered in the kitchen, which was where we always gathered; it was also where my grand-mother ruled supreme. During the worst of the Blitz, and after a bomb had fallen on the house two doors down from hers and utterly demolished it, my father had insisted she move in with us. 'What use will that be?' she told him. 'Do you think your house is so special the Germans won't drop a bomb on it?'

'No, but at least we'll know where you are if it does happen,' he replied.

Even when she hadn't lived with us, my grandmother had, in the manner of Moses laying down the commandments, dictated how things should be done in the family. My parents had happily given her this level of control on the understanding they were permitted to run the business unhindered. Though she grumbled furiously that she was to be excluded from what she and her husband had begun, she put her considerable energy into cooking, washing, and keeping our house spotlessly clean. Any relaxation time she grudgingly allowed herself was spent knitting socks for the troops while listening to the wireless.

'Ach there you are, *Bubala*!' my grandmother greeted me from the stove where she was stirring a large bubbling saucepan that was giving off a deliciously fragrant aroma. Other than when I was in trouble with her, *bubala* – Yiddish for dear – was what she'd called me since I was born. In turn I had always called her *bobeshi*, granny. To an outsider, we were an odd mix, our common language a blend of Russian, Yiddish, Hebrew and English, also liberally peppered with words of our own making. Of all of us, and not surprisingly, my grandmother was the one with the thickest Russian accent and, depending on her mood, could be incomprehensible even to our ears. She took great delight in taking by force an unassuming defenceless English *r* and bludgeoning it with her tongue until it had gained the mighty status of a distinctive Russian *rrrr*.

I crossed the kitchen to her, her round and wrinkled cheek already poised to receive the expected kiss. '*Bobeshi*,' I said, taking the wooden spoon from her, 'say hello to Kitty.' As I watched them greet each other, I admitted to myself that of anyone's approval I most wanted, it was my grandmother's. Being the traditionalist she was, I knew that she would be disappointed that the woman I wanted to marry wasn't Jewish and I mentally crossed my fingers that this wouldn't be an insurmountable obstacle.

My father then appeared in the doorway and smiled at me. For as long as I could remember he had taken great pride in his appearance, but the war had taken its toll and despite his efforts, I could see that since my last visit his jacket was a little shabbier, the fabric worn and discoloured, the cuffs beginning to fray. The pointed corners of his shirt collar showed evidence of having been mended and his tie was shiny with constant wear. Mama's dress was also worn, and knowing that they would have put on their smartest clothes to make a good impression I was greatly touched.

My grandmother, now removing her apron and showing Kitty what she was cooking for lunch – chicken soup with matzo balls, potato latkes and chopped liver – looked the same as she always did. Ever since my grandfather had died she had worn a selection of shapeless black dresses with a dark-coloured cardigan, invariably one she had knitted herself. On very cold days, she would drape a shawl around her shoulders. Her low-heeled, lace-up shoes were also black and immaculately polished. She wore her silver-grey hair in exactly the same style without fail – a bun squashed into the nape of her neck during the day. At night, when she was getting ready for bed, she would sit in front of her mirror plaiting it. I had loved watching her doing that as a young child, largely because she had fixed her eyes on my reflection in the mirror and told me wonderful stories of when she'd been a child, often singing to me as well.

Lunch, pre-empted by a blessing and the menorah candles being lit, was served in the kitchen and was rounded off with my favourite honey cake and lemon tea. My grandmother made the tea herself in her treasured samovar and served it in tea glasses with silver filigree cup holders and her best long-handled silver teaspoons. Before rationing, she would have drunk her tea the traditional Russian way, with a cube of sugar between her teeth, but with sugar such a precious commodity, she drank it without, like the rest of us. Throughout most of the meal I had tried not to think of the food coupons my family must have saved in order to put on such a fine lunch in honour of my visit today with Kitty. I hoped they knew how grateful I was.

I could see that my father was utterly charmed by Kitty, but then he was always comfortable around women, especially the prettier ones. Many times I had wished I was more like him with his easy and relaxed manner, but it was claimed I took after my grandfather, a quiet man capable of intense thought and the ability to hold his tongue for long periods of time, which my father claimed was simply because he couldn't get a word in edgeways with his wife.

Exchanging looks with my mother, I could see I was home and dry when it came to my parents' opinion of Kitty. But although perfectly courteous, my grandmother was not so easy to read. Or rather, I suspected that I was reading her all too well. And that worried me. Trying to ignore my concern, I knew my next step was to get her alone so I could ask her about the ruby ring. But how?

As luck would have it, it was she who engineered things so that we were alone. '*Bubala*, kindly help me with the washing-up,' she instructed when we had finished the honey cake and drunk our fill from the samovar.

'I'll help as well,' Kitty offered brightly.

'No, no,' my grandmother said firmly, 'you are our guest.' To my parents she said, 'Take Kitty through to the parlour and show her some photographs of Yakov when he was a small boy. Be sure to show her the one with him playing the balalaika.'

The use of my name in Russian alerted me to her having more than tidying the kitchen on her mind.

We took up our positions, my grandmother wearing her apron again and in command of the sink, and me at her side with a tea towel in my hand. After a long concentrated silence, I said 'So what is it you want to say to me, *Bobeshi*?'

Without pausing a beat, she said, 'Do you love this girl?'

'Yes,' I said, meeting her candour head on. 'And I plan to marry her.'

'Have you made her pregnant?'

'No.'

'Then marriage is not necessary.'

'*Bobeshi*, are you giving me permission to live in sin with Kitty?'

She whipped round to face me. 'Yakov, do not try to be smart with me! You know very well what I am saying.'

'Yes, you believe because she is a *goy* I can't marry her. Only one of our own kind will do.'

'You see, you know this to be true.'

'I know no such thing, merely that I should only marry the girl I love.'

She sighed deeply. '*Ach*, you always were so headstrong.'

'If I am, I can only think I must have inherited it from you.'

If the matter we were discussing was not so important to her, I knew ordinarily she would have laughed at this comment of mine, but handing me a saucepan to dry, she said, 'First your parents turn their backs on the faith, now you. Such high hopes I had for you. I thought you'd become a doctor, or a lawyer, and that you'd marry one of Rabbi Abie Rosen's four daughters. Naomi is married now, and Anna is courting, but there's still Rebecca and Sarah. Though you would have to wait for Sarah; she is only fifteen. And Rebecca wouldn't be my first choice for you, not with those eyes of hers, they're much too close together to get herself a good marriage match.'

Poor Rebecca, I thought, unable to recall a single thing about the girl's eyes.

She passed me another pan to dry, accompanied with another deep sigh. 'I don't even know what it is you do every day,' she said. 'You never say. Not a word. And now this girl. Am I to have nothing but disappointment in my life?'

I wanted to put my arms around this maddeningly lovable and contradictory woman, to convince her that no matter what I would always love her. But instead of doing that, I said, 'I wouldn't make any of Rabbi Rosen's daughters happy, *Bobeshi*, not when I love somebody else.'

'But you'd make *me* happy, does that count for nothing?'

'What about my happiness? Isn't that important?'

She clucked her tongue impatiently. 'You're too young to understand what real happiness is. For you young people, you think you have to live only for the moment. With this war you think your life could be over tomorrow, so today you have to do everything in a rush.'

'But it's true, isn't it? A bomb could drop down on us at any minute and we could all be dead in an instant. Would you want my last dying wish to be one of regret, that I died without knowing the happiness of being married to Kitty?'

'But what of turning your back on God?'

'It would be a very mean and small-minded god who worried about that when the world he supposedly created is in the process of trying to wipe itself out.'

'There is no *supposedly* created about it, Yakov! If you spent more time reading the Torah you would not say such a dreadful thing!'

The last thing I wanted to do was upset my beloved grandmother, especially by insulting the faith in which she believed so strongly. 'I'm sorry, forget I said that. But tell me honestly, if Kitty was Jewish you would say she was perfect, wouldn't you?'

Pursing her lips, she gave me a plate to dry. 'Perfect is not always the right thing in life. For how can that make a person grow? Tell me, do you really know who you are and where you are from? Do you not have a sense of the great heritage you are turning your back on? Do you not feel anything for who we are and what our ancestors did, the struggles they endured?'

It would have been too easy to blurt out that yes, of course, I knew who I was – I was Jacob Belinsky, part Jewish, part Russian, and part British. I was the sum of my parts. But in essence my grandmother was right, for I had got to be where I was now not really knowing who I was. I had never felt that I truly fitted in anywhere. I had always been an outsider, first at school, then at Cambridge and now at Bletchley. But one thing I did know, until I met Kitty I had been anchorless, like a boat drifting away from the shore. When Kitty came into my world, it suddenly made sense. Moreover, her love gave me an idea of the person I could one day be.

'But I can see your mind is made up,' my grandmother said in the silence as she waited for my reply. 'I suppose that means you want to ask me for your great-grandmother's ring. Am I right?'

'Yes,' I said softly. 'And with it I'd like your blessing. I want you to be happy for me.'

Chapter Thirty-Four

'I know I've said this before, but it just feels so completely surreal this image I'm now getting of Jacob, a man who I was always incredibly in awe of. It sounds crazy, but I'd somehow assumed he'd arrived in the world a fully formed, self-assured man of black-and-white certainty. It's a bit like discovering Father Christmas doesn't exist.'

'I suppose it's impossible ever really to know a person, isn't it?'

Climbing the stairs to the third floor to his office, Matthew said, 'I'm fast coming to realise that. The other thing I keep wondering is how Jacob would feel about me reading something so private. In many ways, beneath the surface veneer of frankness, he was a very buttoned-down person; he never spoke of anything of a personal nature. I keep thinking how mortified he would be that I'm delving into something that was obviously so private and important to him.'

'But from what you say you were pretty close to each other so perhaps he'd like you knowing about this part of his life. Maybe this was the only way he could have ever shared it with you.'

Matthew smiled at Saskia's words and pushed open his office door. 'You're trying to assuage my guilt, aren't you?'

'Only because I felt the same when reading the first notebook, as though I was intruding, and I didn't even know Jacob.'

He dumped his rucksack on his desk and sat down. 'And you know, I'd never have described him as having an ounce of sentimentality in him, yet I'm having to revise that belief now, as why else would he have gathered around him all the things he did?'

'You mean his books?'

'Yes.'

'Sometimes it's not sentimentality that does that; often it's a way to put up a barrier, a wall to hide behind. There again, it could simply have been an inability for him to see what was piling up around him. Heaven knows there's enough of that going on around me.'

Intrigued by her comments, but conscious he had things to do before his meeting with Jim Rycroft, he said, 'I'd better let you get on. Sorry again for calling so early, I just wanted to let you know where I'd got to with the story.'

'No problem, I was already in my workshop. Feel free anytime to keep me posted. Just hurry up and read the rest of the book!'

'I'll try and apply myself tonight,' he said with a laugh, 'though I can't promise anything.'

He rang off, thinking that he probably wouldn't get anything read tonight as he was spending the evening with Fliss.

Switching on his computer, he thought of his reason for ringing Saskia; it had been so he could talk about Jacob. She was the only other person who had read, albeit partially, *The Dandelion Years*, and he valued her insight as somebody who could be entirely objective. Which was something he couldn't be, because every word he read was clouded by what he thought he'd known about a man who'd played such an important role in his life. Saskia was able to take every word at face value without any preconceived ideas that would distort the story that was unfolding. And for that, he valued her input.

But the more he thought about it, it was the level of secrecy Jacob had lived with all his life that he was still trying to come to terms with. It continued to amaze him that Jacob had worked at Bletchley and never once mentioned his involvement. There had been any number of times when

Jacob could have smiled knowingly and admitted, even boasted, of the part he'd played in bringing about an end to the Second World War. Only the other year there had been that announcement about the posthumous royal pardon for Alan Turing – one of Bletchley's most famous code-breakers – and his conviction for homosexuality back in 1952. Then there had been the film, *The Imitation Game*, with Benedict Cumberbatch playing the part of Turing. For pity's sake, Matthew had been to see the film when it was released last November and had commented on it to Jacob. Yet not a word had Jacob said. The sly old devil!

Why then write *The Dandelion Years*?

Matthew had asked Saskia the same question and her answer had been that perhaps that would only become clear when he had finished reading the entire story. She'd asked him if he was tempted to cheat and read the end pages of the notebook: his answer was a categorical no. Just as the way in which he worked, methodically and without taking shortcuts, he would do the thing properly or not at all.

Scrolling through the emails that had come in overnight, looking for anything that was urgent, he couldn't shake off a restless awareness that *The Dandelion Years* – a story that had lain untouched for so many years – was reaching out and instilling in him a growing sense of dissatisfaction with his own life. It reminded him of a remark Jacob had once made, about everybody needing to find their own horizon. It resonated with what Jacob had also written about himself, of knowing exactly who he was. Did Matthew know who he was? Or was he like a boat drifting away from the shore and with no sense of the direction he should be going in?

Noting the time on his computer, Matthew knew that he had to put aside all thoughts of Jacob and finish preparing for the meeting with Jim Rycroft. God help him if he was exposed for not being thoroughly up to speed with the contents of the file he'd been given yesterday afternoon.

*

'How do you feel about a weekend away?' Fliss asked him that evening.

The question took Matthew by surprise. They had just sat down to eat, Fliss having gone to the bother of putting candles and paper napkins on the table, something she had done at the very start of their relationship and which had soon been dispensed with. 'Where were you thinking?' he asked.

'It's my mother's birthday and Dad's treating us all to a trip to Copenhagen.'

'Why Copenhagen?'

She smiled. 'Don't laugh, they both have this thing about Scandi-crime and want to see where *The Killing* was filmed, along with *The Bridge* and *Borgen*. You will come, won't you?'

His honest answer was no. It felt too soon, much too soon to be playing happy families all over again. 'Your family is hardly going to welcome me back into the fold with open arms, are they?' he said carefully. 'Not after what I did to you.'

'I knew you'd think that. But hand on heart, Mum and Dad understand completely that you were going through a difficult time.'

'So they know we're back together?'

'Of course they do.' She reached across the table to him. 'And they're delighted. In fact it was Dad who suggested you join us. Everything's forgiven and forgotten.'

Matthew found that difficult to believe, but not wanting to disappoint Fliss, he said, 'When is this birthday weekend?'

'The weekend immediately after Easter. You are free, aren't you? Please say you are. It'd be much more fun for me if you came.'

'I'll make sure I am free,' he said with a smile.

He hoped the smile disguised his true feelings. Without beating about the bush, the prospect of a reunion with Rod and Sally Campbell and the rest of Fliss's family, namely her two brothers and sister, their partners and raucous children, filled him with dread. But there was nothing else for it but to overcome his foreboding and tough it out. He'd do it for Fliss's sake. It was the least he could do.

In the flickering candlelight, and suspecting from the tense expression on her face that she wanted a more reassuring response from him, he squeezed her hand. 'I've never been to Copenhagen before,' he said, 'it'll be fun.'

'Yes it will,' she agreed, happy relief brightening her face. 'It'll be great.'

Chapter Thirty-Five

When it came to restoration, Saskia was a great believer in retaining as much of the original condition and character of the book as was possible. She hated to see an old book with its heart and soul stripped away through an insensitive repair job. It usually happened when the person restoring had taken a short cut, often to keep the price down, and had not replaced like-with-like materials. Saskia never lied to the customer; she always made it very clear she wasn't a cutter of corners and used only the best materials. She also warned the customer that the process of restoration could be a lengthy one, depending on the amount of damage she had to deal with.

This afternoon she had put the finishing touches to a book called *Antiquities of Cambridgeshire* and which was full of the most beautiful engraved illustrations. Bearing in mind the limited amount of foxing to the pages, the book had been lucky to escape the type of dealer she and Dad hated – the vandal-dealer who would destroy a book by removing the illustrations so they could be framed and sold individually. It was easy money. It was also a crime against books and therefore unforgivable in Saskia's opinion.

With this particular book, and in order to preserve it for many years to come, Saskia had begun by cleaning off the back of the spine and removing all of the original lining and animal starch glue. With painstaking care she had then carried out a resew and put in a new lining. Making a new spine from the best quality goatskin leather, she had then inserted it so that it would blend in nicely and not stick out like an ugly sore thumb. With the original covers redyed she had then applied the gold leaf lettering and lastly given the finished book a good polish.

Not without a warm glow of pride at a job well done, she now gave it a final buff with a soft cloth, put it carefully on the shelf behind her, and rang the owner to tell him he could come and collect it now.

That done, and before she started on the binding of a dissertation, she made herself a mug of tea and went outside to enjoy the afternoon sun. It really was a beautiful day, a day that felt washed clean and bright.

She loved the month of April; it was when spring really seemed to make up its mind that it was here to stay. Dad had cut the grass last night when he'd returned from work and the sweet smell of freshly mown grass still laced the air. If she listened hard, she could make out the sound of lambs bleating from Denston Farm which was the other side of the vivid yellow rape field and the copse beyond. The cherry and damson trees were already in blossom in the garden and the apple trees in the orchard were only a week or so away from flowering. The same was true for the hawthorn hedge, which had now filled out with fat leaf buds bursting open to release soft green leaves like butterflies emerging from their cocoons. Cowslips were growing like Topsy along the hedgerows too.

Yesterday the weather had been just as lovely and Saskia had spent a couple of hours in the garden with Grandpa O planting potatoes, purple sprouting broccoli, peas and French beans. There was something delightfully satisfying about the sight of the newly erected cane wigwams standing to attention in the freshly dug beds.

When the risk of frost had passed, she would help Oliver put up the rows of parallel cane supports in readiness for planting out the runner beans that were coming on in the greenhouse. A stickler for not sowing his seeds in the garden too soon, her grandfather held firm to the maxim that if it wasn't warm enough to park your bare bum on the earth, then it wasn't warm enough for your seeds!

In a few days it would be Easter and hidden in a cupboard in her workshop, Saskia had the chocolate eggs she had bought for her family. She had bought one for Libby as well. It was quite remarkable how easily Libby had slipped into the routine of their lives, especially as no one else had ever done so before her. Saskia hoped she didn't slip out just as easily, it was nice seeing Dad so happy. There was a light-heartedness about him these days that suited him.

No sooner had this thought made its presence felt than the familiar old unease formed a knot of anxiety in the pit of her stomach – it was the fear she had never managed to rid herself of, that of loving another person and the pain of losing them.

Forcing herself not to dwell on anything that would spoil the loveliness of the day, she thought instead of the amusing way in which her grandfathers behaved whenever Libby was around. They bickered less, and like a couple of adolescent boys went to the trouble of sprucing themselves up when they knew she was coming, spending ages in the bathroom showering and shaving, then emerging from their bedrooms drenched in aftershave. And when Libby wasn't around, their conversations were liberally sprinkled with Libby-says-this-and-Libby-says-that.

Her father had noticed it too and after a bit of nervous umming and aahing he had asked Saskia if she was all right with the situation. An echo of the same question Matthew had asked her, she had given much the same answer. It saddened her to think Dad felt the need to tiptoe round her.

For her own part, and whether it was merely the arrival of spring that had raised her spirits, the crabbiness that had so consumed her previously had now gone. But then how could anyone feel crabby on a glorious day like this, when the sun was shining and everything felt as though it was exactly in the right place at the right time? It was days like these that made up for any bad ones. She supposed that was how people like Jacob and Kitty had got through the hardships of the war, clinging to fleeting moments of happiness.

It was three days since Matthew had phoned Saskia early in the morning while he was on his way to work. She had been only too pleased that he'd wanted to share what he'd read with her, but really she was itching to read the second notebook for herself, because while Matthew had given her the bare bones of what had happened in the story, he had undoubtedly glossed over the details.

It had occurred to her that she might be able to hurry the process of Matthew passing on the notebook to her by inviting him to join them for lunch over Easter. She had mentioned it to her father, and he'd been all for it. But then, given his apparent fondness for Matthew and his not-so-subtle attempt at matchmaking, his reaction hadn't surprised her. 'Find out if he's at a loose end on Easter Sunday and invite him for lunch,' Dad had said, 'Libby will be here as well and it'll be good to see him again.'

It would, Saskia thought now, and not just because it might mean she got her hands on the second notebook that much faster. She had to admit that she had come to enjoy Matthew's company. Since spending the day on her own with him at Glaskin House, and then seeing him again when he came to collect the second notebook and the Russian Orthodox Bible Gil had found, she had caught herself thinking of him more and more. She liked the fact that he'd cared so much about an elderly man to whom he wasn't even related and of whom he had nothing but good things to say. It made her curious to know him a lot better, to know what made him tick. Moreover, she was curious to see how she felt being around him again, because, and there was no point in deluding herself by not articulating this growing belief, a small part of her was beginning to feel just a little bit attracted to him. But she would keep that well and truly to herself for now. The last thing she needed was her father revelling in any kind of a told-you-so satisfaction.

She watched Grandpa O appear at the back door and toddle off down the garden towards the greenhouse. She was tempted to go and join him, but thinking of the dissertation that awaited her attention, she stayed where she was on the wrought-iron bench to finish her tea.

Running a hand over the armrest of the metal bench, she rubbed at the paint that was flaking off. It was time to give the seat a new lick of paint. Ever since she'd been fifteen years old she had been the one to take care of the bench and it was a labour of love. Harvey had bought it at a garden reclamation yard the first summer they moved here and back then her legs had been too short to reach the ground when she sat on it. As that young child she had often sat here on her own and secretly cried for her mother who was already beginning to fade from her memory.

How changed she was since then, she thought, as she stretched out her legs in front of her.

Or was she? She might have grown physically, but had she really changed that much from the bewildered and heart-broken child who had sat here and cried for her mother and grandmothers? The child who had been too afraid to go to school for fear of coming home and finding the rest of her family had been taken from her.

And was there not a part of her which deliberately sought out the familiar to avoid the risk of putting herself in harm's way? However that harm was perceived? When was the last time she had put herself in the frontline of life and actually taken any kind of a risk?

After some minutes pondering this, she drank the last of her tea and went back inside the workshop. She had only got as far as clearing a space to start work on binding the dissertation when she made a decision. As risks went it hardly counted, she supposed, certainly not by most people's standards, but to her it did. She hated the thought that Matthew might think she and her family had nothing better to do than constantly issue invitations for him to come to Ashcombe, or worse, that he might think he was being set up with regard to her.

Putting her concern aside, she decided to text Matthew rather than ring and disturb him at work. It would also make it easier for him to refuse – with its recourse to brevity, texting was the convenient way for anyone to wriggle politely out of something they didn't want to do. Guilty of having done it herself a few times, a spoken untruth always felt more of an untruth than a lie in a text.

Chapter Thirty-Six

April Gray had been twenty-one years old when she'd given birth to Matthew and today – Easter Saturday – would have been her fifty-sixth birthday.

His conception had not been planned and the shock of it was enough to unsettle April's boyfriend, a thirty-year-old car salesman who had no desire to be saddled with a wife and child. He stuck around for a couple of years, but then walked away. The last anyone heard of him, he'd found himself a new job and moved out of the area, nobody knew where. Matthew's mother saw no point in trying to track him down so she could force him to accept a share of the parental responsibility – having shown his true colours, she wanted nothing more to do with him.

With admirable pragmatism she put her energy in to accepting that she had repeated the pattern put in place by her own mother who'd got pregnant with her at a similar age and the best thing she could do was to get on with life with a baby she adored. Declaring herself as bad a picker of men as her mother, she vowed to steer clear of them. All that mattered, Matthew once overheard her telling his grandmother, was raising her son not to turn out to be like his father.

Sadly another pattern was repeated when Matthew's mother died of breast cancer, just as her own mother had at the age of fifty.

For Mum's last birthday, a few weeks after she'd been told she had cancer, Jacob had treated them to lunch in Lavenham at The Swan Hotel. It had been a bittersweet celebration, each of them doing their level best to ignore Mum's diagnosis and the likely outcome. Having read up extensively online, Matthew knew off pat the treatments involved and the statistical chances of his mother making a full recovery, but deep down he'd known that the dice was loaded, that history was about to repeat itself.

At Mum's specific instruction, Jacob was banned from ever referring to her illness, other than when she asked him for time off when she needed treatment. 'Please carry on being your usual annoying self,' she told Jacob when Matthew brought her back from the hospital after her third round of chemo, which had left her horribly sick and weak. 'Please don't be sympathetic – I couldn't take that from you.'

Hovering awkwardly in the small sitting room of The Coach House as she lay on the sofa, Jacob had sunk his hands deep into his pockets. 'April,' he'd said gruffly, 'I think this might be the time for you to shut up and do as you're told by Matthew and me.'

'Not while I still have breath left in me,' she'd said. 'And don't ever call me April again. It's Mrs Gray to you, Professor Belinsky.' For the sake of propriety, she had always retained her married status and made a point of always calling Jacob by his official title.

Jacob had known exactly what he was doing; making Mum fight him made her smile and even laugh on occasion. And when she was really ill, towards the end when she could no longer bear to receive visits from concerned friends in the village, he would sit and read to her. Yet as ill as she was, it amused Mum greatly that he was prepared to lower his highbrow standards and read from the romantic novels she enjoyed so much. 'You know this is all nonsense, don't you?' Matthew had heard him saying to Mum one day after reading a particularly schmaltzy ending to a book. 'Real life isn't so neat and tidy.'

'So you would deny me my happy ending even on my deathbed?' had been Mum's reply.

Matthew had never really thought of it before, but in

many ways Jacob had fulfilled an unlikely dual role for the pair of them – a surrogate grandfather to Matthew and a father figure to Mum.

In the light of *The Dandelion Years*, Matthew couldn't help but wonder if, in those last few weeks of Mum's life, when they'd been so close, Jacob hadn't confided in her about Kitty. But whether he did or not, it was immaterial because if he had, Mum had taken the story to the grave with her.

Which was where Matthew was now this Easter Saturday. He'd come here on her birthday to tidy her grave and leave a bunch of her favourite flowers. He knew the peonies wouldn't last long, but her love of them meant no other flower would do. Nothing lasted for ever anyway, he thought with a shrug when, after also tidying Jacob's plot, he left the churchyard and returned to Glaskin House.

Fliss had flown to Barcelona last night for a hen weekend with a bunch of old friends from medical school and with four days away from the office to relish, and the weather set to be fine, Matthew had decided to spend the Easter weekend here. Tomorrow he had lunch to look forward to with Saskia and her family. He was surprised how much he was looking forward to being back at Ashcombe. There was something rather special about the place. And the family who lived there.

Having not read as much of Jacob's second notebook as he'd wanted to during the week, he planned to spend the rest of the day putting that right so he could give Saskia the notebook tomorrow as a surprise. Although he strongly suspected it wouldn't be a surprise. He reckoned she was pinning her hopes on him having finished it by now and expecting delivery of it tomorrow.

A beer in hand, the notebook gripped firmly in place under his arm, he dragged a dusty wooden chair out from the dank, cobwebby outhouse that stank of mould and creosote and took it round to the back of the house to sit in the sun.

Chapter Thirty-Seven

December 1943

It was cold enough to snow.

Snuggled up to me, a woollen scarf wrapped around her neck, Kitty looked out of the window. 'I love winter,' she said softly.

'That,' I said, my voice equally hushed in view of the full train carriage in which we were seated, 'is a big difference between us.'

'You mean that's another to add to all the other differences between us,' she teased, just as out in the corridor beyond our carriage a group of soldiers started up with 'It's a Long Way to Tipperary'. She tugged off her leather gloves and began counting her fingers. 'Firstly you don't like jitterbugging and I—'

'Only because I have two left feet and could no more dance than I could fly to the—'

'Don't interrupt.' She cut me off with a tap of her hand. 'Secondly, you don't approve of my fondness for Spam and you think fish paste sandwiches should only be eaten by cats, and thirdly you think—'

'All right,' I said, interrupting her again, 'you've made your point, which leaves me wondering whether being so incompatible we really should be reconsidering our getting married.'

Curling her fingers into a fist, she punched me lightly on the shoulder. 'How jolly rotten of you to say such a beastly thing!'

I kept a straight face as best I could. 'Better that you should know just how beastly I can be before you're stuck with such a brute forever.'

She looked up at me from beneath half-closed eyelids, a look that never failed to make me want to take her in my arms and kiss her. 'I'll take my chances, thank you very much, as I'm fairly confident I can smooth out the bits of you I find so disagreeable.'

'Care to share what exactly you find so disagreeable?'

'Goodness, no,' she responded with a small laugh, 'the list is extensive and would take far too long.'

Abruptly she leant forward and wiped at the condensation that had misted the carriage window. With everything shrouded in blackout darkness, it was impossible to know precisely where we were, but taking out the pocket watch that had once belonged to my grandfather and which was given to me when I graduated from Cambridge, I said, 'Another twenty minutes and we should be there.'

'Unless there's a delay,' a fellow traveller remarked. He was directly opposite me and until now hadn't so much as peered at us over the top of the book he'd been reading since we'd pulled out of the station. I wondered how much of our conversation he had overheard above the singing in the corridor.

I nodded at him in a friendly fashion, keeping to myself that in this instance I would happily welcome a three-hour delay if it meant I could spend even longer with Kitty.

We were on our way back to Bletchley after visiting my family for a second time. It was the week before Christmas and knowing that I would be working on Christmas Day – and knowing too that my wonderfully contradictory grandmother saw it as an opportunity to be together as a family, despite it being a Christian celebration – I had engineered this day off in lieu so that I could take them a few presents. Gifts were always welcome, no matter my grandmother's beliefs, and so from the limited shops in Bletchley I had scavenged a scarf for my mother, a boxed set of handkerchiefs for my grandmother, a pair of leather gloves for my father, along with a bottle of Billy's damson liqueur which she had thrust upon me in return for my helping to fill out some forms for her for the Ministry of Agriculture. Kitty had leapt at the chance to join me and now that I knew there was nothing to fear from my family, I had readily agreed that we make the trip together. Luckily her request to swap her day off with a colleague was not turned down by her section leader and so we had set off happily this morning.

The day had been a great success and thinking now of the photographs we had posed for in the studio owned by a friend of my father – Kitty had been talking for some time that she wanted some pictures of me – I hoped they would come out all right. Normally I hated having my picture taken because I always looked so awful but Kitty had somehow made me relax and not adopt my usual frozen-faced look when under the focus of a camera lens.

But the best aspect of the day was that, hidden inside my coat pocket, was a small velvet bag containing the ruby ring I would give Kitty on New Year's Eve. My grandmother, true to her word, had handed it over and with her blessing.

When we stepped on to the cold, dark platform at Bletchley, a familiar face appeared through the steam and surge of travellers getting off the train with us.

'Hello, you two,' Chatterton-Jones greeted us volubly and for all to hear. 'What've you been up to, a secret assignation in town?'

'Oh really, Charles, don't be such an ass!' Kitty reprimanded him with the kind of dismissive ease I was incapable of.

'So what *have* you been doing?' he pressed.

'I've been having some portrait photographs done, if you must know,' she improvised smoothly and with partial truth, 'and bumped into Jacob on the train coming back. What have you been up to, more to the point?' It had now become a game for Kitty to mislead and misinform as often as she could. She loved the enquiring glances, the expressions of puzzlement, and the general fascination our regularly being seen together generated. Privately I thought that only an exceedingly stupid person would not guess we were so much more than mere friends.

'Oh, a rather tiresome family celebration with my parents,' Chatterton-Jones said airily, pausing to light his pipe and oblivious to those around him whose way he was blocking. When he'd got the thing going and dispensed with the spent match, he looked directly at me, 'I believe you met my ma and pa down at Fanley Manor not so long ago. They said you caused quite a stir.'

It was inevitable he'd hear of my meeting his parents, but even so, the manner of our meeting and his mentioning it rattled me.

Just lately I had tried several times to get Kitty to tell me what repercussions had followed my visit to Fanley Manor, but she had stuck steadfastly to the line that she had apologised to her parents for her outburst and in the way things always were in her family, it was forgotten and blamed on her emotional state while convalescing. I couldn't bring myself to believe this was true. I was resolutely of the opinion that her parents had me firmly in their sights and were biding their time before forbidding their daughter from further association.

'A stir,' I repeated as nonchalantly as I could, 'doesn't ring a bell with me. How about you, Kitty?'

'No, nothing special springs to mind. But then, with my parents a stir is an everyday occurrence. Oh drat, it's started to rain! Now I shall get thoroughly soaked cycling back to my digs.' We had both left our bicycles at the station that morning.

'No need to worry about getting wet,' Chatterton-Jones said, 'I'll run you back in my car.' He pointed across the road to where an Austin Eight four-door saloon was parked.

'What about my bicycle?' asked Kitty.

'Plenty of room in the back. Which means, old chap,' he looked at me through a cloud of pipe smoke, 'there won't be space for you I'm afraid. But you haven't far to go, have you?'

Anger scorched my being at the effortless way in which this confounded man could take charge, and after helping him shove Kitty's bike into the back of his car I watched them drive off down the unlit street, silently cursing him.

I continued cursing him all the way back to my digs as the rain turned to sleet, spreading a deep, penetrating chill through me as I pedalled hard. I should, of course, have been grateful to this knight in shining armour for saving Kitty from a drenching and catching her death of cold on this bitterly cold night, but I could not bring myself to be grateful. And oh, how I hated knowing that in one single flip of the coin I could go from the ecstasy of love to its polar opposite, utter torment.

Mrs Pridmore pounced when I let myself in and let rip with a predictable scolding for dripping on her precious linoleum and hall runner. When she'd finished ranting, she informed me that I wasn't to think about a bath as there was no hot water.

With strained politeness, and knowing supper would have been served an hour ago – I could smell something unappetisingly cabbagy in the air – I enquired whether there was anything to eat.

'You know the rules, Mr Belsinky, I can't be expected to cook all hours of the night just because you can't keep to the schedule.'

'It's Belinsky,' I said, fighting the urge to grab the woman by her fat, wobbling neck and strangle the life out of her. 'If there's anything cold you have to offer, and which wouldn't be too much bother for you, I'd be grateful.' *Apart from your cold meanness, with which your generosity knows no bounds*, I declined from adding.

'There's a bit of corned beef left over from lunch which I was saving for tomorrow,' she said grudgingly. 'I suppose you could have that with some grated carrot. Take it or leave it.'

'Thank you, that and a cup of tea will be sufficient. I'll be down in a few minutes once I've changed out of my wet clothes.'

Could I have had a more unwelcome return to my digs? Squelching and shivering my way up the unlit narrow stairs, and seriously wondering what the hell Mrs Pridmore did with the food rationing books we were compelled to give her, I pictured Kitty at the farmhouse warming herself in front of the range while Billy served her something hot and delicious to eat. But then I pictured Chatterton-Jones sliding his well-shod feet under Billy's kitchen table and making himself comfortably at home.

Upstairs I hung my wet coat on the back of the door, removed my shoes and stripped off my sopping wet trousers and socks. I knew it would take forever for my clothes to dry in the damp cold of my room, but with no choice, I draped my things over the wooden clothes horse between my bed and the window.

I awoke in the middle of the night feeling far from well. I had a pounding headache and, despite the coldness of the room, I felt hot and feverish. I didn't need a doctor to tell me I was coming down with something. But what had woken me was not feeling unwell, but a dream. I'd dreamt I was about to propose to Kitty, but I couldn't find the ruby ring my grandmother had given me, and searching all over Bletchley Park for it, I found only a rusting old chain-link.

The dream was just a dream, I knew, but it made me realise that I hadn't removed the ring from my coat pocket and put it somewhere safe. Common sense told me it was quite safe in my coat pocket for now, and perhaps it was my feverish state to blame, but I had to know it was still there. Such was my haste to put my mind at rest, I leapt out of bed and stubbed my toe on the leg of the armchair. Letting out a loud and distinct cry of pain, I hopped the last two paces over to the door where my coat hung.

To my horror, and it didn't matter how many times I put my hand inside each and every one of the pockets, the ring wasn't there. I switched on the light and made another frenzied search, pulling the pocket linings out in the dim light as though the ring could somehow be secreted within the folds or stitching.

But no. The ring and the little velvet pouch it had been inside wasn't there. In desperation I checked my trousers in case I'd misremembered where I'd put it.

Yet again I drew a blank. I could have wept with anger and frustration. The ring had been safe for all these years – and after only a few hours in my possession it was lost! How was I ever going to explain that to my grandmother?

And just as bad, how could I ask Kitty to be my wife on New Year's Eve without a ring?

Was this a sign, an omen that we were doomed not to be together?

Chapter Thirty-Eight

December 1943

I was no malingerer, but the next morning I knew the chances of making it to work for my shift that afternoon were slim to non-existent. It would be the first day of work I'd missed due to illness.

The fever I had woken with in the night had worsened; my throat was raw, my head felt as if it had a steel band wrapped tightly around it, and my limbs were heavy and seemingly without strength. A number of my colleagues had gone down with something similar in the last week. To be honest, it was a wonder we weren't all dropping like flies, or dead, given how closely confined we were in the huts and how perishing cold it could be at times.

Yet as ill as I felt, it was nothing to the torment that consumed my mind. How could I have lost the ring? I was not a careless person, far from it; as Kitty often pointed out, I was ludicrously cautious. I certainly wasn't one of those absent-minded people who put things down and then forget all about them.

The only answer I could come up with was that a pick-pocket had targeted me, either on the way to the station from my parents, or while on the train. Or could it have been when we arrived back at Bletchley and Chatterton-Jones had blocked the way on the platform while lighting his pipe? I conjured up the scene in my mind's eye – people in a hurry to get home, people tutting crossly as they'd tried to get round the three of us. Had it been then, when distracted by my annoyance at bumping into Chatterton-Jones, that a professional sleight of hand had relieved me of the ring?

In my near deliriously feverish state it made absolute sense to lay the blame at Chatterton-Jones's door and tell myself that if it weren't for him being on that train, the ring would still be in my possession.

I tried to summon the energy to go downstairs and ask Mrs Pridmore if I could use the telephone to tell them at work I wouldn't be in today, but my body held me captive and eventually I tumbled into a fitful sleep.

At two in the afternoon I surfaced, sweating and shivering, and in desperate need of the lavatory. Emerging from the bathroom, and tightening the belt on my dressing gown, I went in search of Mrs Pridmore and the use of the telephone.

The black Bakelite telephone was a recent addition to the household and Mrs Pridmore regarded it with almost as much suspicion as she did me. Several times I had witnessed the scene of it ringing shrilly while Mrs Pridmore hid in the kitchen waiting for it to cease its disturbing racket. She claimed the handset was yet another thing designed to make her life more difficult and play on her nerves. Which begged the question why she'd had the telephone installed in the first place. Perhaps it was no more than a means to impress those neighbours who didn't have one. I had, however, observed her using it, extending a fat finger and dialling with infinite care and then bellowing into the device as though her voice, unaided, had to carry itself all the way to whoever it was at the other end of the line.

Knowing how dreadful I must look – unshaven and probably smelling none too fresh – I approached the kitchen with trepidation. I went in this direction, to the back of the house, because the front room was as quiet as the grave, as was the dining room, and with the sound of jaunty music playing on the wireless in the kitchen, I concluded this would be where I'd find Mrs Pridmore.

'Mrs Pridmore,' I called out hoarsely, wincing at the sharp

pain it caused my throat and taking myself by surprise at the lack of sound to come out of my mouth.

There was no reply and so I ventured into the private domain that was the kitchen, where no man dare set foot. As lodgers, we had been warned in no uncertain terms against disturbing our landlady when she was in her inner sanctum, her Holy of Holies. I had once remarked to Griffiths and Farrington that this precautionary measure was for our own good, that if we ever saw the process by which Mrs Pridmore put together our revolting meals, we would surely never have the stomach to eat another dish cooked by her.

The door was ajar and, my hand raised to push it open, I hesitated at the sound of voices against the backdrop of music. The voices were low and insistent – quarrelsome, I'd go so far to say. One belonged unmistakably to Mrs Pridmore, the other to a man. At a guess I'd say they were arguing. There was nothing new in that; Mrs Pridmore was the most argumentative person I knew. She argued with the milkman, the postman and anyone who came within range who was not to her liking.

With my ear as near as dammit pressed to the door, I shamelessly listened to the heated exchange taking place and, as the minutes passed, it suddenly all made sense. I had heard of such things happening, but hadn't ever seriously considered it would be going on right under my own nose. I had dismissed Mrs Pridmore as no more than a petty, mean-spirited woman who took sport in goading people for the sheer hell of it. Now I saw that I had underestimated her, for it was all too clear from what I was hearing that she had been systematically depriving us of the food to which we were entitled and selling it from her back door.

Peering in through the gap in the doorway, I could see a box on the table which she was filling with rationed items – cheese, milk, bacon, tea, sugar, jam, biscuits, and tins of fruit and dried egg powder. To the side of her, a balding man with the face of a weasel, dressed in a short jacket with a scarf loosely tied at his neck, was counting out money. I recognised him; I'd seen him coming and going from the house on several occasions. And always by the back door. I had even mentioned him to Kitty once, joking that Mrs Pridmore had a paramour.

The transaction looking to be almost complete, I debated what to do. Should I burst in on them and melodramatically declare the game was up, or quietly withdraw and report what I'd seen to the police? There were harsh penalties for anyone caught committing black-market activity. Mrs Pridmore could face a hefty fine and up to two years in prison for what she was doing. Could I really be responsible for sending her to prison? Did I hate her that much?

Yes, I thought grimly, remembering the way she had treated me last night and all the other times when she had been so appallingly rude. There were also those instances when I had been convinced she had been riffling through my few possessions. Had she been looking for something to sell? How disappointed she must have been to discover that I had nothing of any worth.

No sooner had I thought this than I wondered about the only item of value I had brought to the house – my grandmother's ring. But that was absurd. There had been no opportunity for the ghastly woman to steal it last night. Not unless ... not unless she had crept in while I slept. Surely I would have heard her? Wouldn't I? But in my feverish state, an elephant could have barged its way in during the night and I would very probably have been none the wiser.

The outrageous notion that Mrs Pridmore could have done such a despicable thing fired me up and, without another thought, I pushed open the door, fully prepared to do battle.

But my timing was abysmal. Just then, at the moment two startled faces turned towards me, there came a loud and sudden ring from the doorbell at the front of the house.

*

It was difficult to know who looked more shocked, the two people in the kitchen, or me, but recovering fast, the weasel-faced man scooped up the box and fled through the back door, banging it after him.

That just left Mrs Pridmore and me.

And whoever was at the front door.

'If you'll kindly get out of the way,' she said sharply, brazenly composing herself with impressive speed, 'I need to see who that is.'

I blocked her way.

'No,' I said hoarsely, 'you need to give me some answers. Who was that man and why were you giving him that box of rationed food?'

'That's none of your business!' she snapped.

'I think you'll find it's very much my business. So much so, I'm going to report you to the police for black-market dealing.' My threat would have carried more weight had my voice not been reduced to a pathetic and painful husk.

From behind me came another ring at the doorbell.

'How dare you!' she hissed. 'How dare you accuse me of such a thing! Me, a decent woman with not a brass farthing to my name!'

'I dare all right. What's more, I strongly suspect you of helping yourself to more than just the rationed food you should have been giving your lodgers.'

She prodded me hard in the chest, making me cough. 'Get out of my way *now*, because I'll tell you this for nothing, I'm a respectable woman doing my bit for the war effort by giving you a roof over your head, when by rights you should be seeing active service rather than hiding here. You're a coward! Just like the other two here. Cowards, the whole bloody lot of you! I'll be glad to see the back of you. Because that's what's going to happen, I'm going to report *you* and then you'll be gone, and good riddance, I say!' She gave my chest another vicious prod. 'And it'll be *you* who goes to prison for spreading nasty things about honest, hardworking folk like me.'

Such was her righteous indignation, I lost my nerve. Had I got it wrong? Had I leapt to a hasty and mistaken conclusion? But then I saw the money on the table. 'What's that for, then?'

'That,' she roared, 'is none of your business!'

And propelling her repulsive body forwards, she pushed me out of the way, marched through to the hall and snatched open the front door.

'Yes,' she snarled at the man standing on the doorstep. 'What do you want?'

I couldn't believe my eyes – it was Chatterton-Jones! Dressed in a good-quality suit and cashmere coat, he tipped his hat and smiled at Mrs Pridmore as though she were the most beautiful creature he'd ever set eyes on. Catching sight of me some way behind her, he said, 'I'm sorry to bother you, madam, but I wonder if I might have a word with Mr Belinsky.'

'I suppose you're another one,' she said ungraciously. 'Another lazy, no-good coward!'

Stepping forward and mustering as much dignity as a man can in a dressing gown, I said, 'Mrs Pridmore, I really wouldn't be so rude if I were you because this gentleman is from the Ministry of Food. In view of my suspicions, I asked him to pay a visit.'

Her eyes bulged, her face paled, and her chins wobbled.

'Kindly leave us alone,' I said, adopting an authoritative voice that was laughably at odds with my attire and the soreness of my throat.

I took Chatterton-Jones up to my room where I hoped we'd have a degree of privacy.

'Good Lord, Belinsky, what was all that about?' he asked when we were alone.

'*Ssh!*' I said, listening at the door for the telltale sounds of footsteps coming up the stairs.

'I say, you are all right, aren't you? Pressure of work and all that; it gets to some chaps.'

'Don't be absurd,' I said crossly, 'of course I'm all right.'

He looked at me dubiously. 'I have to say you're giving a fair impersonation of a man tipped over the edge. Not to put too fine a point on it, old chap, you look awful. Completely done in.'

'Look,' I said impatiently, sinking on to the edge of my unmade bed, suddenly exhausted. 'I've come down with that bug doing the rounds at work. But that's not what's troubling me.'

He sat in the armchair opposite and I told him what I'd seen downstairs in the kitchen and how it tied in with the paucity of food served at mealtimes by Mrs Pridmore.

'Ah,' he said with a smile. 'Hence my persona as a bod from the Ministry of Food. That was rather clever of you. Very quick thinking.'

Ignoring his comment, I said, 'Worse still, I think she might have stolen something from me. Something precious.'

'Really? What exactly? Money?'

Reluctant to admit to Chatterton-Jones why I'd been in possession of a ring, I said, 'It's something of a personal nature. I had it yesterday and now it's gone.'

'It wouldn't by any chance be this, would it?' From his coat pocket, he pulled out a small black velvet pouch. 'It's why I'm here. I found it in the back of my car last night after I'd dropped Kitty off. It must have fallen out of your pocket when we were getting her bicycle in.'

'Oh my God!' I murmured, taking it from his extended hand. 'You've no idea how pleased I am to see that.'

'I think I do.' Then, crossing one leg over the other and smoothing down the woollen fabric of his trousers, he went on, 'I presume you're about to propose to the divinely lovely Kitty?'

What could I say? To lie would make me look even more foolish than I already did; after all, I'd as good as accused Mrs Pridmore of stealing the ring, yet here it was. 'Yes,' I said simply.

'You know her parents don't approve, don't you?'

'I'm aware they might feel indifferent towards me, yes.'

'It's nothing personal, old chap, they'd just prefer their youngest daughter marry someone of their ... of their own choosing.'

'I'm aware of that too,' I replied, registering how carefully he had avoided using the word 'class' or 'background'. 'But has Kitty no choice in the matter?'

'Yes, so long as her choice fits in with theirs. You're an intelligent chap, you know how these things work. Besides, isn't it the same for your own people?' Again a careful choice of words from him. He could so easily have said 'you lot'.

In principle he was right, of course, but passing over this, I said, 'And I suppose you'd be a much better choice, wouldn't you? The right background, the right credentials. The right—'

He jerked forward in the chair. 'I say, steady on there, Belinsky! Much as I'm very fond of the girl, you have nothing to worry about from me; I'm not the marrying kind, I like my freedom too much. Lord, I'd hate to have my wings clipped, even by a girl as enchanting as Kitty.'

I stared at him, trying to decide if I believed him or not.

'So what are you going to do about your landlady?' he asked in the absence of a response from me. 'Throw the dragon in clink? Though if I were you, I'd use the power your discovery gives you. Tell her to serve you the food you're entitled to and you'll say no more about the matter.'

Surprised at his suggestion, I gave it a few moments of thoughtful consideration, before finally seeing the sense in it. A smile twitched at the corners of my mouth. 'I could actually have the fire on in my room for as long as I wanted,' I said, my gaze settling on the clothes horse over by the window where my trousers were doubtless still wet. 'And the luxury of more than one hot bath a week.'

Chatterton-Jones smiled at me. 'There you are then. A satisfactory and highly beneficial solution found, and what's more, your ring is now back in your safekeeping. All in all, I call that a good day's work. Talking of which, I should be on my way. Shall I let the appropriate people know you won't be in?'

I nodded. 'Thank you. And ... and thank you for coming here today. I'm very grateful.'

I suddenly found myself regarding the man before me in a new and very different light. Furthermore, I was forced to acknowledge that, very likely I had allowed a shameful inferiority complex to get the better of me and, in so doing, had wilfully distorted Chatterton-Jones's true character. I had learnt an important lesson today.

'Don't mention it,' he said, now on his feet and clapping a hand on my shoulder, 'it's the least I could do. Just glad to be of help.'

I went to open the door for him when I realised that there was still something important I needed him to do for me if I was going to ensure Mrs Pridmore behave as I wanted her to.

'Will you speak to Mrs Pridmore for me?' I asked. 'Keep up the pretence that you're from the Ministry of Food, and tell her that you're giving her a warning to stop her illegal goings-on and that if she doesn't, you'll be back with the full weight of the law at your disposal?'

He grinned. 'Consider it done, old chap! By the time I've finished with her, you'll have her in the palm of your hand.'

I could think of other places I'd sooner have the vile woman, but the palm of my hand would suffice for now.

Chapter Thirty-Nine

With Jacob very much on his mind, Matthew thought how he too had initially misjudged somebody's character.

At their first meeting he had thought Saskia detached and stand-offish, whereas now he was getting to know her, and her family, he could see she was anything but. Admittedly she had a tendency to retreat into moments of quiet introspection, but that was something he often did himself. He'd never been one of those people who felt compelled to fill a lull in the conversation, not when there was usually somebody else only too ready to step in and fill the silence with some random inanity. Jacob had been fond of saying that only an fool utters his whole mind. Another favourite of his had been that if you can't improve the silence, it was better not to speak.

It was advice that Matthew had taken very much to heart and relied upon heavily when called to be an expert witness in court; it was probably why Jim Rycroft had referred to him as an inscrutable bugger.

Here now, in the garden of Ashcombe, Jim Rycroft and the new fraud case to which he'd been assigned felt a long way away, which was an unusual sensation for him as invariably work tended to take up a large part of his weekends and dominated his thoughts. Following behind Saskia as he helped to ferry plates, dishes and cutlery from the kitchen to the large wooden table in the garden, he tried again to put his finger on what it was that made him feel so comfortable being here with this family.

To a degree it was to do with these people, who hadn't

known him for very long, welcoming him so readily into their home, but it was also the sensation of being absorbed into what felt like an oasis of genuine warmth and affection. The more time he spent in their company, the more he was left with the very clear impression that this family genuinely cared about each other, that they were bound together with something far stronger than a mere family connection.

At Saskia's invitation, he sat in the chair next to her and wondered if it had always been as agreeable here at Ashcombe. When the family first came, burdened with their grief, had they struggled to find a way that would make their new life together work? Had there been arguments? Were there times when they'd regretted their decision?

With everything now on the table, it was the turn of Ralph to bring out Harvey's *pièce de résistance*, a large and spectacular platter of roast lamb studded with sprigs of rosemary. Its appearance was met with loud applause and a loud whistle from Saskia. Mopping his brow with a handkerchief, Harvey took a bow, then taking a swig of red wine and arming himself with a fearsome carving knife, he set about the leg of lamb.

Watching the scene, and listening to Saskia teaching Libby how to whistle using the method of sticking her fingers in her mouth, Matthew concluded that this family had achieved something exceptional; they had pulled off the best aspects of communal life but without the clash of egos that so frequently accompanied the arrangement. It was a way of life that many dreamt of, but too often the reality shattered the dream.

Matthew had come across families that proudly flew the flag of supposed normality – in that they weren't considered dysfunctional – but he had seen for himself that often the ones who made the most noise about being perfectly happy seldom were, because sometimes they were so smugly intent on portraying the appearance of harmony, they were blind to the undercurrents of discord going on right under their noses.

He reckoned it was the same with marriage. In the course of his work he'd encountered many a divorcing couple and heard the same story of disbelief that a partner could have strayed without the other knowing. 'But I thought we were so happy,' was the recurrent refrain.

Fliss's parents were a prime example of this. Not long before Matthew met Fliss, and a day after a big bash to celebrate whatever wedding anniversary it had been, Fliss's mother had discovered her husband had been having an affair with a work colleague. According to Fliss, her parents had somehow managed to patch things up and the subject was never referred to again. Having only known the family in the aftermath of this crisis, and therefore unable to make a direct before and after comparison, it seemed to Matthew that the wreckage left in the wake of the affair had resulted in a marriage that was unhealthily tense, as though Rod and Sally Campbell were walking a tightrope. It also meant that family occasions had come to symbolise so much more than a mere celebratory get-together: they were performances freighted with a sort of teeth-gritting artifice with everybody acting a part. No wonder Fliss wanted Matthew there with her in Copenhagen!

'There you go, Matthew,' Harvey said, passing him a plate generously loaded with slices of lamb. 'Help yourself to everything else, no standing on ceremony.'

'I hope we're not being too overwhelming for you,' Saskia said in a quiet voice as she handed him a divided dish that contained new and roast potatoes.

'Not at all,' he replied, 'I'm enjoying myself. It was kind of you to invite me.'

'Not kind at all. I'm sure you're astute enough to know perfectly well that I had an ulterior motive behind the invitation: I want to know how *The Dandelion Years* is progressing.'

'And there was me thinking it was my scintillating company you wanted.'

'Oh yeah, that too. But I think it only fair to say I shan't let you leave here until I've extracted every last scrap of information out of you.'

'I don't doubt it,' he said with a smile. 'I'll fill you in later, shall I?'

She smiled back at him. 'Yes, when I can interrogate you in peace.'

With everyone now served, and as head of the table, Harvey raised his glass. 'Happy Easter to you all, and may I say how good it is to have such delightful guests joining us. To Libby and Matthew, thank you for adding to the occasion.'

'To Libby and Matthew,' the others said in unison.

After they'd all drunk from their glasses, Libby raised hers again, and with her glance directed towards the house behind them, she said, 'To Ashcombe, may it never change.'

Was that the answer, thought Matthew as everyone murmured agreement. Was the house the key to the special atmosphere created here, almost as though it was an additional member of the family, a benign but forceful guiding hand? Could a house have that effect on anyone? Perhaps it could, he thought, for hadn't he always felt perfectly at ease during the few times he'd visited? But surely that was down to its occupants?

'Now come on, everybody; get on and eat before it gets cold!' Harvey instructed them. 'And if there's any mint sauce left, pass it this way, please.'

'You mean the mint sauce I spent an age lovingly making for you?' Oliver said, lifting the pot and passing it down the table. 'And without which this entire meal wouldn't be worth eating!'

'Indeed yes, Oliver,' Harvey said with a wink at Matthew. 'Credit where credit's due, I always say.'

The food was as delicious as the mood was genial and Matthew found himself thinking how much his mother would have enjoyed being here. Just as he hadn't, she had never known what it felt like to be a part of a big and happy family; she had only had her mother and Matthew. And then Jacob.

It was probably because yesterday had been the anniversary of his mother's birthday, but certain memories of her kept popping into his head when he least expected them to. It made him wonder if, after all this time, Saskia experienced the same thing: that a certain memory or a feeling could still creep up on her from nowhere.

Realising that Ralph was talking to him – he'd asked if probate was any nearer to being completed – he said, 'I'm told it should be all wrapped up sometime in the coming week.'

'And what will you do then?' Ralph asked.

'It sounds pretty feeble on my part, but I still haven't decided.'

'Presumably there's no rush,' Libby said from across the table.

'No, but common sense dictates I have to make up my mind soon. All the advice I'm getting is that a house that isn't lived in deteriorates faster than a house that's a proper home and permanently occupied. It already needs a lot of work doing to it; I'd hate to see it get any worse.'

'What about Jacob's books?' Saskia asked. 'What will you do with those?'

'If I sell the house, which probably I should, I'll have to sell the books. Perhaps not all, but certainly the bulk of them.'

'I know a chap who could help you on that score,' Oliver said, pausing with his fork and indicating Ralph with it. 'Decent sort, and as reliable as the day is long.'

'Ignore my father,' Ralph said good-humouredly, 'but as I've said to you before, if you do need any help from me, just say the word.'

'Thank you. I was hoping you'd suggest that. Now isn't the time, but I'd value talking to you in the coming days.'

*

'I wish it could be like this forever,' Ralph said wistfully.

'You mean you stuck there up to your elbows in soapy water doing the dishes and me drying them?' Libby said with a laugh. 'I had rather hoped for more from life.'

He smiled, rinsed out a large mixing bowl that was too large for the dishwasher and put it on the draining board. 'You know what I mean.'

She picked up the bowl and started drying it. 'Maybe I do, maybe I don't. What exactly is it you want to go on forever?'

He pointed through the open kitchen window to where his father and Harvey were snoozing in comfortable garden chairs in the shade of the cherry tree. They both wore paper hats, which Saskia had fashioned from the sports pages of the *Sunday Times*, and with a soft breeze occasionally stirring the blossom, a small shower of petals floated down from the branches and came to rest on them and the grass. 'I want those two to stay like that forever,' Ralph murmured. 'And,' pointing further down the garden to where Saskia and Matthew were playing a game of croquet, he added, 'I'd like Matthew to be a permanent fixture in Saskia's life.'

'You old romantic, you.'

He turned and faced Libby, and perhaps buoyed by a surfeit of good wine, good food and good feelings, he said, 'And I'd very much like you to be a permanent fixture as well.'

After a brief hesitation, she gave him a small awkward smile. 'You know, for some reason that doesn't sound so romantic.'

'Oh,' he said, not knowing what else to say. Had he misjudged things between them? He had thought Libby was as committed as he was to the idea of their relationship continuing. Everything seemed to be going so well. She had even taken the step of staying here for the bank holiday weekend. She'd arrived on Friday evening with a small wheelie suitcase and, unpacking her things, she'd placed her toothbrush next to his in the en-suite bathroom.

But after two nights was she now regretting that? Had she

witnessed the reality of life here at Ashcombe and thought twice about digging herself in any deeper? Could anyone really blame her? With a daughter still living at home and two elderly men in his care, she'd have to be mad to want to get any more involved! Assailed by doubts, and appalled at how upset he was at the thought of losing her for a second time, he swallowed anxiously. To compound his fear, he thought of her comment earlier in the garden about Ashcombe – *may it never change*. Was that her way of saying her presence wasn't going to be around much longer?

Unable to bear her looking at him the way she was, he turned away and reached for a Le Creuset pan to clean. Scrubbing hard, his good mood now thoroughly evaporated, he wished he'd never opened his mouth. He should have known better. What the hell made him think any sane woman would willingly take him on? Madness. Stupid, stupid *madness*! He scrubbed all the more.

But then he felt a hand on his shoulder and Libby was standing next to him. 'Stop that,' she said, 'or you'll take the enamel off and be through to the cast iron. Then you'll have Harvey's wrath to deal with.'

He shook his head. 'I'll take my chances,' he muttered, his humiliation growing.

'Ralph, stop it, please.'

He did.

'Now dry your hands,' she said, passing him a towel.

He did that too.

'Now kiss me.'

'I ... I don't think I can right now.'

'Why's that?'

'Because I think it might be a farewell kiss. That afterwards you'll go upstairs and pack and ... and I'll never see you and your wheelie suitcase again.' For some reason the thought of that small suitcase disappearing out of the door, never to be seen again, pained him enormously.

'How, in the blink of an eye, did we go from you wanting

me to be a permanent fixture to imagining kissing me good-bye?' Her voice, so soft and melodious, added to the dull ache of pain somewhere deep in his chest.

'Your look said it all. And your words about Ashcombe never changing. I'm sorry if I've been too quick to assume we wanted the same thing. Forget I ever said anything. Blame it on too much wine and sun.'

'I'd sooner blame it on stupidity,' she said. 'I think you've dried your hands quite enough now.' She took the towel from him and put it on the worktop. 'Ralph,' she said, taking his hands in hers, 'I'd love nothing better than to be a permanent fixture in your life.'

He stared at her. 'Really? But ... but you said it didn't sound romantic and ... ' His words trailed off.

She smiled. 'I meant I thought there were nicer ways of saying you wanted things to be more lasting between us. It's what I want, too. We lost each other ten years ago; I don't want that to happen for a second time.'

'So it was semantics?'

'A woman, no matter how old she is, likes a romantic gesture to be properly dressed up.'

Relief flooded through him. 'I'm sorry. What an idiot I am.'

'Yes you are. But I can think of a good way for you to make amends.'

He smiled. 'Funnily enough, so can I.'

He took her in his arms and kissed her.

Retrieving her red wooden ball from the flowerbed beneath the kitchen window, Saskia looked through it and saw her father and Libby kissing. Moving quietly away from the flowerbed and throwing her ball out of hearing of her father and Libby, she gave it a light thwack with the mallet.

'Did you just cheat?' Matthew called out to her.

She put a finger to her lips. Misunderstanding, he glanced towards her sleeping grandfathers. 'Sorry,' he mouthed.

She shook her head and went over to where he was about to knock his ball against the winning post. 'I was saving my father from any unnecessary blushes,' she said, 'he and Libby are in the kitchen and let's just say the washing up isn't getting done.'

'Oh, I see,' he said with a smile. 'How very considerate of you.'

'That's me. Go on,' she added, pointing to the coloured wooden post, 'finish the game and put me out of my misery. Jacob clearly taught you far too well, you've totally annihilated me.'

'Sorry,' he said, tapping the ball against the post, 'that was extremely ungallant of me, but knowing how well your family treats guests, I wondered if it was an Ashcombe house rule to let the guest win.'

'We have many rules, but that's not one of them.' She took the mallet and ball from him and put them in the wooden box, along with hers.

'Is that how you've made things work here, having rules?' he asked when she'd lowered the lid of the box.

'I've never thought of it that way, but I suppose it is,' she said. 'If there are rules, they're unspoken ones, mostly a respectful understanding that there are certain lines better not crossed.' She smiled. 'Such as not tapping on the kitchen window and embarrassing Dad and Libby, tempted as I was.'

'Doesn't seem odd to me,' he said, 'just a pity more families don't adopt the same tactics.'

'Mind you,' she went on, looking behind her, 'the house helps; it being as large and rambling as it is, it means there's always somewhere to hide if the need arises. And I have my workshop, of course.'

'Do you think you'll ever leave?'

The question took her by surprise and made her go on the defensive, as though he was accusing her of something. 'When the time is right,' she said stiffly, 'yes. Why wouldn't I?'

He turned to look at the view across the fields. 'I'm not sure I'd be in any hurry to leave, it's perfect here.'

She relaxed, as much as from his words as the smile that was now on his face. She liked the fact that he enjoyed being here, that, in short, he got it. During their game of croquet, while he was bringing her up to date with Jacob and Kitty, he had referred to Ashcombe as having a uniquely special atmosphere that he'd felt it the first time he'd visited. When she'd asked him if Glaskin House felt as special for him, he'd shaken his head. 'Not in the same way. But maybe it did for Jacob. Perhaps houses speak to people in different ways.' It was, she decided, a perceptive comment from him.

'You're lucky,' he said now, 'to have such a great family. And to live somewhere so beautiful.' But his face instantly clouded. 'I'm sorry, I can't believe I said that, what with you losing your mum and grandmothers.'

'It's OK,' she said. 'You're witnessing my family as it is now, and you're right, I am extraordinarily lucky.' Wanting to put him at ease again, she said, 'Come with me, I want to show you something.'

She took him down to the furthest end of the garden, out of sight from the house, and with a view across an expanse of gently sloping pastureland. 'This is where I love to come and think,' she said, climbing over the wooden fence and settling herself on the top rung. 'I love being here late at night in the summer listening to the owls. They live over there in the woods.'

'I can see why you come here,' he said, sitting next to her and following the direction of her gaze. 'It's like being in the middle of nowhere, as if the rest of the world doesn't exist.'

'That's what I like most about it; the sense of peaceful solitude it creates.'

He nodded and continued staring into the distance.

The quietness was immense, just the way Saskia liked it, and as the sun shone warmly down on them and a ridiculously large bumblebee flew drunkenly near their feet, then lumbered away to inspect a patch of clover, she said, 'When I was little I used to come here for picnics with my grand-fathers. Usually during a break from them home-schooling me.'

He turned to look at her. 'You were home-schooled?'

She explained why. 'I suppose that's partly why I've ended up being something of a loner,' she said. 'Listen, can you hear that?' It was the cry of a buzzard. She pointed up into the cloudless pale sky where the bird, circling higher and higher, was catching the thermal currents.

'I can't remember when I last had such an enjoyable day,' Matthew said some moments later. 'Thank you again for inviting me.'

The buzzard now no more than a dot in the sky, Saskia turned to look at him and found he wasn't looking up at the sky, but at her. 'We've enjoyed having you here,' she said.

His gaze intensified. 'I've never met anyone like you be-fore.'

Taken aback by his remark, she said, 'Oh dear, am I that weird?'

'No. You're far from that. It's just that I see something in you that I've never come across before. I see myself in you.'

'Is that a good thing?'

He hesitated before answering. 'I'm not sure, if I'm honest. And there's something else I'm not sure about.'

'What's that?'

He tilted his head and continuing to stare at her through slightly narrowed eyes, as if thinking hard, he said, 'I find I suddenly want to kiss you.'

She tried to affect an air of ambivalence, as if a remark like this was an everyday occurrence for her. 'Do I have any say in the matter?'

'If you have any sense you shouldn't let me.'

He spoke and looked at her with such grave solemnity, it caused her heart to miss a beat. 'What if I'm not feeling particularly sensible?' she said.

Lowering his eyes from her face, he took hold of her hand. And for what felt like a very long time, while she held her breath and myriad thoughts spun around inside her head, he just sat there contemplating her hand. He then raised his gaze, leant towards her and kissed her very lightly on the mouth.

At first it was no more than a coming together of their lips, a tentative kiss to test the waters perhaps. But then he kissed more surely and very deeply. It was a kiss as perfect as the day itself and Saskia sank into his arms, not wanting the moment to end.

Chapter Forty

Matthew drove back to Glaskin House mystified by what he'd done. He felt awful. He had never – that was *absolutely never* – cheated on anyone before. It was completely wrong what he'd done; he knew that. But even so, he tried to assuage his guilt by telling himself that he hadn't cheated in the true sense of the word. All he'd done was kiss Saskia.

That's right, he'd *only* kissed her.

And if only it had been just the *one* kiss, he might be persuaded by that argument. But it hadn't been just the one kiss. In all, he'd kissed Saskia three times. And to make matters worse, he'd enjoyed himself. He'd enjoyed the response he'd got from her as well.

His hands gripping the steering wheel, he flinched at the recollection. What the hell had he been thinking? He couldn't even claim he'd had too much to drink – knowing he'd be driving home he'd kept a close watch on how much he'd consumed, so had been stone cold sober.

Yet while he might well have been sober in the sense of not having an excess of alcohol flowing through his blood, something else had got into his system, because before he'd kissed Saskia he'd had no more idea of doing it than he'd had of staying at Ashcombe for as long as he had. His intention had been to spend the afternoon and leave around four o'clock, but instead, urged on by Saskia, he'd stayed to watch the sunset from the end of the garden and before he knew it, supper was being pressed on him along with a game of Risk, a game he hadn't played in years, not since college. Now, as he drove past the church to turn into the driveway of Glaskin House, he saw the clock face on the tower showing that it was ten minutes to midnight.

Being at Ashcombe, he decided, was like disappearing into a black hole: time seemed to stand still there. Certainly the outside world, along with any sense of right and wrong, had no longer existed for him during his visit today.

Maybe that's why he'd kissed Saskia; it hadn't felt real. He latched on to this thought, desperate for something to explain – and more importantly justify – his behaviour. Was that what he'd fallen foul of, an enjoyable day that, like a very pleasurable dream, had beguiled him into acting out of character?

OK, that sounded plausible enough, but where did that leave him? Precisely back where he'd started – a boyfriend who'd just cheated on his girlfriend, that was where! What was more, he'd cheated on Saskia as well. He reckoned her opinion of him would hit rock bottom if she knew the truth.

But then, and in spite of being furious with himself, he recalled how good it had felt sitting with Saskia at the end of the garden. How peaceful it was. And how he'd been so in tune with her. *I see myself in you*, he'd said. It was true; he did. He still wasn't sure what it was he saw in her, but somewhere along the line there was an empathy between them. It seemed unlikely that they could be kindred spirits, but that was about as close to it as he could get.

There had been no awkwardness on Saskia's part after he'd kissed her the first time – or indeed the subsequent two times. She didn't even comment on what he'd done. She'd simply turned to look across the meadow and said matter-of-factly, 'Can you hear the woodpecker? *There!* There it goes again.'

When she'd turned to look back at him again, she'd offered him a vague smile, a smile so alluringly vague it had made him want to kiss her once more. Which he had.

He'd kissed her again when finally, and reluctantly, he'd left. She'd come outside to say goodbye to him and, standing next to his car, he'd kissed her goodnight. Just a small kiss, this time. Not that that exonerated him in any way.

He let himself in at Glaskin House and, without bothering to switch on any lights, he went upstairs to the bedroom he'd used ever since Mum had died and Jacob suggested he stay over with him.

Standing in the semi-darkness, the room lit by a pool of light from the moon, he emptied his pockets, placing his things on the chest of drawers next to the bed in the order he always placed them – Jacob's pocket watch on the left, his wallet in the middle, his mobile to the right.

Out of habit, he checked his mobile for any missed calls or messages. There were two missed calls from Fliss and one text from her wishing him a Happy Easter.

The message further compounded his guilt: he'd forgotten all about wishing her a Happy Easter. In fact, he'd barely given her a thought all day. What was more, and this really was the crux of the matter, why had he never mentioned Fliss when he was with Saskia and her family? Fair enough she had only reappeared in his life just recently, but even to his mind it now looked bloody odd that not once had he uttered her name while at Ashcombe, or here at Glaskin House when Saskia had spent the day with him. And that, he feared, bore all the hallmarks of a deliberate deception. How else would Saskia and her family see it?

But he hadn't done it deliberately, he really hadn't. It was just ... he shook his head, at a loss to come up with an explanation. He genuinely had no answer.

Shamefully, the nearest he'd got to thinking about Fliss today was when he'd been seized with the urge to kiss Saskia. *If you have any sense you shouldn't let me*, he'd said to her. So yes, the tiny voice of his conscience had surfaced fleetingly to remind him that he was in no position to go around kissing girls other than Fliss. Of course, by rights, if his conscience had been doing a proper job it should have been yelling *What the hell do you think you're doing?* at full volume, but perhaps, like him, his conscience had been mellowed by the beauty of his surroundings while sitting on the fence with Saskia.

Which, as metaphors went, was one he really wasn't inclined to dissect. Not now. It was too late.

Better to go to bed and sleep the worst of his guilt away. The rest he'd deal with in the morning. He'd also have to figure out a way to deal with the aftermath of his actions. He couldn't lead Saskia on. On the other hand, he couldn't tell her the truth. If he did that, he'd never be able to face her father again, and he wanted Ralph's help with selling Jacob's books.

In one easy stride, he'd got himself into one hell of a mess.

With the window open and the duvet wrapped around her, Saskia rested her elbows on the sill and leant out into the cool, limpid silence.

The air smelled sweetly of thatch from the eaves just above her head and of dampening earth below her. It was a beautifully clear starlit night with a three-quarter luminescent moon shining down, and far away, from within the depths of the silvery light, came the hoot of an owl. She sighed happily. Was there ever a better night for indulging in a little harmless musing?

She smiled to herself and softly whispered his name out loud – *Matthew Gray* – as though offering it up as a wish into the magical sky. Enjoying the sensation and how it made her feel, she said his name over and over – *Matthew Gray, Matthew Gray*. She then had to cover her mouth with her hand to stifle a giggle. How silly she was being. And how differently the day had turned out from what she thought it would.

The owl hooted again, nearer this time, and seconds later, she caught the sight and sound of the distinctive flap and glide of the bird sweeping across the garden, homing in on its prey, an unfortunate mouse perhaps.

She stayed at the window for a few more minutes, then decided to get into bed. But her mind was too active to be lulled into sleep and not unlike the owl homing in on its prey, her thoughts returned to Matthew.

When, she wondered, would she see him again? And what would happen next between them?

Oliver lay in his bed thinking what a perfect day it had been. Best of all, he saw a future that would contain many more such perfect days.

He foresaw Libby moving in permanently with them at Ashcombe and in turn that would set Saskia free – free to lead the life she was meant to lead. No more would she have to worry about abandoning them here. More to the point, she could allow herself to fall properly in love for the first time, knowing they were in safe hands with Libby.

Not that he would breathe a word of this to anyone. Good Lord no – that would be a disaster. Better to keep these thoughts to himself. He could see, though, that the crucial element in his hope for the future would be Matthew having the patience to pursue Saskia on her own terms and then very gently, oh so gently, prise her away. It would take some doing, but from what Oliver had seen of the lad, he seemed the quiet, determined type. Just what Saskia needed. And they clearly liked each other. Oh yes, Matthew Gray would do very nicely. Why, he was practically family already!

Thank goodness he was infinitely better than that last chap Saskia had gone out with. What was his name again? No. He couldn't remember it. And didn't that say it all, an unmemorable name for an unmemorable boyfriend? Dull as ditchwater, quite frankly. Oliver had never really taken to him. He'd always suspected the lad had resented Saskia being so close to her family. He'd never played Risk with them like Matthew had this evening. Matthew was a good sport and fitted in well here.

Smiling to himself, Oliver recalled Matthew and Saskia

in the garden when they'd been perched on the fence like a couple of secretive lovebirds. They might have thought nobody had seen what they were getting up to – not that Oliver been spying on them – but he'd seen them kissing. Oh yes, he'd seen them all right. They'd have to be up early to get one over him!

At half past three in the morning and unable to sleep – clearly his guilty conscience wasn't going to let him off so easily – Matthew switched on the bedside lamp and reached for Jacob's second notebook.

Chapter Forty-One

January 1944

'You know, I'm rather fond of the effect I have on you.'

Knowing exactly what Kitty was referring to – my exponential desire for her: the more I made love to her the more I wanted to lose myself in the mind-spinning joy of her beautiful body with all its soft curves and sensuous litheness – I said, 'Funnily enough I'm rather fond of the effect you have on me.'

Raising herself on to an elbow, she gazed down at me. 'Will it always be like this, do you think?' she asked solemnly, her eyes dark and intense. 'Will it always be just as perfect?'

'It'll be even better,' I replied. 'For one thing we'll have a bed large enough to accommodate us without risk of one of us falling out.'

She wrinkled her nose. 'I don't think I want a bigger bed; I much prefer a small one because it makes things more romantic and intimate.'

I smiled and cupped her face with my hands. 'There's so much I plan to give you, my darling Katyushka, and a bigger bed is just the least of it.'

'I don't need anything else, only you. I wish we could stay here forever.'

I rolled her on to her back and kissed her. 'You deserve more than a cold, damp outhouse on Billy's farm, my darling, and when this war is over I promise to give you everything I possibly can.'

As always, she saw through me and guessed what I was

really promising her. 'You're not saying that because of my upbringing, are you?'

'I'm saying it because I love you and want the best for you.'

'Shouldn't I be the one to decide what I see as best for me?'

'Of course. But—'

She tapped a finger against my lips – lips that had earlier covered almost every delicious inch of her silky smooth skin. 'I hope you're not going to turn into one of those awful dictatorial husbands who refuses to listen to his wife,' she said sternly. 'I won't stand for that. I have a brain I intend to put to good use when this war is over.'

'Of course,' I repeated, sensing we had strayed into an area where I needed to tread warily. 'Do you have anything specific in mind?'

'I want to do what you did; I want the chance to learn, I want to go to university.'

This was news to me and stupidly I blurted out the first thing that came into my head. 'But that will separate us.'

Her brow furrowed, she said, 'Darling, nothing is ever going to separate us, certainly not something as trivial as a little bit of physical distance. Besides, you could get a job near where I'll be studying.'

Alarmed at how upset I felt at the thought of the future I'd had pictured for us being snatched from me, I asked as calmly as I could, 'How long have you been formulating this idea?'

One of her hands absently stroked my chest. 'For ages, I suppose.'

'Why did you never mention it before?'

She shrugged. 'I don't know. I didn't see it as being some-thing to discuss.'

'Really? But it impacts on our life together and surely anything that does that is worth discussing?'

'We're discussing it now, aren't we? And if I'm not

mistaken I don't think you're terribly overjoyed about it, are you?'

She was right. I hated the idea. I hated the thought of her not being with me, of her living a life that wasn't closely entwined with mine. I didn't want to settle for anything other than the whole of her. I wanted her to be waiting for me when I came home from work. I wanted to know that she would be there every night in our bed. I needed the certainty of knowing that whatever else went on beyond the walls of our home, and wherever it was, she would be mine. Entirely mine. Sharing her with people I didn't know had not figured in my thinking of the life ahead for us.

I sat up abruptly, my back turned resolutely towards her. 'I'm just trying to keep pace with you. One minute you're saying you don't want anything to change, that you wish we could stay here forever, and the next you're leaving me to go off to college.'

'You're taking me too literally.'

'Are you really sure you want to get married?' I asked, my back still to her. 'Frankly, it doesn't seem that you do, not when you're so eager for us to be apart. Or maybe that's your idea of how a marriage works, not spending any time together.'

In the crashing silence that followed, and with the harshness of my words reverberating in the small, dimly lit room, I sat rigid in agonised dread waiting for her to speak, hoping with all my being that she would say the words I needed to hear, that she would bend to my will.

And while I waited for Kitty to speak, I suddenly regretted that I hadn't gone ahead and proposed to her on New Year's Eve as I'd originally planned. But as it had many times before, work had prevented us from being together that day and so I had put my plans on hold, deciding to wait for a more auspicious date to propose to Kitty – her birthday in the summer seemed the ideal time. What did a few months matter when the whole of our lives stretched out before us?

I had thought. A short evaluation of my thinking, and my regret, revealed how absurd I was being. Would a ring on Kitty's finger have stopped this conversation from happening? Would her wearing a ring make her more malleable to my wishes? Of course not! I knew her better than that.

To my mortification, Kitty didn't speak. Not so much as a word or a tut of frustrated annoyance, and the longer the silence went on the more defensive of my feelings I became, until I found I couldn't speak or even begin to articulate the countless emotions battling within me. And although I strongly suspected pride was at the root of my reaction – I was burning with self-righteous anger – there was nothing on earth that would make me retract the words I'd just spoken. Words I had uttered because I meant them. At the same time the last vestiges of my rational self whispered that I was behaving like a petulant child.

Yet still the silence continued, the weight of it pressing in on me. Oh how badly I wanted her to be the one to apologise and release me from this torment!

Unable to bring myself to turn round, knowing I would see the worst kind of judgement in her expression, I reached for my clothes, reasoning it was better I left than stay and submit myself to further damnation.

'You're not running away, are you?' she asked when I began pulling on my trousers.

'It's time I was going anyway,' I muttered, now on my feet.

'Liar! Coward!'

The severity of those two words slapped me hard. As the truth always does when one is forced to confront it head on, especially an uncomfortable truth.

'It's late,' I tried half-heartedly.

She leapt from the bed and, standing before me in all her splendid nakedness, her hands on her slim hips, she said, 'You didn't think it was late five minutes ago.'

Oh, I was hopeless at this. How could I stay cross with

her? How could I deny her the right to be the woman she wanted to be? But what of *us*? What of *me*? How would marriage work between us when we couldn't be together?

Unable to meet her eye, I lowered my gaze and stared at her small feet and the delicate toenails she had painted with pearly-pink nail varnish. I suddenly remembered the first time I saw her toenails and the effect they'd had on me. For some reason they had always seemed so dainty and doll-like, and so very vulnerable. Not that there was anything vulnerable about Kitty. Certainly not in the way she was staring at me. 'I'm sorry,' I murmured.

'What are you actually sorry for, Jacob? For doubting my commitment to you? Or are you sorry that you don't want to be married to someone who would like to pursue her own dreams and aspirations? If so, you should ask yourself why that is.'

'You're over-simplifying it.'

'No, it's you who's over-complicating it. Do I have to remind you that your mother has always worked and your grandmother before that? How would they regard your stand right now?'

'That's different! My grandmother had to work when she and my grandfather arrived in this country. They had no choice.'

'And your mother?'

'But *your* mother doesn't work,' I said without answering her question, horribly conscious that my reason was being shredded and I was being reduced to an appallingly illogical, bleating state. I was conscious too that I was on the verge of destroying the one thing that had come to mean the world to me. Why could I not stop myself? Why was I so intent on this course of destruction?

She stepped towards me – her pearly-pink toes almost touching my feet. 'Jacob, what's this really about?'

'It's about me loving you,' I said gruffly, 'and wanting you to be my wife.'

'Are you sure it's not about trying to replicate my life at Fanley Manor? Of you believing you have to keep me in the style to which I've become accustomed? Which is nothing more than wanting to keep me in an airtight box.'

'Is that how you see it?'

'I see my parents' way of life as one of the many ways to live, but not the life I want to lead. We live in a different time to the one in which my parents started married life. What they have has worked for them, but it won't work for me. It won't satisfy what's in here,' she tapped her head, 'and here,' she added, placing a hand between her perfectly formed breasts. 'Don't you want me to be happy?'

'I want nothing else but for you to be happy.'

'Then you have to allow me to be free to make my own decisions and to follow my own dreams.'

'But do I feature in your dreams?'

She smiled at me sadly. 'Oh, Jacob, how could you ask such a question? Of course you do. When will you understand and accept that, as different as we are, the only barrier between us is your lack of belief in my love for you. Why can't you believe in me?'

Because I don't actually believe in myself, I realised. I had no real identity, I was merely a vague somebody I had become through my family's longing to give me everything they had never had the opportunity to experience. Their sacrifice and aspirations had given me so much, yet at the same time had denied me the one thing everybody needs: a true knowledge of oneself. Who was I? Who was Jacob Belinsky? He was all things and he was nothing.

In contrast, before me stood the most beautiful woman I'd had the good fortune to know, and in her magnificent nakedness she had need of not the slightest subterfuge. Right from the word go she had probably known who she was and what she was capable of, sure in the confident knowledge that doors would always swing open for her.

As if reading my thoughts, as she frequently claimed she

was able to do, she held her hands out to me. 'Jacob,' she said softly, 'the one thing you do not have to do is pretend to me. I fell in love with you because you are *you*, not because I hoped to change you into something you weren't. If you love me, as you say you do, you'll show me the same respect.'

I held her hands and stared deep into those wonderful eyes of hers. A clear choice was before me. I could throw aside all my doubts and insecurities and be a part of the wonderful adventure she had in mind for us, or I could give in to my greatest fear – the constant dread of her waking one morning and seeing through the persona I had carefully constructed for myself. With the scales gone from her eyes, the real me would be thoroughly exposed to her – the me that was riddled with the tawdriness of a weak and possessive nature.

'Maybe I need you to change me,' I ventured.

'Maybe we'll grow and change together,' she responded.

'Will you always have an answer for every question I ask?' She smiled. 'I imagine I will.'

'You must be frozen,' I said, bending to retrieve my shirt from the chair to put around her.

'I don't care about the cold,' she said, resisting my efforts to wrap her. 'I only care about you. About *us*. There is going to be an *us*, isn't there?'

Chapter Forty-Two

From somewhere very far away there was something buzzing. And buzzing loudly.

Roused from a deep and all-consuming sleep, Matthew realised the noise was coming from his mobile on the chest of drawers. He stuck his hand out for his glasses, but unable to find them he fumbled for the mobile instead. He had the phone almost to his ear, when the buzzing stopped. But then another noise caught his attention; it was the sound of something dropping with a soft thud on to the floor. Leaning bleary-eyed over the side of the bed, he saw that it was Jacob's notebook. It was then he clocked that the bedside lamp was still switched on, and that it was light outside. He looked for his glasses again and, discovering he was wearing them, realised he must have fallen asleep while reading.

He was just rubbing his face, trying to wake up properly and checking who had called him – it was Fliss – when the mobile buzzed and vibrated in his hand. It was Fliss again.

'Morning!' she said cheerfully, her wattage as bright as the light pouring in at the window.

'Hi,' he said, trying, but failing to match her cheery tone. 'Sorry I missed you a few moments ago, I was asleep.'

'At nine-thirty? That's not like you. Late night?'

'A bit.' Deflecting the conversation away from himself, he asked how her weekend was going in Barcelona. In the background he could hear an assortment of voices and the rumble of traffic.

She gave him a detailed account of things she and her friends had been getting up to, including the club where they'd been until two in the morning. 'You'd love it here,' she enthused, 'we should come for a weekend together some time. So what've you been up to?'

'Oh, you know me, mostly working.'

'Matthew, I've told you before, you work too hard.'

'But look at it this way, at least I'll be free to spend more time with you when you're back.'

'I'll look forward to that. What are you doing today?'

'I'll spend it missing you.'

Fliss laughed. 'That's either the nicest thing you've ever said to me, or the cheesiest.'

'I suspect it's the latter. Am I forgiven for my crimes against cheese?'

'On this occasion, yes.'

In the minutes after he'd said goodbye, Matthew considered all that he hadn't said to Fliss. Not liking where that left him, he threw aside the bedclothes and decided that instead of spending the day here, as planned, he would head back to Cambridge immediately. Being here wasn't good for him. He needed to get away from Glaskin House. More importantly, he needed to distance himself from Ashcombe.

In his present frame of mind, Cambridge represented safety. Life was normal there. It didn't lead to him telling outright lies to Fliss. Such as saying he'd spent most of yesterday working. He'd lied, of course, to avoid any mention of Ashcombe and the seductive effect the place had on him. There had been a moment last night when he'd been getting ready for bed and swapping his contact lenses for glasses, when he'd been in favour of an all-out confession to Fliss, but now, in the cold light of day, he deemed the better course of action was to keep quiet. It was a one-off event that Fliss didn't need to know about, in the same way that she didn't need to know anything about Saskia and her family. Just as soon as he'd sold Glaskin House and Ralph had helped to sell Jacob's books, there would be an end to his association with the Grangers.

He was taking his lead from Jacob who, in the pages Matthew had read before falling asleep, had appeared to be on the verge of throwing away the one good thing in his life, and over something that was nothing but an issue of pride. Matthew wasn't about to be as reckless. And if that meant telling a few white lies to protect Fliss, then so be it. He'd hurt her once before, he didn't want to put her through any further upset.

As for Saskia, judging by her nonchalant reaction after he'd kissed her, almost as though it hadn't happened, he was pinning his hopes on her regarding the matter as of little or no consequence.

It was that coolness of Saskia's that occupied his thoughts while driving back to Cambridge. He was forced to admit that it was something that intrigued him about her. The more he thought about it, the more he began to consider the possibility that what he found himself admiring in her – her refreshingly self-contained composure – was something he had admired in Jacob. It was a character trait that must have rubbed off on him, because he also never had a problem being on his own. As a child he had once declared that when he grew up his intention was to live just like Jacob, in a big house, alone, surrounded by lots of books. Mum had wagged her finger and warned him to be careful what he wished for.

He was on the outskirts of Cambridge and still thinking about Jacob, and in particular the future of Glaskin House, when he realised he'd left Jacob's notebook on the bed in his bedroom. *Damn!* Now he would be left wondering how Jacob had responded to Kitty's question – *There is going to be an us, isn't there?* More annoying still, he wouldn't know the answer anytime soon as the week ahead was a full-on busy one, leaving him no time to get back to Glaskin

House. Then next weekend he would be away with Fliss in Copenhagen.

Which was probably a good thing, all said and done. The longer he went without seeing Saskia, the better.

Chapter Forty-Three

The Easter good weather continued for the rest of the week and on Friday, when still it showed no sign of breaking and the sky was once again bright and clear, and dotted with the lightest and fluffiest of white clouds, Saskia was having a day off from her own work to look after the shop while Dad, taking Libby with him, had gone to Woodbridge to check out a collection of purportedly Agatha Christie first editions.

Whenever Saskia helped in the shop, it revived a series of snapshot memories. As a young child she had hated the freezing cold and poorly lit upstairs loo and had held on until she was home rather than risk using it. She had also been convinced it was haunted by a ghost dragging a clanking chain in its wake. Of course it wasn't haunted, just subject to the vagaries of bad plumbing – the clanking was the sound of the ancient pipes banging against each other whenever the chain to flush the loo was pulled or a tap was turned on or off. Even so, she had been hugely relieved when Dad had got the builders in to change the layout and modernise things.

Her happier memories were of her imagining herself to be so very grown-up when Dad had allowed her to take the money from the customers and give them back their change. Following Dad's instructions she had carefully to count out the coins so the customer knew they were getting the right amount. Funny how, as a child, a job like that was so appealing. Funny too that nowadays nobody ever counted out change; instead it was clumsily shoved into the customer's hand in a jumbled fistful. It was one of her habits always to check her change; a habit that she knew infuriated the person who'd given it to her, as though she were questioning their ability or honesty. Which she was, but then she questioned most things, rarely taking anything at face value.

Honesty and openness were important to her, although ironically she didn't always display it herself, but nonetheless she demanded it from others. And that included Matthew. She was doing her best to pretend she wasn't disappointed to receive only the one message from him since last Sunday – a terse thank you text – but there was no getting away from it, she was confused by his silence. The only conclusion she could reach was that he regretted kissing her.

Through the shop window she observed a man browsing the books in the display boxes out on the pavement. Books were regularly pinched from the wooden boxes and while the principle rankled with her – who were these people to think they could brazenly help themselves? – Saskia accepted that there was little to be gained from challenging anyone. Not that the books that were stolen were of any value, they were very much the chaff of what they sold; the wheat was kept safe and secure inside. Sadly even then they still occasionally had books stolen from the shelves in the shop.

But after five minutes of browsing the man proved to be an honest punter by pushing the door open and coming in to pay. He parted happily with fifty pence for an out-of-date car manual and went merrily on his way.

No sooner had the door closed behind him than it opened again and a familiar figure, dressed in a white T-shirt with paint-spattered overalls, poked his head in through the doorway. It was Will Swinton.

'Hi, Will,' Saskia greeted him. 'If you're looking for Dad, I'm afraid he's not here.'

'That's OK, I was just passing and thought I'd let Ralph know that I've had a change of jobs and I can make a start on the shop on Monday, if that's all right with him.'

'He'll be delighted to hear that.'

For some time now Will had carried out all their decorating

work, both here at the shop and at home. He'd once lived in London but after suffering some sort of breakdown had walked away from a high-stress job in the City. Opting for a complete career change, he'd moved to a cottage on the outskirts of Chelstead and after doing a painting and decorating course, he'd set himself up in business. That had been almost six years ago and as he'd gained a reputation for being reliable and extremely good, he was never short of work; once people had got themselves on his client list, seldom did they go elsewhere. The downside was that his popularity meant that customers had to get in line and patiently wait their turn for him to fit them in.

'I don't suppose you fancy going out for a drink this evening, do you?' he asked.

Saskia smiled. 'Does that mean you're back on the market?' It had been a long-standing joke between them that he only ever asked her to go for a drink when his love life stalled.

He laughed. 'You've got me all wrong. I only dare to ask you out when I reckon your dad and grandfathers will let me get away with it.'

'And you dare now?'

'Your father needs the shop painting so I have him over a barrel!'

She laughed too. 'Goodness, you know how to flatter a girl.'

'I'm a bit out of practice, so say yes to a drink and I'll try to do better.'

'In the absence of any better offers, I'll risk it then. What time?'

'What time will you be finished here?'

She flicked her gaze to her watch. 'In about two hours.'

'I'll go home for a wash and then cruise by to pick you up.'

'No need, I have my car. Name the pub and I'll meet you there.'

'How about The George in Cavendish? We could extend things to include a bite to eat, if you like?'

'Oh Lord, that must mean you have a worrying amount of heartbreak to pour out.'

'No more than the usual amount.' He gave her a wave goodbye and after pressing his nose against the window, and she shooing him away, he sauntered down the road.

His invitation was just what Saskia needed because, as much as it pained her to admit it, her vanity had been severely wounded by the lack of communication from Matthew. To make matters worse, and clearly mindful of her feelings, her father and grandfathers were tiptoeing around her with all their customary subtly, veering from carefully avoiding any mention of Matthew, to just as carefully asking if she'd heard from him. Honestly, could they be more unbearably annoying? She was not made of glass. Anything but!

Yet it was odd that Matthew had suddenly dropped off their radar. Perhaps it really was, as she suspected, a case of embarrassed regret for kissing her. Maybe he was concerned she might have read too much into it, which, naturally, she had. Wouldn't any girl in her position? If it had been a solitary drunken kiss, she could easily dismiss the exchange, but what had passed between them had been something more. Or so it had felt to her.

After dealing with a steady stream of customers, she rang home to say she'd been invited out for supper. 'Matthew's been in touch at last, has he?' Grandpa O said.

She counted to five. 'I'm spending the evening with Will Swinton,' she said, straining not to sound waspish.

'Oh,' her grandfather said. 'That's nice.'

'Yes, isn't it?'

At five forty-five she locked up and, after double-checking that all was secure, she set off to the other end of the market square where she'd left her car early that morning.

*

Will was already at the pub when she arrived. As usual when he was out of his overalls, he was a man transformed – clean jeans, a well-ironed blue-and-white shirt, the sleeves rolled up to his elbows. He smelled good too, and the stubbly shadow of his beard she'd seen that afternoon was gone. He steadfastly refused to say what age he was, but the commonly held view was that his fortieth birthday was a few years behind him.

'Had I known I would be going out this evening, I'd have made more of an effort with what I put on this morning,' she said, joining him at the bar where he was chatting up a pretty member of staff.

'You look fine to me,' he said, his eyes sweeping over her from top to bottom. 'As you always do. What do you want to drink? And do you want to sit inside or out?'

'A small glass of Pinot Grigio would be perfect. And inside suits me fine.'

It was too early for the place to be busy so, with the pick of the tables, they took their drinks over to one in the window.

'Come on, then,' she said, once they were settled. 'What's the latest with you?'

'Does there always have to be a latest?'

'To the best of my knowledge there always has been – why would this be an exception?'

He smiled. 'Why don't you tell me your latest news first? Are you still going out with Alan? Or was it Pete?'

'His name was Phil, and for some reason everybody seems incapable of remembering that.'

'From your use of the past tense I take it he's no longer around?'

She shrugged. 'Old news. He shipped out in the New Year when I refused to consider moving up north with him.'

'Any regrets you didn't go?'

'Not a one. We'd run our course anyway. What about you?'

'Funnily enough, a similar thing. Chrissie claimed she

admired me for what I'd turned my back on in London, but when push came to shove she thought it was time I stopped trying to prove a point and picked up where I'd left off. Funny how the novelty of dating a painter and decorator soon wears off. Initially she saw me as some kind of brave warrior fighting the system, then she realised I was no such thing, just a bloke who was happy to do his own thing.'

'That doesn't sound at all similar to Phil and me,' Saskia said.

'No? You don't think Phil had his own agenda going on and wanted you to change for his benefit? You don't think you had to fit in with what he wanted, rather than him fit in with your plans?'

'On that basis, aren't we all guilty of the same crime?'

'Hang on, I came here for a sympathetic shoulder to cry on, not sensible, objective advice.'

Saskia laughed. 'You should have said.'

'Didn't think I'd need to. Just assumed an old friend would know the right thing to say.' He took a long swallow of his beer. 'Anyone new since Phil?'

'Nah.'

He tapped his watch. 'Time's running out, girl. You need to get your skates on or you'll be left with just the duds to choose from.'

'What, the duds like you?'

'Hey, you could do a lot worse.'

'And there was me thinking this evening out would cheer me up.'

He raised an eyebrow. 'Why do you need cheering up?'

Watching a couple making themselves comfortable at a nearby table – they looked about the same age as her father and Libby – she said, 'No real reason.'

'You're such a poor liar, Saskia.'

She didn't bother to deny the accusation, but in the moment of silence while they each drank from their glasses, she noticed Will's gaze fall on the pretty girl who had served them at the bar. She was perfectly used to his roguish eye – as Grandpa O referred to it – and wanting to change the subject, she said, 'Will, can I ask you something?'

'Ask away.'

'We've known each other for a few years now, why have you never flirted with me?'

He laughed loudly. 'Are you mad? You're untouchable for somebody like me.'

'What do you mean?'

'I mean your family would hound me out of town if I made so much as a move on you.'

'You make me sound like a princess held captive in a tower,' she said with a frown.

'Aren't you?' he said, his face suddenly serious. 'Just a bit?'

She gave him a scornful look. 'You wouldn't say that if you knew how obsessed my family have recently become over hooking me up with a certain person.'

'Aha! So there is somebody you're holding back on! C'mon, tell Uncle Willy all.'

'Only if you promise not to laugh or say I'm being stupid and behaving like a teenage girl with her first crush.'

He leant in closer, his aftershave coming at her in a fresh wave. 'This sounds like it's going to be interesting.'

Pushing him away, and deciding that with all his years of hustling girls into bed with him he might actually be of help, she told him about Matthew and how he'd kissed her and that apart from one brief text, and despite her reply, there'd been nothing from him since. 'It sounds pathetic now I hear the words out loud,' she said with self-disgust, 'there was nothing previously in his manner really to suggest he regarded me in any particular way, but—'

Will stopped her words mid-flow. 'But when a fella kisses you, especially in the manner you've just described, you'd be forgiven for thinking he meant something by it. Unless you're a lousy kisser, Saskia, and that put him off.'

She punched his arm. 'Pig!'

'Maybe I should try kissing you to see if I'm right.'

'The only bit of me you'll kiss is the flat of my hand if you carry on like this!'

He smiled. 'Fighting talk! And no less than I deserve. But I stand by what I said: I agree with you totally, it is odd behaviour from the guy. Tell me again what he said, the bit after he'd asked to kiss you.'

'He said, "If you have any sense, you should refuse me."'

Taking another long swallow of his beer, Will stared contemplatively into the glass, then towards the window where outside a car was making a hash of squeezing into the space between two other vehicles. Finally he turned back to Saskia. 'He's already in a relationship, that's what his problem is. Obvious, isn't it? He knew he was crossing a line, but was somehow justifying his actions by handing over the responsibility to you.'

Saskia shook her head. 'No way! He's never once mentioned a girlfriend. Not once. Not in any of the conversations we'd had, and we've had plenty.'

'Did you ever ask if he was seeing someone?'

Will's question was an uncomfortable echo of a conversation she'd had with her father when she'd first met Matthew. 'No,' she said flatly.

'And you don't think it would be a natural thing to mention in a conversation when getting to know another person? Unless you deliberately want to deceive that person?' He paused. 'I'm guilty of doing it myself once.'

'Really?'

'I'm afraid so.'

She frowned. 'Why are men so horrible?'

'Because we never know when we're well off. And don't look so shocked; I wasn't always this perfect specimen you see before you. My ego back then, when I was flying high on the excesses of too much money and all it offered, led me to believe I was entitled to anything and everything.'

Saskia took a long and thoughtful sip of her wine, trying to take in what Will had told her. Not about his own behaviour, but that of Matthew. Had she really got him so badly wrong? But then a far worse thought occurred to her.

'What if he's actually married?' she said.

Will tutted. 'If he is, he is, but don't you go beating yourself up; you've done nothing wrong. It's him who has to deal with his conscience, not you. Now how about we get the menu? I'm starving and I'm in the mood for a big juicy steak.'

The only thing Saskia was in the mood for was a showdown with Matthew Gray, because much as she didn't want to believe Will, his theory was beginning to ring true for her.

Chapter Forty-Four

In a simply furnished, bleached-white hotel room a twenty-minute drive from Copenhagen, Matthew was lying on the bed thinking about the one and only time he'd come close to arguing with Jacob: it had been about Fliss.

'Do you think she's the girl you're going to marry?' Jacob had asked one evening during a game of chess, just minutes after their game had been interrupted by Fliss ringing Matthew on his mobile.

The question came so out of the blue it had momentarily thrown him. 'How could I possibly know that?' he'd answered Jacob. 'We haven't been a couple for long enough to consider such a step.'

'Trust me, Fliss has,' Jacob had replied, head down, and taking Matthew's last remaining bishop with his knight, he added it to the growing number of captured pieces.

'How could you possibly know that when you've only met her the once?' Matthew had said, annoyed that he'd carelessly taken his eye off his bishop and allowed Jacob to take it so easily. Sticking to his tactics, he moved his rook forward.

His gaze on the chequered board, Jacob's slightly trembling hand hovered over his queen. 'The girl has a look about her,' he said at length.

The remark made Matthew laugh. 'A look about her?' he'd repeated, spotting the manoeuvre the old man had in mind with his queen. 'I'm afraid you're going to have to do better than that.'

'She's in love with you,' Jacob responded matter-of-factly,

his eyes hidden beneath his bushy eyebrows, but still fixed on the board, where he seemed to have gone off the idea of moving his queen. 'The next logical step for her is marriage.'

'I think you're getting ahead of yourself; love certainly hasn't been mentioned or discussed.'

Jacob lowered his hand to his lap. 'Do you love her?'

With the old man continuing to keep his sharp and penetrating gaze on the board, Matthew was able to disguise his embarrassment at the unvarnished directness of the question. 'Not yet,' he said, adopting an easy carefree tone.

'Ah, so you imagine one day you will. How very certain you sound. Is that how you believe love works?'

'I certainly don't believe in love at first sight, if that's what you're getting at.'

'I never had you for a fool,' Jacob muttered under his breath, his trembling hand back on his queen again and moving it to threaten two of Matthew's pawns.

'You don't think that's a bit harsh? A difference of opinion is permitted, surely?'

'Not if it clouds your judgement.'

'I'm not aware of any such thing happening to me.'

Jacob grunted and reached for his glass of whisky.

'I presume that grunt signifies you disagree with my statement,' Matthew said, swooping in with satisfaction on Jacob's queen with his rook.

Seconds passed while Jacob took another sip of whisky, then carefully settled his glass on the table to his left. 'You presume correctly,' he said, a finger tapping the top of his bishop. 'You've left your king exposed and at the same time comprehensively trapped. Checkmate.'

And so it was. While relishing taking the old man's queen, Matthew had missed the obvious line of attack on his king. 'That was disappointingly short and sweet,' he said.

Now Jacob did look directly at him. 'You need to take more care, Matthew. Sloppy thinking begets sloppy behaviour and leads to disastrous consequences.'

Irritated that the old man was being so unsubtle, he said, 'I have no idea why you've taken against Fliss, but I'd sooner you kept your opinions to yourself about her.'

'I haven't taken against the girl,' Jacob said gruffly, 'I'm perfectly indifferent to her, having only met her on the one occasion. I just know that she's further on in the relationship than you are. She's always ringing you when you're here with me. Doesn't that worry you? It's as if she can't bear for you to have any time with me.'

Matthew strongly suspected that Jacob's comments were triggered by jealousy. Mum used to say that he needed careful handling at times, that he liked to have a person's full and undivided attention, more so as he grew older. And since Jacob gave total loyalty and maximum consideration to those he cared about, he expected no less in return. Matthew had always believed it a fair exchange, but in that split second, sitting across from Jacob, he felt a strong desire to resist that expectation.

'What makes you such a relationship expert, Jacob?' he asked. 'You've never even been married.'

'I'm an expert for that very reason! My objectivity gives me the ability to see things as they really are and not as people want to believe they are. Self-delusion is the very worst kind of deception.'

'Is that what you're accusing me of?'

'I'm tired of this conversation,' Jacob said with a weary shake of his head. 'You're intelligent enough to grasp what I'm saying, but if you choose not to take my advice, that's your decision. Now if you'll excuse me, I'm going to bed.'

The conversation, which had taken place two months before Jacob's death, was never referred to again by either of them. Matthew had dismissed it as the out-of-sorts ramblings of a tired old man and had thought no more about it.

Until now.

A combination of things had conspired to make the memory resurface. Firstly, reading *The Dandelion Years* and discovering the extent of Jacob's jealous and insecure nature as a young man, and secondly, a question posed by Fliss a few minutes ago before she went to take a shower. She had asked, quite unexpectedly, if Jacob had disapproved of her.

They had arrived four hours late after their flight had been delayed by a fuelling problem and had missed the chance to have dinner with Fliss's parents and the rest of the family who'd all arrived on an earlier flight. Personally, Matthew had been glad they'd arrived so late because it meant there was only time for a limited exchange of friendly fire in the bar while he and Fliss wolfed down a drink and a snack.

Now, emerging from the bathroom wrapped in a towel, her hair tied up on the top of her head, Fliss said, 'Well, I've given you ten minutes to come up with an answer for my question, so do you have one? *Did* Jacob disapprove of me?'

'I've been lying here wondering what on earth could have made you think that he did?' Matthew said, deliberately not answering her. He watched her go over to the mirror. Removing the scrunchie from her hair she brushed it out with long vigorous strokes.

'Because that was the impression I had when I met Jacob,' she said.

'Did you feel he was rude to you?'

'Oh no, quite the opposite. He was charming.'

'So what made you think he didn't approve of you?'

She put the hairbrush down and looked at Matthew in the mirror. 'It was the way he spoke about you and your mother. There was a distinctly proprietorial edge to everything he said. I sensed I was being warned off, as though I shouldn't consider myself good enough to join your close-knit little gang of two. Actually, I sensed that he'd exclude *anyone* who had the temerity to climb over the wall and break in.'

'You got all that in just one meeting?'

'Think about it, was there ever a time, when your mother was alive, when it was more than the three of you? According to what you've told me, your mother never married again and that was of her own choosing.'

'That's right. She always said she was happy with how things were.'

'Did Jacob ever encourage her to marry again?'

'I think you're being unfair; Jacob wasn't Mum's jailer. Or my jailer, for that matter.'

'Are you sure about that? How many friends did you have to come and play. Or to stay?'

'I had Laura next door.'

'And who else?'

'I've told you before, I was a full-on professional nerd; I didn't need anyone else.'

Fliss turned around to look at him. 'I hope that's changed.'

He frowned. 'What do you think?'

'I think it's been a long day and we should get some sleep.'

'You're right,' he said.

Some time later, when he could hear the steady rise and fall of Fliss's breathing, Matthew lay on his back, his head turned towards the television where the standby light glowed like an omnipresent, all-seeing red eye in the dark of the unfamiliar room.

Fliss's comments about Jacob had left him wound up too tight to sleep. Was there any truth in what she'd said? Had she seen something in Jacob's behaviour that he never had? Was it, just as Jacob had said, only the objective eye that was capable of seeing things as they really were?

Or was there an element of jealousy colouring Fliss's opinion, just as there had been with Jacob? To imply Jacob was some sort of jailer for him and Mum was laughable. And yet there was the young Jacob as revealed in *The Dandelion Years* to consider, a young man who couldn't bear the thought of Kitty having a life outside of their relationship.

The more Matthew couldn't settle to sleep, the more these thoughts spun round inside his head, and the more he couldn't sleep, the more he regretted not having brought Jacob's second notebook with him to read.

What had Jacob said to the woman he loved when she'd asked if they had a future together? Had he blown it there and then and insisted Kitty do as he wanted and give up on the idea of going to university when the war was over?

Whatever the answer, it was of no consequence when compared to what *he* needed to address right now. Because what really mattered was why Fliss had asked the question she had, and the subsequent comments she'd made about Jacob. It mattered also that once again Matthew had lied – in this instance by omission – to protect her, because no way could he admit the things Jacob had said. Was this how it was going to be from here on, a series of omissions and lies between them? Was that how most relationships worked? If so, he had to ask a far more fundamental question of himself – what did he really feel for Fliss?

It was all very well them getting back together again and him agreeing to support her by coming to Copenhagen and participating in a big family gathering, but what did that mean?

Did it have to mean anything? What was wrong with merely living in the moment? Why was there always this compulsion to look beyond today? Why did things have to change?

And why the hell couldn't he answer that one, all-important question, without resorting to bombarding himself with a string of other questions?

His hands clasped behind his head, he breathed in deeply, then let out his breath slowly and quietly so as not to waken Fliss.

Chapter Forty-Five

'I think we should go; it would be an interesting day out. What do you think?' Harvey waited for his granddaughter's answer. And waited. 'Saskia?' he said when it was obvious she hadn't heard a word he'd been saying.

She turned to look at him, a small frown on her face. 'Sorry, what was that?'

'I was asking whether you'd ... oh, never mind that; it can keep. Why don't you tell me what's bothering you?'

Saskia steered the trolley she was pushing round another that was causing an obstruction in the aisle. 'Is something bothering me?' she asked.

A bottle of balsamic vinegar added to the contents of the trolley, Harvey ticked it off on his list. 'I know you well enough to know that your mind is elsewhere and you've probably not listened to a word I've been saying since we left home.'

'Not true!'

'An exaggeration perhaps,' he said, 'but you get my drift. So what's up? Anything I can help you with?'

'I'm fine, just a little narked with myself. Rewind to the bit I missed and I'll listen properly this time.'

Aware, just as the rest of the family was, that as the week had gone on Saskia's mood had plummeted markedly with each day that passed, he put on hold his exploration to find out why, and repeated his earlier suggestion to plan a day out to Bletchley Park.

'When were you thinking?' she asked as he scanned the shelves for the *trofie* pasta he was after.

'Next weekend perhaps? Oliver's all for it. Practically champing at the bit!'

'But it's the Long Melford Book Fair next weekend. I always help Dad.'

Treading warily, Harvey said, 'Ralph's going to talk to you about that, apparently Libby's offered to step into your shoes and help him. That's if you don't mind.'

'Of course I don't mind,' she said, visibly bristling. 'Why would I?'

Giving up on finding the *trofie* pasta, Harvey selected a packet of *farfalle*. 'Because Libby's arrival at Ashcombe means life is changing for us and we've all got to adjust in our different ways.'

'I'm not a child, Harvey. I am capable of accepting change without throwing a hissy fit. Have I once shown the merest hint of not liking Libby? Have I once given anyone any reason to think I'm not happy with Dad seeing her? Have I?'

Seeing the colour rising to his granddaughter's face, he said gently, 'No you haven't, sweetheart, and I wasn't suggesting you had.'

'Good. Because I'm sick of people tiptoeing round me!'

Conscious that he was doing precisely that, Harvey indicated she move the trolley further down the aisle. 'So how about it,' he said when they'd turned the corner. 'Can you bear to spend the day with your grandfathers at Bletchley Park?'

'Of course I can.'

Knowing he was pushing his luck to the limit, and pretending to check his shopping list, he said casually, 'Oliver and I wondered if you'd like to ask Matthew to join us. After all, it's thanks to Professor Jacob Belinsky and his notebook that our interest has been piqued.'

'I expect he'll be too busy,' she said flatly.

'He wasn't too busy last weekend to join us.'

'He was probably at a loose end and it suited him to spend Sunday with us. I wouldn't count on it happening again.'

'Saskia, has he done something to upset you?'

She brought the trolley to a stop. 'Let's just say I have reason to believe he hasn't been entirely honest with us.'

The tilt of his granddaughter's chin and the tightness in her voice told Harvey all he needed to know: she was upset and holding back on something. 'In what way not honest with us?' he asked.

'If you must know, I reckon he's in a relationship. Who knows, he might actually be married and for reasons of his own he hasn't shared that with us. Not that it really matters, he can do or say whatever he wants, he's merely a client who will disappear from our lives when Dad's sold the book collection for him and we'll never see him again. Good riddance, I say!'

Standing in the middle of a supermarket freezer aisle was far from the ideal place to have this conversation, particularly as Harvey could see how troubled Saskia was by it. He regretted now forcing her to admit what was wrong. He should have waited until they were in the car driving home. But no, urged on by Oliver who'd been muttering all yesterday and this morning that one of them had to tackle her, he'd stupidly volunteered. Better him than dear old Oliver blundering in and making a hash of things, had been his reasoning.

'But what makes you think Matthew's married, or in a relationship?' he asked, trying hard to mask his surprise. And disappointment. Along with Oliver and Ralph he'd had such high hopes for Saskia and Matthew; they'd seemed such an ideal couple. God knew Saskia deserved somebody special.

She began pushing the trolley again. 'It's just something I feel,' she said. 'Call it intuition.'

Harvey was doubtful. He didn't want to accuse Saskia of leaping to any hasty conclusions, but surely she was mistaken? Surely Matthew wouldn't have hoodwinked them? He just didn't seem that kind of a young man. 'No more than a feeling?' Harvey probed, his every instinct warning him to take care. 'It's not much to go on, is it?'

'It's enough,' she said emphatically. 'Ask yourself this, what's he actually told us about himself? He's talked a lot about Jacob and his mother, and work, but he's never spoken about what he gets up to outside of work.'

'Perhaps he's not the sociable sort. And if he had a partner, wouldn't he have spent Easter Day with her?'

For a moment he could see Saskia debating this with herself. 'What if they'd had a row or something, and he'd come to us to spite her?' she said.

'Now you're making him sound horribly petty.'

'That might well be the least of his crimes,' she said with fervour.

'You're really convinced, aren't you?'

'I am.'

'But why? So far you've given me nothing but a gut feeling. You have to have something more tangible to think so badly of him.'

'OK, how's this? When I was with Will last night, he opened my eyes to the type of person Matthew Gray really is. The Matthew Gray who's made a fool of me. And of *us*.'

Once more Harvey was taken by surprise. 'Will? Does Will know him, then?'

'No, but he knows the *type*. He admitted he'd played a similar game with a girl some time ago.' She suddenly switched her gaze to further down the aisle, towards the fish counter. 'Do you know what I'd really like to eat tonight?' she asked, signalling the subject of Matthew Gray was now closed.

'What?' asked Harvey.

'Smoked fish pancakes – you haven't made those in a long time.'

'That's because Oliver always complains about the smell.'

'You can blame me if you like.'

'No need.'

There'd be absolutely no need, thought Harvey unhappily. With the news he was about to relay when they returned home, Oliver wouldn't raise so much as a squeak of complaint about the smell of smoked fish cooking. He'd be far more concerned about Matthew and whether or not he had been playing the rascal with Saskia and had deliberately led her up the garden path. Heaven help him if he had, because they'd have him within an inch of his sorry life.

Which was stuff and nonsense, because what on earth could they really do?

But what if Will had been talking rubbish and had stirred things up for his own ends? As amusing and interesting as the chap was, they all knew his reputation when it came to the fairer sex. What if he was now trying his luck with Saskia and had employed the old trick of divide and conquer?

They were in the car, the shopping piled on the back seat of Saskia's Mini when Harvey said, 'What exactly did you tell Will about Matthew that made him reach the conclusion he did?'

'I'd rather not say.'

'Was it something to do with Matthew kissing you?'

She took her eyes off the road and briefly looked at him. 'How do you know he did?'

'Oliver saw the two of you.'

'Oh, that's great; no wonder you've all been fussing around me!'

'I wasn't aware we had been fussing.'

She shot him another look. 'So avoiding all mention of Matthew when you realised he hadn't been in touch with me isn't fussing?'

Harvey shifted in his seat. 'You know what we're like. We care about you.'

'I know,' she said with a sigh. 'But sometimes I wish you didn't. Not so much anyway. I'm thirty-two years old, not ten.'

'Sorry,' he said, 'our problem is we can't switch the caring on or off; it's simply the way we are. Just as you're constantly looking out for us. More so now we're so decrepit. Ever thought how that might make us feel? Like we can't be trusted to put on our own socks. Which I agree might be true of Oliver, but' – he sat up straight and puffed out his chest – 'I'm very much a fit young buck still in my prime.'

She laughed. 'And as mad as a hatter into the bargain.'

'That's better,' he said, 'I've missed the sound of your laughter these last few days.'

'And I'm sorry for being such a pain. I guess I let my imagination run away with itself over Matthew. I was really beginning to like him.'

'No harm in that, but how about you give him the benefit of the doubt and invite him to join us on our little jaunt down to Bletchley? Let's see if the three of us can get to the bottom of the mysterious Mr Matthew Gray.'

'You mean trap him into an admission?'

'Why not?'

'Because it's sneaky and duplicitous.'

'And you have a problem with that?'

She smiled. 'None whatsoever. I say let's do it.'

'That's my girl!'

Chapter Forty-Six

One big happy family.

That was the message being broadcast loudly and clearly, and as hard as Matthew tried to embrace his place back within the Campbell fold, there was no getting away from it, his heart simply wasn't in it. Not that it ever had been. Not really.

Being with Fliss was fine; it was the rest of the Campbell clan that was the problem. He had nothing in common with any of them and, as usual, being unable to discuss anything meaningful, he was reduced to a bored onlooker, nodding his head in feigned interest with their constant talk of golf, cricket and rugby – the men of the family having played all three in their time. Such was Matthew's chronically poor coordination as a youngster, he'd experienced nothing but humiliation on the playing fields of his school and consequently he had zero tolerance for the subject of sport. Which in turn meant he had his work cut out trying not to admit to Fliss's family that it had as much appeal to him as did constantly hearing about the younger members of the family – four-year-old twins, Dylan and Cosmo, and six-year-old Poppy. If Poppy's parents were to be believed, the girl was a child prodigy – a violin virtuoso *and* a mathematical genius into the bargain – but from Matthew's perspective she had all the makings of a despotic leader the way she bossed her younger cousins around, not to mention her parents.

On top of all that, and as if on a permanent loop, was a never-ending discussion amongst the female members of the family about the arrival in four months' time of the newest recruit to the Campbell clan – a baby which they knew was a boy. Fliss's youngest brother's wife, Amy, had asked Matthew at lunch today if he would like to feel her bump. 'You can feel him kicking like mad,' she'd said happily. 'He's clearly going to be just like his father, a constant fidgety-pants. Here, give me your hand.'

Matthew's instinctive reaction had been to say he'd sooner touch the white-hot coals of a tandoori oven, but Amy had grabbed his hand and placed it firmly on the ballooning surface of her surprisingly hard stomach. His face must have shown his discomfort because everyone around the table had burst out laughing, with Fliss's father claiming Matthew was suddenly looking a bit green about the gills. Which had to be a blatant lie, his face could only have been one colour: scarlet. After feeling something that he now couldn't stop thinking of as a baby octopus being incubated, he'd lost his appetite for the *smørrebrød* of marinated herrings in front of him.

Now, after spending the day sightseeing, they were on the train heading back to the hotel in Skodsborg. As luck would have it, he and Fliss had a seat a few rows away from everybody else. 'Why do I get the feeling you're not enjoying yourself?' she asked in a quiet voice.

'I am,' Matthew said as convincingly as he could and trying to adopt his best I'm-having-fun face.

She looked at him doubtfully. 'You don't look like you are.'

'You know what I'm like; I'm never at my best in large gatherings.'

'It's not because you're still embarrassed, are you?'

'What about? Touching Amy's bump?'

She smiled. 'You looked like you were worried the baby might bite your hand off.'

'I think he had a go. He's going to be some brute when he's born.'

She smiled again and nestled in closer to him. 'Actually,

I wasn't referring to that particular embarrassment, I was meaning the awkwardness of facing my family again.'

'I can't pretend I'm entirely comfortable with the situation,' he said, seizing all too readily the convenience and plausibility of the excuse. It was better than saying he couldn't stick her self-satisfied, overbearing brothers.

'Well, you shouldn't be embarrassed. Everybody's delighted about us being back together. It's as if our splitting up never happened.'

Yes, Matthew thought, turning to stare out of the window at the passing scenery, that was something else to be swept under the carpet. This family was good at that.

Or had he got it badly wrong? Why couldn't he accept that Rod and Sally had put the affair behind them and recommitted themselves to each other with renewed and strengthened love? Why did he have to have such a distrustful nature and suspect that the patch-up job couldn't be effective? He supposed it was because he'd witnessed one too many acrimonious marriage breakups in the course of his work.

Fifteen minutes later, and probably to the enormous relief of the other passengers who'd had to put up with the twins, Dylan and Cosmo, running amok in the aisle of the train compartment in a game of improvised chase, causing Poppy to shriek at them to behave, while their parents and grandparents looked on with smiling indulgence, they clambered noisily off the train at Skodsborg station. After a quick head count they walked the short distance back to the hotel. It was a shame they weren't actually staying in the centre of Copenhagen, but Sally and Rod had picked Kurhotel for its renowned spa, together with its close proximity to the beach, the latter for the benefit of the children.

Unfortunately the Danish weather had put a dampener on any hope of the children playing on the beach; it was much too cold for that. Waking that morning after only a few hours of restless sleep, Matthew had looked out at the grey churning sea across the road from the hotel and felt it mirrored the growing unease within him.

He felt that same unease now as he stood at the window in their room while Fliss enjoyed a soak in the bath. He knew what the problem was, and the more he tried to ignore it, the more it insinuated its way into his thoughts – it was the memory of that perfect day at Ashcombe and his kissing Saskia. OK, he'd done nothing more than kiss her, but it was the fact that one, he'd done it, and two, he'd enjoyed it. That he'd known exactly what he was doing and had almost convinced himself at the time that so long as he handed over to Saskia the responsibility to say no, that it in some way lessened his part in it. It served him right that the memory of what he'd done would sneak up on him at the most inopportune moments. Usually when he thought of Fliss, and especially when he kissed her. With increasing insistence, his conscience was clawing at him that the only way to expunge the memory was to confess to Fliss.

The thought appalled him, and not just because he didn't want to hurt Fliss, but because it would expose him as being no better than her father, a man who he had previously and rather arrogantly dismissed as a wife-cheater, a man who had betrayed his wife in the pursuit of some moment of selfish pleasure. Perhaps that was the real reason he wasn't enjoying himself here; his crime might not be on the same scale as that of Rod Campbell's, but being around the man punctured Matthew's ego and the misguided belief that he was in some way better. He wasn't.

But why couldn't he just keep quiet? Why did he keep feeling the only way he could be free of the guilt was to unburden himself by confessing what he'd done to Fliss? And what if he did offload the guilt on to her, what then? Did he expect her to forgive him and carry on as though nothing had happened, just as her parents had done?

No, he thought tiredly, he couldn't do that. He'd sit tight and wait for the guilt to pass, because ultimately it would. If nothing else happened to fuel that reservoir of guilt inside of him, it would simply run dry.

Which meant no more chats with Saskia, and no more visits to Ashcombe with all its enchanting and seductive charm.

He shook his head and smiled wryly. So now he was blaming a house, was he? Yeah, that was about the long and the short of it – blame anything or anyone for his actions and perish the thought he'd lay the blame where it was rightly due!

Something he still hadn't squared in his head was why he hadn't mentioned anything about Fliss in his dealings with Saskia and her family. He still believed it wasn't intentional on his part, there had just seemed so much else to talk about, mostly Jacob related. But there again, he rarely felt the need to divulge more than was necessary about himself. A trait he believed he shared with Saskia.

As they had before the words *I see myself in you* echoed in his head. Not wanting to explore the thought any further, he dismissed it fast. But whatever the reason for the oversight, in view of what had transpired, it looked glaringly calculated, and certainly Fliss would have every right to view it that way. As would Saskia.

Hearing Fliss calling to him from the bathroom, he remembered he was supposed to be ordering drinks from room service. 'Just doing it,' he called back, reaching for the telephone on the desk. He'd got as far as dialling the first number when his mobile buzzed with a text.

He stared at his mobile in disbelief when he saw what the message said and who the sender was. The freaky coincidence of it was acutely unnerving.

My grandfathers & I are planning a trip to Bletchley Park next weekend and we wondered if you'd like to come with us. Saskia.

In view of the decision he'd just reached, the answer was no.

No, no, *no*!

Absolutely not.

A day out with Saskia was asking for trouble.

He dialled the number again for room service, ordered the drinks, and then sat in the uncomfortably rigid chair in front of the window. But instead of looking at the view of the sea across the road, he pictured Bletchley Park, or rather the Bletchley Park Jacob's notebooks had conjured in his head. How could he not take the obvious next step in the unfolding story of *The Dandelion Years* and explore the very place where Jacob had lived and worked in such secrecy all those years ago?

But he could visit Bletchley any time he wanted, he told himself, hastily countering the temptation to accept the invitation. Moreover, he could do it alone. He didn't have to go with Saskia and Harvey and Oliver.

His mobile still in his hand, he read Saskia's message again.

Wasn't he overreacting in all of this? Surely he could spend a day with Saskia and her grandfathers without doing anything stupid again? Of course he could. If nothing else, it might prove to him that he'd got the whole episode out of proportion. He could also, if it was necessary, use it as an opportunity to try and apologise to Saskia for crossing a line with her that day. He wouldn't have to say anything about Fliss, but he could make it clear it had been a one-off event, that he wasn't looking to repeat what he'd done.

What was more, he'd tell Fliss where he was going and why. Which would mean telling her about *The Dandelion Years*.

Satisfied he was making the right decision, he quickly sent a reply to Saskia.

Then he heard Fliss calling to him. 'Coming,' he said, suddenly feeling a lot more positive. Crossing the room to the bathroom, he began to think that maybe now he could finally begin to enjoy this weekend away.

Chapter Forty-Seven

It was Monday afternoon and if those weathermen were to be believed, East Anglia was in for a mighty good soaking after the agreeably warm dry spell. With this in mind, and knowing the job would be more easily done when it wasn't raining, Oliver felt compelled to deal with something that had been annoying him for some days.

Strictly speaking he should wait for Saskia and Harvey to return from the surgery in Chelstead where Harvey was getting an eye infection checked out, but really, it was such a simple job and would take no more than a couple of minutes to do. He'd have the ladder back in the garage in a trice and nobody would be any the wiser.

Some years back Ralph had laid down the law after Oliver had taken a tumble while atop the ladder pruning the fruit trees. That had been the start of his dodgy knee, along with the diktat from Ralph that ladder use for anybody over the age of sixty had to be carried out while in the presence of a responsible adult. Cheeky devil! Little did Ralph know, Oliver had often broken the rule, but he'd had the sense to keep his mouth shut. Let on to half of what he got up to and Ralph would ban him from getting out of bed in the morning!

He opened the door to the garage and stepped into the gloomy, petrol-smelling interior. The ladders lay on the floor, pushed against the wall behind the sit and ride mower. Pushing the mower out of the way, Oliver braced himself and hauled the aluminium ladders on to his shoulder. When he was satisfied he had the balance of them right, he set off down the garden. A gusting wind was now stirring the tree-tops and the sky was ominously dull. Rain was on its way.

He paused at the midway point to his destination to reposition the ladders. They weren't that heavy, but they were cumbersome and the buffeting wind wasn't helping. Hefting them back up on to his shoulder, and with a couple of nosy hens following him, he pressed on to the far end of the garden towards the corner where a white carrier bag had lodged itself in the branches of the hornbeam. It had been there since Friday, probably snatched up by the wind and blown into the tree.

Things like that bothered Oliver. The garden was his domain and he liked it to be shipshape. He'd mentioned the bag to Ralph, but Ralph had other things on his mind right now, namely Libby, and who could blame him? The man was in love and Oliver for one couldn't be happier for his son. It was about time he had something else in his life other than work and the family. It was a damned shame Ralph had let Libby go when he first had the chance to share his life with her. Still, you had to admire his loyalty to the family by putting them first. But then it was what they had all done; for the sake of the family nobody had wanted to break rank and disrupt things.

Stopping again to shift the ladders to his other shoulder, Oliver couldn't help but think that maybe that fierce loyalty had been a mistake, for hadn't it also trapped them? Look at Saskia, thirty-two and still living at home. She should have left home a long time ago and instead here she was, forever running around after them. Right now she was probably sitting in the surgery waiting room, bored out of her mind, while Harvey saw the doctor. Not that she would ever complain, that wasn't her style. Just as it wasn't his style to ask her to go clambering up the ladder to remove the carrier bag for him. In his opinion this was a job for a man, which he knew was something he shouldn't say aloud; a comment like that was tantamount to insulting the whole of womankind. He couldn't help it, though; he was old school. He believed in old-fashioned things like holding a door open for a woman and standing up when one came into the room. It was a mark of respect. And there was precious little of that around these days. Nor manners and decency.

If what Saskia believed was true, then that rascal Matthew Gray could do with learning some respect and decency. Who did he think he was, getting his feet under the table here and making fast and loose with Saskia? Outrageous!

On the other hand, the lad deserved the right to explain himself; after all they had no actual proof that he'd lied to them. It wouldn't do to be too hasty in their condemnation, but they'd certainly smoke him out next Saturday when they went to Bletchley, if there was anything to smoke out. He wouldn't stand a chance under their combined interrogation!

The ladder now fully extended and in place against the tree, the top of it resting against the branch where the offending plastic bag was snapping in the wind like a tacky flag, Oliver put a foot on the lowest rung and tested his weight on it. Happy that the ladder was securely placed, he began slowly to climb up.

There'd been a time when he would have scaled the ladder like a monkey. He'd been a devil for climbing things as a child and had reduced his poor mother to a perpetual state of anxious dread whenever he was out of her sight. His father had been more sanguine, advocating the view that a few bumps and scratches never hurt anybody. Oliver had been the same with Ralph, he'd practically encouraged his son to take as many risks as he could, but with Saskia, his attitude had been altogether different.

From the day she was born and he had looked into her beguiling gaze, with her wondrously perfect face so alert and full of promise, he had wanted to keep her safe. Whenever she had stayed with them as a baby and then a toddler, he had watched her like a hawk, terrified she might come to harm. To keep her safe he'd filled in the pond in the garden, put safety locks on all the kitchen cupboards and upstairs windows, installed stair gates, and removed any pieces of furniture with corners sharp enough to cause damage to a tender and precious little head.

He could remember the day when Saskia had figured out how to open the gate at the top of the stairs. Having managed it, and looking down at him where he stood at the bottom, she'd stretched out her arms on either side of herself and cried, 'Look, I can fly!' To his horror she had flung herself off the top step, causing him to pitch himself forward to catch her. She'd thought it fantastically funny, but he'd damn near had a heart attack.

To his surprise his wife had been a lot more relaxed about their treasured only grandchild in the house than he ever was. 'I know you love her dearly,' she would often say, 'but you can't wrap the girl in cotton wool.' Just watch me, was his private response.

He was now almost at the top of the ladder: two more steps and he'd be able to lean across and reach the offending plastic bag. He took the next rung and willed his legs to stop trembling – it seemed the higher he climbed the more his legs took on a life of their own, particularly his right. It was probably because he was concentrating so hard; it had made his body unnaturally tense and his legs were rebelling.

Tentatively putting his weight on his left leg, the one with the replacement knee joint, he tried to loosen the muscles in his other by sticking it out and flexing it. For good measure he gave it a bit of a shake. The ladder gave a shake too and, tightening his grip on it, he moved his leg back to the safety of the rung. Except it wouldn't move, it was locked. Far from loosening the muscles he seemed to have increased the tension. He gave the leg another shake but all that did was make the ladder wobble.

So seized tight was the wretched leg he couldn't do a thing with it. It dawned on him then that unless he could make the leg bend, he was stuck. The realisation made his heart beat faster and in response his left leg began to shake again. The movement reverberated through the ladder and, clinging on tighter still, he cast his gaze downwards to where the hens that had followed him were pecking at the grass. But it was a mistake to look down. A bloody awful mistake, because the safety of terra firma looked a hell of a long way down.

OK, he told himself as his heart continued to beat faster, he mustn't panic. The important thing was to stay calm. But his body wasn't listening. His breathing was all over the place and as if the blood was draining out of him, he felt lightheaded and the tree branches in front of him began to blur. Worse, his head started to spin and he could feel his bowels loosening with fear.

Gripping the ladder so hard his hands were numb, he squeezed his eyes shut in the hope it would help him to keep his balance. He hoped also that Saskia and Harvey would come home soon and rescue him. They'd be furious with him, but he didn't care, just so long as they got him down from this bloody ladder. Oh, why hadn't he stuck to Ralph's rules! Why did he always have to know better? Then from nowhere came the thought that he hadn't put the casserole in the oven as Harvey had asked him to. Harvey would be cross with him. Oh, he'd be very cross. 'Can't you even be trusted to do that?' he imagined him saying. 'One simple instruction and you couldn't do it, could you?'

He risked opening his eyes and tried again to still the trembling of his body, but it was no good; if anything he was shaking all the more. And now the rain had started, fat drops splashing on to his head and running down his face. He wanted to wipe the raindrops from his eyes, but he daren't let go of the ladder.

A fresh wave of fear took hold of him. Was this how his life was to finish? Clinging miserably to a ladder? He'd always believed he'd be ready for death when it came, now he wasn't so sure. Dammit, he didn't want to die! He wasn't ready. He had things he wanted to do. He wanted to see Jo again in Canada. He wanted to see Ralph and Libby married. And, most of all, he wanted to see Saskia happy and free.

The rain was pelting down hard now and to his horror he realised his face was wet not just from the rain, but from tears. And with that realisation came the certainty that with his left leg buckling beneath him, he couldn't hold on for much longer.

Finished at the doctor's surgery, Saskia and Harvey – having been warned by Oliver to bring them – put up their umbrellas, and hurried through the downpour of rain to the chemist to get Harvey's eye-ointment prescription made up. Then they called in next door to the bakers for a lardy cake and the finest cream eclairs for miles around – Oliver's favourite. From there they popped in to see Dad and Libby and found Gil enjoying a mug of tea and a gossip with them.

'Hi, Gil,' Saskia greeted him. 'How's life?'

'Same as it ever was: mucky and unrewarding.'

'And yet you look so well on it,' she said with a smile. Gil always made out he was on the verge of bankruptcy – never mind that he drove around in a classic Jag and had more holidays than anyone they knew.

'Appearances are deceiving,' he said darkly. 'How'd you get on with the notebook hidden inside that Russian Bible I found for you?'

'I gave it to the rightful owner and sadly haven't seen it since.'

'That's a shame.'

Isn't it, just? Saskia thought a short while later when she and Harvey were on their way home.

She was pleasantly surprised how easily she had shaken off her disappointment with Matthew. Sharing her suspicions about him with her grandfathers, and then Dad and Libby, had helped; having it out in the open had stopped her brooding over him. And now that she and Harvey and

Oliver had the plan in place for next Saturday, she was actually looking forward to seeing Matthew again. She couldn't wait to see the expression on his face when he realised he'd been rumbled. The only downside to their scheme was that she might not ever know the ending to *The Dandelion Years*. The best she could hope for was that Matthew would bring her up to date with what he'd read, and only then would they spring their trap on him. It was devious of her, but frankly, given Matthew's underhandedness, she wasn't going to lose any sleep over it.

'And what will you do if you're wrong and he's innocent?' Dad had asked.

It was a good question, but since her instinct had her convinced Matthew wasn't innocent, Saskia didn't feel the need to have an answer. Matthew's continued lack of communication, apart from responding to her invitation and a subsequent text message confirming the arrangements, told her all she needed to know.

The rain pounding the roof of the car, they bumped along the puddled and rough surface of the narrow track that led to the house. On either side of them the cow parsley in the hedgerow drooped wearily in the heavy downpour. As a child Saskia had picked armfuls of the lacy cream flowers and decorated the house with them. She'd been about twelve years old when the man who had rethatched their roof – a local man, born and bred in the area, who had seemed about a hundred and ten to her then – had told her he'd been brought up to call the plant cow mumble. It was a name that always made her smile.

She must have been smiling now because it provoked Harvey to say, 'Is that a private joke you're enjoying, or can it be shared?'

'No joke, just something I was remembering from a long time ago.'

Dropping her speed, she turned in through the gateway of Ashcombe. 'I'm going to do some work for the next couple of hours,' she said 'unless you need any help with anything?'

'No, I've taken up enough of your time today. You get on and I'll see what Oliver's been up to.'

'If he's had any sense he'll have had a quiet afternoon snoozing in his armchair.'

Saskia had only got as far as selecting the right marbled paper to use for the repair of a rather gruesome anatomy book from the 1850s when, sheltering beneath an umbrella, Harvey poked his head round the door, a worried look on his face.

'I can't find Oliver,' he said. 'He's not in the house.'

Peering through the rain-blurred window, Saskia said, 'He wouldn't be gardening in this weather, but how about the greenhouse?'

'I looked there. And he's not in his shed either.'

'He could have gone for a walk.'

'In this weather? Besides, he'd never miss *Pointless*. You know how obsessed he is with it. And he hasn't put the casserole in the oven, as I asked. I'm worried about the old fool, Saskia. Where is he?'

'OK,' she said, seeing how concerned Harvey was. 'Perhaps he's tinkering with something in the garage and has lost track of time. Let's go and have a look.'

There was no sign of Oliver in the garage, but Saskia spotted straight away that the mower had been moved and the space where the ladders were kept was empty. Remembering her grandfather muttering at breakfast about the carrier bag that was stuck in the branch of the hornbeam, a terrible thought occurred to her.

As if reading her mind, Harvey followed after her as she rushed outside into the rain. But he was left well behind when, halfway down the garden, she broke into a run.

Chapter Forty-Eight

Saskia knew at once that her grandfather was dead.

With the hens gathered around him as though they were standing guard, he was lying unnaturally still on his back, the ladder across his legs, his arms outstretched, his face turned upwards, his eyes wide and staring as the rain dripped down on him from the leafy branches of the hornbeam tree. His mouth was open too, as if he'd just taken one last final deep breath.

Removing the ladder from his legs, then dropping to her knees on the sodden grass, her tears mingling with the rain streaming down her own face, Saskia knelt beside him. She knew it was useless, but she put her ear to his chest to check for a heartbeat. Opposite her, Harvey was also on his knees and feeling for a pulse at Oliver's neck. After what felt like an age had passed, she raised her head and saw that Harvey had closed Oliver's eyes and mouth.

'We need to get him inside,' she said. 'He can't stay out here in the rain.'

'I know, love, but we can't lift him on our own. I'm going to call for an ambulance.'

'An ambulance,' she repeated dully. 'What use is that; he's dead.'

'And then I'm going to ring your dad,' Harvey continued without answering her. He stood up and held out his hand to her. 'Come with me, Saskia. Come inside with me. Please.'

His words seemed to her to be spoken unnecessarily slowly and overly pronounced as though he was worried she might not understand. She understood perfectly and shook her head. 'No. I can't leave Grandpa O. Not like this. Not here on his own. You go. I'll stay with him.'

'Are you sure?'

She nodded mutely.

'All right. But I'll be back out just as soon as I've made the calls.'

She watched him set off at a hurried pace across the lawn towards the house, then taking hold of one of Oliver's hands – a hand that felt frozen to the touch – she pressed it tightly to her heart as if she could will him back to life by the sheer force of her love for him. 'Why, Grandpa O?' she sobbed. 'Why did you have to leave us now? How will we manage without you? Things won't ever be the same now.'

Through eyes blurred with tears, she looked reproachfully up at the plastic bag in the branch of the tree above her. A gust of wind blew and filled it with air like a balloon. She felt so angry knowing that it was responsible for her grandfather's death. How could something so insignificant have such devastating consequences?

She returned her gaze to Grandpa O. Drenched to the skin, he was somehow already diminished, his thinning hair plastered to his pale scalp, his cheeks seemingly sunken by death. His hearing aid, she noticed now, had fallen out from behind his ear and lay on the ground. His end should not have come about this way, she thought sadly, lifting his head on to her lap and cradling it tenderly. Not in this cruelly trivial manner and with no one with him to say goodbye. She should have been here with him. Why hadn't she come straight back with Harvey after they'd been to the doctor's surgery? Why had they wasted precious time going to the bakers, and then calling in to see Dad and Libby?

Remembering the eclairs they'd bought, and knowing that her grandfather would never eat his now, she sobbed all the more.

*

Ralph dialled the number again for his sister in Canada. It was nine-thirty in the morning there. He'd tried three times already without success and each time he'd been unable to bring himself to leave a message, knowing that if he left one saying 'Please ring me as soon as you can,' Jo would know there was something wrong and illogically he didn't want her to have that moment of concern without him on the other end of the phone. Normally he would speak to her using Skype, but again, illogically, that felt wrong: Skype was for good news, not this kind of news.

He listened to the dialling tone and waited. Please be there this time, he silently urged his sister.

Finally his wish was granted and at the sound of Jo's voice he struggled to speak, suddenly overcome with the memory of having to make a similar call on the day of the car crash when Evie and their mother and Ester were killed.

'Hello,' she repeated, this time with a trace of impatience to her voice.

'It's me,' he managed to say, 'Ralph.'

There was a pause.

'What's happened?' she asked. 'It's bad news, isn't it?'

Typical Jo, straight to the point. 'Yes,' he said, steeling himself. 'It's Dad. He's—'

'In hospital?'

'Worse. He's … I'm so sorry, Jo, he's gone … he's dead.' Hearing the words aloud caused his chest to tighten. He swallowed back the lump in his throat. 'We can't be completely sure, but we think it was an accident.'

'Oh God, what was he doing?'

'He was up a ladder. He must have fallen.'

'Not a heart attack, then? I always thought that would be the way he'd— ' Now it was Jo's turn to struggle to speak.

'He was alone,' Ralph said, 'so we're only guessing what happened at this stage.'

'Does that mean there'll be a post-mortem?'

'I think so.'

'How's Saskia?'

'In shock. She and Harvey found him out in the garden.'

'The poor kid. Look, I'll clear my diary and be over as soon as I can. Bob too.'

'There's no rush. The funeral won't be until—'

'I want to be there with you,' she said before he could finish.

When he came off the phone some minutes later, Ralph looked up to see Libby standing in the doorway of his study. 'How did it go?' she asked. 'No, don't answer that, it was a silly question.'

He rubbed his hands over his face, then stood up and went to her. 'What a bloody awful day,' he said with a tired sigh.

She put her arms around him and he sank gratefully into the comfort of her embrace. 'I'm so glad you're here.'

She tilted her head back from him. 'If you'd rather I didn't stay the night as planned, I'd quite understand.'

'Why wouldn't I want you here?'

'Don't be obtuse, Ralph, this is family time.'

'I want you here,' he said without hesitation. 'I *need* you here.'

'But Saskia and Harvey need you.'

'And they have me. Please stay. Besides, you're family now.'

'If you're absolutely sure ...'

'I am. Where's Saskia?'

'Putting the hens to bed.'

Ralph let out a small groan and shuddered. 'That was always Dad's job. He ... he said he didn't trust the rest of us to do it right.'

'I know, he told me he liked to tell them a bedtime story.'

'Daft old devil! Beneath the gruffness he was nothing but a big softie. He cared deeply about everything. He didn't always show it, but he did.'

'I saw that in him the first time I met him. I saw how much he loved you all and the bond you had.'

Ralph held Libby close again.

Alone in the kitchen, Harvey sat at the kitchen table with his head in his hands. He missed Oliver deeply already. They'd been like brothers. Or how he'd always imagined brothers would be, for he'd never actually had one. Yes, they'd wound one another up at times, but never over anything that really mattered. When it came to the important issues, they'd always been in agreement.

Behind him the uncooked casserole they should have been eating this evening lay abandoned and unwanted. Nobody felt like eating anything. He should put it in the fridge for to-morrow, but feeling as though the stuffing had been knocked out of him, he couldn't summon the energy, or the will, to move.

Poor Oliver. Why had he worried so much about that bloody bag stuck in the tree? Why couldn't he have left it to Ralph? Or at least waited until somebody else had been around. But no, the stupid, stubborn old fool had to pretend he was still a player and deal with it himself.

Nobody liked accepting the reality of advancing years and the restrictions old age brought with it, but why for the love of God had Oliver been so obstinate? Why couldn't he have given in more graciously?

Because that wasn't the man he'd been. And that was why they'd loved him. He was predictably pig-headed over the slightest thing, like all the times he would deliberately leave stuff lying around in the kitchen just where he knew it would annoy Harvey most.

They were such petty little battles between them, and Harvey would give anything to wake up tomorrow morning knowing that Oliver would deliberately put the basket of eggs precisely in the wrong place. Oh, to be able to tut and roll his eyes at his dear old friend again and then settle down together and enjoy a coffee while watching *Homes Under the Hammer* or *This Morning*. It had been one of their secret guilty pleasures that occasionally they watched *The Jeremy Kyle Show*, each of them shaking their heads in disbelieving morbid fascination at people so desperate to have their fifteen minutes of fame on the telly. Oliver had said once he'd like to go on the show and bang a few heads together and Harvey had joked that he'd pay good money to see that.

At the sound of the back door opening, he looked up to see Saskia, her face ravaged by tears. She hadn't put on a coat and her clothes were wet through and clinging to her. 'You're soaked,' he said.

'It's still raining,' she answered, going over to the sink to wash her hands, 'and it took ages to round up the hens. It's as if they know Oliver isn't here for them anymore. I wouldn't be surprised if they stop laying.'

Trying to rouse himself from the table, but feeling too leaden to move, he watched Saskia wash her hands then dry them. When she turned round to look at him, she said, 'I wish he hadn't died alone. I can't stop thinking about those last awful moments for him. I'd give anything to change that. I wish we'd been here.'

The heartfelt frankness of her words echoed Harvey's own thoughts. He didn't think there was anything worse. He hoped to God he didn't die that way. And he would be next. Of course he would. It was only a matter of time before his worn-out body would be lying in a morgue stripped of all its dignity. Just like poor Oliver.

The thought was too much and brought forth a choking sob from him. Powerless to stop it, and with Saskia's arms suddenly around his shaking shoulders, he began to weep for his dear old friend who'd been his constant companion all these years.

Chapter Forty-Nine

It was Thursday lunchtime and, having been at his desk since seven that morning and with Jim Rycroft safely out of the office for the day, Matthew had decided he'd earned a longer than usual lunch break. He had thought he'd go for a browse in Heffers, but in need of giving his mind a thorough reboot, a walk along the Backs had seemed the better option, especially as the sun was shining after several days of heavy rain.

With Pembroke Street now behind him, he crossed the road, turned into King's Parade, then cut through King's College to take the path down towards the river. The sun had brought the students and tourists out in equal numbers and, dodging around a tour group that had stopped to take photographs, he hurried on. At the bridge he turned right and, sidestepping yet more tourists who were watching a double scull row by, the blades of their oars cutting through the water with barely a splash, he dropped his speed to a leisurely pace. Looking ahead, he could see the stately willow trees that marked the river frontage to Merchant College, a college that was squeezed in between Clare College and Trinity Hall. When he was level with it he was tempted to veer off from the main path and take a wander through the lawned quads. Not for the first time in the last few weeks he wondered at the coincidence that he should be working on a case brought against Jacob's old college. Taking a moment to admire the immaculate lawn and the ivy-clad walls of the seventeenth-century chapel that was a fraction of the size of its neighbour's, he thought it was a shame the college hadn't

349

taken as much care with their finances as they had with the lawns and buildings.

Sir Desmond Leamington had initially queried the college's investment portfolio when it came to his notice that, along with the usual dubious companies listed – tobacco manufacturers, fossil fuel and arms companies, some of which included nuclear warhead and drone production – the name of a Russian gas company was included. The name set off an alarm bell for Sir Desmond as it was widely suspected it had holdings in a subsidiary gas company with some very dodgy connections, specifically a history of money laundering and links to the Russian mafia. Furious that his *alma mater* could have made such a colossal error of judgement, he complained in the strongest terms.

In common with many others over the years who'd had to justify investments made in arms companies, the college trotted out the usual meaningless line that it had a moral duty to ensure its investments weren't in conflict with its charitable status and so would look into matters. Not content with the response, Sir Desmond looked into matters himself and discovered a number of irregularities that led him to a sizeable discrepancy in the accounts, a discrepancy to the tune of nearly nine million pounds. Initially it was put down to a simple miscalculation, the kind of mistake that could happen to anybody when dealing with such large amounts of money.

But Sir Desmond was having none of it and took his concerns straight to the door of Scotland Yard. The college was lucky he had such a deep sense of loyalty to where he'd studied and didn't go to the press, because once they got hold of the story they'd undoubtedly go to town. Matthew reckoned it was only a matter of time before the story was leaked – how could something like this be contained? And on the face of it, it was a jackpot of a story. Apart from the fact that Cambridge University was the wealthiest university not just in the UK but in Europe, the place was a sitting target for complaints and accusations because, for many, it represented everything bad in society – elitism for the over-privileged and a woeful lack of accountability.

Matthew would be the first to challenge the view as being overly simplistic, for Jacob had not come from a privileged background, just as he hadn't.

He walked on, stepping to one side to let a dark-haired girl in a Magdalene sweatshirt jog by, and thinking that she reminded him a little of Saskia – something in the intensity of her expression – he wondered why he hadn't heard any more from her about Saturday and the planned trip to Bletchley Park. He hadn't pestered for an update because frankly he'd been too busy. Plus, he was trying to stick to his resolution to keep his distance. Perhaps this evening he'd send a text and see what the state of play was.

He was looking forward to the outing. He had a picture in his mind of what it was like – or more to the point, how it had once been – and he now wanted to slot Jacob into place. He supposed he could always go on his own. No reason why not. Except he liked the idea of sharing the trip with some-body who knew about Jacob's time there. And, of course, that person was Saskia.

During the flight back from Copenhagen he had told Fliss the whole story about *The Dandelion Years* notebooks and how they'd been found by a book restorer, the daughter of the bookshop owner who had carried out the probate valuation of Jacob's book collection. He'd told her about the arranged visit to Bletchley next weekend as well. Predictably Fliss had asked him why he hadn't mentioned any of this before, and just as predictably he'd made light of it, saying it just hadn't cropped up, what with them getting back together and her being away over Easter and him being so busy with work.

Her next question was to ask if the leather notebook she'd come across in his bedroom had something to do with what he was talking about. When he'd confirmed it did, she'd given him a long hard look. 'You really didn't want me to read it that morning, did you?' she'd said at length.

Remembering how he'd felt at the time when she'd been flicking through the pages, and unable to come up with a credible response, he'd asked her if she'd like to read the notebooks when they were back. With a dismissive shrug, and while pouring the contents of a miniature vodka bottle into her tonic water, she had told him she wouldn't dream of intruding on something that was clearly such a private matter.

'Don't be like that,' he'd said.

'Like what?' she'd challenged him.

'Upset with me,' he'd said quietly, convinced the man on her left was only pretending to read his Kindle.

'You think I'm upset with you, do you? Well, that must be a first, you actually noticing something about me. But don't you worry yourself, Matthew, you go off and have fun with your new friends on Saturday. Meantime, I'll be at Vicki and Emma's joint baby shower party. As I think I told you. You see, that's the difference between us, I *tell* you things. I *share* what I do with you. Whereas *you* keep things hidden.'

Her reaction was unprecedented; he'd never seen her act petulantly before. But could he really blame her? Just as well he'd kept quiet about spending Easter Sunday at Ashcombe; that certainly wouldn't have helped. Especially as he'd already lied and said he'd spent the day at Glaskin House working. As his mother had frequently drilled into him, the first lie always leads to another, and then another.

Since arriving home from Copenhagen, there had been a definite chilliness from Fliss. He was being taught a lesson. A lesson he richly deserved.

Passing the Bridge of Sighs on his left, he picked up his pace and pushed on and took the path through his old college, St John's. With living and working on the doorstep, he'd long since lost the nostalgic urge to drop in and have a look round for old times' sake. The last time he'd done that had been with Fliss when she'd wanted to see where he'd been a student. Emerging on to Magdalene Street, he turned right for Bridge Street and after calling in at his favourite sandwich shop, he walked back to Hills Road and the office. He'd passed Emmanuel College and had just crossed from St Andrew's Street to Regent Street when he did a double take. At the same time, the man coming towards him did the same thing.

'Hello, Ralph,' Matthew greeted him, 'fancy bumping into you here. How are you? I've been meaning to get in touch with Saskia to ask about the arrangements for Saturday.'

At the curiously blank expression on Ralph's face, Matthew hesitated. 'The trip to Bletchley Park?' he further explained. 'Saskia invited me to join her and her grandfathers. Or perhaps there's been a change of—' He stopped abruptly. Something was horribly wrong with Ralph. Beneath the blank expression on the man's face was something more, something Matthew recognised all too well.

'I suppose Saskia hasn't told you,' Ralph said gravely. 'My father died on Monday afternoon.'

'Oh God, I'm so sorry! What happened? He seemed so well when I saw you all at Easter.'

'An accident. He fell off a ladder in the garden.'

'I'm sorry,' Matthew repeated, surprised how saddened he was at the news. He'd hardly known the man, but he could empathise with the family's shock and distress. 'How's Saskia?' he asked.

'Devastated, as you'd expect.'

'And you?'

Ralph shrugged. 'I'm OK. I've just spent the last hour with Oliver's solicitor going through a ridiculous amount of paperwork.' He indicated an office a few yards further down the road.

'That's the last thing you need at a time like this,' Matthew said. 'If you need any help with anything of a financial nature, just give me a call.'

'Thanks. I'll bear that in mind. Though I doubt my father will have made things unnecessarily complicated. He always claimed he'd made life difficult enough for everybody while living, he refused to be a bother when he was no longer around.'

Matthew smiled tentatively. 'I can imagine him saying that. Will you pass on my best wishes to Saskia and Harvey, please?'

'I will.'

There seemed nothing else either of them could say, other than an awkward goodbye.

Seated at his desk, a spreadsheet of Merchant College accounts in front of him, Matthew ate the ham and mustard sandwich he'd bought. His mind, however, refused to concentrate on the columns of figures, he kept thinking of Saskia and how upset she would be and how different the atmosphere must now be at Ashcombe.

He wondered about sending her a card. When Mum died he'd received a flood of them from people in the village, some of whom he didn't know. That hadn't mattered. What had counted, and what he'd appreciated, was the trouble they'd gone to because it showed how popular his mother had been. He still had the cards; he hadn't been able to bring himself to throw them away. The same had happened when Jacob died.

How would Saskia react to a card from him? From somebody who had known the family for so little time?

And why was he even asking himself this question?

He looked out of the window down on to the busy street below. The only conclusion he could reach was, just as he'd told her that day at Ashcombe, he had never met anyone like her before. It sounded a bit odd, but she was an enigma to him. He'd thought once before that she seemed to present a different aspect of herself to him each time they met, and really, it was true. The net result of that was he felt he never really knew quite where he stood with her.

Was that the attraction? he pondered as he chewed on the last of his sandwich. He didn't like to think that he viewed her merely as a challenge, but perhaps he did, and maybe that was why he had kissed her that day in the garden: he had wanted to see how she would react.

Try explaining that to Fliss, he warned himself as his mind strayed treacherously to the memory of watching the setting sun with Saskia, a sight that had been just as glorious as she'd said it would be.

By the time he finished work that evening, it was too late to find a proper card shop still open, so he called in at Waitrose on the way home in the hope he'd find something suitable. He didn't want one of those cards that contained lines of cloying verse that made his toes curl, nor did he want anything that would look as if he'd picked it up from a supermarket on his way home.

Luckily he found a card that fitted the bill and with a book of first-class stamps in his wallet and the address for Ashcombe stored on his mobile, he decided to write in the card there and then and post it straight away.

But what should he write? He'd never actually written a condolence card before and all he could think of were those awful things teenagers wrote on social media sites, *RIP dude* and *love you forever babes*.

He gripped the pen in his hand and concentrated hard. It didn't have to be anything clever, just a few words of sympathy. How difficult was that?

Dear Saskia, he wrote, *I bumped into your father this afternoon and he told me about your grandfather. I'm so very sorry for ...*

He was about to write *for your loss,* which was the last thing he wanted to say, it was such a cliché.

But what to write instead? *I'm so very sorry for ...*

... the difficult time ahead for you all.

... the upset you must be feeling.

... the sadness you must all be going through.

He tapped the pen against his mouth, then finished the

355

sentence with – *the difficult and sad time you must all be going through.*

Kind regards,
Matthew.

P.S. If there's anything I can do to help, please don't hesitate to give me a call.

He looked at that last sentence and hoped that Saskia would know the sentiment was genuinely meant, not just one of those things people were inclined to say in the circumstances. Slipping the card inside the envelope and sticking a stamp on it, he posted the card in the postbox on the way home.

Letting himself in at the flat and hearing James speaking on the phone in the kitchen, he decided that with the outing to Bletchley Park now cancelled, he would drive over to Glaskin House and spend a quiet weekend there. He would use the time to finish reading Jacob's notebook and discover what had happened to him and Kitty.

With a bit of luck, by the time he returned to Cambridge on Sunday evening, Fliss would have surfaced from her sulk and be receptive to yet another apology from him.

Chapter Fifty

February 1944

Things were never going to be the same again and it was my own stupid fault.

As a result of my blinkered vision of the future I'd had for us, I had caused Kitty to look at me through new eyes. Naturally I had apologised for the remarks I had made regarding her desire to go to college when the war was over, but I knew she wasn't convinced. How could she be? My outburst had been wholly instinctive, a revelation of my true colours.

Whether or not it was to test me, but sometime after that night Kitty announced she had been invited to join a group of Wrens at a dance at a nearby American base. I was appalled at the thought but knew better than to say anything and kept my mouth firmly shut when, along with a couple of Wrens and with her precious clothing ration coupons in her handbag, she took the train to Watford to find something new to wear for the dance. I hated the idea of her wearing something new and specially chosen for the benefit of some brash US army soldiers intent on seducing her with packets of nylons and chocolate.

Yet not a word did I say. Not even when she showed me the dress, and, with my chest tightening with an inner pain, I could visualise how beautiful it would make her look.

As the evening of the dance drew near, I arranged to pass the time with the Chess Club in the vain hope that it would divert my thoughts from imagining the woman I loved being held in the sweating arms of some wholly disagreeable jitter-bugging swine. At no stage had Kitty asked me if I minded her going to the dance; of course she wouldn't, that would have been counter to what she was forcing me to accept, that she was a woman who could make her own decisions and was fully prepared to do so. More importantly, she was forcing me to prove that I trusted her.

And all the while I had my great-grandmother's ring in my possession, just waiting for the right moment when I could put it on Kitty's finger and claim her as mine, believing that once that ring was on her finger I would never have to endure an evening like this one again, that as a married woman she wouldn't dream of going to a dance without me. But I couldn't bring myself to propose now for fear she would refuse me.

Before Kitty had come into my life, I had never imagined I would fall in love and have my emotions so sorely tested. I had somehow imagined myself an island, impervious to everything that I was now coping with. I had begun to argue with myself that it was the life I had been thrown into at Bletchley Park that exacerbated matters, that the close-knit community with its pressure-cooker environment heightened my emotions and magnified my flaws and weaknesses.

If anyone had told me before that I could behave so irrationally I would have scoffed. I had always believed I was one of the most reasonable and level-headed people who existed. How wrong could I have been! I was fast turning into the kind of person I had always despised, capable of pettiness and profound self-centredness. I was proud and judgemental too, and a lot more besides. In short, I was a thoroughly disagreeable human being. Why on earth would Kitty want to marry me?

Oh how effortlessly I could talk myself out of this chance to be happy. Why could I not be more like the other fellows I knew and take a more light-hearted approach to life and love? Come to that, why did I find human contact of any sort so overwhelmingly challenging?

Kitty had often joked that she was my saviour. 'What are you saving me from?' I'd asked in all seriousness the first time she had said this.

'Yourself, of course,' she'd replied.

The day of the dance arrived and after my shift ended I went over to the canteen for a bite to eat and then to the library in the Mansion where the Chess Club was putting on a mini tournament that evening. The usual faces were there, as well as a new chap who'd recently arrived at the Park. His name was Victor Stein and standing next to him in the bay window was a fair-haired girl I didn't recognise. New recruits were a constant reminder of the vital necessity of the work we did here – if our numbers ever started to dwindle we'd have every reason to believe the war was almost won.

Stein waved me over and weaving my way through the tables and chairs and the awaiting chessboards, I greeted him politely. He was, I sensed, similar to me in that he felt something of a fish out of water here, and had taken it upon himself to acknowledge me whenever our paths crossed. I had no idea what he had been recruited to do at the Park, other than knowing he hadn't been assigned to Hut 8 where I worked.

However, from our limited conversations I knew that he suffered not just from a mild stammer but also asthma and had therefore been deemed unfit for active service in the same way I had with my weakened arm. He'd been a Classicist from Balliol College, Oxford, and had been plucked from a prep school in the north of England where he had been teaching boys the rudiments of German and Latin – boys who had probably relished the sport of mimicking his speech impediment.

He had left behind him the kind of teaching post I imagined for myself when the war was over. Question was, did Kitty still see herself as the wife of a schoolmaster buried deep in the countryside somewhere? Would that life be enough for her? A few weeks ago I would have answered with an unequivocal yes, but now I doubted it.

'D-d-d-do you know each other?' Stein asked, indicating the fair-haired girl at his side.

'No,' we said simultaneously, which caused her to blush furiously, her pale cheeks instantly stained with two vividly pink circles.

'I'm Jacob,' I said, extending my hand and realising that I was in that rare position of feeling the most experienced and confident of the group. 'Jacob Belinsky.'

'Molly Pearson,' she said, regarding me shyly from behind a pair of wire-framed spectacles.

'I haven't seen you around before,' I remarked with the kind of nonchalance I normally envied in others.

'I only arrived a couple of days ago,' she answered. From her accent I guessed she was from somewhere in the Midlands.

'So probably finding it all rather strange,' I replied.

She nodded. 'It's the first time I've been away from home. Nothing's at all what I thought it would be. Not that I'm complaining. Really I'm not. It's just there's so much to take in.'

'You'll soon find your feet,' I assured her, 'everybody does. How are your digs?'

'Not too bad; the couple I'm billeted with are quite elderly and rather sweet. Last night we played cribbage together while we listened to the wireless.'

'L-l-l-lucky you,' Stein said, 'I'm with an old b-b-boy who's as deaf as a post and keeps a p-p-p-parrot which never stops shrieking.'

I had a sudden and utterly inappropriate mental picture of the parrot mimicking Stein's stutter. 'We all have to draw a short straw sooner or later,' I said, as a swell of activity behind me started up – voices raised and chairs being pulled out. 'Looks like things are about to get under way.'

'I've never been to a chess club before,' Molly said. 'I've only ever played at home with my father and brothers. I wasn't going to come, but Victor said I should, that it would help me to settle in and make new friends. Do you think everyone feels homesick at first?' she asked.

Her candour stirred an emotion quite unexpected within me: the urge to counsel her. 'Victor's absolutely right,' I said gently, 'you'll have so many new friends you won't have time to think about home.' I kept to myself that what would keep her from dwelling on the relative comfort of home would be exhaustion, that the workload would be so intense, home would become but a distant memory. 'Perhaps you'll join the group when we go for a drink afterwards?' I said.

She smiled and once again her cheeks were suffused with colour.

Throughout the games of chess I played for the next couple of hours, I occasionally glanced around the library to see who she was playing against and how she was doing. I had the strangest feeling of wanting to take her under my wing and protect her. Thank goodness Chatterton-Jones wasn't a chess player and here to inflict himself upon her innocence.

Although, in fairness to the man, ever since he had gone to the trouble to deliver the lost ring and played his part in helping to get the upper hand with Mrs Pridmore, I had reviewed my opinion of him. We would never be the best of friends, but at least now I rubbed along companionably enough with him during our shifts together.

As for Mrs Pridmore, the strain to be polite had to be killing her and I often wondered if she would one day explode and come at me not caring about the consequences. I once dreamt that I awoke to find her standing over my bed clutching a carving knife and about to plunge it into my chest. My fellow lodgers were staggered at the improvement in our meals and prayed that whatever had caused the miraculous change didn't stop. I was tempted to tell them what had happened, but decided to keep quiet – the only person I had told was Kitty, although just to keep Mrs Pridmore on her toes I would occasionally raise the subject of black-market goods with Griffiths and Farrington while she was slamming our meals on to the table. They had no idea what I was up to, but the expression on our landlady's face could have single-handedly sunk the entire German navy and made our code-breaking work redundant.

I acquitted myself sufficiently to come a decent second in the tournament and after we'd tidied away the chessboards and pieces, we set off for The Shoulder of Mutton, our regular haunt on these evenings. Noticing that Victor was deep in conversation at the bar, I spotted Molly on her own. Biting the nails of one hand, she couldn't have looked more forlorn and anxious so I went over and offered to buy her a drink. 'Oh no, I couldn't possibly,' she said, all of a flutter.

'Why ever not?'

'I'm not really a drinker.'

'You say that now, but give it a month and you'll be a drinker like the rest of us – I guarantee it. How about a sherry?'

She looked doubtful. 'My parents wouldn't approve. They say drink is the gateway to letting the devil into your life.'

'Just a small one,' I said with a smile, 'and I promise to stand guard at the gateway to stop the devil.'

Her cheeks flushed once more. 'Well ... perhaps just a small one.'

'A sherry it is,' I said, rather enjoying my newfound role as avuncular seasoned hand.

When I'd returned from the bar, we said cheers and knocking back a decent mouthful of my whisky, I watched her tentatively try her sherry. To my amusement, within no more than a few sips, her face was charmingly pink and she was smiling at me, her eyes bright and twinkling behind her spectacles. It occurred to me then, caught in the beam of her obvious delight, that this would show Kitty that she wasn't the only one who could enjoy an evening in the company of somebody else.

'It's very kind of you to befriend me like this,' she said,

leaning in closer, 'especially as I'm sure somebody as popular as you must have any number of friends here. I hope I'm not boring you.'

'Of course not,' I said, amazed at her naivety and her hugely mistaken assumptions. 'How did you find the evening?' I asked, as somebody jostled my arm from behind, nearly making me spill my drink. When I turned to see who it was, I saw a balding man pushing his way through the crowded pub. Something about him looked familiar but I couldn't place him. My attention back on Molly, I said, 'Will you be joining the Chess Club, do you think?'

'Oh yes, I signed up before we left the library. You know, I've never seen a house as large as the Mansion; it's beautiful, isn't it? Honestly, if my family could see me here, they wouldn't believe it!'

I nodded non-committally, lacking the heart to tell her that there were those who believed it to be one of the ugliest houses in the whole of Christendom, a ghastly hotchpotch of architectural features that no person of any real taste and breeding would have dreamt up.

'You know, that sherry wasn't too bad at all,' she said. She held out her now empty glass and giggled. 'Perhaps I could try another.'

I smiled. 'Why not indeed?'

Forty-five minutes later, when she was merrily suggesting a third glass, I advised against it, saying that perhaps it was time to call it a night. Helping her into her coat, we stepped outside into the cold night air. The street was in darkness and knowing that I had drunk more than my usual fill, but worse, that I had unwisely encouraged Molly to drink more sherry than was good for her, I offered to walk her back to her digs.

'I couldn't possibly put you to all that trouble,' she said, visibly swaying.

'Better that I do,' I insisted. 'Which way do we need to go?'

Scrunching up her eyes behind the lenses of her spectacles, she peered into the blackout darkness and then hiccupped loudly. 'Oh, pardon me!' she exclaimed, slapping a gloved hand to her mouth. When she hiccupped a second time, she began to laugh. It was such a happy sound, I couldn't help but laugh with her. Then, reminding her that I needed directions if I was going to get her home, she indicated we should cross the road.

'You're sure?' I asked.

'As sure as sure,' she said with a giggle while stifling another hiccup.

When she missed her footing on the pavement the other side of the road and nearly went over, I put a firm hand to her arm. 'Now which way?' I asked when I had her upright. 'Left or right?'

But she wasn't looking at the road; she was gazing up at me through her spectacles, which had become skewed on her face. She suddenly looked so awkward and vulnerable that I felt something stir within me and, before I knew what I was doing, I'd raised my hands to straighten her spectacles. But then, and in a fumbled rush, she pushed her face against mine and kissed me. I was so surprised, I kissed her back. Afterwards, her face hot and flushed, she smiled self-consciously. 'Goodness, I've never done anything like that before,' she said breathlessly. 'What must you think of me?'

'Come on,' I said, the taste of sherry now on my lips, 'let's get you home before you freeze to death. Which way do we need to go?'

'Right,' she said. 'No, I mean left.' Flustered, she let out a small laugh and pointed to the left. Again I put my hand to her elbow and steered her in the way she'd said. She was humming now, something jolly but indistinct, and increasing my grasp on her arm, I regretted, in my desire to appear more worldly than she, that I had pressed that first glass of sherry on her. It was the grossest of irresponsible and shameful acts, for which the poor girl would pay dearly in the morning with a hangover. What was more, I should not have kissed her. What had I been thinking? I was mortified with myself.

We were almost at the end of the road when behind us I heard footsteps. I glanced over my shoulder and in the shadowy darkness made out what looked like two figures. Another glance, and I realised they were moving at a faster pace than Molly and I were and not only that, there were actually three figures, each wearing a cap pulled down low, their faces partially hidden behind scarves, the collars of their coats turned up. Instinct told me to increase my grip on Molly and make her get a move on. 'Which way now?' I asked as a car drove slowly by, its headlamps barely showing through the masks that covered them.

She pointed across the road junction. 'Over there and then to the right.'

I hurried her over the road and when I looked back over my shoulder, the three figures were gaining on us, their boots beating out a tattoo on the pavement.

They might just be going in the same direction as we were, I told myself. It was coincidence, nothing more. So why then did they have such a menacing look about them? And was it fanciful of me to think that one of the men was the man who'd jostled me in the pub?

It was just as Molly complained that we were going too fast, that I realised why I thought the man was familiar: he was Mrs Pridmore's black-market partner in crime. Now I really was worried.

'Please,' Molly said, shaking my hand off her, 'you're hurting my arm.'

'Perhaps you should listen to the little lady,' came a gruff voice from the darkness behind us.

'Who's that?' Molly asked, turning to look.

'Ignore them,' I said, taking hold of her arm again and dragging her down the street.

'That's not very polite of you. Nobody likes to be ignored. Least of all us.'

'What do you want?' I demanded.

'Let the girl go, we want to have a word with you.'

'Why?'

'Just do as we say. Unless you'd like your lady friend here to receive the same message we have for you?'

'What message?' I asked.

'One from a mutual friend of ours, somebody who isn't happy with you right now. No more than we are.'

'I can't imagine we have a mutual friend,' I said.

The taller of the three men stepped forward and loomed menacingly over Molly, making her cower. 'How about you toddle off home, sweetheart? We've got business here to attend to with Mr Belinsky.'

'Go on,' I said to Molly, 'you can find your way home from here, can't you?'

Her face stricken, she nodded, and clutching her handbag to her chest, she hurried away.

I had been in only a few fights in my time, both times at school, both times for no other reason than I was a Jew. I had broken a boy's nose during the last altercation and had been severely reprimanded by the headmaster. Right now I felt like breaking more than a nose, and I raised my fists, lashed out and made contact with a jaw. But not enough to inflict any real damage.

I threw another punch, but I wasn't dealing with a couple of schoolyard bullies now, these men meant business. And it was three against one. The first blow caught me on the side of my face. The next made me lose my balance and, stumbling back, my arms flailing wildly, I found myself being grabbed by the collar of my coat and thrust against a wall. With my head making contact with the rough brickwork behind me, I waited for the next blow. It came, a vicious punch to my stomach that would have had me doubled over in pain had not an equally vicious jab caught me on the jaw and smashed my head back into the wall.

'That's for interfering in business that doesn't concern

you!' one of the men said when a succession of punches had been dished out. 'And don't even think of reporting this to the police. Do that and we'll come after your sweet little girlfriend.'

'She's not my girlfriend.'

One of the men laughed nastily. 'A true gent this one, trying to protect his lady-love by denying his feelings for her.' The man's breath stank of cheap soapy beer and tobacco and with his fingers suddenly digging into my windpipe and squeezing hard, he said, 'We saw you in The Shoulder of Mutton together, and we just saw you kiss her, so don't lie to us.'

With the blood pounding in my ears, and accepting that it was easier to let them think what they needed to, I tried to swallow but couldn't. The man's grasp on my throat was painfully tight.

'Do we have a deal, then?' the man said. 'You leave us to continue with our business as before and we'll leave you and your girlfriend alone?'

I nodded.

They left me gasping for breath on the pavement, and just as I was picking myself up, I heard the sound of running and whistles being blown.

'This way!' came a high-pitched voice. 'He's down here!'

Chapter Fifty-One

February 1944

'My poor, poor darling, I can't bear to see you this way. It's absolutely scandalous what those ghastly men did to you. As though there isn't enough fighting going on in the world!'

I opened my mouth to say something, but Kitty shook her head, 'No, not a word, Jacob, you need to sleep.'

Thinking that sleep would be a long time in coming with Kitty determined to articulate her outrage so animatedly, I tried to arrange my swollen face into something that I hoped resembled a smile of amusement. Judging from her expression my attempt fell somewhat short of the mark.

We were in my room at Mrs Pridmore's. It was the first time Kitty had been in it and it felt odd seeing her move about the cramped space, drawing curtains, folding clothes and fussing with the bed coverlet. Odder still, and far more worrying, was the ingrained fear I had that Mrs Pridmore herself would march in any minute and create merry hell.

But that was never going to happen. Mrs Pridmore and her black-market cronies were in police custody and very likely on their way to prison. I had been told that I was lucky I wasn't heading for the same destination as well, as by rights I should have informed the authorities what was going on.

'You kept quiet for your own personal gain,' the detective inspector had said, his speckled grey moustache quivering as he breathed out heavily through his hair-filled nostrils. A man who was about fifty years of age and too old to fight for king and country, he was fighting hard here on his patch.

'Not entirely,' I had argued, focusing on the man's moustache, using it as a means to contain the indignation I felt at being questioned at the police station before I'd even been allowed to have my injuries looked at. 'I was also thinking of my fellow lodgers; we'd all been cheated by the woman. I just wanted us to have the rations to which we were entitled and with the least amount of trouble.'

'So you gave her a second chance, did you? How very magnanimous of you.'

'I agree I'd misjudged matters,' I'd replied, 'but naïvely I had hoped she would change her ways for the better. It has been known, surely?'

'You're one of those clever types from up at the Park, aren't you?' he'd said, abruptly getting to his feet and coming round to my side of his desk. He made it sound like working at the Park was a crime in itself. He shook his head disparagingly. 'Clever but as green as grass.'

The questioning and sneering accusations had continued, the implication being I had been involved in the black-market ring. But finally I was considered innocent of any real crime, other than foolhardiness. As with so much in life, my propensity to take the course of least resistance had not gone as smoothly as I'd have liked.

My injuries were far from life-threatening – two black eyes, a few cracked ribs, a thumping headache and a variety of cuts and bruises. However, and not yet twenty-four hours on from the attack, Kitty was intent on treating me as some sort of heroic invalid who had single-handedly taken on a vast crime ring.

Needless to say, this was not how I regarded myself. Indeed, the one person who I believed deserved to be applauded was Molly Pearson, for it was she who had fetched help in the form of a policeman and returned to where she'd left me. While I didn't believe Mrs Pridmore's cohorts had intended to kill me – their purpose had been merely to rough me up and scare me off – I was grateful to Molly for her prompt action.

But worse than the physical injuries I had been left with was the sense of deep, deep shame I felt. My intentions had been far from honourable towards Molly; I had used her to make myself feel better about Kitty and inadvertently involved her in something her parents would find far more horrifying than an hour or two spent in a public house drinking sherry.

I must have fallen asleep, for when I woke there was a cup of tea on my bedside table, a biscuit in the saucer. Through painfully swollen eyelids and observing Kitty moving about in the dimly lit room inspecting my few possessions, I suddenly felt the pitiful need to confess my actions. I wanted her forgiveness, to be told that I had done nothing that couldn't be forgotten with a hug and a kiss.

She had come here straight from finishing her shift, having heard on the grapevine that I had been attacked in town late last night. Griffiths had answered the door to her and brought her upstairs. I hadn't wanted her to see me this way, so bruised and battered, but she was having none of my squeamish need to protect her finer feelings. Or my foolish need to protect my vanity. I had told her everything about the episode, everything apart from kissing Molly.

'How was the dance at the American base?' I asked. My question was not fuelled by the jealous need to know with whom she'd danced – I had lost that right to resent her wanting to have fun with her friends the moment I had not resisted Molly's mouth upon mine – it was asked in the genuine hope that she had had a good time.

Startled at the sound of my voice, she turned round from the mantelpiece where she had been looking at a photograph of me with my family.

'It was fun.'

'Did you dance?'

'Of course, that was rather the point of the evening.

Where are the photographs we had taken of us the last time we visited your parents?'

'Carefully hidden.'

She frowned. 'Why?'

'I didn't want Mrs Pridmore seeing them when she was carrying out one of her snooping and prying exercises.'

Her frown deepened. 'How jolly unlucky you are to be billeted with such a vile woman.' She came and sat on the edge of the bed. 'Why don't you drink the tea while it's still hot, I've only just brought it up for you.'

I carefully eased myself into a sitting position and drank the tea. It was black and sweet, just how I liked it, a reminder of how my grandmother made it when rationing allowed.

'So where did you hide the photographs of us?' Kitty asked.

'Guess,' I replied, taking a hungry bite of the biscuit.

Smiling, she looked around the room. 'On top of the wardrobe?'

'First place the old dragon would look.'

'Hmm ... behind the wardrobe?'

'Second place she'd look.'

'I give in.'

'That didn't take long.'

'I don't want to wear you out. Tell me.'

'You were very close before. They're in the fireplace.'

She turned her head towards the wall opposite the bed. 'But it's blocked off with that small electric fire in front of it.'

'Which makes it the perfect hiding place because one, Mrs Pridmore wouldn't think I would go to the trouble of dismantling it, and two, she would never dirty her hands by rummaging around in it herself.'

'Can I see?'

'If you want.'

Seeing her eagerness, and knowing what else was hidden there, I made a snap decision. It wasn't the romantic moment I had envisaged for us, but more than ever I needed to know that she still wanted to marry me – the real me, battered and bruised, and with my manifold faults and insecurities.

Which also meant I had to confess what had happened last night with Molly Pearson: that I had selfishly and wilfully used the poor girl to bolster my pathetic ego in order to prove a point. I really couldn't embark on married life without Kitty knowing the depths to which I could sink.

Chapter Fifty-Two

'*Don't do it!*' Matthew wanted to yell. 'Just don't do it!'

So exasperated at what Jacob was about to do, Matthew couldn't read on. He slapped the book shut, rubbed his face hard and sighed. Then pushing his chair back, he went over to the digital radio he'd bought Jacob several Christmases ago. When he'd come in to the library this morning to work, he'd switched it on, the first time he had since Jacob's death, and hearing the Radio 3 announcer introducing the next piece of music had given him a sense of comforting connection to the old man. Jacob had always preferred the radio to the television, citing the latter as a pernicious idiot-box, designed to destroy the last residue of intellect and humanity left in the world. Considering some of the rubbish Matthew occasionally found himself watching, it was difficult not to agree with Jacob.

He switched the radio off. The Brahms piano concerto of before had been fine as pleasant background music, but now the relentless high-pitched scraping of violins playing something he didn't recognise was getting on his nerves.

In the silence that fell on the room, he went back to the desk and looked out at the garden. It was a drearily wet day; the rain had started just as he'd arrived last night from Cambridge. It might be May, but the temperature had dropped dramatically and after breakfast he'd resorted to putting on the heating. Jim Rycroft had called him twice during the day, both times interrupting Matthew while he slogged through the epic amounts of documents he'd brought with him. At six o'clock he'd called a halt to work and, in need of something to clear and refresh his head, opened Jacob's second notebook.

He looked at it now and thought how, with each page he'd turned, he'd experienced a moment of dread that Jacob would give in to the need for yet another bout of self-laceration. It saddened him enormously that Jacob hadn't been able to allow himself to be happy, that he preferred to give in to his doubts and keep punishing himself. Why? Why could he not simply be content with being with the girl he loved? Why the perpetual desire to scupper his chance of happiness? Was it merely the fear of not living up to expectation, of feeling himself an outsider, so better to pull the rug out from beneath himself before anyone else had a chance to?

The similarity between Jacob's situation and Matthew's, in that they had both knowingly crossed an identical line, was unnerving. Matthew could understand Jacob's need to absolve himself, but he couldn't help but wonder if that was enough for Jacob. Was he subconsciously aiming much higher, destruction at the very least? Clearly he hadn't believed he was good enough for Kitty, so what better way to prove it than to push her to the outer limits of her love for him and wait for her to walk away?

There was no similarity between Matthew and Jacob in that respect, Matthew wasn't hell-bent on any kind of destruction, but what he now knew, without a shadow of a doubt, was that he didn't love Fliss with anything like the intensity that Jacob had loved Kitty. And never would. He certainly didn't feel the depth of emotion for her that would lead to a lifelong commitment.

It had gradually become clear to Matthew in the last few days that the reason for his recent restlessness was very straightforward and very unoriginal – he simply didn't know what it was he wanted in life anymore. On the other hand, he knew what he didn't want. He didn't want to carry on as he was.

For so long he'd been led by his ambition, initially at school, then at Cambridge and then with work. While it was true he'd relished the challenge of the academic treadmill, it was also true that a lot of what he'd done had been to please his mother and Jacob. In return for everything they had done for him, he'd wanted them to be proud of him.

When he'd woken this morning to the sound of church bells coming from next door, he'd lain in bed and asked himself the dangerously loaded question – is this it, then? Because if it was, what did it really amount to? What did his career give him, other than a decent salary and a ferocious workload? There had to be more, surely?

But work aside, what of his relationship with Fliss? If he now knew that he didn't love her, then what was the point in continuing? It wasn't fair to her. Not fair at all. It had been all too easy to slip back into the relationship they'd had once before, but it had been a mistake. He'd probably known intuitively from the start that it was wrong and wouldn't work long-term, and maybe that's why he hadn't mentioned the fact that he had a girlfriend when he was getting to know Saskia and her family. Perhaps that was also why he had kissed Saskia. Had he been truly happy being back with Fliss, he would never have felt drawn to Saskia.

Or had he, with an entirely different motive in mind, kissed her in a deliberate act of courting disaster, just as Jacob had?

It was impossible to answer the question. But one thing he had to find an answer for was how to tell Fliss the conclusion he'd reached, and without causing her any more upset. And having received no word from her for several days, there was always the chance she was having second thoughts of her own.

He suddenly yawned. He was dog-tired. And not just tired through lack of sleep and working the long hours he had this week on the Merchant College case, but tired of seemingly going round in endless circles. He needed to make some decisions and sort out his life, because for too long it had felt as if he was stagnating and going nowhere.

Something else he needed to do, now that probate had been completed, was get in touch with Ralph to make a start on selling the bulk of Jacob's books. Obviously now wouldn't be appropriate because the family had a funeral to get through, so he'd have to wait a respectful couple of weeks.

Thinking of Ralph and how awful he'd looked yesterday in Cambridge, Matthew wondered if his condolence card had reached Saskia this morning. He hoped so. He wanted her to know that he cared. He regretted that he hadn't asked Ralph if it would be all right to ring Saskia. But then why wouldn't it be all right? Wouldn't it be more usual for a friend to call as soon as he or she had heard there'd been a death in the family? What if his card hadn't arrived yet and her father had mentioned he'd run into Matthew yesterday: wouldn't she think badly of him for not getting in touch?

But he was hardly a close friend of the family, was he? He was merely an acquaintance. An acquaintance who'd been fortunate enough to be welcomed into their home. An acquaintance who'd sat on a garden fence on a warm and sunny spring day and kissed an intriguingly fascinating girl. A girl who reminded him of himself.

He lowered his gaze to the notebook on the desk. It was this that had led to that moment in the garden at Ashcombe; without it they would never have made the connection in the way they had. Saskia probably wouldn't be interested in reading the notebook in the coming days, but just as soon as she did want to, he would give it to her.

After making himself some supper, Matthew took his plate through to the library and was about to sit down and eat when he saw the screen of his mobile was illuminated. Checking it, he saw he'd just missed two calls – yet another from Jim Rycroft and one from Ralph Granger.

Chapter Fifty-Three

Saskia loved her aunt dearly and it was good to have her here at Ashcombe, but a little of her went an extremely long way.

Despite speaking so regularly on Skype, the in-the-flesh reality of Auntie Jo always came as a shock after a lengthy period of not seeing her, mostly because she was so scarily efficient and organised, and an eminent believer in speaking her mind. She claimed it was the teacher in her that made it second nature to give out orders. Dad reckoned that it was the other way around, that her bossy nature was the reason she became a teacher because no other profession would tolerate her. Grandpa O used to call any face-to-face exchange with his eldest child akin to hand-to-hand combat and it was always better to go into battle with her well prepared.

From the moment they had picked Auntie Jo up from the airport, she had somehow taken command, instructing Dad on the best way to stow her luggage in the boot of the car and insisting that Harvey was to sit up front with Dad, she would be quite happy in the back with Saskia, she wanted no special guest privileges. Saskia knew enough about grief to know that this was her aunt's way of coping, staying busy and getting things done was so much easier than allowing oneself time to dwell.

In much the same way Saskia was in her workshop working on one of the many dissertations she had to bind. She had left her aunt sitting at the head of the kitchen table with Dad and Harvey on either side of her going over the arrangements for Grandpa O's funeral next week. There seemed no point in Saskia joining in; Auntie Jo had it all in hand.

Moreover, Saskia needed some time alone. For just a few brief minutes, she wanted to think about something other than the practicalities of organising Grandpa O's funeral, which she understood had to be done, but she wanted to think about the man he'd been, not how the remains of him were to be dealt with.

She was still struggling to come to terms with the shockingly needless manner of her grandfather's dying, and all because of his stubbornness and determination to get rid of that bloody bag caught on the tree branch. If he'd simply waited for Saskia or Dad to do it, he'd still be alive with the prospect of years ahead of him to enjoy. For them all to enjoy. Silly, silly old man, she thought with great sadness.

Her eyes filling with tears, she brushed them away and raised her gaze from her workbench and looked out at the garden where in the rain one of the hens was perched on the roof of the hencoop. Saskia had often seen the bird there since Grandpa O's death; it was as though she was keeping watch, anxiously waiting for him to come back from wherever he was. They were probably missing his grumpy chunterings, which had always been a source of amusement for the family. 'Better he grumbles at the hens than us,' Harvey used to say.

Her attention drawn back to the workbench, she switched on the anglepoise lamp that provided the extra light she needed, selected some gold leaf and set to work on the lettering on the spine. It was a step in the process that she liked, the careful precision of lining the letters up and getting the spacing just right.

The spine finished, she then completed the front and afterwards she stood back to give her work her most critical scrutiny. Perfect, she thought with a satisfied nod, then standing up straight she worked the tension from her neck and shoulders. Going over to the window, she saw that the rain had stopped, but the hen was still keeping watch from the roof of the coop. What a sad and bedraggled sight the poor bird looked. How long before it gave up waiting for Oliver to reappear?

In the days since word had gone round the village of Oliver's death, they had been inundated with cards and messages of sympathy. There had been flowers as well and even plastic storage boxes of home-baked cakes, adding embarrassingly to what Harvey was stockpiling in the larder and freezer. Every time Saskia went into the kitchen, there was Harvey weighing, stirring, beating or kneading some sort of cake, pudding or dough mixture. He said he was doing it in readiness for the funeral because afterwards people would roll up at the house for refreshments, but she had her doubts: she could foresee many days of intense distraction-baking in the months to come.

In her head Saskia could hear Oliver muttering that Harvey was a daft old bugger and as usual was over-catering. 'How many people do you think are coming?' she imagined him saying. 'Who's going to bother attending my funeral when they have better things to do?' To which Harvey, in this imaginary conversation, would say, 'They won't be there for you, you miserable old devil, they'll be there for my cakes!'

If the number of cards and messages they'd received was anything to go by, the turnout looked as if it would be big. The service was going to be held in the village church; while none of them in the family had been regular attendees, Oliver had been a keen bell-ringer and had only given up a few years ago. The four of them had also taken part in the church quiz night, an event that took place twice a year and which Oliver had taken ridiculously seriously, swotting up for weeks in advance. Saskia doubted they would enter the quiz again without Oliver: it wouldn't feel right, not having their team captain with them.

The garden wouldn't feel right without him either. The sight of the cane wigwams for the peas and beans, one of the last jobs Saskia had helped Oliver do in the vegetable patch, was going to be a sad reminder of Oliver's absence. Just as everything he had already planted and which they would later harvest and eat was going to be a poignant milestone.

Hearing the sound of a car, Saskia craned her head and saw Libby's red VW Golf sweep in through the gateway. Libby had been wonderful over the last week and had taken on the running of the shop, leaving Dad free to deal with the inevitable bureaucracy of Grandpa O's death. Even in death, or perhaps especially in death, there was a depressing amount of paperwork to sort out – notifying the tax people, the various banks and building societies Oliver had used, the charities he supported, the mailing lists he was on, the dentist, and so much more.

Out of her car, Libby spotted Saskia in the window and changing her mind about going to the house, she followed the path towards the workshop.

Saskia opened the door and let her in. 'How was the shop today?'

'It was fine,' Libby said, 'the usual Saturday, a nice steady flow of punters. Oh, and that interior designer from Bury called in again; she's after about five hundred shelf-decoration hardbacks for a gastro pub she's working on.'

'That shouldn't be a problem, should it?'

'No problem at all, there's easily that much on the top floor at the shop.' She tapped her handbag. 'And I have a few more sympathy cards which were dropped off during the day. Do you want to read them?'

Saskia shook her head. 'Let the others see them first, I'll look at them later.'

Looking about the workshop, Libby said, 'You've been doing some work then?'

'I needed something else to occupy my mind, other than the obvious.'

Libby smiled. 'Sometimes work is the best thing. If you've got a minute, there's something I'd like to ask you.'

'That's odd, because there's something I want to ask you too.'

'Really?'

'Yes. But you go first.'

'It's about the garden. I was ... well, it's occurred to me that Oliver loved it very much and derived great pleasure from everything he planted and grew and I was wondering, because it would be such a shame if it fell into ...' Her words trailed away and she frowned. 'Oh dear, this is more awkward than I thought it would be.'

'Perhaps I can help you,' Saskia said. 'You see, that's what I wanted to talk to you about; I wanted to ask if you'd like to take the garden on. Not the lawns, Dad'll see to those as he always has, but the vegetables and everything else. I'll help you as well, if you'd like, but I'm no expert, I always did as Oliver told me, I was his under-gardener. And I know it's a lot to ask of you, but I saw how much he enjoyed talking to you about it. He once said to me, "That Libby knows her onions!"'

A slow smile spread over the other woman's face. 'Do you really mean that? Because that's exactly what I was going to ask you.'

'I can't think of anyone Oliver would have trusted more with his pride and joy.'

'Goodness, I don't know what to say. I was so worried you'd think I was overstepping the mark, you know, muscling my way in. After all, you haven't known me for that long.'

'Long enough to know that you make my father exceptionally happy, so that's all I need to know.'

'I have one more question.'

'Go on.'

'Can I hug you, please?'

Later, when Libby had gone across to the house, Saskia thought how sad it was that Libby had asked for permission to hug her. Was that how she came across, aloof and unapproachable? Or was it merely another example of

Libby's extreme care in not upsetting the apple cart here at Ashcombe?

It worried her also that Libby had felt the need to ask *her* and not her father about the garden. On the other hand, it could simply be consideration, and for that she should be applauded; not every woman in her shoes would go out of her way to ensure all parties were kept happy. And for that Saskia liked Libby even more.

She was just settling down again to start work on binding another dissertation, when, and after a perfunctory knock, the workshop door opened and her aunt poked her head in.

Of her own admission, it had been Auntie Jo's unfortunate bad luck in life to inherit her father's looks rather than her mother's. She had the same coarse grey hair, which she had cut severely short by the same barber who cut Uncle Bob's hair. She had been a great athlete when younger but in recent years, as age had begun to take its toll, her knees and hips had been giving her problems and her sporting prowess was now limited to cycling and hiking.

'Is it your intention to stay here all night?' she demanded. 'If so I'll arrange for a camp bed to be brought out for you.'

Saskia checked her watch. 'It's not that late, it's not even seven o'clock.'

'True, but this may come as a surprise to you: I'd like to see something of you while I'm here. Come and help me put the hens away.'

'Does that mean you want to talk to me in private?'

'Yes.'

Saskia smiled and knowing she would get nothing but honesty from her aunt, said, 'In that case, answer a question for me. Do I come across as aloof and unapproachable?'

Walking across the sodden lawn, her aunt answered her question. 'At times, yes,' she said. 'That's because you have a tendency to sit back and observe rather than join in. You've always done that. You did it when you were a toddler. You'd sit watching everyone as though you were a fly on the wall.'

'Do you think it's a bad character trait?'

'Depends how far you take it.'

'But it's fair to say I'm an outsider, aren't I?'

'Not within your own family, no. As for life beyond Ashcombe, that's another matter. I'd say you've deliberately distanced yourself from the rest of the world, and will keep on doing so if left to your own devices. It was what my father was most concerned about whenever we chatted.'

'He spoke about me with you?'

'Of course he did! Your happiness was his top priority. It always was.'

Saskia's eyes welled up. 'He didn't have to worry about that, I *am* happy.'

'Are you?'

Managing to get hold of one of the hens, Saskia held it against her chest. 'Obviously I'm not happy now, but generally yes, I'd say I'm happy with life.'

'He wanted so much more for you, you know that, don't you? The last conversation he had with me was that he wanted you to fly the nest and have some real fun. An adventure.'

'Is that why you've been on at me so much lately to visit you?'

'In part, yes. But, Saskia, visit Bob and me by all means, but for heaven's sake, there's a whole world out there for you to explore. Staying with us should be a springboard for you.'

'But I like it here, this is my world.'

'And that's great, but there's nothing wrong in exploring somewhere else even if it then confirms to you that this is where you belong. What are you scared of, Saskia?'

Saskia deposited the hen safely inside the coop and looked at her aunt. 'I'm not scared of anything. What on earth makes you think I am?'

'For starters, your total reluctance to change things.'

'You know me well enough to appreciate that I don't

believe in change for the sake of it. It's highly overrated.'

'Come on, Saskia, everything changes at some point, look how things have already started changing here. First Libby, now Oliver.'

'That's called evolving. But what are you really getting at?' Rounding up another of the hens, Saskia could feel herself becoming defensive.

Her aunt stopped what she was doing. 'OK, it's this,' she said. 'Your love life. Or, to put it more bluntly, the lack of it. What happened to that chap you were telling me so much about, Matthew Gray? Ralph says you've decided he's already in a relationship, though you haven't a shred of evidence to prove he is.'

'Dad told you that? I'd have thought he had more important things to discuss with you.'

'Apparently he bumped into Matthew in Cambridge when he went to see Oliver's solicitor yesterday.'

'I know about that. And I've read the card he sent me.'

'So? Does the fact that he went to the bother of sending you a card as soon as he heard about Oliver sound like a two-timing rotter? Seems to me like he's not all bad.'

'And your point?'

'That maybe you're cutting your nose off to spite your lovely face. Why not simply ask him whether he's seeing somebody else?'

'Don't you think I'm much more concerned about Grandpa O at the moment?'

'And what do you think my father's advice to you would be?'

'That's neither here nor there; the question is why are you so keen to push me into the arms of somebody you've never even met?'

'Because my father was a good judge of character and he told me he liked this Matthew a lot; what's more, in his last chat with me he said he was firmly of the opinion that you were more than a bit sweet on him.'

Saskia rolled her eyes. 'How quaintly put.'

Dismissing her sarcasm with a wave of her hand as she roughly scooped up the last remaining hen, her aunt shoved the poor bird unceremoniously into the coop. The door shut, she stared at Saskia. 'Ralph and Harvey have confirmed everything Oliver told me. So here's what's going to happen: at my request your father's just invited young Master Matthew Gray to the funeral, and if he comes, I shall check him out and ask him directly if he's currently in a relationship.'

Saskia was appalled. 'Oh, for heaven's sake, that's ridiculous! I can't believe you've gone behind my back and done this. I'm ... I'm staggered! I'm staggered that you'd meddle to that extent.'

'I'm meddling because I strongly believe my father would approve.'

'What about my feelings in all of this? Do I not have any say?'

'You can have your say after the event. For now you're going to do as you're told.'

'Auntie Jo, can I remind you that I'm thirty-two years old, not ten?'

'You can remind me all you like, but it won't change a damned thing. Wheels are in motion. Suck it up, as you young folk say.'

'I assure you that is not something I have ever said,' Saskia said primly.

Her aunt laughed. 'I thought not, somehow. Come on, that's the hens done, let's go inside and see about supper. I've given Harvey the night off.'

'I bet he didn't take kindly to that.'

'He put up a bit of a fight – but let's face it, an exhausted, grieving octogenarian is no match for me.'

Despite how cross she was with her aunt, Saskia smiled. 'You're a bloody nightmare, you do realise that, don't you?'

'Sure I do. And each and every one of you will be hugely

relieved when I leave. That's my purpose in life, to make you realise how lucky you are that I live so far away.'

Saskia linked her arm through her aunt's as they made their way to the back door. 'You're completely mad, but I do love you.'

'Oh shucks, don't go getting all sentimental on me! Anything but that.'

'It's called quid pro quo – expose your Achilles heel to me and I'll poke at it to punish you for the mayhem you're intent on creating.'

Her aunt laughed. 'See, beneath that cool, unapproachable exterior lies a heart that does beat after all.'

Saskia laughed too, grateful that Auntie Jo had achieved the impossible: she had actually taken her out of her grief. If only for a few minutes.

Chapter Fifty-Four

Matthew couldn't have been more surprised by the message Ralph had left on his voicemail.

He was touched that the family had invited him to Oliver Granger's funeral, an occasion that was inherently a very personal and primarily a family occasion. He would definitely go. He just had to hope that Jim Rycroft wouldn't object to him having time off.

His supper eaten, he took his plate through to the kitchen, grabbed another beer from the fridge and went back to the library. Making himself comfortable, he opened Jacob's notebook and picked up where he'd left off.

Was Jacob about to throw away his chance to be happy with Kitty?

Chapter Fifty-Five

One of the many things I have learnt about myself since meeting Kitty is that my nerve constantly fails me. It's the one thing I know I can rely upon, the ability always to fall at the last hurdle.

That night, as I sat up in bed, bruised and battered and full of guilty recrimination for my behaviour, I looked at Kitty's lovely face and knew I could never confess what I had done. The thought of causing her a moment of anguish over my stupidity put a stop to my selfish need to absolve myself. Rather, I took a perverse kind of solace in accepting that perhaps the beating I had received from Mrs Pridmore's thugs was my just punishment. It would serve us both better to put the whole incident behind me and mentally wipe my own slate clean. There was no need to destroy Kitty's belief in me.

At my direction she found the things I had hidden inside the blocked-off fireplace and when she saw the little velvet pouch, her curiosity was roused. 'What's this?' she asked.

I took it from her. 'It's for you,' I said. 'My plan was to give it to you at a more auspicious time, certainly a moment that contained a modicum of romance to it, but I've changed my mind.'

She frowned. 'Does that mean you're not going to give it to me? What a tease you are.'

With nervously clumsy hands, I opened the pouch and felt for the ring inside. It was still there, thank God!

Withdrawing the ring and showing it to her, I explained it had once belonged to my great-grandmother in Russia. 'I'm wholly unworthy to ask you this,' I went on, 'but would it be beyond the realms of possibility for you to consider wearing this ring and become my wife?'

Her eyes, bright and shining, moved from the ring to my face. 'You absurdly silly man, of course I'll marry you! There's nothing I want more. And to think I'd been worrying that you'd gone off the idea of marrying me. I kept waiting and waiting for you to propose. Officially, that is. And now, finally, you have!'

'You're sure about this?' I asked. 'You're absolutely sure it's what you want? Your family may well not be so keen on our getting married.'

'Jacob, please don't spoil things by worrying about my family. Just put the ring on my finger and kiss me!'

I did. Amazingly, the ring fitted perfectly.

'See,' she said, raising her hand to admire the oval-cut ruby that was flanked on either side by small clusters of diamonds, 'it was meant to be. This ring was destined to be worn by me. It's beautiful.' She kissed me gently at first and then more passionately. 'Why don't I get into bed with you?' she said with a smile. 'With no ghastly Mrs Pridmore on the prowl, who's to stop us?'

I smiled too, and despite my aching body pulled her into bed with me.

I half expected Kitty to want to keep our engagement secret until she had told her parents, but no, she wore the ring proudly and straight away showed it off when she went in for her next shift. 'They were queuing up to see it,' she said when she returned to visit me, her face wreathed in happy smiles.

By the end of the week I was well enough to return to work and no sooner had I crossed the threshold of Hut 8 than Chatterton-Jones congratulated me with a hearty slap on the back. 'So you convinced Kitty's parents you were the right man for the job, after all. Well done!' When I admitted that we had yet to inform them of our intention to marry, he sucked hard on his pipe and after wishing me luck with that, asked if we had set a date, but that was something we had yet to do.

Something else I had to do was speak to Molly Pearson. With no idea where she worked at the Park, I spotted Victor Stein at lunch that same day and sitting in the space next to him, I asked if he knew where I could find her. 'As a matter of fact, I can,' he said, pointing towards the entrance to the cafeteria with his knife. 'She's just walked in.'

No time like the present, I thought. 'I'll be right back,' I said, hurrying over to where Molly had joined the end of the lunch queue. I'd spent ages in my head preparing what I had to say and it came out in one long rush, that I owed her an enormous debt of gratitude and an apology.

'Really, there's no need to apologise,' she said, stepping away from the queue so we couldn't be heard. 'I should never have drunk that sherry. If I hadn't, I certainly wouldn't have embarrassed you by kissing you.'

'You didn't embarrass me,' I said, 'it was I who was at fault; I should have told you that I was seeing somebody.'

'Well, yes, perhaps you should have, although I believe I didn't give you much of an opportunity to do so.'

'It's no excuse, but I wasn't myself that evening and I'm mortified that you ended up getting involved in what you did.'

A small smile lifted the corners of her mouth. 'Actually, it was all rather an adventure. So don't worry, no hard feelings. I'm just glad you're all right.'

As she regained her place in the lunch queue, I thought how much she had changed in the few days since I had last seen her. Not once had she blushed, or displayed a hint of shyness, she was a wholly more confident young woman. Evidently life at Bletchley Park suited her.

*

Ten days after our engagement Kitty and I sat down together and wrote to our parents – a job long overdue. A job that I knew would provoke a stand-off with Kitty's parents. Even she must have known this by now as otherwise she would have written to them before with the news.

We both received a letter back on the same day. My mother wrote to say that they were all delighted with my news and wanted to know when they'd see us next. In contrast, Kitty's father wrote to say he was on his way to Bletchley.

He arrived twenty-four hours later. Doubtless with his Foreign Office connections he was able to cut through the usual security measures and gain access to the Park without too much difficulty. He had made it plain in his letter that he wanted to speak to Kitty alone, a request she refused point-blank.

So the three of us sat on a bench overlooking the lake with the house behind us. It was a cool March day, but beneath my shirt and tweed jacket I was sweating as though I had a fever. I was as nervous as hell but determined not to show it. I was, after all, going to be Kitty's husband, and I had to prove once and for all that I was no coward; that I could fight for the woman I loved.

'This nonsense will stop as of now,' the man said without preamble. 'There will be no more talk of an engagement and certainly no more talk of a wedding. Have I made myself clear?'

I opened my mouth to speak, but Kitty beat me to it. 'Daddy, please listen to me – Jacob and I love each other and we plan to marry as soon as we can.'

The man's face quivered and I saw his hands ball into tight fists on his lap, the knuckles turning white. He whipped his head round to face us both, his expression one of thunderous disbelief that he was being subjected to such insubordination. 'I forbid it,' he said in a barely controlled voice. 'And that is my last word on the matter. Disobey me and there will be consequences.'

It was as I feared, and Kitty being cut off cut off from her family being the last thing I wanted for her, I found my voice. 'I can quite see how our announcement has taken you and your wife by surprise, but is there a specific reason why you're so against our marriage?' I knew I was treading on dangerous ground, but there was nothing else for it but to challenge the man and his prejudice.

He looked at me in disgust. 'I would have thought our reasons would be abundantly clear.'

'It still might be helpful to know just what they are, sir.'

He continued to regard me with disdain, his steely gaze taking in my face, which still bore the signs of the attack I'd suffered and which I knew made me look like some sort of disreputable ruffian.

'You might have fooled my daughter,' he said, 'but you're not fooling me, young man. You're an upstart on the make for a good catch, a wife to give you and your family the respectability they crave but will never have by any other means.'

Kitty gasped and jumped to her feet. 'That's an inexcusable thing to say, Daddy, take it back this instant!'

'I will not. Since making Mr Belinsky's acquaintance, I've made it my business to do some careful checking on him. Oh yes, he may well have excelled at Cambridge and carved out a place for himself here, but did you know his father is nothing more than a Jewish barber in the East End of London?'

Now it was my turn to get to my feet. 'With all due respect, my father is a decent, hard-working man who would never criticise another human being for being different to him. It's a pity there aren't more like him in the world, in my opinion.'

He glared at me again, his face reddening with fury.

Kitty took my hand in hers. 'I know all about Jacob's family, Daddy, I've visited them and they couldn't have been sweeter to me. I do wish you could show the man I love the same consideration.'

'I'm not going to argue with you, Kitty. You're too young to understand what you're doing. You've got yourself caught up in something through the stress of working here. This man's been nothing but a diversion for you, something to take your mind off the strain of the war. I know how these things happen. But take it from me, if it wasn't for the war, the two of you would never have met and we wouldn't be having this confounded conversation.'

'We're having this *confounded* conversation because you're treating me like a child!'

'That's because you're behaving like one! Now stop being so obstinate and accept that your mother and I know what's best for you.'

For the first time ever, I saw Kitty's face crumple and she began to cry. I put my arm around her but that only seemed to make things worse; she leant against me and sobbed. Over her shoulder, I looked at her father and knew real hatred. I didn't doubt for a single second that the feeling was mutual.

'That's enough, Kitty,' her father said. 'Please don't be so childish and cause a scene.'

She raised her head from my chest and sniffed. 'Daddy, there's something you need to know. Something important. I'm expecting Jacob's child, so you see, we must be married and sooner rather than later.'

It was a close call as to who was the more shocked, her father or me, but wanting to seize the high ground straight away, I pulled myself together. 'Kitty's right,' I said, 'and while we both appreciate the situation is far from ideal, I'm sure you'll agree that for the child's sake we should marry immediately.'

If I had expected the man before me to capitulate and concede that matters had gone well beyond his jurisdiction of angry, defied father, I had miscalculated him. He rose slowly from the bench. 'I might have known this would be the way you'd force the issue; it only goes to prove that you are no gentleman.' Then, quick as a flash, he flung his arm wide and

393

struck me on the side of my head with the palm of his hand, and with such force my teeth rattled inside my head.

Kitty let out a scream of alarm. Then she turned on her father. 'You're mad, Daddy! Completely mad. Now please leave before you do anything else to shame yourself.'

After he'd gone, we sat down again and for a few seconds sat in silence. From behind us in the house came the incongruous sound of music playing; it was Glenn Miller's 'In The Mood'. It broke the tension between us. 'Why didn't you tell me you were pregnant?' I said.

She tucked her hand in mine and stared straight ahead to where two girls had laid a blanket on the grass and were lying reading. 'Because I'm not really sure that I am,' she said. 'I'm only a week late. But I'm never late. So there's a jolly good chance I *am* pregnant. Are you very shocked?'

'I'm more shocked by the way I heard the news.'

She turned to face me; her eyelashes were still wet with tears. I took a handkerchief from my pocket and wiped them. 'I'm sorry you had to hear it that way,' she said. 'I really didn't want to blurt it out like that at my father, but I didn't know how else to make him listen to us. He'll come round eventually. Once Mummy knows about the baby, she'll convince him there's no point in staying angry with us, but I'm sorry he hit you.'

'It could have been worse,' I said with a smile, 'he could have thrown me in the lake.' Kissing her forehead, I drew her closer to me. 'Funny to think we might be about to become parents.'

'Do you think we'll be any good?'

'We'll be disastrous.'

'Don't say that.'

'I'm joking. We'll muddle our way through, just as all parents do. But we'll need to find somewhere to live. I don't think we can impose on Billy to that extent.'

'She'd love having a baby at the farm.'

'I'm sure she would, but we have to be sensible; Honeysuckle Cottage isn't big enough for the two of us, never mind a baby as well.'

Two days before, following Mrs Pridmore's fall from grace, Griffiths, Farrington and I had been rebilleted. I was now staying with two elderly spinsters and their flatulent King Charles spaniel called Bertie. It was streets ahead of anything I had experienced at Mrs Pridmore's, but it wouldn't work for a married man with a wife and baby. Our plan before had been for me to squeeze in with Kitty at Honeysuckle Cottage once we were married. Billy had already agreed to our request but had said that while she knew perfectly well what we got up to when we were alone at the farm, she wouldn't have us openly living together, not when it would incur the wrath of Kitty's parents.

That wrath had now been incurred, and who knew what the consequences of it would be.

Chapter Fifty-Six

June 1944

It was the third week of June when we decided the silence from Kitty's parents had gone on long enough.

Their cruelty astounded me. They flatly refused to accept our forthcoming marriage and in a terse one-page letter they all but disowned their daughter, informing her that unless she promised never to see me again, that's how things would remain.

Her sister Ruthie had written to say how disappointed the family was by Kitty's defiance. Did Kitty have no sense of what was expected of her? she wanted to know. Did Kitty have no understanding of the spiritual torment she was inflicting on their parents by wanting to marry a man – a *Jewish* man at that – who would never be fully accepted in the circles in which they moved?

Ruthie's letter had arrived two days after the D-Day landings in Normandy, when we were glued to the wireless for further news updates. Frankly, the juxtaposition of what was going on in France and Ruthie's petty concerns for the family good name truly sickened me.

Shortly afterwards Kitty received a letter from Nanny Devine in which she asked if I had thought of converting to Catholicism, as that might be a satisfactory way to smooth the troubled waters. 'I'll convert to whatever they want if it'll bring them to their senses,' I told Kitty.

'You'll do no such thing,' she said, 'I won't have my family dictating what we should and should not be doing!

So what if they all think I'm condemned to burn in hell for loving you!'

I knew that the strength she was using to stand up to her family was stoked by indignation and fury, and an iron streak of stubbornness. I also knew that it would only last for so long before that strength ran out and she began to question what she was doing. Which meant things could not go on as they were; we had to find a way to break the deadlock. There was nothing else for it; we would visit her parents and talk things through in a calm and rational manner. That was the plan.

With Kitty's pregnancy now officially confirmed, for the sake of appearances we had to marry as soon as possible. Our going to London to talk to Kitty's parents was a last ditch attempt to resolve matters before the wedding because the following week we were to be married in the church at Bletchley. Billy had offered to lay on a few drinks and sandwiches after the ceremony and Peggy was to be bridesmaid with Chatterton-Jones acting as my best man, something I could never have foreseen this time last year. My family was in regular contact and when I broke the news to them that Kitty was pregnant, they expressed nothing but joy. Since learning she was to be a great-grandmother, my grandmother had stopped knitting socks for the troops and had moved on to blankets, bootees and matinee jackets. Much to my surprise, and not without a degree of subversive glee on her part, she confided in me that my mother had been conceived out of wedlock.

Nanny Devine had written again to say that Kitty's parents would be at the house in London for the weekend of the twenty-fourth and twenty-fifth to celebrate an old friend's birthday. She would be there too, in order to see a cousin who lived in Pimlico. In view of the latest spate of bombings in the city, I was unhappy about our visit, especially as only a week earlier a V-1 flying bomb had caused extensive damage in nearby Rutherford Street. But so keen was Kitty to resolve matters with her parents that she maintained lightning couldn't possibly strike twice in the same spot so we shouldn't worry.

The V-1 flying bombs were the latest in Germany's armoury against us. Pilotless, jet-propelled aircraft, they were capable of carrying nearly a ton of high explosives. With its distinctive engine noise, the device had already been nicknamed the buzz bomb, or doodlebug. People had been warned that if they could no longer hear the engine, they should take cover immediately. It was a deadly device, causing considerable destruction and loss of life throughout the south of England. One had been dropped not that far from Fanley Manor.

We arrived in Milton Place shortly after ten forty-five. Nanny Devine opened the door herself and greeted us warmly, especially Kitty who she clucked over like a mother hen, quizzing her on her condition and insisting she sit down so she could be thoroughly inspected and questioned. Was she eating enough? Was she sleeping properly? Was she getting enough fresh air?

'Yes to everything, Nanny,' Kitty replied, 'but never mind all that, where are Mummy and Daddy? They are here, aren't they? I hope we haven't come all this way only for them to refuse to see us? You did tell them I was coming, didn't you?'

'Hush, child, don't take on so, it's not good for the baby.'

'And is it good for the baby to be ignored by its grandparents?' she demanded fiercely. Though it was too soon for there to be any physical evidence of the child she was carrying, Kitty put a protective hand to her stomach.

It was an instinct I felt too. With each day that passed which took us one step closer to becoming parents, I could not believe how protective I felt both of Kitty and our child. If somebody had told me this was how impending parenthood would be, I would not have believed it. I would have claimed that it was impossible to form an emotional attachment to something one could not see, hear or touch. I had been proved profoundly wrong on that score.

This intense new instinct manifested itself in other ways; it made me want more than ever for the war to be over. I did not want a child of mine to be born into a world that was so full of danger and hatred. I wanted a peaceful world in which our son would grow up.

And yes, I was utterly convinced our child was a boy. I could already picture him so clearly, a dark-eyed boy with a frank and open face just like his mother's. He would have her smile too, a smile that would warm the coolest of hearts and possess a quickness of thought that would be mine to guide and instruct. I would teach him to have the kind of confidence and self-belief that I did not have. He would enjoy learning for the sheer joy it brought to his enquiring mind, and together we would explore the world through the written word.

One of the things I had always loved most about my time at Cambridge was the college library; it had been a sanctuary for me, a place of refuge and great reward. I wanted that same experience for my son.

But above all, I wanted him to be loved as my family loved me, and that was why I was here by Kitty's side, patiently waiting for her parents to dispense with their pride and their prejudice. I wanted them to acknowledge that I was the father of their first grandchild and to believe that I would do all I could to ensure his and his mother's happiness.

'Your parents will be here shortly,' Nanny Devine assured Kitty. 'Your mother had to visit a friend who's poorly and your father was urgently required at work.'

An hour and a half later, with still no sign of them and with time of the essence – we both had to be at work that evening – I made a decision that I would regret for the rest of my life.

Although the purpose of our visit to London was primarily to see Kitty's parents, if there was time we also wanted to see my family. When a further hour had gone by and still neither Kitty's mother nor father had appeared, I decided I would go to the East End on my own and return later so we could leave for Bletchley together, whether or not her parents had deigned to meet us. Kitty wasn't happy to be left, but I was in agreement with Nanny Devine that she shouldn't overdo it by traipsing across town, or be put at unnecessary risk, what with the Germans dropping their wicked little air bombs on innocent folk, as Nanny Devine referred to the V-1s.

I hadn't told my family that we would be in London in case we weren't able to find the time to see them, and now, as I left Milton Place, the thought of surprising my parents while they were at work appealed to me. Surprising my grandmother was another matter; she would be her usual self and greet me as though I had been expected and was in fact late. The thought of sipping hot sweet tea from her precious samovar and discussing my plans for the future put a spring in my step, and I set off, determined that nothing Kitty's family could do would spoil my happiness. They could do their worst and it would be their loss, not ours. Whatever wrongs they were prepared to commit, I would compensate by loving Kitty and our child all the more.

I had been walking for some time, trying to navigate my way through this unfamiliar part of London, with its elegant squares and streets, hopefully in the direction of Westminster where I would catch a bus, when I heard a strange noise. It sounded like a lorry engine, although not from the road I was standing on, but from above my head. I noticed then that the people around me were looking skywards. Following their gaze, I saw something that resembled a bomb with wings flying through the sky. In the seconds it took for me to process what I was seeing, the drone of the engine noise stopped and an air-raid siren sounded.

Cries of '*Run!*' rang out, and suddenly everyone was doing exactly that. Instinct made me run too, despite not having a clue where I was running. But those around me seemed to know and I followed them blindly, my heart pounding in my chest, my legs powered by panic. As one, we turned a corner and I saw that people from all around were running towards the entrance to Westminster Underground station. Just as, with huge relief, I joined the mass of humanity in its bid for survival, I heard a terrifying explosion that battered my eardrums and took what was left of my breath clean out of me.

Once we were below street level, people started to talk.

'Pity the poor devils on the receiving end of that,' I heard a man say.

Another said: 'Bit close for comfort.'

'Bloody Germans and their doodlebugs,' somebody else commented.

'It's a cowardly weapon of terror and no mistake,' a woman muttered. She had a baby in her arms and it was crying. I wondered where she'd left the pram in her haste to take shelter. And then I thought of Kitty and my own child. From nowhere, a fear greater than the one that had propelled me through the streets to escape the bomb made me cry out. The woman with the baby looked at me and perhaps not liking the expression on my face, held her child all the tighter and took a step away from me.

I didn't care what she thought. All that mattered was getting out of here and back to Milton Place to make sure Kitty was all right. I pushed my way through the crush of people, ignoring their tuts of annoyance as I rudely barged them out of the way, not heeding their instructions that I should wait until the all-clear was given.

I emerged on to the street and again ran, even faster. This time there was far more at stake than the trivial matter of my own survival.

I came to a junction and couldn't for the life of me remember which way I had come before. I mentally tossed a coin and turned left. On I ran, the sweat pouring off me, my breath ragged, and my legs threatening to fold beneath me. At the acrid smell of burning filling the air, I forced my legs to continue through the pain. Please God, I prayed, as I hurtled round the corner into Milton Place, not here, anywhere but here.

But my prayer went unanswered. Milton Place was a confusion of rubble, smoke and dust. Several fires raged and the air was so chokingly thick I had to cover my mouth and nose with a hand. Houses that hadn't been completely destroyed stood with their stuccoed fronts ripped away, the rooms obscenely exposed, broken furniture scattered like matchsticks, blackened papers fluttering like birds caught on the thermal heat of the flames.

I stumbled towards Number Ten, or what remained of Number Ten. An ARP warden blocked my way, 'Best stand back, sir, you never know if another explosion is likely to happen.'

'I don't care,' I said. 'I have to know. I have to find—'

My words were drowned out by the arrival of a fire engine, its siren blaring. The warden's attention caught by it, I slipped past him and started to climb over the mounds of rubble. Somebody else shouted to me to keep back, but I ignored the advice.

But it was useless; there was no house to enter. No room I could walk through to find Kitty. What remained of the building looked as though it had taken a direct hit and absorbed the full impact of the bomb. Reason told me that nobody could have survived such an explosion, but my heart screamed that Kitty and our son had to have survived. They simply could not be dead.

Chapter Fifty-Seven

July 1944 and June 1949

Kitty's funeral was held a week later. I didn't go. I didn't trust myself. I didn't trust myself to look her parents in the eye and not hold them accountable for her death.

For they *were* responsible. If they had loved their daughter selflessly, as I loved her, she would still be alive: there would have been no need for us to go to London to try and gain their approval.

But blaming them was a short-term measure. Once that had run its course, I would blame myself for putting the woman I loved and our unborn child in danger. While it was Kitty who had wanted to go to London and defy the Germans and their latest deadly weapon, I should have known better. And for that I would pay dearly for the rest of my life.

Through Chatterton-Jones, whose parents attended the funeral, I heard that it took place in Sussex and her body was buried in the churchyard just a few miles from Fanley Manor. One day I might be brave enough to visit.

Nanny Devine's body was buried the same day, in the same churchyard. Nobody in the house in Milton Place at the time of the blast survived. Had I stayed, I would have died as well.

It was about a month later that I received a small package in the post. There was a piece of writing paper with the words – *Returned to rightful owner* – written on it. With it, and wrapped in several layers of white tissue paper, was the ruby ring I had given Kitty. I didn't know whether to be glad to have the bittersweet memento in my possession again, or be wild with fury that, even in death, her parents could not bear for her to have any connection with me. The thought of somebody prising the ring off my darling Katyushka's finger in order to return it to its *rightful owner*, was just too cruelly spiteful and macabre for me to contemplate.

It is now five years to the day since I lost Kitty. The war is long over and the world is a very different place to the one it once was.

In the months after her death, it would be no under-statement to say that I descended into a hellish state of indescribable pain and dark despair, but somehow I stayed sane enough to function sufficiently so as to be able to stay on at Bletchley Park. With hindsight, it was all that kept me from going mad with grief.

I remained at Bletchley until VE Day and then returned to my parents in the East End. My grandmother never saw peacetime again; she died unexpectedly in her sleep on New Year's Day 1945. I'm glad she never lived to hear about, or see the images, of the true horror of Hitler's Final Solution and the evil that had gone on in the concentration camps.

Victor Stein stayed in touch with me sporadically and, through a friend of his, I was given the opportunity to take up a teaching post in a boys' prep school in Kent, just as I had thought I would. But my heart wasn't in it and within a year I returned to Cambridge to further my own education by embarking on a course of Slavic Studies with a view to teaching at university level.

The last I heard of Chatterton-Jones, he was working for the Foreign Office and making a name for himself somewhere overseas.

In the time since, not a day has passed when I have not regretted leaving the safety of Bletchley for London and visiting Milton Place with Kitty. I regularly dream that she survived the explosion and comes to me, staggering through the smoke and rubble, her hands outstretched. I'm told the pain will lessen, but I cannot think how. Have I contemplated suicide? you're probably wondering. Frequently, yes. However, each time the lure of death has reached out to me, the thought of Kitty's disgust at such an idea has chased it away and somehow I fight on to live another day.

I took the decision to write our story – employing a few flourishes of artistic licence to preserve the ethos of secrecy and anonymity that so marked my time at Bletchley Park – in the hope that committing it to paper would exorcise the worst of the pain. And to honour the woman who loved me. My plan now is to put away these two notebooks – to hide them – along with the ring I gave Kitty. It is not my intention ever to read them again.

In that case, throw the books away, I hear you say. But that would deny our place in history. I also want to live knowing that the books exist, because if the unthinkable happens and my memory fails me when I'm an old man, then I will need to remind myself of my darling Katyushka and our time together. And though I'm hopeful my mind will stay sharp until the day I die, I'd like to think I have a backup plan.

Another of my intentions is never to discuss this chapter in my life again. It is now closed and is to be kept strictly between Kitty and me. It's our secret. Our very own *Dandelion Years*.

And if Kitty is right about an afterlife, and I rather hope she is, I look forward to the day I meet her there, if only to hear her say, 'You see, Jacob, I was right!'

I'm sure you will have gleaned from these pages that I am the least perfect of beings and that I have at times a wilfully weak and contrary nature. But the truth is, we are all contrary one way or another: we all say one thing and do another.

And who, might you be thinking, do I imagine is reading this? I have no answer. But if you have discovered my

405

notebooks and read the entire story, you will be somebody who cares and for that I thank you. If you had not cared, you would not have read to the end.

So now I bid you and my story adieu and finish with the words: if you love someone who lights up your world, do all in your power to make yourself worthy of that person's love. Do not make the mistake I constantly made: do not keep doubting yourself, or the object of your heart. If you find yourself focusing on your shortcomings, find a remedy to overcome them. Be brave and do the thing you fear the most. Take as many risks as you can, let yourself be happy – and believe in the impossible.

I've never understood what Kitty saw in me, but I'll always be grateful that she discerned something worthwhile in me. Perhaps there's a lesson to be learnt from that, that we never truly know ourselves, or see ourselves as others do.

Lastly, and it's a question I have often asked myself – would I relive that time again if I had the chance, even though I would have to go through the agony of losing Kitty again?

Oh yes, in a heartbeat.

Chapter Fifty-Eight

Matthew turned the page of the notebook and saw that Jacob had made one last entry, as if with one final important thing to say he had been unable to lay down his pen.

He recognised the words immediately, it was '*Im Abendrot*' ('At Sunset') by Joseph von Eichendorff. Jacob had considered him to be one of the finest German Romantic poets and had insisted, when the time came, that the poem was read at his funeral service. Matthew had performed the task and read the poem in English as it was written here in the notebook.

Through sorrow and joy
we have walked hand in hand;
now we are at rest from our journey
above the silent land.

The valleys descend all about us,
the sky grows dark;
only two larks yet soar
dreaming in the haze.

Draw close and let them fly;
soon it will be time to sleep;
let us not lose our way
in this solitude.

O boundless, silent peace!
So deep in the sunset!
How weary we are of our journeying –
can this be death?

Now, after reading *The Dandelion Years* in its entirety, and knowing of Jacob's love for Kitty and her death, the poem made perfect sense and was all the more poignant.

As was the music Jacob had wanted for when they exited the church with the coffin. He had chosen the final song in Richard Strauss's cycle of the 'Four Last Songs', which was inspired by *'Im Abendrot'*. Jacob had explained to Matthew that Strauss had been drawn to the poem and written the music especially for it. What was more, it had been written not long before the composer's death, as though he had a sense of his demise fast approaching. Perhaps just as Jacob had in those last months of his life when he had grown increasingly melancholy, and had discussed with greater frequency how he wanted his funeral to be conducted.

Interspersed with the melancholy, however, there had been bursts of sudden cheerfulness. Matthew could remember during one of his weekend visits, coming upon Jacob in the library and finding him staring into the flames of the fire quietly smiling to himself, as if he'd just recalled a funny joke.

At the time Matthew had put it down to his presence having a positive effect on the old man's spirits. Now he wondered if that had been somewhat arrogant of him. Maybe Jacob had been secretly imagining being reunited with Kitty at long last and was picturing their glorious and much-awaited sunset together.

How Matthew wished the old man had spoken to him of Kitty. Why had he kept that part of his life such a secret? Why leave so many unanswered questions? Had it simply been too painful an experience for him to discuss? Or was it all wrapped up in the secrecy of his time at Bletchley Park?

Returning his attention to the notebook, Matthew reread the previous page where Jacob had written that he had wanted to commit the story to paper so that if he ever needed to, if the memories grew so faint, he could remind himself of Kitty. Matthew didn't think for one minute – not even with the onset of age and all that brought with it – had the memories ever faded for Jacob. Quite the reverse, he suspected. That was why he'd never needed to unearth the notebooks from their hiding places.

Darkness had fallen, and sitting in the pool of light cast from the lamp on the desk, Matthew speculated whether Jacob had regarded him as the child he'd never known – the child he'd wanted to guide and instruct and with whom he could share his extensive knowledge. If that was the case, and he had somehow filled a void in Jacob's life, then Matthew was happy for that.

He closed the notebook and, placing it on top of the first notebook, which he'd brought with him from Cambridge – the ring and Russian Bible he'd left behind – he decided to ask Saskia, when the time was right, if she could bind the two together to create a proper book. Such a story deserved to be properly preserved.

As did the samovar he and Saskia had found upstairs, he suddenly thought. He couldn't be certain, but very likely it was the samovar that had belonged to Jacob's grandmother. He hadn't looked at it since they'd unearthed it, and having spent the day doing nothing but read, Matthew needed something physical to do now, so he went upstairs to fetch the samovar. In the kitchen he rummaged through a selection of cleaning products and cloths, but on reflection, and anxious not to cause any damage, he opted to use just hot water and washing-up liquid.

Removing the top section, the interior released a strong odour of metallic mustiness. He rubbed gently at the exterior, its tarnished surface soon giving way to a pleasing shine.

An hour passed as he methodically cleaned the samovar, carefully rubbing at the ornate handles, the tap and its base, along with the areas where it was intricately patterned. He risked some silver polish and when he'd finished, he stood back to admire his handiwork. Not bad, he thought, replacing the top section and giving it a final rub. Not bad at all.

At the time they'd discovered it, Saskia had said that after a good clean and a polish, it would be worth keeping: she was right. He guessed it was made of brass and silver-plated, and while he didn't think it would be of great value in monetary terms, it was a handsome thing. And if it was the samovar that had belonged to Jacob's grandmother, it was also a poignant keepsake for Matthew to have.

Such was his satisfaction with the transformation he'd wrought, Matthew was tempted to take a photo and send it to Saskia, just to let her know he'd taken her advice. But then he remembered about her grandfather and thought better of bothering her with something so trivial.

He put the cleaning things away, locked up, turned out the lights and climbed the stairs to bed.

But the sadness of Kitty's death and what it must have done to Jacob returned to Matthew's thoughts when he tried to sleep. Had Jacob intentionally spent his life being faithful to Kitty? Had he sworn never to love another? Or had there been others, but they had never come close to his first and one great love?

The questions provoked the memory of that evening when Jacob had challenged Matthew over his feelings for Fliss, accusing him of self-delusion. How condescending Matthew had been to assume that Jacob couldn't possibly know what it was to be in love because he'd never been married. Jacob had been right about Fliss, though, her feelings for Matthew had been stronger than his for her. Which was going to make their breaking up that much harder. There again, and in view of this last week when Fliss had scarcely been in touch, she could well be one step ahead of him and already had her exit strategy planned.

From nowhere came the thought of what Jacob's opinion of Saskia would have been. Would he think Matthew was deluding himself again because he wanted to get to know Saskia a lot better; that he believed there was a connection there between them? Would Jacob say he was merely attempting to recapture that enjoyable day at Ashcombe when he'd sat on the fence at the end of the garden with Saskia? A day that now felt like a dream.

Immediately he put a stop to that line of thinking. Why bring Jacob into it? Besides, not until he had ended things with Fliss should he think about Saskia and what it was about her that he found so intriguing.

Instead he directed his restless mind to mapping out the changes he planned to make with his life. *Be brave ...* Jacob's voice growled at him in the darkness. *Take as many risks as you can ...*

He woke to golden sunlight streaming in through the gap in the curtains, and the familiar sound of a bell ringing. He rolled over, fumbled for his glasses on the chest of drawers, and checked the time on his fob watch: it was seven o'clock.

He lay back and by the time the bell had stopped ringing in the church tower, he was wide awake and full of resolve. He had figured out what he was going to do. No more stagnating. It was crunch time.

His first task of the day would be to ring Fliss. He'd prefer to have the conversation face to face, but he didn't trust himself to speak to her on the phone solely to arrange a time to meet without giving himself away. And nor did he want her thinking he wanted to meet to apologise and that then everything would be OK again, that it was just another little glitch they were experiencing, a simple lovers' tiff. It would be better all round to get it over and done with.

Which was normally how he lived his life, decisive and proactive. He was not a capitulator by nature, but somehow he'd become one since Jacob's death.

Jacob had had many conundrums, but this had been a favourite of his – 'If you're playing Russian roulette with somebody, is it better to go first to pull the trigger, or second?' Matthew's answer was always the same: that it was better to go first when the odds were stacked better in your favour.

'But the other chap could go first and fire the bullet into his head and you'd be home and dry,' Jacob would argue.

'I'd sooner take my chances,' Matthew would say.

And that's what he would do today.

He was dressed and down in the kitchen scrambling eggs for his breakfast when his mobile rang. It wasn't seven-thirty; who'd be ringing him at this early time on a Sunday? He switched off the gas so the eggs wouldn't spoil, and scooped up the phone.

It was Fliss and her first words, and in such a conciliatory tone, wrong-footed him. 'Matthew, I'm sorry,' she said, 'truly I am.'

When he left too long a pause before saying anything in reply, she said, 'You're not still angry with me, are you?'

'No,' he said at length. 'I'm angry with myself, I—'

'Don't be,' she cut in quickly. 'I don't know what got into me, but I was jealous and being silly, and I've been sulking ever since. You are still at Glaskin House, aren't you? James said you'd gone there.'

'Yes. I'm just making some breakfast. Look, Fliss, there's—'

'That's good,' she cut in again. 'Because guess where I am?'

'Err ... not a clue.'

'Try looking out of the window.'

He did, and at the sight of Fliss's car at the bottom of the drive, his heart sank.

'A peace offering,' she said with a smile, holding up a carrier bag. 'Eggs, dry oaked-smoked salmon, and a bottle of Bucks Fizz! Oh, and some Krispy Kreme doughnuts as a treat to finish up with.' She began emptying the bag on to the kitchen table. 'I wanted to surprise you with breakfast in bed,' she continued. Pushing her sleeves up, she went over to a drawer, found a pair of scissors and started to open the packet of smoked salmon.

Wracked with guilt that she'd gone to so much trouble

to apologise and put things right between them, Matthew watched her moving about the kitchen. He had to stop her. He had to pull the trigger and tell her. He couldn't bear to witness the excruciating cheerfulness of her demeanour, not when he knew he was about to crush it. She'd come here with such good intentions, and he wished he felt differently about her, but he didn't. He couldn't fake it. Ultimately, that would humiliate her more.

'Fliss,' he said, removing the smoked salmon and scissors from her hands. 'There's something I have to tell you. And you're not going to like it. Why don't you let me make you some coffee and we can talk?'

All at once she was staring at him intently, something, he realised, she hadn't done until now. Until now her words had been directed at him, but she hadn't met his eye. Not once. 'What is it?' she asked in a low and anxious voice. 'Or ...' she hesitated, 'or is it so obvious even a fool like me can work it out?'

'You're not a fool. Far from it.'

'Then why am I feeling like one? Why, after I've driven all this way to surprise you and to say I'm sorry, do I get the feeling I've made a massive fool of myself?' She swallowed. 'Is there somebody else?' She turned towards the doorway. 'Is ... is she here with you now? Upstairs? In your bed?'

Before he had a chance to reply, she was through the doorway and making for the stairs.

'There's nobody else here,' he called after her.

But Fliss wasn't listening to him, and with there being no point going upstairs to confirm what she needed to discover for herself, Matthew waited for her at the foot of the stairs.

When she came back down and stood on the bottom step so that she was at eye level with him, he said, 'It's really not what you think.'

'So what is it, Matthew?' she asked angrily. 'Because I'll tell you for nothing, your face is giving me a very different story. You look like you're the guiltiest man on the planet.'

'You're right,' he said. 'I do feel guilty, but please, let me try and explain.' He took her hand and indicated they sit down on the stairs. 'If you're really honest with yourself,' he said gently, 'you'll agree with me that it's not working between us second time around. Wouldn't that be fair to say?'

'Please don't tell me what I should or should not think, or talk about what's fair! We probably have quite different views on the latter.'

'You're right. But the thing is, Fliss, whatever we once had, it isn't what I want anymore. I thought it was, but it isn't.'

'What *do* you want?'

'Not this. I don't want to upset you.'

'It's a bit late for that. Are you sure there isn't somebody else? What about that girl you told me about, the book restorer; the one you were going with to Bletchley yesterday.'

'We didn't go. Her grandfather—'

'I'm not interested in the grandfather,' she snapped. 'Tell me about the *girl*.'

He shrugged and pushed a hand through his hair. 'There's nothing to tell.'

'Matthew, I've known you long enough to know you're not being honest with me – or with yourself, by the look of things. What's so special about her, then? What does she have that I don't?'

He gave in, recognising that while it wasn't the whole truth, a tangible reason, such as somebody else in the equation, would help Fliss to accept it really was over between them.

'It's difficult to explain,' he said. 'I hardly know her, but at the same time, I see part of me in her and that makes me feel as though I *do* know her, when actually I don't. Does that make sense?'

'Not a lot. Are you sure it's not just a case of infatuation? Which doesn't last, you know that, don't you?'

'Yes. But it's not like that. There's been barely anything between us.'

'Have you kissed her?'

He nodded.

Fliss made a noise at the back of her throat that told him precisely what she thought of that admission. 'Does she know about me?'

'No.'

'Nice going, Matthew! I didn't have you down for a two-timer, I thought you were better than that.'

'Me too.'

'How long has it been going on?'

'Nothing's been going on. Not in the way you think.'

'So, what is it, then, just a bit of intellectual banter, oh, and a kiss? Let's not forget you kissing her. When did that happen?'

'Easter Sunday. I spent the day with her. Her and her family.'

She inhaled sharply. 'You bastard! You told me you were working that day.'

'I'm sorry.'

'You should be. Were you texting her while we were in Copenhagen? Were there secret little messages flying backwards and forwards between the two of you?'

He'd been totally honest with her so far, so he went for broke. 'There was only the one text,' he said, 'and that was to invite me to go to Bletchley with her and her grandfathers.'

Fliss let out a scornful laugh of disbelief. 'And when did you think you'd get around to telling me about this change of heart of yours?'

'Today. I was going to ring you after breakfast. Cowardly I know, not planning to do it face to face, but I wanted to avoid causing you any unnecessary pain.'

'How considerate of you.'

With the sound of the church bell striking the hour – it was now eight o'clock – it seemed to bring about a natural conclusion to the conversation.

'No point in me hanging around here any longer,' Fliss

said, rising to her feet, 'I'm going back to Cambridge.'

'Don't you want to stay and have something to eat?'

She looked at him with a grimace. 'What do you think?'

'I think I've behaved abysmally and you have every reason to be furious with me. But why not have a quick cup of coffee, what harm would that do?' He was pushing his luck, but he really didn't want her driving while she was still angry and upset.

'It would probably choke me, Matthew,' she said tartly. 'Either that or I'd throw the cup at you to stop you being so bloody contrite and civilised about splitting up with me.'

Matthew got to his feet too. 'I understand.'

'No you don't!' she rounded on him. 'You don't understand one little bit. I loved you. I really did. I just hope you realise what you're throwing away.'

Without another word, she grabbed her bag and went.

Chapter Fifty-Nine

While it certainly wasn't his intention, there was a danger that Matthew's second pull of the trigger that day could be construed as crass and insensitive.

But reminding himself that compared to what Fliss would be thinking of him now she was back in Cambridge, crass and insensitive would be practically complimentary. She was probably right now ringing round all her friends to say what a bastard he was and how he'd humiliated her and lied to her. Sadly, she'd have every reason to be angry and hurt.

After she'd left him, he'd resisted the urge to watch her drive away, feeling a curdling mixture of relief and impotent sadness. He'd upset her badly, the very thing he'd wanted to avoid. He was sorry for that. Not surprisingly he'd lost his appetite for any breakfast and after tidying the kitchen and drinking a mug of strong black coffee, he'd settled in the library at Jacob's desk and worked for a couple of hours, dealing with an email from Jim Rycroft sent at six-thirty that morning – did the man never sleep or take a minute to relax? It was when Matthew had ticked off the last of the items on the list of things he'd been told to investigate further, and was staring absently out of the window that his second big decision of the day came to him.

Now, as he turned off the main road in the village of Melbury Green and followed the narrow track down to Ashcombe, the trees and hedgerow were so dense on either side of the car, he felt as if he were driving through a tunnel of green. Would there be light at the end of it? he mused.

*

Ralph had just manoeuvred the sit-on mower out of the garage when he saw the car turn in through the gateway and it took him a moment to realise who it was behind the wheel. Switching the mower engine off, he went over to say hello.

'What brings you here?' he asked when Matthew was out of his car.

'A long shot,' he said, 'and one I hope you don't think is inappropriate, given what you're going through.'

'If it's something that will take our minds off Friday and the funeral, then I'm all for it.' He pointed towards the mower. 'As you can see, we're trying to get on as though it's business as usual. So what's this long shot?'

'I've brought Jacob's second notebook for Saskia to read. I wondered if it might, as you've just said, take her mind off things.'

In view of how cross Saskia still was over Ralph inviting Matthew to the funeral, it was anybody's guess how she would receive their visitor. 'Why don't you ask her yourself,' he said, 'she's somewhere in the garden with Libby. They were talking earlier about planting the broccoli Oliver had sown from seed in the greenhouse.'

'As long as you're sure I'm not intruding,' Matthew said.

'Not at all. Come on, let's see if we can find her.'

They had rounded the side of the house where, in full sun, the climbing roses grew most prolifically, when Ralph faltered in his step. He knew it wasn't his place, and that according to Saskia he and Jo had meddled more than enough, but the protective father in him couldn't resist wanting to know for himself what Matthew's intentions were when it came to Saskia. The very fact that he was here with the notebook for her to read implied an act of kindness on his part. But was it the act of a friend, or somebody who wanted to be more than a friend? And was Matthew in a position to be more than a friend?

'What is it, Ralph?' asked Matthew.

Without realising it, Ralph had come to a stop. He glanced

at Matthew. He couldn't very well ask the question outright – are you playing fast and loose with my daughter? – so he settled for a warning salvo. 'It might be nothing more than a misunderstanding,' he said, 'but I think you should know that you've upset Saskia.'

From the look on Matthew's face, it was clear this was the last thing he expected to hear. 'How?' he said. 'What have I done?'

'Perhaps it's better you ask her that.'

'Do you know what it is I've done?'

Feeling even more awkward, Ralph shook his head. 'I shouldn't have said anything, but from a father's perspective, all I'd ask of you is to be completely honest with Saskia. Can you do that? Because if you can't, then I don't think you should be here. Especially not at a time like this.'

No longer meeting his gaze, Matthew shifted the notebook from his right hand to his left, then back to his right. 'There is something I want to discuss with Saskia,' he said slowly, 'but I didn't think now would be the right time.'

'Perhaps you should let her be the judge of that.'

They resumed walking. 'If I've upset Saskia,' Matthew said, 'can I ask why you invited me to Oliver's funeral? It seems an odd thing to do, if you don't mind me saying.'

'The idea actually came from my sister who's flown over from Canada for our father's funeral. I didn't know he had, but apparently Oliver had often spoken about you to Jo and she's curious to see for herself what he liked about you so much.'

'That sounds like I'm up for scrutiny?' Matthew said with a frown. 'Am I?'

Oh hell, thought Ralph, he'd left the door wide open for that. That was his trouble; he was too damned honest for his own good and in this instance he was making a first-class hash of things. He was going to get it in the neck good and proper from Saskia if she got wind of this conversation. But then, based on Matthew's reaction just now, it would appear that he hadn't been totally honest with them. But how to explain why his sister wanted to size Matthew up without letting on that he and Harvey and Dad had had high hopes for Matthew and Saskia?

'When it comes to my sister, we're all up for scrutiny,' he said, trying to sound enigmatic.

They found Saskia alone in the vegetable patch; she was on her knees, trowel in hand, a tray of seedlings at her side. She looked as startled to see Matthew as he'd been a few moments ago when Ralph had warned him to be honest with her.

'Matthew's brought something for you, Saskia,' Ralph said. Not waiting to witness how things would go from there, he mentioned something about finding Libby and beat a hasty retreat.

Trowel still in hand, and looking far from pleased at the sight of him, Saskia stood up, her jeans stained from kneeling on the damp ground.

In view of what Ralph had just told him, Matthew was suddenly nervous and doubted the wisdom of coming here. If he didn't know better, he'd say Saskia and her father knew about Fliss. But how? 'I've brought Jacob's second notebook for you,' he said, 'I know you'll have other things on your mind, but I thought it might be a distraction.'

'Thank you,' she said, making no attempt to take it from him. 'I'll let you hang on to it for now. My hands are all mucky.' She tapped the trowel against the palm of her hand. Matthew didn't know whether to interpret the gesture as nothing more than drawing his attention to the veracity of her statement, or as a subtle threat – one wrong move on his part, and she'd use it on him!

'How are you?' he asked, for something to say. The question was absurd, he could see for himself that grief had sapped the life from her – her hair was tied back severely, her face was dull and pale, and below her eyes the skin had a bruised appearance. She looked beyond tired, as if she hadn't slept properly in a very long time.

'I've been better,' she said non-committally.

'And Harvey, how's he?'

'It's hit him hard. He and Oliver were like brothers.' Her gaze moved away from Matthew and took in the garden and the house behind them. 'The place seems very quiet without him,' she said her voice suddenly soft and devoid of all the edge of before. 'I keep expecting to see him in my workshop, or out here in the garden rounding up the hens.'

'I know the feeling,' Matthew said. 'I keep expecting to see Jacob by the fireside in the library, and after all this time I still have occasional moments when I think of ringing my mother to tell her something.' He paused a beat. 'Your father mentioned that your aunt is here. For the funeral,' he added unnecessarily.

Her blue-grey eyes back on him, she said, 'Yes, she's taken us all in hand. She's good like that. She was the same when my mother and grandmothers died. It's strange how some people are naturally good in a crisis.'

He nodded and steeled himself. He hadn't ever intended to tell Saskia about Fliss, other than to say she had been a girlfriend, but with Ralph's words echoing in his head – *you've upset Saskia ... be completely honest with her ...* he felt compelled to heed the advice. 'There's something I'd like to discuss with you, Saskia,' he began, 'but if you'd rather wait until another day, when ... when you might feel more inclined to chat, it can wait.'

'That rather depends what it is you want to discuss.'

He looked the length of the garden, through the billowing blossom of the orchard, down towards the fence where they'd sat that memorable Easter Sunday. 'Could we talk there?' he asked.

In the pleasantly warm sunshine, they walked wordlessly to the end of the garden, the grass wet from yesterday's rain and dampening his shoes. When they were settled, and with

Jacob's notebook safely balanced on his lap, Matthew said, 'I'm afraid I haven't been one hundred per cent honest with you.'

'I know.'

'You do? But how?'

'A friend who's an expert in these things reckoned your behaviour fitted the bill perfectly of somebody already in a relationship. Are you married?'

'*No*!'

'But you're with someone. You have a girlfriend, a partner, a significant other, call her whatever you like. Or maybe it's a him?'

'It's a girl. And she *was* my girlfriend. We split up after Jacob died, then ... then we got back together again, shortly before Easter.'

'So when you kissed me you were back together?'

'Yes.'

'That wasn't very nice of you. To her, or to me.'

'I know. When I left here that night, I felt awful.'

'Not so awful that you told me the truth, though,' she said accusingly.

'I was confused. I'd thought it was the right thing getting back with Fliss, but then I knew it wasn't.'

'What made you change your mind?'

'If I'm honest, it's a number of things, but you had a lot to do with it.'

'You're not trying to blame me, are you? Because I really wouldn't advise that.'

'No one's to blame but me,' he conceded. '*Mea culpa*.'

'How are things between you and Fliss now?' she asked, after spending a moment contemplating the dirt under the nails of one of her hands.

'It's over. And before you ask, yes, I was honest with her and admitted I hadn't behaved very well behind her back.'

'You told her about me?'

'Not by name, but I confessed that I'd kissed you, yes.'

'Did you also tell her that you'd deliberately misled my family, and that not once did you refer to a girlfriend? Not once.' She gave a contemptuous shake of her head. 'It strikes me that you can be very selective in what you do and say.'

Aren't we all selective when we want to be? Matthew wanted to respond, but he knew that wouldn't help his cause. 'I can't really explain it in a way that would justify what I did, but being here that day with you – and your family – it felt as if I had escaped to somewhere tranquil and quite separate from the world I normally inhabit. I liked the feeling it gave me. I've never experienced that anywhere else, or *with* anyone else.' He paused, then added, 'And, perhaps most important of all, I enjoyed being with you.'

She turned, and lowering her chin, gave him a long, penetrating, unblinking look, as if appraising him like she would a book in need of restoring. 'None of which gives you the right to mislead people,' she said at length.

'You're right. But I want you to know that I've never cheated on a girlfriend before. This was a first, and a last, and I'm not proud of myself.'

'And now that you've got all that off your chest, what do you want from me?' she asked bluntly.

It was a good question. 'If you'd agree to it,' he said, 'I'd like to start afresh with you. I'd like us to spend more time together getting to know each other better.'

'Why, so you can find out if I was worth ditching poor Fliss for? Then when you decide you've made a mistake, you'll go back to her and beg for forgiveness. Is that how it works?'

It was not the response he'd hoped for, but then he hadn't thought he would end up having to make the confession he just had. 'No,' he said firmly, 'that isn't going to happen. It's definitely over with Fliss.' He ran a hand through his hair. 'I'm sorry I wasn't honest with you. Really I am. I didn't mean for anything like this to happen. Do you think you can forgive me?'

She nodded slowly. 'I don't believe in holding grudges, but the question I'll have to ask myself is: can I trust you? Who's to say you're telling me the truth now, and that you'll continue to do so in the future? Maybe you're a serial liar.'

'I promise you I'm not lying now. But I can see that you need time to consider what I've said, so why don't we leave things as they are? Then if you think you'd like to see me again, you have my contact details. There's no pressure. And if you'd rather I stayed away from your grandfather's funeral, just say the word. By the way, your father explained why I was invited, that it was because your aunt—'

'He did what?' she interrupted him sharply.

'He told me about your aunt being keen to give me the once-over.'

Saskia's pale face suffused with colour. 'What on earth possessed him to say that!'

'I'd hazard a guess he thought much the same the second the words were out. Why would your aunt be interested in me?'

'No reason,' she answered with a shrug, turning to watch a pair of swallows darting acrobatically across the meadow in front of them.

He pressed his point. 'Are you sure?'

Swinging her legs, she tapped the heels of her shoes lightly against the fence. 'If you must know,' she said at last, 'it's because we all liked you and then when you dropped off the radar and we didn't hear from you, we suspected you'd been lying to us. I think Oliver was the most disappointed.' She gave him a melancholy smile. 'And I'm almost ashamed to admit it, but if we'd gone to Bletchley, as arranged, my grandfathers planned sneakily to interrogate you, and if necessary, make you squirm for your deception. Though for the record, they did want to give you the benefit of the doubt.'

'Something I didn't deserve.'

'No, you didn't,' she murmured.

'I'm sorry for many things, but I'm particularly sorry I disappointed you and your family.'

She left his remark hanging in the air and taking her lead, Matthew remained silent.

The peaceful, still hush went on for some minutes and with birdsong filling the space between them, accompanied by the low call of a wood pigeon, Matthew once again felt the magnetic pull of Ashcombe and the sense of calm being here gave him. Or was it the magnetic pull of Saskia he could feel?

'Did Oliver like me because he thought you and I might get on well together?' he said, when she started swinging her legs again.

Once more her appraising gaze was on him. 'Whether he did or not is irrelevant, it's what I think that counts, wouldn't you say?'

'But did he?'

She sighed. 'If he'd had his way, he'd have donned a Cupid outfit and fired arrows at you. As it is, he'd probably have punched you in the face for lying to me.'

Matthew couldn't help but smile. 'He was quite a man, wasn't he?'

'He was. And as stubborn as hell once he got an idea into his head. But I loved him dearly.' Her voice wavered and pursing her lips, she lowered her head.

Unable to ignore her obvious distress, Matthew risked putting an arm around her shoulder. She stiffened at his touch and for a split second he considered removing his arm, but he didn't. 'If it would make you feel any better, you could always punch me in the face on Oliver's behalf,' he said lightly.

She raised her head. 'As tempting as that offer is, I'll pass, thank you very much.' Then: 'Do you know what it feels like to experience a sadness so profound it's as if a heavy weight has been laid across your heart?'

'Yes,' he said simply. 'I've experienced that twice, when my mother died and then later with Jacob.'

425

She sighed. 'I can't help but think we'd be better off not knowing the love of a person; it would spare us so much heartbreak.'

'You don't think experiencing that level of pain makes us better people, stronger and more compassionate, and more able to empathise with someone else's suffering?'

Her gaze met his and lingered with such intense sadness that he longed to comfort her properly. But without answering him, she turned to stare once more across the fields.

Some time later, leaving Jacob's notebook with her, he left Saskia sitting at the end of the garden and drove back to Glaskin House, then on to Cambridge.

Chapter Sixty

It was the day of the funeral and Saskia's one and only wish had been granted: it wasn't raining.

With scarcely a breath of wind in the cool morning air, and with the sun shining down from a pale cloudless sky, she trudged across the dew-soaked grass to the hencoop in her grandfather's old boots. They were much too big for her, even with a pair of thick socks on, but she liked the thought of following, quite literally, in Grandpa O's footsteps.

Since he'd died the hens had not been themselves, producing fewer eggs and even giving Auntie Jo a vicious peck on the ankle one evening when she and Saskia were putting them to bed. Grief did that; it made you act out of character. It dropped you from a great height into a world turned upside down, where, in a state of angry confusion, you say, think and do things that ordinarily would never cross your mind.

The hens greeted her with mild curiosity, yielding just the three eggs – an improvement on yesterday by one. She tried talking to them in the way her grandfather used to while letting them take grain from his hand. But they weren't interested in anything she had to say. They were more interested in the boots she was wearing and, as though recognising them, they grouped around her feet pecking at the rubber.

It had been her aunt's idea for her to wear her grandfather's boots, in the thin hope it might make the hens feel more settled. It was not the sort of idea Saskia would expect from her aunt, a woman who had no truck for animal sentimentality – a woman who had threatened to roast the hen who had dared to nip her ankle.

At the back door, and carefully holding the eggs against her chest, Saskia heeled off the boots and keeping the thick socks on, padded through to the kitchen, where she found her aunt and Harvey discussing the catering arrangements for the day. Sharing his domain had not been easy for Harvey, especially with somebody as forthright as Auntie Jo, but he'd done it with good grace. Perhaps privately he was grateful for her help; after all, it was a lot for anyone to do at his age. But just as Grandpa O had had his pride, so too did Harvey, and Saskia knew he'd never admit he couldn't manage.

'Anything I can do?' Saskia asked, knowing full well what the answer would be. Something along the lines of too many cooks spoiling the broth.

'Yes,' her aunt said, 'you can beat it, kiddo, we've got it all in hand here.'

'How about I make some breakfast for everyone?' she tried.

'No, you'll just get in our way. Help yourself to a bowl of cereal, or a bit of toast, and then scram.'

Harvey exchanged a heartfelt look with Saskia, a look that bore more than a trace of his feelings that he'd be glad when all this was over and they could get back to normal.

Saskia smiled complicitly at him and went over to the toaster. She'd just put a slice of bread in when Uncle Bob appeared. He'd arrived yesterday afternoon and having him here acted as a buffer against Auntie Jo. He was the opposite in character to his wife, quietly spoken, slow to anger and with a nice line in dry wit, which he used to good effect in a marriage that, from the outside looking in, appeared to be weighted entirely in one direction. It was an easy mistake to make, because the truth was that he was the steadying influence in the partnership. Through dint of humour and quiet, steadfast persuasion he was the one person to whom Auntie Jo turned for advice and relied upon. Grandpa O once said that without Bob at her side, Jo would be utterly lost – he was her rock.

'Oh, good heavens, not another person to get under our feet!' Auntie Jo exclaimed when she saw him.

'And a good morning to you, dearest,' he said.

She thumped a large dish on to the table. 'Save your sarcasm, Bob, I don't have time for it today.'

'Toast, Uncle Bob?' Saskia asked him.

Skirting round his wife, he went over to Saskia. 'That would be great. I'll make some coffee, shall I?'

'Perfect. Any sign of Dad and Libby yet?'

He lowered his voice. 'I think they're hiding in bed, keeping out of harm's way.'

'Bob Cranshaw, I heard that!'

With an hour until they were due at the church, Saskia was in her bedroom getting dressed. Having hunted through her wardrobe earlier in the week and realising she had nothing suitable to wear for the funeral, she had gone shopping in Long Melford with Libby. After rejecting just about everything she'd seen, she'd chosen a full-skirted black dress decorated with tiny red and pink appliqué rosebuds. In another shop they'd found a cropped black cardigan and lastly Libby had spotted a pair of soft suede red ballerina pumps that went perfectly with the outfit. The shoes were staggeringly expensive, but Libby had insisted on buying them for her.

Looking at herself in the mirror now, as she brushed her hair and tried to decide whether to wear it down or tie it up, Saskia wondered if Matthew would actually come to the funeral. She hadn't really made him feel welcome when they had spoken last Sunday. But then what else could he expect when he had pretended to be something he wasn't?

After he'd left, Dad had come and found her at the end of the garden and she had told him everything Matthew had said. 'At least he's been honest with you now,' he'd responded.

'But has he?' Saskia had asked. 'How do I know that?'

429

'You won't unless you decide to get to know him better.'

'Maybe I don't want to know him better.'

'And that,' Dad said, 'is absolutely your prerogative. But remember why he came here. He brought you Jacob Belinsky's book to read. We can think well of him for that, can't we?'

Reading the final part of Jacob and Kitty's story last night was far from the cheeriest way to pass the time before her grandfather's funeral today, but Saskia was glad she had. And her father was right, she *was* grateful to Matthew for sharing it with her.

When she'd read of Kitty's tragic death, Saskia couldn't fail to be moved by Jacob's profound loss and empathise with how it must have affected him for the rest of his life – just as her father and grandfathers had had to live with the loss of the women they loved. Her initial reaction had been to think that it reaffirmed precisely what she'd tried to explain to Matthew, that loving another person was too great a risk when it made one so vulnerable to being hurt. But then she had thought of Jacob's declaration that he would willingly go through the agony of losing Kitty all over again if it meant he could relive their happy times together. She supposed that had to be the definition of genuine, selfless love.

A knock at the door roused her from her thoughts. 'Are you ready?'

She opened the door to her father. 'Just about,' she said. 'What do you think? Would Grandpa O approve?'

'You look beautiful,' he said, 'and yes, Oliver would strongly approve.' Dressed in a dark charcoal-grey suit with a white shirt and a black tie, he walked over to the armchair by the window and sat down. 'We thought we'd have a drink before leaving. Something to stiffen the nerve, as Harvey put it.'

'That's probably a good idea,' she said. 'So long as we don't turn up at church reeking of hard liquor and slurring our way through the order of service.'

He smiled. 'I think Oliver would get a kick out of that, don't you, his family turning up roaring drunk?'

Liking the way her father referred to her grandfather in the present tense, Saskia watched him pick up the notebook on her bedside table. 'Have you finished reading it?' he asked.

'Last night.'

'I'm assuming it didn't have a happy ending.'

'No, they were about to get married and she was killed by a bomb in London. She was expecting their child.'

Her father returned the notebook to the bedside table, then fiddling with his tie, something he rarely wore, he looked pensive. It was a look Saskia knew well.

'Something on your mind, Dad,' she asked, 'apart from the obvious?'

He let go of the tie. 'Yes. I've been thinking about Matthew.'

'Why?'

'Because of Dad. He was seldom wrong about a person and he liked Matthew.'

'But he hardly knew him.'

'Sometimes you don't need to know a person for long to know that you like them.'

'First impressions aren't always right.'

Her father stood up and smoothing down the legs of his suit trousers, and stooping slightly because the window was so low, he stared out at the garden with his back to Saskia. 'Within seconds of meeting your mother I knew she was the one for me,' he said finally. 'It really was love at first sight.'

'I know,' Saskia said quietly, 'you've told me that before. And that she was engaged to somebody else at the time.'

He turned round. 'I knew it was wrong, but even though she'd just told me her fiancé was in that same room with us, I still made a move on her. I was obnoxiously arrogant with it, too. I was so cocksure she'd find me irresistible. That she'd think I was by far the better man than the one she planned to marry.'

Saskia smiled. 'Luckily for you she thought exactly that. So what's your point?'

'My point is this: when you're attracted to a person, you sometimes just forget all the rules by which you know you should play and you cross lines you know you shouldn't cross.'

'Meaning that I should forgive Matthew for lying to me?'

'Meaning he made a mistake. He should have been straight with you, but he wasn't. He crossed a line, which he now regrets. It would be a terrible shame if you made a decision that you might come to regret one day.'

'You make it sound like I'll only ever have this one chance.' And feeling she was being backed into a corner, added, 'Look at you and Libby; you got your second chance.'

'Yes, but how many years did I have to wait for that? All I'm saying is that it's very clear to me that Matthew is attracted to you, and that before your suspicions were roused, you liked him, so why not give him the benefit of the doubt and let him have a second chance to prove he's not as bad as you think he is?'

From downstairs came the unmistakable klaxon of Auntie Jo's voice: 'Are you two ever coming down for a drink?'

Her father smiled and put a hand on Saskia's shoulder. 'Come on,' he said, 'better do as we're told or we'll be sent to the naughty corner for the rest of the day.'

Saskia didn't notice Matthew until they were outside and grouped around the coffin, waiting for the awful moment when it would be lowered into the ground. Oliver had always been adamant that he didn't want his remains to be cremated when the time came. As a child he'd suffered nightmares of being burned alive and it had been with great reluctance that he'd acquiesced to the known wishes of his wife that when she died, she was to be cremated. Her ashes, along with those of Harvey's wife and Saskia's mother, had been interred here in the churchyard when they'd moved to

Melbury Green, and now Oliver's body was to be laid to rest alongside them. Saskia couldn't bear to think which one of them would be next.

It was when she was doing her best to avoid looking at the coffin that she spotted Matthew. He was standing slightly apart from everybody else, in the shadow of an overhanging tree branch. At first, and because he'd had a brutally short haircut and was wearing a suit and tie, she didn't recognise him; he looked so different. Most men looked older when they put on a suit, but for some reason the years vanished from him and he could have passed for a sixth-former going for a job interview. She wondered if that worked against him in his job, if he wasn't taken seriously, perhaps. Or did it work to his advantage? Fooling people into underestimating your ability was probably a useful weapon to have up your sleeve. Question was, had she underestimated Matthew? Or was he fooling her?

Staring down at the ground, his expression was of intense concentration, as if he was trying to remember something important. Or was he actually deep in prayer? Was he the sort to pray? He raised his head abruptly and looked directly at her, catching her staring at him. Her cheeks instantly aflame, she ripped her gaze away from his and stared for all she was worth at Grandpa O's coffin, which was now being lowered into the ground. At the same time, her father to her left and Harvey to her right reached for her hands and the three of them stood united in their love for a unique and special man.

When it was over and people stood around in small groups quietly chatting while they waited to be given the go ahead to move on to Ashcombe, Auntie Jo leant in to Saskia. 'Is that Matthew Gray, over there,' she whispered, 'the one who looks like he's leaving already?'

'Yes,' Saskia answered.

'But he can't possibly leave now, I haven't had a chance to have a word with him.'

Saskia put a restraining hand on her aunt's forearm. 'Perhaps it's better that you don't.'

'Nonsense! I owe it to my father.'

Powerless to stop her, Saskia watched her aunt stride purposefully across the cemetery like an avenging one-woman army. For a crazy moment Saskia wanted to laugh. It wasn't a good sign. Grief manifesting itself in the form of hysterical laughter was not advisable. Pulling herself together, she went over to keep her Uncle Bob company.

'Is that the young man everybody keeps talking about?' he asked when she was at his side, his eyes on his wife as she approached Matthew.

'I don't know why he should be such a focus of everybody's thoughts, today of all days,' Saskia muttered.

'Sorry,' her uncle said. 'I'm exaggerating, of course.'

'I wish that were true, but I fear for some inexplicable reason certain people have got it into their heads that we're a match made in heaven.'

'Any harm in you giving it a go?'

'Oh, please don't you start as well.'

He held up his hands in surrender. 'I'm just playing devil's advocate. Unlike your aunt, who looks like she's got your friend dangerously cornered.'

'Let's make a move back to the house,' Saskia said, not wanting to think what her aunt might be saying to Matthew. 'It'll signal to people it's time for the next part of the proceedings and they can start to relax.'

No sooner had she and Uncle Bob taken a few steps when Auntie Jo came full tilt towards them.

'Saskia,' she said, 'I've had a word with Matthew and he's determined not to join us back at the house. Surely you can convince him otherwise?'

'Why would I do that? If he doesn't want to come, that's his decision.'

Her aunt's eyes bore into her with one of her formidable death stares. It was probably the sort of stare that had

434

instilled heart-stopping fear in many a terrified Canadian schoolchild. 'He feels he would be intruding,' her aunt said. 'I've told him that's rubbish, that along with everybody else here, he's most welcome.'

Saskia sighed and looked over to where Matthew was standing. Seeing him alone and awkwardly trying not to look as if he was on his own, her annoyance finally gave way to compassion. 'Oh, for heaven's sake,' she said, 'what choice do I have?'

'That's more like it. Now off you go and tell him you'd be glad of his help with serving lunch to the guests. That way he'll feel he's being useful rather than a spare part. Go on, spit-spot!'

Chapter Sixty-One

'I'm next,' Harvey said gloomily.

'Don't,' Ralph said. 'Don't ever say that.'

The two of them were catching a respite from the rounds of guests offering their condolences and commenting on what a lovely day it was – *thank you* and *it's just what Oliver would have wanted*, was their automatic response. It was a lie, of course. Ralph knew this wasn't what Oliver would have wanted: he'd have preferred to be alive and giving everybody hell!

Tired of the pleasantries, and not wanting Harvey overdoing things, Ralph had collared his father-in-law and forced him to sit down with a glass of wine and eat something. 'Leave everything else to Jo and the rest of us,' Ralph had implored him, 'just for once take it easy.'

'I don't want to take it easy,' Harvey said now, 'that way lies the end.' He took a mouthful of wine, then another. 'And whether you want to face it or not, the truth is, I *will* be next. Because let's face it, we thought the old devil would live forever, didn't we, and now he's gone and proved us wrong. And in dying he couldn't have provided a better reminder that time is running out for me.'

'Please, Harvey, I can't handle this kind of talk. Not today.'

They sat in brooding silence, each with their thoughts. Then, and as Libby walked by with a tray of canapés, Harvey said, 'Are you going to marry her?'

'Yes,' Ralph said simply, his gaze following Libby as she moved about the garden chatting with guests and offering them something to eat. His heart still raced that little bit more when he looked at her. Every day he counted himself lucky that she had walked back into his life.

'Good,' said Harvey.

'It's not every father-in-law who would view his daughter's replacement so positively.'

'After all these years I'd be a pretty poor father-in-law if I didn't want you to be happy. You should never have let her slip through your hands before.'

'I was frightened to rock the boat here.'

'I know. Perhaps we've all been a bit too self-sacrificing in that regard.'

'I disagree. The right time for Libby and me is now. It wasn't back then. I have no regrets.'

Again they sat with their private thoughts and drank their wine. Once more it was Harvey who broke the silence. 'If you'd like, when you and Libby marry, and assuming you're going to continue living here, I'll move out.'

Ralph turned sharply to look at Harvey. 'You'll do no such thing!'

Harvey stared back at him staunchly. 'You and Libby will need your space, you won't want an old codger like me getting in the way.'

'You'd never be in the way, Harvey. This is your home.'

'Yours, too. And Saskia's.' He paused. 'She needs to spread her wings, Ralph. She's stayed here with us too long.'

'I know. But the last thing I need is for her to feel she has to leave when Libby and I marry.'

'Maybe it wouldn't be such a bad thing. It could be precisely the impetus she needs.'

'You make it sound like she's settled for second best by staying with us.'

'Hasn't she?' He breathed in and let out a long expansive sigh. 'I know how she loves it here,' he said, 'how we've all loved it. Ashcombe is a special place, but wherever Saskia is in the world, Ashcombe will always be here for her.'

'She'd be furious to hear us talking like this.'

Harvey nodded. 'And there is the girl herself.'

Ralph twisted round to glance back towards the house where his daughter was just stepping out of the back door with Matthew behind her. They each carried an assortment of wine and soft drinks bottles in their hands.

'Looks like they might have patched up their differences,' Harvey said.

'I wouldn't count on it. The one thing Saskia inherited from my father, along with my sister, was his stubborn streak.'

Harvey's expression darkened. 'And didn't I always warn him it would be the death of him? If he hadn't been so determined to climb that bloody ladder he'd still be here.'

Ralph laid a hand gently on Harvey's hand next to his. 'On the upside, if it wasn't for Jo's dogged determination to see for herself why Oliver thought Matthew was good news for Saskia, he wouldn't be here today.'

A moment passed. 'I keep wondering why we've acted in the way we have,' Harvey remarked. 'We've never interfered with Saskia's love life before, why this time?'

'I think it's because we saw something of ourselves in Matthew. I felt it the first time I met him; he seemed so very alone. Sort of lost. But then when he was here, he appeared at home and somehow more carefree, as though he was more himself. And the more relaxed he became, the more I found myself watching the way he was with Saskia, how he made her smile and laugh. And I know this sounds far-fetched, but I couldn't help but think he fitted in perfectly and was meant to be with us as a family. I'd never experienced a reaction remotely like that with any of Saskia's previous boyfriends.'

'Oliver and I felt the same way. He had a theory that we instinctively picked up on Matthew being recently touched by grief and that was bound to have its own resonance for us as a family. But us having a fondness for the lad means diddly-squat if Saskia doesn't feel the same.'

Ralph continued to watch his daughter as she topped up

guest's glasses, then he watched Matthew moving among the guests. Without realising they were doing it, they were each mirroring the other – the movements, gestures and polite smiles practically identical. 'See,' he heard his father's gruff voice saying, 'that's how ideally matched they are, they're ruddy well synchronised, what more proof does the girl need?'

She wants to be able to trust him, Ralph silently answered his father.

Chapter Sixty-Two

Six weeks after Grandpa O's funeral, and in a poignant reminder of the trip she and her grandfathers had wanted to make, Saskia agreed to go to Bletchley Park with Matthew.

In the time that had passed since the day they'd buried Oliver, and since Auntie Jo and Uncle Bob had returned to Canada, there had been a steady flow of texts and emails between Saskia and Matthew. Initially Saskia had contacted him to thank him for his help the day of the funeral and to apologise for anything her aunt might have said. He'd replied that no apology was required and then asked, if she had the time, if she would be able to preserve Jacob's two notebooks by binding them together. She had sent him a selection of sample ideas – leather-bound and decorated as much or as little as he wanted. Secretly she hoped he'd agree to a design she'd sketched out that would include the seed head of a dandelion.

Occasionally Matthew's communications were an echo of something her father had told her regarding the sale of Jacob's books, which Dad was now organising. A good number had been sold at auction, and without exception had exceeded their reserve price. An assortment of collectors were in regular contact with Dad via the website and gradually the collection was being passed into the hands of people who, hopefully, would cherish the books. Jacob's old college – Merchant College – had been in touch with a view to buying some of the more esoteric volumes of East European history and art, particularly the ones in their native language, including the many texts in Hebrew, ancient and modern.

They were also keen to acquire his extensive collection of books about the Holocaust.

On the morning of the trip to Bletchley, Saskia arrived at Glaskin House exactly on time, the arrangement being she would meet Matthew there as early as possible and he would drive them down.

When she turned into the driveway the first thing she saw was a for sale board, with an additional sign declaring it Sold Subject To Contract.

'I don't know whether to be pleased or disappointed,' Matthew said when he opened the door to her and she remarked on the sold sign. 'It suddenly feels very final. No sooner had the board gone up than an offer of the asking price was made.'

'You could always change your mind.'

He shook his head. 'I'd be nuts to do that – the house and its upkeep is too big a commitment for me to take on just now. Common sense dictates somebody else should enjoy living here.'

'Do you know anything about the person buying the house?' she asked.

'It's a couple with young children moving up from London in search of a rural idyll. They'll probably tear the place apart to suit their needs, but that's to be expected.' Jiggling the bunch of keys in his hands, he said, 'Let's get going, shall we?'

They drove out of the village, and thinking of his ex-girlfriend, Saskia wondered what other commitments were too big for Matthew to take on just now.

The talk during the journey was at times heavy going and interspersed with long pauses. When they did chat it was mostly work related – she talking about a commission she'd recently taken on to restore a collection of flood-damaged books, and he telling her about a nightmarish man he worked for called Jim Rycroft, and a fraud case he was on – a case he couldn't go in to in any detail for professional reasons. He appeared to be as reluctant as she was to stray into an area that might lead to touching on what had previously passed between them. She was glad of that. She was glad, too, to see his hair had grown since the funeral. She liked him better with longer hair. He seemed more himself. Although that wasn't entirely true: there was a distinct edginess to his behaviour this morning, as if he was preoccupied. She hadn't seen him this uptight since the day they'd first met. Perhaps work was bothering him.

He drove fast but not recklessly fast. Having lost three members of her family in a car crash, it was hardly surprising she made for a nervous passenger, but thankfully he wasn't one of those drivers who scared her by constantly turning their head to look at her while speaking. Or maybe there was another reason, other than safety, for keeping his eyes firmly on the road ahead.

Following the instructions on the satnav, they soon arrived in Bletchley and easily found their destination. There were stewards on hand to show them where to park, and to point them in the right direction for buying their entrance tickets. Opting to join an organised tour around the Mansion House and the huts where the code-breakers had worked, they had thirty minutes to wait before it began. Matthew proposed they go for a walk down to the lake.

Happy to go along with his wishes, Saskia fell silently in step beside him, respecting that being here would mean so much more to him than her; this was his private exploration of the secret life Jacob Belinsky had once lived. A man he had known for nearly all of his life, a man he had thought he'd known.

When they reached the lake, Saskia watched Matthew take a photo of it, then turn towards the house. In his telling of the story, Jacob had implied that a person's opinion on the building depended on their background – some thought it grand and impressive, and others thought it a hideous monstrosity. Seeing it for herself, Saskia could understand both points of view. At first glance it looked all right, but on closer inspection its mishmash of architectural foibles and additions became more apparent and unsightly. She tried to imagine how it must have felt for Jacob and everyone else who came here to work and saw the house for the first time. For many it would have been at night, when the building must have loomed large and eerily foreboding in the shadowy darkness.

His photos taken, Matthew steered them towards a nearby bench. 'What were you just thinking?' he asked when they were seated. 'You looked deep in thought.'

She told him.

'I was thinking much the same,' he said, 'that for many of the people who worked here it was their first time away from home and this must have been quite a place to pitch up. It's hardly a home from home, is it?'

'From everything I've read online, it sounds as though they got used to their surroundings pretty quickly,' she said.

'I guess there wasn't much time for navel-gazing.'

She smiled. 'That's an affliction of the modern world, I suspect – too much time on our hands.'

He twisted round to look back at the house and drummed his fingers on the back of the bench. Once again Saskia was reminded of the first time they'd met, when he'd drummed his fingers restlessly on the mantelpiece in the library at Glaskin House. Whatever was making him so jittery today, she wished he would let it go and relax.

'Do you remember that part in the story when Jacob turned up for the concert in the hope of seeing Kitty, but was sick in the bushes in front of her?' he said.

Saskia laughed. 'I really felt for him, reading that bit. Poor man, he was so in awe of her, wasn't he?'

Matthew drummed his fingers some more on the bench. 'I can sympathise with him on that score,' he murmured.

'Really? I wouldn't have thought you'd have that in common. Was that how it was with you and Fliss, then?'

He removed his sunglasses and with a slight tilting of his head, looked directly at her. A slow frown creased his forehead and his hazel eyes narrowed fractionally. 'No, not with Fliss,' he said slowly. 'With you.'

'Why on earth would you ever be in awe of me?'

The frown increased. 'Because I never know for sure just what you're thinking. It's one of the things I like most about you; I find it intriguing. But ironically, as I now realise, it also unsettles me because my brain is wired to be logical and with you I can't join up the dots.'

She stared back at him stunned. 'Wow! I had no idea all that was going on inside your head. But I assure you; it's not something I've worked at. I'm not even aware I do it.'

As though she hadn't spoken, he said, 'Can I ask why you agreed to join me here today?'

'I wanted to see for myself the world in which Jacob and Kitty inhabited.'

'You could have done that anyway. Why today with me?'

She studied his tense angular face before replying, speculating why he was pressing her. 'What's the answer you'd like to hear?' she asked at length.

'Your honest answer, of course.' Then pulling out his pocket watch, he stood up abruptly. 'Come on, we'd better go; the tour starts in five minutes. And lunch will be on me if it doesn't land us smack in front of the entrance to the gift shop.'

'You old cynic, you,' she said, bemused by his behaviour. 'And for the record,' she added, getting to her feet, 'I thought spending the day with you here might be a step in the right direction in getting to know you better.'

He suddenly looked pleased that finally he had got the admission out of her that he'd clearly hoped for. 'And for the same record, I'm glad you thought that,' he said.

Their guide was a dapper ex-military type, and if he was working from a script, he was doing it in a lively and informative way that disguised the fact that he probably did the tour several times a day and was repeatedly pestered with the same questions. The well-dressed man led them around the Park, sharing anecdotes about men and women who had worked there during the war. One or two of the stories Matthew had already read online, such as the one about the mathematical genius Alan Turing arriving for work in his pyjamas, but gratifyingly everything he heard and saw resonated with what Jacob had written.

It was when they were taken inside Hut 8 that Matthew's interest was really piqued. It was just as he had imagined it, so much so he felt that if he closed his eyes he could smell the smoke from Chatterton-Jones's pipe and picture Jacob hard at work at his desk.

The group was turning to leave when Saskia leant in close to him. 'I've got goosebumps,' she whispered, 'it's as though I can feel Jacob watching us in here.'

Without thinking, and because her words articulated perfectly what he'd just felt, Matthew slipped his hand through hers and squeezed it. 'I knew you'd get it,' he said. 'That's why I wanted you to come with me.' But then he registered what he'd done and self-consciously removed his hand. She made no comment, didn't even look at him. But what else should he expect, she was, after all, one of the most inscrutable people he knew.

'Looks like lunch is on you,' Saskia said, when the tour came to an end and they hadn't been deposited outside the gift shop.

'Me and my big mouth,' he said.

The café was housed incongruously in what had been Hut 4, its original occupants having been responsible for translating and analysing German naval Enigma messages decrypted by the likes of Jacob and his colleagues in Hut 8.

After they'd chosen something to eat and drink, they sat at a table inside rather than venture outside to where a party of boisterous schoolchildren had commandeered the tables and chairs. Matthew felt jarred enough as it was without having his eardrums pummelled by a horde of overexcited kids.

He unwrapped his ham and tomato sandwich and tried to summon the courage to reiterate the comment he'd made before. It was absurd that he felt so rattled spending the day with Saskia, but he was; he was terrified of doing or saying the wrong thing. He badly wanted her to know that he was serious, that he truly valued their friendship, as precariously balanced as it was – and hoped for more than just friendship. 'I meant what I said earlier,' he said at last, distracting himself from her watchful gaze by prising open the two slices of bread of his sandwich to check the contents. 'I'm genuinely glad you agreed to come here today. It wouldn't have been the same without you.'

'I'm glad you invited me,' she said, her appraising blue-grey eyes on him.

'You're not just saying that?'

'I think you know me well enough to know that I wouldn't say something I didn't mean. But – and don't take this the wrong way – I wish you'd stop giving me the kid-glove treatment, it's getting on my nerves.'

He pushed the slices of bread back together. 'In that case, you're going to have to help me out,' he said. 'Can you give me a clue how you'd like me to treat you?'

Adding some milk to her tea with studied care, she looked at him from beneath her dark eyelashes. 'That's rather a loaded question, isn't it?'

'How about we narrow it down to friend or foe?'

'Now you're being silly,' she said with a smile.

It was a smile that gave him hope that she wasn't about to pull the rug from beneath him. 'And you're being evasive.' He tapped the table with his finger. 'Answer, please, Miss Granger.'

Her smile widened. 'You know the answer; it's friend. Why else would I be here?'

'But don't forget I never know what's going on in your head. You take inscrutability to a whole new level.'

'I'd have thought I was anything but inscrutable. Nobody's ever described me in that way before.'

'Maybe you've allowed them to get to know you better than you have me.'

She lapsed into silence while she stirred her tea thoughtfully. He watched her hand, the way her pale, slender fingers held the teaspoon so precisely, stirring clockwise first, then anti-clockwise. Momentarily mesmerised by her hand, he found himself wondering what it would be like to be stroked by those pale fingers. He'd wondered a lot of things in the weeks since he'd last seen her, not least how much he regretted having upset her. For some people what he'd done would barely register, but Saskia wasn't most people; trust was clearly a major issue for her and more than anything he wanted to win her trust.

'Is that a question or an accusation?' she asked when she'd replaced the spoon in the saucer.

He put down his sandwich. 'It's neither,' he said, brushing the crumbs from his fingertips. 'It's a statement of fact. I just want you to enjoy being around me as much as I enjoy your company.' He rolled his eyes and groaned. 'And that, my learned judge and jury, has to be the neediest thing I've ever said in my life! Can I retract it, please?'

'Absolutely not!' she said with a laugh. 'I rather like it. Now, please may I eat my lunch without the cross-examination?'

He drew an imaginary zip across his mouth. 'Be my guest.'

When they'd finished eating they resumed their exploration of the Park. In the main exhibition area was one of the famous Bombe machines that Alan Turing and Gordon Welchman had helped develop. Frankly Saskia could make neither head nor tail of the giant decryption device, but Matthew had read up on it and was fascinated by its intricate workings and set

447

about closely examining its dials, cogs and wires. Noticing his interest, an attendant came over to chat with him.

Leaving them to it, Saskia wandered off to find something else to look at. She was enjoying herself immensely, much more than she'd expected to. She certainly hadn't expected Matthew to be so full of surprises. Fancy him thinking her so inscrutable. She didn't see herself that way at all; she was merely quieter than your average chatterbox. Now if she could just find a way to make Matthew relax around her, the day would be perfect. But then after the hard time she'd given him, it was little wonder he was so jittery in her company. She had hoped that by coming here today, he would realise she had forgiven him for what he'd done, but she was beginning to think that things would only be right between them if she heeded something Grandpa O had strongly believed – that forgiveness counted for nothing unless it was uttered aloud to the person who'd earned it. 'And hasn't Matthew earned the right to be forgiven?' she imagined her grandfather asking bluntly in his distinctive gruff voice. The answer was yes, of course, which meant she had to be the one to restore things to how they'd once been.

She stood motionless for a long moment, abruptly paralysed by the memory of her grandfather's voice. The sadness, as it always was, hit like a large stone crushing down on her heart. It was so swift, so powerful, she had to catch her breath. She missed him so very much. Not a day went by without her experiencing the pain of his absence. He'd been such a dear man, thoroughly infuriating at times, but always the kindest and wisest, and most loyal and encouraging supporter of anything she undertook. His love for her had been boundless, as was hers for him.

Doing her best to compose herself, she dug around in her handbag for a tissue. She blew her nose and focused on what she was now standing in front of – a row of glass-fronted rooms that had been staged to resemble the interior of a wartime home. Looking at the small bedroom with its narrow bed, wooden clothes drier, and meagre homely touches made her think of Honeysuckle Cottage and how Kitty and Jacob had turned it into their very own special place. As cold and as miserably damp as it had been, they had counted themselves lucky to have it.

How easy it was to think that happiness had to come wrapped in five-star, gilt-edged luxury.

How easy it was too, to believe it didn't come without myriad problems and challenges.

Sensing the presence of somebody hovering close by, she turned sharply to her left.

'Sorry,' Matthew said, 'I didn't mean to startle you.'

'That's OK – I was miles away, thinking of Jacob and Kitty.'

They moved on to look at the rest of the exhibits, including the famous Enigma machine. Next they went to see the library and ballroom. When they'd finished inside the house, Matthew said he'd like to go and sit by the lake again.

The bench where they'd sat before was free and once again they claimed it. 'There's something I want to tell you,' Matthew said, the lightness slipping from his face as if a cloud had passed across it.

'Actually there's something I want to say as well,' she said. 'But you go first.'

He cleared his throat. 'When we were driving here,' he began, staring ahead of him, as if addressing the lake, 'and I was talking about what's going on at work, I omitted to tell you something. I've decided to hand in my notice. I'm going to see this case I'm working on through to the end and then I'll leave.'

'But why? I thought you enjoyed your job.'

'I do, but I'm ready for a change. I'm thirty-four and feel as though I've done nothing fun or interesting with my life. I need to shake things up.'

'Is that why you went ahead and put Glaskin House on the market?'

'In part, yes.' He turned to look at her. 'But this feeling of dissatisfaction with my life has been coming on for a while.'

'What are you going to do, run off and join the circus?' she quipped. 'If so, I might join you.'

'Now there's an idea!' he said with a small smile. 'Do they still exist? They must surely have been outlawed by the fun police.'

'I expect they have. But come on, circuses aside, what do you plan to do?'

'I want to go travelling.'

'For how long?'

'Six months, eight months, a year … I'll take it as it comes.' He shrugged. 'Who knows, I might be bored with my own company within a couple of weeks and return home before anyone's had a chance to miss me.'

I'll miss you, thought Saskia. 'Where are you hoping to go?' she asked, keeping her voice upbeat.

'Europe, the Far East, maybe North America – wherever they'll have me.'

'That sounds quite an adventure. When do you think you're likely to go?'

'As soon as this latest case I'm working on is completed. Jim Rycroft's appointed me the expert witness for when it goes to court. We're hoping it won't drag on for too long because the evidence is stacking up massively in our client's favour, and with any luck the whole matter could be settled before we get to court. That would mean I could be free to leave in September.'

September. She swallowed her disappointment. Why did he have to disappear just as things were … Just as what? she interrupted herself. Just as she'd allowed herself to trust the feelings she had for him? 'Will you stay in touch while you're away?' she asked. 'I'd love to see an occasional photo of you bungee jumping, or doing something equally nuts.'

He shifted his position so he was facing her head on. 'I could do that,' he said slowly, 'if that's what you'd like. But, and please don't reject what I'm about to say without first giving it some thought, why don't you join me for part of the trip? Or all of it?'

'*Me?*'

He made a pantomime of looking around where they were sitting. 'Yep,' he said, fixing his gaze back on her. 'As I thought, it's just you and me sitting here, so yes, I just asked *you* if you'd like to come with me. We could have an adventure together. It could be fun. Like today's been fun.'

'It's hardly fair to compare a single day out to that of several months away together,' she said astonished. 'What if we argued? What if—'

He stopped her flow of words by reaching for her hand. 'Either one of us would be free at any time to call a halt and fly home.'

'But my family! I can't just leave them. Dad hasn't said anything, but I'm pretty certain he and Libby are going to break the news any day that they're getting married. I couldn't miss that.'

'Of course you couldn't. And obviously there are any number of reasons why it's completely crazy for you even to consider the suggestion, but promise me you'll think about it.'

'But we hardly know one another.'

'This would be one way of rectifying that.'

She looked at him dubiously. Then at his hand still holding hers. 'There's my work,' she said. 'I can't just abandon everything. And there's the small matter of money— '

'As I said, any number of reasons why you shouldn't come with me ... It's a bonkers idea. You'd be crazy to do it. But have a go at looking at it from a different perspective, try thinking of a couple of reasons why it might be fun.'

'I ... I've never done anything like that before,' she said faintly.

'Nor have I. But consider where we are. People like Jacob and Kitty came here without a clue about what they were letting themselves in for, and yet they did it without a backward glance.'

'But that was different, they did it out of a sense of duty, it was for King and Country against a common enemy.'

He smiled. 'All I'm saying is that they took a leap of faith and made the most of an extraordinary situation and opportunity.'

She looked beyond him towards the house. She stared at it thoughtfully, and then at the lake.

'Dare I ask what's going through your head?' he asked, letting go of her hand.

'I was thinking that this was where it all began. If Jacob and Kitty hadn't been sent here to work, Jacob would never have written *The Dandelion Years* and we wouldn't have got to know each other the way we did, and ... and maybe you and Fliss would still be together.'

'Hey,' he said with a frown, 'you were doing fine until that last bit. Fliss and I were *never* going to stay together.' Then in a rapid change of subject, he said, 'What was it you wanted to say to me?'

She looked at him blankly. 'Sorry?'

'Before I stole the show with my announcement, you said you had something to say.'

'Oh. That. It's ... it's nothing much. I just wanted to let you know that ...' She stalled. She could hear the words in her head – *I forgive you* – but to say those three little words aloud now seemed childishly prim and patronising.

'Go on,' he gently urged.

Mentally taking a deep breath, she forced herself to say the words. 'OK, it's this. You asked me before my grandfather's funeral if I could forgive you for misleading me, and, well—'

'And you can't?' he cut in. He looked crestfallen.

'*No!* I mean, *yes*! Yes, I do forgive you.' Flustered she could feel her cheeks reddening, especially so as his hazel eyes were fixed with such intensity on her.

'But do you trust me?' he asked. 'Because that's what really matters, isn't it? To you and to me.'

She nodded. 'I trust you enough to want you to kiss me again.'

The corners of his mouth lifted into a small smile and putting a hand to her cheek, he touched it lightly. 'Are you saying you trust me enough to give me a second chance?'

'That's exactly what I'm saying,' she said, smiling, 'and if I were you, I'd kiss me before I change my mind.'

He did. But no sooner had their lips made contact when from behind them came the sound of high-pitched voices and laughter – descending on the lake like a marauding army was the crowd of noisy children they'd managed to avoid at lunchtime.

'As with comedy, timing is all when it comes to kissing,' Saskia said with a smile.

'It certainly seems to be where you're concerned,' he said, laughing. 'Let's go, shall we? I really don't feel like having my technique critiqued by a bunch of kids.'

If they had researched things more, they might have had a chance to find where Jacob had been billeted with the ghastly Mrs Pridmore, and also locate Billy's farm, but as it was, and following a brief and unsatisfactory look around the town, they put Bletchley behind them and headed for home.

Saskia had wondered if Matthew would want to mention to an official at Bletchley Park that he was in possession of what amounted to an historical record of somebody who had worked at the Park, and as he'd made no attempt to do so, she asked him in the car why he hadn't.

'I thought about it,' he said, 'but I decided it could wait. Besides, Jacob's story isn't going anywhere, is it? It can keep for another time.'

Yes, she thought, just as it would keep for her to wait a few days before breaking it to Matthew that she couldn't possibly drop everything and take off with him. Deep down he had to know that. Her life was at Ashcombe. That was where she belonged.

Chapter Sixty-Three

On a pleasantly warm late September afternoon, and with summer seemingly reluctant to depart, Saskia was on her way to say goodbye to Matthew.

In the months since they had visited Bletchley Park, and to her great relief, Matthew hadn't gone out of his way to change her mind to go travelling with him. He would, however, occasionally ask if she'd had second thoughts. Her answer was always the same: as fun as his trip sounded, she couldn't just up sticks like he could and go; she had commitments and responsibilities. Primarily she was still concerned about Harvey and didn't like him spending too much time on his own, not when it gave him the opportunity to brood on Oliver's death. As they were all still inclined to do.

Rather exasperatingly Dad had kept up a steady barrage of reasons why Saskia should go away with Matthew. He seemed to think his own admiration and envy of Matthew's plans was reason enough for her to pack a bag and go swanning off around the world. Tired of his remarks, she'd suggested that if he thought it was such a brilliant idea, why didn't he and Libby do something similar. 'Who knows, maybe we will one day,' he'd said.

But there was no getting away from it; she was going to miss Matthew enormously. They had been seeing each other as often as possible, alternating their get-togethers between Cambridge and Ashcombe. They'd had some memorable moments punting on the Cam and walking along the river and she had grown to be very fond of the place, seeing it through new eyes with Matthew as her guide.

Last weekend she had helped him pack up the remaining boxes of his things at Glaskin House. The new people were moving in sometime this week and she felt sad that she would never visit the house again. As odd as it sounded, the house was a keynote in their relationship; it was where they'd met.

And yes, they were in a relationship, much to her family's delight. Her aunt had whooped and cheered when Saskia broke the news to her in one of their weekly Skype chats. 'I take all the credit, of course,' she'd crowed, clapping her hands, 'I knew my intervention would bear fruit. *Bob!*' she'd bellowed, turning away from the computer screen. 'Saskia and Matthew have finally sorted themselves out. *Bob*, did you hear what I said?'

'Yes, dear,' came Uncle Bob's barely audible voice, 'I imagine most of the neighbourhood heard as well.'

Saskia had warned her aunt not to get too excited; it was early days.

Which was very true, and conscious that Matthew was going to be away for an indefinite amount of time, Saskia knew that she shouldn't get her hopes up too much. A lot could happen in those months. He could meet any number of girls on his travels who could easily make him forget all about her. She had to be realistic. And that meant she had to keep a tight hold of her heart to keep it safe from being hurt.

Something in her manner must have given him cause to wonder, and he challenged her to be straight and tell him what was wrong. When she'd explained, he'd said he'd cancel the trip if she continued to think so poorly of him. 'I thought you trusted me,' he'd said.

'I do.'

'Doesn't sound like it.'

The conversation had taken place the first time she stayed the night with him in Cambridge. It was also the first time they made love and lying in bed with him, his arms wrapped around her, he'd said that he had no intention of not coming home to her. 'You say that now,' she'd said, 'but you don't know what lies ahead, or what could happen in the heat of the moment when you're thousands of miles away from me. I don't want you to feel you're tied down with the baggage of a girlfriend back at home.'

'I know what's in my heart,' he'd responded, taking hold of her hand and placing it against his chest. 'I promise you I'm not interested in meeting anybody else, or being distracted by some random encounter.'

At Heathrow, and after a few wrong turns, Saskia found the departures car park. She'd made good time and, being nearly thirty minutes early, she wondered if she'd arrived before Matthew and James. She had offered to pick Matthew up from Cambridge and drive him to Heathrow herself, but he'd said that rather than add an extra hour or so to her journey, James would do the honours.

Once inside the departure hall, she looked for the Virgin check-in desk for New York and at once spotted Matthew with his large rucksack on the floor at his feet. Staring intently at his mobile phone he didn't see her approach. It was only when she was directly in front of him that he looked up from the phone. 'You made it,' he said, kissing her on the mouth for a very long moment.

'Of course. Where's James?'

'He's gone already, said he didn't want to intrude on our goodbyes. We've got time for a quick coffee if you want.'

With Matthew guarding his rucksack at a table, Saskia queued for their drinks, then carried them to where he was sitting. Once more he was checking his mobile. Was it her imagination, or did he look anxious? Was he beginning to regret going away? Selfishly she wished he wasn't going, but she would never admit that to him.

'Everything all right?' she asked, pushing a cappuccino and a packet of biscuits across the table to him. 'You seem a bit worried.'

He put down his phone. 'It's the thought of missing you,' he said with an awkward smile.

'Don't say that. You'll have a great time and I'll be here looking forward to hearing all your latest news. Well, obviously not here in the airport, I'm not thinking of moving in, but back at Ashcombe.' Her words came out in a nervous rush to lighten the mood; he looked so very tense.

'You could always change your mind and join me at some point,' he said, taking a mouthful of his coffee.

'You know I can't,' she said softly. 'I don't want to leave Harvey feeling like a lone gooseberry stuck between Dad and Libby. Not so soon after losing Oliver. And somebody has to keep an eye on him, even if he doesn't like the idea of it.'

'Is there nothing that would change your mind?' he asked.

The gravity in his expression made her heart swell. 'Don't, Matthew, don't make it any harder for me, please.' The last thing she wanted was their final moments together to be spoiled, not when she was so near to tears at parting with him. 'Just think of the welcome party we'll have for you when you come back!' she said with a smile, trying to inject a cheerier tone to the conversation.

'I could always amend my plans and shorten the time I'm away,' he said.

She shook her head again. 'No, you mustn't do that. I'd hate for you to change your plans because of me. You'd always regret it and then you'd blame me.'

'I can't win, can I? You have an answer for everything, don't you?'

'I like to think so,' she said lightly.

Smiling, he leant across the table and kissed her. 'Oh,' he said, when he sat back in his seat, 'you're frowning; was that not to your liking?'

'I'm frowning because ... if I'm not mistaken, I've just spotted my father with Libby and Harvey. Look, over there. I'm not seeing things, am I?'

But instead of looking across the concourse to where she

was pointing, Matthew took hold of her hand. 'Saskia,' he said solemnly, 'I want you to promise me that in the next few minutes you're not going to be cross with me. Or with your family.'

She looked at him confused. 'What are you talking about?'

He rose from his chair and hefted his rucksack on to his shoulder. 'Let's go over and say hello, shall we?'

'I thought you were all going to Aldeburgh for the day,' she said when she was face to face with her family. 'What on earth are you doing here?'

'We've come to say goodbye,' her father said. 'Why else would we be here?'

It was then that Saskia noticed the rucksack he was carrying. A terrible feeling came over her. 'What's that?' she asked.

'It's yours,' her father said. 'Libby filled it for you.'

'You'll find everything you need, plus a few extras,' Libby said, smiling.

The terrible feeling grew and her mouth went dry. Saskia stared at her father, then at Libby, then Harvey, and finally Matthew.

'You knew,' she said. 'You've arranged this between you, haven't you?'

'Don't be cross with us,' Harvey said, stepping forward. 'It had to be done. We just want you to stretch your wings and see something of the world.'

From nowhere the threat of hot angry tears pricked at the back of her eyes. 'But my work! I can't just leave customers in the lurch, you know that.'

'It's all been taken care of,' her father said, 'I've explained the situation to them and they're quite happy to wait.'

Her head was spinning. This had to be a joke! This couldn't be happening! 'And just what situation did you explain to them?' she demanded.

'That you were going on a surprise trip of a lifetime, which is true. You and Matthew are going to have a great time together.'

'But haven't you forgotten a small detail? I don't have any flight tickets, I don't even have my passport with me.' There! That was an end to their silliness.

Libby opened her handbag and pulled out a leather travel wallet. 'Tickets and passport and your boarding card – you're all checked in. We did it yesterday. And there's some currency in the wallet as well.'

Saskia battled the tears that were threatening to do their worst. Whether it was defeat or acceptance, she didn't know, but the anger had gone and she was filled with another emotion now. It was love for her family because they had gone to so much trouble behind her back.

She turned to look at Matthew. His expression was tight with apprehension. 'Is this why you were looking so anxious earlier when you were checking your mobile?'

'Yes,' he said, 'Libby was texting me updates and the nearer they got to being here, the more nervous I felt. You're not too cross, are you?'

'I don't know what to think,' she said. 'I'm in shock. I can't believe you've all been so devious.'

'We had to get our timing just right,' Harvey said, laughing, 'we couldn't take the risk of catching you up on the way here and overtaking you because that would have put paid to our surprise.'

'And talking of surprises, there's another for you,' her father said. 'It's your destination. Matthew, do you want to tell Saskia?'

'We're going to stay with your aunt and uncle in Canada for a couple of weeks,' he said, 'and at the end of that you can decide whether to stay on with me for the rest of the trip, or just part of it, or come home. It will be your decision. And in case you're wondering, it was your aunt and uncle's suggestion that we started the trip with them; they've been in on the plan more or less from the beginning.'

'But I thought you were going to New York first? You told me to meet you at the Virgin check-in desk for New York.'

He smiled. 'I didn't want to give the game away. Now I hate to hurry the goodbyes, but we'd better get a move on and check in our luggage.'

After they'd dropped their bags off, as though in a dream, Saskia found herself being hugged by Harvey, then Libby and then her father. The tears had begun to flow now. 'I'll miss you all,' she sobbed. She hugged Harvey again. 'You take care, and don't overdo things. Promise me that.'

'I promise,' he said, kissing her cheek. 'And in return, promise me you won't worry about me. Your father and Libby will do that for you. All you have to do is have a wonderful time. And remember, we've done all this because we love you. It's also what Oliver would have wanted.'

She gulped back another sob and clung to her grandfather. Then she hugged her father and Libby again, her tears wetting their cheeks as well as her own. 'Don't you dare get married while I'm away!' she managed to say shakily.

'Not a chance,' her father said. 'We'll wait for when you're back, I swear.' Then to Matthew, he said, 'Look after her, won't you?'

'You can count on it.'

They were almost at the front of the queue to go through passport control when Saskia ran back to them. 'What about my car? It can't stay here the whole time I'm away.'

'All taken care of,' her father said. 'We have your spare set of keys and Libby will drive it back to Ashcombe. Now go or you'll miss your flight!'

Matthew had one more surprise in store for Saskia and it wasn't until they were boarding the plane that she realised what it was: he'd paid for them to travel first class. When she gasped at the expense, he hushed her with a kiss. 'With the house now sold, think of it as Jacob's present to us. I'm sure he'd approve.'

'I don't know whether to love you for doing this, or to hate you,' she said with a smile.

'How about you decide in a few weeks' time?'

The plane was in darkness and most people were sleeping, including Saskia. But Matthew was wide awake. He still couldn't believe that she was here with him. Although, in truth, she really hadn't stood a chance in the face of her family's commitment to the cause, including her scheming aunt in Canada. Ralph had been the most instrumental in making things happen and whenever Matthew had lost his nerve, Ralph had stepped in and convinced him the plan would work.

'She deserves this chance with you,' Ralph had said. 'She took on far too much responsibility at too young an age. This is her chance to let go and have a little fun.'

But as always with Saskia, Matthew had had no idea how she would react. He'd been terrified she would be furious with him, and her family. Ralph and Harvey had assured him they would deal with any fallout. They'd also said that, if all else failed, he had their full permission to carry her over his shoulder on to the plane if he had to!

He wondered what Jacob would make of what he'd done, jacking in his job and taking off. He liked to think the old man would have applauded Matthew for daring to step out of the box. Mum would have been harder to win round; she would have been concerned that after all the hard work he'd put in at school and college, he was throwing away a perfectly good career. He might well have done precisely that, but it was a risk he had to take. He didn't want to live to be as old as Jacob and look back over his life and regret the path not taken.

Maybe in time he would return to a role similar to the one he'd resigned from, but for now he was determined to take each day as it came, with the girl he loved beside him. He had yet to tell Saskia he'd fallen in love with her, but he'd wait for the right moment to do that, just as Jacob had wanted to wait for the perfect moment to propose to Kitty.

He closed his eyes and it wasn't long before he felt himself falling into a deep sleep. He dreamt of a lake. On the lake was a rowing boat and in it were two people: Jacob and Kitty, their happy carefree laughter drifting across the water. Kitty was holding a dandelion up for Jacob to see. But then the boat turned around and it wasn't Jacob and Kitty, but Matthew and Saskia in the boat. Her mouth poised just inches from the seed head, Saskia blew on the dandelion in her hand. 'Look,' she cried, the seeds floating away on the light breeze, 'there they go, catch them, Matthew!'

'No.' He laughed. 'Let them go. Let everything go!'

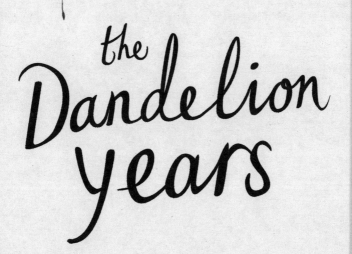

the Dandelion years

Reading Group Notes

About the Author

....

With an insatiable appetite for other people's business, Erica James will readily strike up conversation with strangers in the hope of unearthing a useful gem for her writing. She finds it the best way to write authentic characters for her novels, although her two grown-up sons claim they will never recover from a childhood spent in a perpetual state of embarrassment at their mother's compulsion.

The author of many bestselling novels, including *Gardens of Delight* which won the Romantic Novel of the Year Award, and her recent *Sunday Times* top ten bestseller, *Summer at the Lake*, Erica now divides her time between Suffolk and Lake Como in Italy, where she strikes up conversation with unsuspecting Italians.

For Discussion

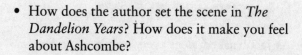

- How does the author set the scene in *The Dandelion Years*? How does it make you feel about Ashcombe?

- 'Fitting in had never been a priority for her.' What are your first impressions of Saskia?

- 'In my experience girls always want to change something about a man.' Is this your experience?

- 'Saskia couldn't help but wonder whether a secret of that magnitude [Bletchley] could be maintained in this day and age.' Do you think it could? Has society changed so much, or does Saskia's thought say more about her, and her relationship with the wider world?

- How does the author create the world of wartime Bletchley?

- 'It was typical of the self-sufficient to be content with their lot.' Why do you think this is?

- 'Love was all too frequently held up as being the cure-all to many of life's difficulties, but was it?' What do you think?

- 'A possessive nature was a wholly destructive nature.' Is Jacob right?

- 'If we are to take away belief what does one have left?' What do we have left?

- As Jacob asked; does everybody need to find their own horizon?

- 'Why are men so horrible?'
  'Because we never know when we're well off.'
  True, do you think?

- 'Self-delusion is the very worst kind of deception.' Do you agree?

- What are some of the parallels between the actions of Jacob and Matthew?

- 'But the truth is, we are all contrary one way or another: we all say one thing and do another.'
  Are we?

- Is 'navel-gazing' an 'affliction of the modern world.'?

In Conversation with Erica James

....

Q 'More often than not she preferred the company of a room full of books to a room full of people.' Do you sometimes share Saskia's preference?

A I realized a very long time ago that I'm a very self-contained person. That's not to say I'm anti-social, I'm not, I enjoy being with people, but I'm more than happy to be alone. However, a bookcase full of books vastly improves my own company!

Q Is living in the past 'the safer option'?

A That would depend on the past, wouldn't it? Personally I see nothing wrong in choosing to opt out of the here and now if the past brings more comfort. I love the idea of people who are so fascinated with a particular era, the thirties or forties for instance, that they decorate their homes in the style of that period, along with wearing the fashion of the time. I think it must be nice to tune out of today's busy world and lose oneself in a completely different one. Perhaps that's what I was doing in writing *The Dandelion Years*, I enjoyed losing myself in a very different time and place.

Q What drew you to the world of wartime Bletchley?

A In a nutshell I think it was the secrecy surrounding Bletchley Park that intrigued me, along with the intense pressure everybody was under who worked there. When I began to get the feeling that I would like to write a book with a Bletchley Park storyline I knew it was the angle of the human story I would pursue, rather than that of a code breaking story, after all that had been done to great effect by Robert Harris with his novel *Enigma*. One aspect that intrigued me was the throwing together of so many people, which meant that paths crossed when ordinarily they might not have. But then war does that, doesn't it? It's a great leveller.

Q 'Something else he'd believed was that his aptitude to throw himself one hundred per cent into a task was a strength, but now he was effectively being told his ability to lose himself in the absorption of a challenge – the more in depth and all-consuming the better – was actually a weakness.' Strength or weakness?

A It's a strength, in my opinion, as otherwise everything I do would be classed as a weakness! I have a great capacity to lose myself in my writing, blocking out everything else I deem as an unnecessary and irritating disturbance. Woe betide the person who telephones me when I'm struggling with a chapter! Now that could be considered selfish by some, but it's the only way I know how to work. Of course, anyone who feels excluded by somebody else's ability to lose themselves in their work, might well see it as a fault, just as Fliss did with Matthew.

Q 'Jacob always claimed that diaries, other than appointment diaries, were strictly for the self-indulgent – or the maliciously inclined with an axe to grind.' Do you agree with Jacob?

A Not necessarily. But there do seem to be an awful lot of diaries and memoirs written by politicians, which are subsequently published and seem deliberately written with the sole purpose to malign others.

Q How difficult was it to adopt the correct Forties speech patterns? How did you go about it?

A I read lots of books written at the time, or before, such as one of my favourites *Diary of a Provincial Lady*. Agatha Christie came in very handy also, as did reading first hand accounts of those who'd worked at Bletchley. Basically it was a matter of absorbing myself in the language and nuances of the period. Funnily enough, Jacob's voice came to me straightaway, followed quickly by Kitty's and once those two characters were in my head, I was off.

Q 'I suppose it's impossible ever really to know a person, isn't it?' Do you agree with Saskia?

A Yes. I truly believe that we never know what a person is capable of doing, or indeed what we ourselves are capable of doing when push comes to shove. Extreme circumstances can bring out the best and worst in a person.

Q 'A spoken untruth always felt more of an untruth than a lie in a text.' Why is that?

A Perhaps it's only me who thinks this, but spoken words, especially unkind words, or a lie, can never be unsaid, whereas a text can be deleted.

Q 'She questioned most things, rarely taking anything at face value.' Are you like Saskia?

A Yes, I'm always looking for the subtext and analysing a situation. Sometimes it's helpful, but often there's nothing to be gained from it, other than reducing myself to a state of inertia. And that way madness lies!

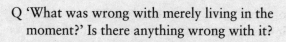

Q 'What was wrong with merely living in the moment?' Is there anything wrong with it?

A I suppose that rather depends on the extent of 'living in the moment' and how much risk is involved. There's a danger that while it can be fun to throw caution to the wind, it can be an act of selfishness to do so and comes conveniently with blinkers to block out potentially harmful consequences. Maybe that's an overstatement, but short-sighted behaviour can often be followed by regret with a side order of guilt.

Q 'You don't think experiencing that level of pain makes us better people, stronger and more compassionate, and more able to empathise with someone else's suffering.' Does it always?

A I believe it does. Without true empathy, I don't think we can understand another person's sadness or suffering.

Suggested Further Reading

....

Enigma by Robert Harris

The Year of Taking Chances by Lucy Diamond

Circle of Friends by Maeve Binchy

The Shell Seekers by Rosamunde Pilcher

The Ship of Brides by Jojo Moyes

The Bletchley Girls by Tessa Dunlop